DAI HOUYING

The author taught Chinese literature at Shanghai
University, and has recently taken a new teaching
post in Guangdong Province. STONES OF THE
WALL is her second novel.

Frances Wood is Head of the Chinese section at the
British Library. She read Chinese at Cambridge before going to Peking University to study history. A
frequent visitor to China, she lives in London.

Dai Houying

STONES OF THE WALL

Translated by Frances Wood

Translation copyright © Frances Wood

First published in Great Britain in 1985 by Michael Joseph Ltd.

Sceptre edition 1987

Sceptre is an imprint of Hodder and Stoughton Paperbacks, a division of Hodder and Stoughton Ltd.

British Library C.I.P.

Houying, Dai
　　Stones of the wall.
　　I. Title
　　895.1'35[F]　　　PL2098.I165

　　ISBN 0-340-41241-0

Printed and bound in Great Britain for Hodder and Stoughton Paperbacks, a division of Hodder and Stoughton Ltd., Mill Road, Dunton Green, Sevenoaks, Kent (Editorial Office: 47 Bedford Square, London, WC1B 3DP) by Richard Clay Ltd., Bungay, Suffolk. Photoset by Rowland Phototypesetting Ltd., Bury St Edmunds, Suffolk.

STONES OF THE WALL

CONTENTS

TRANSLATOR'S NOTE

Some of the worst struggles of the Cultural Revolution were fought in China's universities – the background of this novel. It is set in the years immediately following the death of Mao, the arrest of the Gang of Four (including Madam Mao), and the end of the Cultural Revolution.

University teachers and administrators had already suffered more than almost any other group during the Anti-Rightist Campaign of 1957, in which intellectuals who had been encouraged to speak out against corruption, maladministration and bureaucratic restrictions were subsequently persecuted for their outspokenness, and sent off to the countryside for 'reform through labour'.

In the Cultural Revolution, students were deliberately used as 'Red Guard' shock troops to attack 'experts' who, by current definition, could not be both 'red' and 'expert'. The Red Guards quickly split into different factions and fought armed battles within the universities (1966–69). All staff and students were forced to take sides; some were instantly condemned, while others, whether out of fear or conviction (often to be regretted in hindsight), joined the various groups and attacked their colleagues in other factions.

With the death of Mao and the arrest of the Gang of Four – the group most strongly associated with the worst excesses of the Cultural Revolution – there was general celebration throughout the country at the thought that those days of terror and suspicion were over. But though they rejoiced, the aftermath of the Cultural Revolution meant that many Chinese still had to face the extraordinary situation described in the novel. Throughout China, victims of the Cultural Revolution and the Anti-Rightist

Campaign, rehabilitated and back in their former jobs, have to work side by side with those who denounced them and drove other colleagues to suicide. Though some of the greatest villains may have been imprisoned, most of the torturers are now back at work with those they tortured, creating the atmosphere described by Dai Houying where people have to come to terms with their own past and with current relationships seen against the events of that past.

Frances Wood

LIST OF PRINCIPAL CHARACTERS

PART ONE

In everybody's mind, a bit of history
is stored, with its own independent
existence.

ONE

ZHAO ZHENHUAN

History can be treacherous. It sometimes makes a surprise attack
on me in the night. My hair has gone white.

I'm struggling to swim. The floodwaters seem endless. I don't
know where I've come from, nor where I'm swimming to. I don't
know how long I've been swimming, nor how long I will have to
swim. All I know is that I must follow the girl who is bobbing in
the water ahead of me, her slim arms moving strongly, her two
short plaits bouncing. All the time I've been watching her, that's
all I've been able to see. I can't see her face. Yet I feel that I
know her, know her well, love her.

I want to reach her, to tell her what I feel.

I've never swum so well before, proper breaststroke, arms
and legs perfectly synchronised, sliding quickly and easily through
the water.

The distance between us is immense, but I pursue her steadily.
Suddenly I bump into the floating carcass of a dead cow. Shocked
and disgusted, I try to swim away, but something drags at my
legs. Suddenly, all my strength is gone. I can't swim any more.

The girl swims further and further away. In my agitation, I
shout after her, using words that I haven't used for a long time.
Only she and I can understand them. Finally, she turns towards
me. An oval face with arched eyebrows and fine lips. Slightly
prominent cheekbones. I was right! It's her!

I want to laugh, and also to cry. My arms stretch out to her. But something holds me back, something like a creeper wrapped around my neck. The girl is swimming ahead. I struggle to free myself but the creeper wraps itself ever tighter. Now I've lost sight of her.

I start to weep noisily. I mustn't lose her.

'Have you had another nightmare?' – a woman's voice in my ear.

Does she mean me? Have I been dreaming? No. Can one see so clearly in dreams? Who is this woman who talks such rubbish? Why is she so close to me? It's strange, everything is getting more confused. The woman's face is at my shoulder. I can't see it but I know those pretty cloying features, like a paper mask, hovering in front of me. The mask provokes reflex reactions: a sensation of acute misery, and another notion: wife. My wife, Feng Lanxiang, her hand clutching at my neck, that maddening creeper. I fight free of it and ask, reproachfully, 'Why did you drag mc back?'

'What do you mean, drag you back? Haven't you woken up yet?' Feng Lanxiang asked, half-alarmed, half-amused as she tweaked my nose.

At last, things were becoming clearer. I had been dreaming.

'Who were you dreaming about? You cried again.'

Feng Lanxiang let go of my nose. Why did she let go? She might as well have stifled me and been done with it. She wouldn't even let me finish my dreams. I turned away and pulled the quilt over my head. She pulled it back down again.

'What's the matter with you? You're always having weird dreams. You cry and shout and then you won't speak to me. And you don't make love to me anymore.' She sounded plaintive, aggrieved.

I began to feel sorry and turned back to her: to her uninspiringly pretty face. Her eyebrows are strong and thick but she plucks them half out to make them finer. Her smile is pretty enough, why does she pluck her eyebrows into that coy arch? I felt like turning away again but I stopped myself. I felt I should comfort her but I couldn't think of anything to say. So I smiled.

'Who do you dream about?' she asked, again.

Who did I dream about? Who was the girl? Why did I still feel so peculiar?

'I wasn't dreaming. I felt dizzy and stifled,' I said rather inaccurately. Accuracy isn't essential when comforting people.

She laughed. 'You drank too much yesterday. You wouldn't stop. Still, it was your birthday.'

Birthday? Now I remembered. Yesterday, I, Zhao Zhenhuan of the *Daily News*, celebrated my forty-fourth birthday. Everything went well. In my village, four was a lucky number. My friend and colleague, Wang Panzi, had said I really ought to have a great party for this doubly auspicious birthday. Besides, there were three other reasons for celebration. Firstly, in the ten disastrous years of the Cultural Revolution, I had been remarkably lucky and hadn't been affected at all. He, on the other hand, as a 'rebel', still had not been cleared or assigned a job. Secondly, I had a happy home and my wife, Feng Lanxiang, was an acknowledged beauty as well as being gentle and considerate. My daughter, Huanhuan was clever and lively and showed promise as a dancer. What was more we had two rooms to live in which was not bad at all. Thirdly, in an assessment meeting at the newspaper, I'd been praised as the most efficient editor and I'd just been promoted to the highest grade. I had an official's black silk cap on my head which covered my grey hair. It was true, everything was just fine.

Fully awake now, I remembered how Lanxiang had agreed with Wang Panzi. She had used some money she'd saved to buy an overcoat to prepare a party for me. But I knew they both wanted something in return. Wang Panzi hoped that I'd put in a good word for him at the office so that he could return as a reporter; Lanxiang was afraid of whoever it was I dreamt about and worried that I'd leave her. If people want something from you, it shows you still have something to offer. But why does everyone want to hear good things from people, want to be needed? I was no different; despite their ulterior motives, I'd still been pleased by the attention. Finally I agreed, let's have a party. Let everyone congratulate me. Everything is just fine!

I'd never had such a birthday celebration before. Just to think of it made me feel dizzy again.

A room full of friends. A table laden with food and drink. We drank and played 'guess-fingers' [a drinking game similar to scissors, stone, paper]. 'Man's life must be spent in pleasure. Never lift an empty glass to toast the moon. Come on! Let's play!' I said this to everyone, and each time we played I stuck out two fingers. I didn't win very often. 'Six, six, six in sequence!' Everything was just fine. 'One less, one less!' 'All down, all down!' The women played a different drinking game, 'Tiger!' 'Stick!' The tiger eats the bird, the bird eats the insect, the insect gnaws the stick, the stick beats the tiger. It's a very simple game but it's full of dialectic. Strong and weak, winner and loser, all in opposition.

Music and dancing. Fashionable pop music. Huanhuan performed a dance she had made up herself. Her feet hardly touched the floor but she managed to overcome the noise in the room. Lanxiang dragged me out to dance heaven knows what sort of dance. When I was at university, I loved the weekend dances. My partner was always the same, the girl I'd just lost in my dream. The first time we'd danced together, it was to a song which went, 'Find, find, find a lover, hold, hold, hold his hand'. She sang the two lines and then laughed. I laughed with her and seized her hand.

Spinning. People spinning. The table spinning, losing its corners. The room spinning. The earth spinning.

I turned, smiled and raised my glass, 'I must use my talents; a thousand pieces of gold, once scattered, can never be recovered.'

'Old Zhao's drunk! He can't even quote a poem straight!' shouted Wang Panzi.

'Penalty! Penalty!' I knew I had to pay a penalty for misquoting. I drained my glass in one gulp and reached for a bottle.

Someone took my glass and put me onto the bed.

Rocking. The bed was rocking. It was like lying in a small boat. I couldn't open my eyes. I remembered my father being drunk once. He lay on the bed and waved his fists in my face, shouting, 'Laugh at me! Laugh at me!' How old was I? Eight? I couldn't behave like that in front of Huanhuan; I couldn't behave as oddly as my father had done. Huanhuan was standing by the bed. Carefully she lifted my eyelid: 'Happy birthday, daddy.'

I could just make out her small figure as she knelt down. That's right, I told her, and explained that at New Year and birthdays when I was small, I'd often kowtowed in front of grown-ups, offering respectful congratulations on their longevity.

Huanhuan was a bright child, and Wang Panzi, Lanxiang and the others were all laughing and encouraging her: 'Kowtow forty-four times, four more, keep on kowtowing!'

My father had schooled me in the traditional ways. When I was three, my grandfather died. I hadn't liked him and didn't want to go to the mourning hall, but my father had pushed my head down and said, 'Bow your head in front of your grandfather's spirit tablet! Kowtow! Kowtow again!'

I wanted to weep. I wanted to carry Huanhuan off alone and weep, but I had no strength. All I could do was push her and say, 'Off you go, little one. Wait till Daddy . . . wait till . . .'

Then the tears had begun to well up, and I buried my face in the pillow.

And after that? The flood came after that.

Seeing me stare at her so fixedly, Lanxiang moved closer, her smile even more ingratiating and sweet. I pushed her away harshly. Hurt, she turned her face to the wall and after a while, her shoulders began to heave; she was crying. Slightly guilty, I stretched out a hand to touch her shoulder – but immediately pulled it back. Why should I comfort her? Who comforted me? And if it hadn't been for her, I'd never have lost Sun Yue . . .

Sun Yue! The girl I'd been chasing in my dreams was Sun Yue. Not Sun Yue now, but Sun Yue when she was young. By now, the daughter we had together must be almost grown up.

What was the end of the dream? It was odd, yesterday had been so busy that I hadn't had time to think of Sun Yue. But at night I dreamt of her. And what happened in the dream was so like what had happened to us.

It was just after we had graduated from lower middle school and we were walking home together. The roads were flooded, so we had to take a small boat to get back to the village. Sun Yue was irrepressible. She dangled her legs over the side of the boat and kicked water at me. 'If you fall in, I won't save you,' I threatened her, knowing she couldn't swim. 'Oh no?' she said, and suddenly, whether on purpose or by accident, she was in the river. Horrified, I jumped in, and I grabbed her. Though she'd swallowed several mouthfuls of water, she was still laughing. I pushed her into the boat. I didn't want to get back into it myself and my clothes were already sodden, so I swam alongside as we laughed. Her laughter led me, swimming, for three miles. When we reached home, my mother said I must have been possessed by the devil. I looked stupidly at Sun Yue, and she blushed. From that day on, my feelings for her were different. We went to the same upper middle school and we went to the same university, the most envied couple amongst all our fellow-students. All the men in the class were particularly jealous of me. Finally, we married.

Who would have thought that we would be divorced after five years of marriage? And that it would have been me who asked for the divorce?

We married after we graduated from university. Sun Yue proposed, but it was for my sake. I'd been assigned a job in Guangzhou, over three hundred miles away from Shanghai, where she was to stay. I didn't mind leaving Shanghai but I did mind leaving Sun Yue. I tried to think of a way of staying there with her. 'We can't make individual appeals to the Party; I belong to you, so why don't we go home and get married in the village?' I was overjoyed at her proposal but also very worried – my father was bedridden, and at home in the village my half-dozen brothers and sisters were very poor; we'd never be able to buy furniture and utensils. None of this worried Sun Yue, and after we got back, she came to live in my home. My mother was delighted by her unconventional daughter-in-law. Every day, at lunch, she'd surreptitiously slip a fried egg into Sun Yue's bowl of noodles and Sun Yue would equally surreptitiously slip the egg into my little sister's bowl . . .

> *When young, they held hands and danced,*
> *Loved for ten years and married,*
> *A thousand miles between them and a river,*
> *Exchanged letters written in their hearts' blood,*

Their wings broke as the sea turned into mulberry fields,
Who can lick the blood and soothe the pain?
Head bowed, I hear a loving mother call,
There is no shelter in the wide world.

Sun Yue sent me those verses just as I was about to send her the demand for a divorce. I tore the poem up in front of Lanxiang; but it tore at me, and I've never forgotten a word of it.

How can I explain?

When my mother heard we were divorcing, she rushed to Guangzhou to ask me why. I resorted to a lie and said, 'She's a good woman and I'm not worthy of her.' My mother cursed me and, as she was about to leave, said I could never return to the village and that she wished she'd never given birth to me. I didn't see my mother again until last year, when she was dying.

Finally, Lanxiang turned towards me, unable to bear my silence any longer. Clinging pathetically, she asked, 'Do you regret it?'

I pretended not to understand. 'Regret what?'

'Marrying me.' She looked at me as she spoke.

I laughed and stroked her hair. 'When have I ever regretted it? How could I? Since I married you I've been well provided with clean pressed clothes. I can live up to my reputation as a handsome well-groomed man! Sun Yue! She never took care of me. All she thought about were her ideals!'

'Why do you think you've gone grey so quickly? You're only just forty-four and you're half-white. People might think I don't look after you.' She picked at my hair, looking petulant.

My heart sank. When my mother had seen my white hair she'd forgiven me. 'You brought it upon yourself, my son. Go to Sun Yue's parents and tell them you were wrong. If you don't, I shan't be able to die peacefully.' That was the last thing my mother said. I never went to see Sun Yue's parents. After the burial, I left immediately. I wanted to bury all my memories. If Sun Yue knew my hair had turned white . . .

'In those days, everybody liked workers. You respected me then. Now intellectuals are back in favour, so you're bound to think Sun Yue would be better than me.' Lanxiang was talking half to me, half to herself. I began to get irritated.

'If that's what you want to think, then go ahead. I'm going to sleep.' I snapped the light off and closed my eyes, leaving her to toss and turn.

Was I unfeeling? Perhaps. But she couldn't begin to understand me; how on earth had I managed to fall in love with her? Marry her? This was the nightmare. As everyone knew, she was an important figure at the Press, a worker-member of the Revolutionary Committee. She'd married late but she had previously had an abortion. How could I respect someone like her? Yet I had married her.

It had been a time of senseless upheaval. Rebel, rebel, everything up and down, complete and unending chaos. Sun Yue used to write to me every week, and then less regularly. After a couple of months without a letter, I finally received a telegram with only the two characters for 'peace' on it. That meant she was still alive.

Right at the beginning of the campaign, she'd been labelled 'an inveterate conservative'. After that the 'hats' [epithets] came thick, fast, and increasingly slanderous until she was finally described as 'concubine of the Shanghai University Party Secretary'. I dismissed the slanders, but it was awful to think of her standing in an auditorium with a card round her neck labelled 'concubine' and her head bowed before the masses. Soon, I began to resent her political activism: I felt she should be by my side, fulfilling her wifely duties. Further, I was finding it increasingly difficult to live alone. Then, just around that time, Wang Panzi introduced me to the circle which included Lanxiang; and soon I started seeing her on her own.

'Lots of women are abandoned by their husbands. Does it ever happen to men?' Lanxiang asked the very first time she came to my place. She was looking sourly at the wedding photograph pinned on the wall. Sun Yue leaning happily on my shoulder, my head against hers.

'You're jealous!' I laughed. I didn't look in the mirror at the time but I knew that if I had, I would have seen a man without shame.

How could I have behaved like that?

I'd taken the wedding photograph down and put up one of

Lanxiang in the same frame. Things changed quickly after that. I grew more and more to enjoy criticising Sun Yue in front of Lanxiang. Instinct took over from self-control, and within two months she became pregnant. I was just beginning to realise my mistake.

'The error of a moment became the regret of a lifetime.' Surely the person who wrote that must have experienced something like me?

Lanxiang and Sun Yue: there's no comparison. Sun Yue was naturally beautiful, while Lanxiang has to create her prettiness. Sun Yue was a lover in the real sense, Lanxiang is just a woman. Though I didn't live with Sun Yue for long, I have countless rich memories of her; my time with Lanxiang has been so ordinary as to be completely forgettable. I can't distinguish last year's events from this, yesterday's from today's. I don't see how our marriage can survive.

But to divorce again? What would become of Huanhuan? How would Sun Yue react? Could she still forgive me? I'm so afraid. Trying to avoid the problem, throwing myself into work, cheerfully asking friends back home for a meal or a drink so they can see my happy family life; it's been pointless. The past can be treacherous. It sometimes makes a sudden attack on me at night. My hair has gone white. I so long to see Sun Yue and the child. And beg their forgiveness.

'It's too late for regret. Sun Yue must have remarried by now. Things must have changed for the better for her. You think she still loves you? Didn't she change the child's name?'

Lanxiang wasn't asleep. I paid no attention to her. I knew that Sun Yue hadn't remarried. But it was true, it was too late for regret, far too late.

TWO

SUN YUE

The past and the present are indivisible.
I'm tired of it.

Xi Liu, the Party secretary, asked me to see him. I didn't want to go. Seeing his wife, Chen Yuli, makes me remember those ghastly, painful days.

Chen Yuli was there. She's over fifty but there isn't a wrinkle on her round, pale face. Just like her name – a slab of jade. She went off to make tea, while I tried to conceal my fear.

Xi Liu handed me a copy of the university journal and told me to look through it. Glancing at the table of contents, I saw an essay by Xu Hengzhong, a teacher in my department, 'The literary line of the Gang of Four'.

'Did you know about Xu Hengzhong's article?' Xi Liu asked.

'He's mentioned it.'

'Does that mean you share his views?' He put the question forcefully.

'The Party branch hasn't looked at it. Do you think we should?'

'As a member of the departmental Party branch, is that all you can say? It's not good enough.'

I stared at him. He was angry. His face looked longer and stiffer than ever. I didn't respond.

'What qualifications does Xu Hengzhong have to criticise the Gang of Four? He supported them!' Xi Liu said with venom.

I remembered a scene from those years. Xi Liu, so thin he could hardly stand, with his head lowered as the rebel leader Xu Hengzhong made a speech. Chen Yuli and I both had placards labelled 'Xi Liu's concubine' round our necks, and we stood amongst his old colleagues who were frail and sick.

'He was vicious to us. He destroyed my family. He hated us old cadres. Did you know he comes from a landlord background?' Chen Yuli said as she came in. Her voice was brittle, almost too brittle to have come from that smooth throat. When she'd stood with her head lowered at that meeting, she'd been different, terrified, ter- rified into silence. At the meeting there had been a bombshell of a revelation and she'd been so scared she couldn't stand up. Xu Hengzhong had read out a love letter from Xi Liu to her. Her own husband and children were all there in the audience and they'd supported her, believing she'd been slandered.

What a letter! 'I'd like to be your dog and . . .' I hadn't been able to listen to any more. I thought my head would burst. I felt as if I'd been turned into a dog by Xi Liu, that my life as a human being was over. If Xi Liu hadn't admitted that he'd written the letter, I'd have assumed it was a fabrication. I'd always thought of him as a very serious and puritanical person, a noble man, faultless. He was always criticising me: 'Little Sun, you must improve your world outlook. You've been influenced by nineteenth century capitalist literature and you've filled your head with sentimentality. You are in a vulnerable position in the class struggle.' He had helped me make a thorough self-criticism about the capitalist ideology I was so full of. Once, in a meeting of the entire student body, I'd described the poisonous effect that foreign capitalist literature had had on me. Not being committed to class struggle, I'd been susceptible to the influence of humanism and other theories which denied the class character of human nature; I'd even got to the point of contemplating marriage with a rightist. After I'd finished, Xi Liu had spoken for me: 'Sun Yue is as brave and optimistic as any man. Reading capitalist novels, however, weakened her spirit. Today she's completed an excellent self- examination. I believe that from now on she will be a committed ally of the proletariat.'

I wept when he said this, he was such an example for me. And yet he could write a letter like that. What sort of class influence was he under? After that revelatory meeting, I wrote to my husband Zhao Zhenhuan, telling him I would never defend Xi Liu again. It hadn't upset me terribly to be branded as his 'concubine' since I believed that some day rain and wind from the skies would wash the world and cleanse me. But from that day, I lost my faith. Dirt seemed to stick.

Shortly afterwards, Chen Yuli got divorced from her husband. Xi Liu's wife died. Their families had been ruined. Nevertheless . . .

'Do you mean to suggest that Xu Hengzhong was responsible for everything?' I asked rather sharply.

Xi Liu's face became very ugly. His eyes were always prominent but now they threatened to burst from their sockets. He spoke slowly: 'You've forgotten your history. We should never forget that time. If we forget it, we might easily lose everything all over again.'

I couldn't stop myself arguing with him. 'I haven't forgotten. Nor can I ever forget. But I don't like your partiality: you're not being fair. You Ruoshui was much more powerful than Xu Hengzhong and did much worse things. A lot of people still hate him. Why don't you investigate him instead of appointing him head of the Party office? You're remembering selectively, Xi Liu. You've broken up families yourself. At one time you were far more powerful than Xu Hengzhong ever was.'

I said it all in one breath and startled myself by what I'd said.

'What are you getting at?' asked Xi Liu sternly. Chen Yuli echoed him.

Images of people suddenly appeared in my mind. One was a boy from my class, Little Xie, a 'returned overseas Chinese'. Just because his mother ran a small shop somewhere abroad, Xi Liu refused to allow him permission to visit her. At one meeting, Little Xie had criticised Xi Liu and so he was labelled a rightist and sent off for 'reform through labour' for four years. He didn't dare tell his mother. But later, when he was rehabilitated, he wrote and told her all about it. The shock was too much for the old lady. She went crazy. She's still in a mental hospital abroad.

When Xie finally left to visit her, I went to see him off and he wept silently.

Then there was He Jingfu, who was also branded a rightist because he had defended this fellow-student against an unfair accusation. He'd been expelled. When I thought of them, I felt guilty myself. Why should Xi Liu get away with it? Yet I couldn't say any more to him. I just wanted to leave. 'Is there anything else?' I asked.

'You must be more careful. Tell Xu Hengzhong that if he wants to publish any more articles in future, he should send them elsewhere. And you can tell the editorial board of the journal not to publish anything else by him for a while.'

'But that's not Party policy. It's contrary to the constitution.'

'Your attitude has changed a great deal. Why? You'd better think about it. I'm disappointed in you. When I got my job back, I had you recalled from the middle school and put in charge of the department here. I little thought . . .'

Xi Liu looked hurt, and Chen Yuli chimed in: 'Little Sun, we've all been through a lot. But I warn you, people are saying dreadful things about you. You ought to see less of Xu Hengzhong. His wife has only just died.'

'Yuli!' Xi Liu cut her off.

I stood up. Classes were not yet over but I didn't want to go back to the faculty, I wanted to go home.

At the main gate of the dormitory block, I met Xu Hengzhong. Strange coincidence. He was carrying a couple of pairs of worn-out cloth shoes. Man's shoes, a child's shoes.

'You're home early!' he greeted me.

'Are you going out?' I forced myself to speak to him.

'Our shoes are worn out. I can't afford new ones. I'll have to get them patched.' He held the shoes out with a rueful smile on his thin, sharp face. I felt sorry for him. Both he and his wife, who had just died, had been fellow-students of mine. We'd studied together for five years and later worked together. Just before she died, his wife had asked him to fetch me. In front of Xu Hengzhong and their small boy, Little Kun, she begged my forgiveness for what Xu Hengzhong had done to me in the Cultural Revolution. I promised to take care of Little Kun. I can still hear her appeal, 'Please forget old grievances, Sun Yue . . .'

Now I decided to be firm with myself, and said to Xu Hengzhong who was still standing there, 'I'll make shoes for Little Kun. That would be better than patching old ones.'

His eyes seemed to shine briefly. Chen Yuli's warning was still on my mind so I left him and went quickly home.

I picked up a shoe sole. Little Kun's old shoes were so worn that his toes poked out. On sixty yuan a month, a father and son should be able to get by, but since his wife had died Xu Hengzhong had to support his father-in-law as well.

Ssh-ssh, the sound of the thread being pulled through the shoe sole was monotonous but rhythmic, like a finger lightly brushing a *qin* string in a lonely and melancholy mood.

Dirty water. Dirty water. Wherever people go they always find dirty water. Especially women. And women like me, even more so.

'Ow!' I exclaimed. I'd stabbed my finger, quite deeply. At first the wound was white, then purple and finally it began to bleed. Tiny drops of red blood ran down to my finger tip. There's blood everywhere in a human body, and nerves. When it's cut it bleeds and it hurts. When an old wound has healed, blood will flow from a new wound, and it will hurt. Endlessly flowing blood, endless pain, until death.

I put my finger in my mouth and sucked it. Mustn't let anyone see. Some people are bloodsuckers and like taking blood from new wounds for 'scientific experiments'. They want to find out how to turn people's blood into dirty water and splash it on the ground.

I should never have come back to the university. I'd been content teaching in the middle school. But I came back, happy to think that Xi Liu had changed after the experience of those years. I never thought that in his eyes history would have been reduced to three sentences: In the past, I had power. I suffered for ten years. Now I have regained power. He didn't quite say that, but it showed in every word and gesture. Though I'd been disappointed in him after the letter, I was infinitely more disillusioned today. All his good points, his wisdom, his ability, his understanding of people, had vanished. He used to care about students and teachers and their living conditions – now he only cared about his own power. Xi Liu had returned to his job, but only with part of himself, the base part, the annoying part.

I thought seriously of going back to the middle school, back to being among innocent children.

Ssh-ssh . . . the dismal sound tugged at the thousands of strands and loose ends in me. I stopped sewing and put the sole down.

I'm not really an emotional character. I've changed. I've never wondered before whether the change is for better or worse, whether it's good or bad. What's the use in wondering? If a person can change, can't they change again? Perhaps not. But I'm supposed to be Party secretary. How can I manage when I'm so confused?

'Sun Yue! Sun Yue!'

As soon as I heard the voice, I knew it was Li Yining. Like a spring wind, she brought life into the house with her round, laughing, dimpled, childlike face. She's over forty and still likes to wear brightly coloured clothes, but she never looks vulgar. Today she had on a crimson nylon blouse.

As soon as she came in, she seized my arm and said, 'Guess what I did today!'

I couldn't guess. She went over to the door, shut it and said, 'Where's Hanhan?'

'She's probably out somewhere with her schoolfriends. She gets lonely at home so I don't usually see her till suppertime.'

'You should change your life; I feel sorry for the child,' said Yining. Tears filled her eyes. She is very child-like. 'That's why I've come to see you!' And she was cheerful again.

I laughed at her. She paid no attention but began to describe a possible husband she'd found for me: a well-known writer, fifty-eight years old, never married but now he's getting on, he'd like to find a wife in a university. It didn't matter that he was from a different city, he was quite prepared to move for marriage. When she'd finished, she looked at me with her beautiful almond eyes.

'So . . . a writer advertises for a wife. A nation-wide call goes out to all female university lecturers. Special feature: is prepared to move house when he gets married so no interruption to your career. You want me to leap up and answer the advertisement, don't you?' I laughed as I spoke but I didn't want to laugh. I felt terribly sad.

Yining's eyes widened. 'Whatever I say, you twist it. I thought it was good news for you. And it wouldn't cost anything.'

I was afraid she'd get angry so I said, seriously, 'But you know that I won't accept any introductions. It's like offering yourself for sale and letting other people choose the goods they want to buy.'

'And it's different if you do the choosing?'

'No. I don't want to buy or sell. When it comes to love, the only thing that matters is mutual attraction, not buying and selling.'

'The sort of love you talk about doesn't exist in the real world. I bet that ninety-five women out of a hundred just put up with their husbands.'

'Yes, but at least they put up with them and they may possibly be happy. And the ideal lover does exist. Didn't you allow five percent?'

'Well then, you tell me about your ideal lover! Tell me where he is and no matter how far, I'll find him for you. I just want you to be happy.'

Tears filled Yining's eyes again. She isn't very well suited to her work teaching politics in my old middle school. We met when I was posted there as a literature teacher after my 'rehabilitation', and soon became friends. I was very unhappy at the time, and she was always thinking of ways to cheer me up. She was a great comfort, but despite her efforts I couldn't change myself into a happy person like her. I thought it must be because she had a stable, loving family. She didn't agree. 'It's because I can be happy anywhere. I have no illusions. Do you think I've got a heart of stone? I know that the sun dazzles, that ice and snow freeze, that flowers are beautiful and that birds can fly, but I can bring my sensitivity to these things down to a very low level!'

'It's not a question of bringing things down,' I said. 'As a teacher of politics, can you accept political fluctuations?'

She laughed, 'When I read a politics textbook, it's just like reading a cookery book or a knitting pattern. They're all reference books and they don't move me at all. Maybe I'm just stupid.'

I know I'm equally stupid in my own way. I'm very fond of her, I admire her a lot – but I can't be like her.

'Well, don't you want to tell me about your feelings?' she asked, laughing.

No. I didn't want to. It wasn't that I thought she'd laugh at me but she talked a lot and it might get around. That would be like exchanging one basin of dirty water for another. The last few years have taught me that the best thing to do with my most important feelings is to hide them. Things that have been confused don't easily straighten themselves out. Things that have been blurred don't suddenly become clear. Anyway, how could I describe my 'ideal man' with any clarity when there was no reality to grasp? For the last few years I'd felt like a feather tossed in the east and west winds, longing for a strong hand to hold me and say, 'Your place is here. You are not going to be blown away again.'

I had a dream in which this happened, but it was blurred and illusory. I would find myself unaccountably in an unfamiliar place: a cold wasteland reached by a muddy track, yet filled with all sorts of people, all waiting to be registered. The control was invisible but it could be felt. I was quite alone though the others seemed to be in groups, so I was pushed to and fro and began to panic. The distant sound of horse's hoofs came closer and a large man on a horse galloped past. I was covered in dust. Suddenly, people began to shout at him, 'Hey! Sun Yue is here!' For a moment, the shouts calmed me and filled me with a sort of peace. Then I suddenly realised that he was looking for me, and I was there waiting for him. But who was he? I hadn't heard his name. When I woke up, I thought for a long time and the longer I thought, the more depressed I felt. I had no idea what I was waiting for, or hoping for. There was no point in trying to explain this to Yining – she'd think I was crazy. After a long hesitation, I shook my head and said, 'I've never really thought about it.'

Yining's face clouded. She sighed, 'You think I'm too shallow to understand you, but I do. I know you know what love is and that you'd give everything for it. But just because you can't find it, you're prepared to sacrifice a prospective husband. Sometimes I could weep for you.'

I hugged her. 'Let me wait. It's better to wait than to be disappointed.'

She sighed again, heavily. 'Waiting is the same as being disappointed. If you wait forever, you'll give up hope.'

We didn't say any more. I wanted to change the subject. After a long silence, she picked up the shoe sole I'd been sewing and said, 'I don't think you realise that if you make a mess of this, people will gossip.'

'They've already started gossiping.' I took the sole back from her, and paused for a moment. 'I don't really know what to do about it. I was at university with his wife. She died and asked me to take care of the child. What can I do? And anyway, I've been through it all myself, being a political untouchable. Friends and relatives stopped coming to see me, and if they met me they'd ignore me. It was awful. I couldn't ever behave like that to anyone.

'Some people will say that I don't know where to draw the line. Yining, you teach philosophy, do you think we should draw lines round people? Isolate them? Must we draw lines around friends who've made political mistakes, to prove our revolutionary fervour? I thought we wanted to liberate all mankind. And what's so terrible about Xu Hengzhong by comparison with You Ruoshui? How can someone carry on in a position of power and not even give permission for articles to be published? Is that fair?'

'What's so unusual about it? It's always been like that – it's only you that gets upset about it. I don't worry myself about things like that. Anyway, from what you've just said, you must have a soft spot for Xu Hengzhong. Aren't I right?'

I waved the shoe-sole at her. 'I won't let you talk about your strange ideas again. You've just tried to sell me that writer and now you're pushing Xu Hengzhong. If I'm going to fall in love with Xu Hengzhong, do I need your help?'

She laughed. 'As for me,' I continued, 'I haven't forgotten the past. The past and the present are inseparably linked. Yining, I can't explain, but that link is strangling my future. I'm so tired of it.'

After supper, I had a splitting headache and went to bed early. I was just dropping off to sleep when Hanhan came in and announced, 'There's a man to see you. I don't know who he is.'

I'd never have guessed that the visitor would be He Jingfu. I've never in my life sought to make enemies, but He Jingfu had a thousand, ten thousand reasons to despise me. Where had he come from? Why had he come? His eyes were red, as if he'd just been crying. I told Hanhan to go over to her friend's house and watch television.

He watched Hanhan go. 'Children grow up fast,' he said softly, and held out his hand to me. 'Is this a surprise?'

I nodded: 'Yes, it is.'

'I've often thought of coming here. Today I felt I had to. Zhang Yuanyuan has died; I've just come from her memorial meeting.' As he spoke, he took a stool to sit on and pulled out his tobacco pouch. It was the first time I'd seen him smoke his peasant's pipe and it made me feel uncomfortable. It was as if he was using it to say, 'We are different people. You were one of those who pushed me along that long and bitter road.'

Automatically, I put out an ashtray for him but he pushed it to one side. He looked so sad. I knew what Zhang Yuanyuan's death must mean to him. When we were students, she had been general secretary of the Chinese literature department; but then she'd been sent to a middle school for 'shielding rightist students'. You Ruoshui had taken over from her. Among the 'rightists' she had 'shielded', He Jingfu was the most prominent. Xi Liu had wanted to brand him a rightist but she had resisted. Her reasons had been very simple: 'I encouraged them to speak out. Now you want me to attack them as rightists because they spoke out. Isn't that setting a deliberate trap for them? Besides, they're all children.'

Xi Liu publicised his disagreement with her within the Party and a discussion ensued. Naturally, Zhang Yuanyuan lost the argument. She was described as 'an old mother hen who hatched rightists and then protected them'. She was severely punished by the Party and banished to the middle school as deputy head. A few years later, she retired because of ill health. She'd always looked on He Jingfu as a son. I'd heard that when he was sent away to the countryside, she'd gone to see him off. He cried on her shoulder. When he was being beaten up, he hadn't shed a single tear.

I wanted to comfort him but how could I? What could I say? I stayed silent.

'Do you think it's only because Zhang Yuanyuan supported me that I find her death so upsetting?' he asked. 'It's not just that. I'm upset for the Party too. She was so good, she was worth so much more than Xi Liu. Not enough people realise that. He could get his old job back, she couldn't. It's criminal, whatever anyone says.'

Why had he come to my house to discuss the relative merits of Xi Liu and Zhang Yuanyuan? Because I was one of the 'protect Xi Liu group'? I forced myself to reply, 'Xi Liu is worth what Xi Liu is worth.'

He smiled. 'Yes – Xi Liu has always been highly esteemed. He was really brave that year. In the fifties and sixties he was a very good cadre though he had his hypocritical side. But now his only worth lies in demonstrating how low a Party member can sink, and how rigid and narrow his thinking can become.'

'He had a very bad time, you can't deny that,' I argued, more on my own behalf than Xi Liu's.

'Suffering doesn't affect a man's worth negatively. It can improve him or submerge him.' He paused, looking at me curiously. 'I can't believe you can still have faith in him.'

He had seen my wounds. 'You're right, though. If Xi Liu goes to hell, I go with him.'

Blushing, I turned away. I didn't want to behave this way.

'I can see I shouldn't have come. I've disturbed you.' I heard him leave but I did not move.

That night I could not stop crying. Events in the past were so clear. How they grind people down.

THREE

HE JINGFU

I treasure history because I want to use it as a gauge against the future. I am walking towards the future but it is a long road.

I shouldn't have gone to see her. I've survived long enough without Sun Yue. She talked so coolly, as if she was trying to get rid of an unwanted guest.

Why did I go – to discuss Zhang Yuanyuan and Xi Liu? Did I want to discuss all that with her and get a cold reception?

The strange thing is the yellow flower. Zhang Yuanyuan's husband gave it to me at the memorial meeting, a small yellow flower. I put it in my buttonhole, weeping. There wasn't a trace of a tear on his face but the sight of his eyes was unbearable. They were so full of loneliness, the loneliness of old age, of the widower.

The hall was decorated with a photograph of Zhang Yuanyuan, but all I could see was this little yellow flower made of paper. I've had very few close friends in my life: now there is one less. Who could ever understand and care for me as she did? Who would give out flowers at my funeral? No one but myself.

I hardly ever cry in front of others, but this time I couldn't help it. It was as if I was in mourning for my own life, hoping for someone to hear me and comfort me; for someone to mourn me.

I treasure that flower. It is a token of the grief of the living for the dead and the esteem in which they've been held. And it led me to Sun Yue. I wanted to talk to her about it but she acted so coldly that I forgot.

Why, Sun Yue? You must know that you are the most precious person in the world to me. We've never talked very intimately, never exchanged gifts, but the position you hold in my life is so important, and constant.

If I'd shown her the flower and said, 'Sun Yue, if I died, would you wear a flower like this for me?' she might have behaved differently. She might have said, 'Though I appear cold, I love you, deep down.' But instead I talked about Zhang Yuanyuan and Xi Liu. She must have thought I was taunting her.

Sun Yue, am I so hard to understand? I couldn't possibly taunt you. When we were students I loved you but you rejected me. That's the only love I've ever felt, the one and only love. I write it all down in this diary: will you ever consent to read it?

I've pressed the yellow flower between the pages.

If anyone read this, they'd probably think I was mad. A sort of tramp loves a married woman who doesn't love him and doesn't even know he loves her. He pours his heart out in a diary he's keeping for himself, the only response to which is something he gave it – a small flower made of the same material he's writing on. The whole thing is evidence that Freud was right!

Would Sun Yue tie it up with a red ribbon and treasure it?

I grew up ugly. It didn't bother me because I wasn't that interested in girls. But as soon as I met Sun Yue, I lost my equilibrium.

I was a member of the faculty student committee, deputed to meet new students. She arrived in a three-wheeled tricycle cart with Zhao Zhenhuan. Their clothes and luggage showed they'd come from a village, but I was struck by their beauty and vitality. Helping them down from the tricycle, I asked, 'Is this the first time you've been to Shanghai?'

'Of course it is. I cried when I heard I had a place here. I didn't want to come. It's got a bad reputation,' the girl answered.

'Who says so?' I asked, interested.

'I've read about it in lots of novels,' she said with assurance.

'They all describe Shanghai before liberation. It's changed now,' I said.

'Changed? Hardly! Crossing the bridge just now, some people came up and helped us across. I thought perhaps it wasn't such a bad place after all, but when we were over the bridge they all held out their hands for money. I was so disappointed. They won't get me next time!' She spoke quite angrily and shook her fist in front of my face as if I'd asked her for money. She seemed very young so I teased her, 'Then why did you apply to the university here? Why didn't you go to Beijing?'

She blushed, paused and then, pointing to Zhao Zhenhuan, said, 'He told me to apply here. I do what he says. I'd have loved to go to Beijing – I'd have gone to see the Great Wall every week!'

Zhao Zhenhuan was listening to her, smiling. He looked very happy.

When I was allocating them beds in the dormitories, it emerged that neither had brought a mosquito net. It was too late to borrow any from the office so I moved Zhao Zhenhuan into the bed of a student who was home for the weekend, and gave my net to Sun Yue.

'Whose is this? It's not yours is it? I won't take it,' she said. 'Let the mosquitoes bite me for a night. I've got very bitter blood, they won't bother me.'

I told her it belonged to a student who hadn't yet returned to the university; only then would she accept it. She didn't thank me but smiled, a natural and friendly smile. I was already captivated by her. That night, I was bitten so badly I couldn't sleep. 'My blood is bitter too, Sun Yue. They don't bother me,' I thought.

I often bumped into her in the library, her eyes filled with tears as she pored over a book. She loved foreign literature, and read with impressive concentration and speed. She spent a few days once engrossed in *First Love*. All the seats were occupied and she stood at the bookshelf, reading and weeping, oblivious of everyone else. I remember teasing her then, telling her not to ruin the book by crying all over it. She turned her back on me, brushing the tears away with the back of her hand, and went on reading.

By the end of the first term, she had already demonstrated her multiple talents. She was an outstanding student; her poems and essays appeared constantly in the university journal; she was in the university gymnastics team; and she was a member of the faculty drama group. All the boys fancied her, but at the weekend dance she would only partner Zhao Zhenhuan.

I decided to apply to join the drama group, and had a word with the director. 'You need all sorts of characters on stage, why not take me?' He let me join. They were preparing to stage *Put down your whips* to commemorate the anniversary of the December 9th student revolutionary movement. Sun Yue was playing the girl leader, and I managed to get the part of her father because the director felt it suited my temperament. I was overjoyed with the casting. No one guessed that it would cause problems on the day of the performance.

Sun Yue acted marvellously but she threw me into total confusion. As soon as I got on the stage, I forgot every single word. Fortunately there was a prompter and I struggled on until we reached the point where the girl says to her father, 'It's not surprising, father, they are starving!' and flings herself into his arms, weeping bitterly. Sun Yue was really crying at this point, and I was shaking so much I completely forgot about the play. Gently raising her head from my chest, I stroked her hair, looked at her and said in a low voice, 'Sun Yue!' People must have thought I was mad. She just looked blankly at me, her mouth open, and forgot to say, 'Father' again.

I don't remember how I got off stage. Before we'd removed our make-up, the director stormed in, shouting, 'What on earth were you doing on-stage? Having a sentimental chat?' Sun Yue turned and ran, her eyes furious with me. I was elated. I'd been acting my own part. I'd found my love.

I began writing letters to her, a letter a day. I never got a reply. Whenever I saw her, she gave me a cold stare. I couldn't understand why she seemed to dislike me, so I disguised my writing and wrote anonymously, 'I have something I must discuss with you. Please be at the park gate at seven on Saturday evening.'

She turned up and gave me her usual cold look. 'Don't you know I've got a boyfriend?'

'I had heard. But I love you.'

'You are behaving improperly.'

'I hadn't thought of it like that.'

In fact, I had thought about it but I couldn't see anything wrong with my behaviour. My love for her was pure; I wanted to tell her I loved her; I wasn't going to harm Zhao Zhenhuan and he couldn't harm me.

'Well, think about it. And if you write again, I'll send the letter back.' She ran off, her pigtails bouncing. 'I'll walk you home!' I shouted. Without turning her head she said, 'I'm not alone.' Zhao Zhenhuan was standing there. She took his hand and walked away.

I stopped sending letters after that. But I couldn't stop my love and I poured it out in my diary. Every day I wrote, describing each turn of feeling, each twist: every day until the awful moment in 1957 when my most secret pages were turned in evidence against me.

In the spring of that year, I had stuck up a big-character poster entitled, 'Let us hope that Comrade Xi Liu will behave more humanely', in which I criticised his treatment of the Overseas Chinese student, Little Xie. It was just at the beginning of the Hundred Flowers Movement/Anti-Rightist Campaign, and Little Xie's mother had fallen ill and asked him to come and see her. On the grounds that the campaign was more important than anything else, Xi Liu refused permission for Xie to go abroad; furthermore, he demanded that Xie make a clean break with his 'capitalist mother'. Xie refused and wrote posters to publicise the argument, which stirred up a storm amongst the students. My poster was written in sympathy, and criticised Xi Liu for placing Xie's mother in the enemy camp and for insinuating that family feelings were incorrect feelings. I said that if we were supposed to be humanitarian when faced with the enemy's unrelenting attacks on the revolution, surely we should be generous towards an ordinary working woman? I called on Xi Liu to correct his error immediately and allow Xie to leave the country.

Over a thousand people eventually signed my poster in agreement. I looked carefully at all the names and finally, in a corner, I found hers. Zhao Zhenhuan had not signed. I was ecstatic at the thought that she might compare me with him, and find that her ideals were closer to mine.

I don't know how long my happiness might have lasted had it not been for Xu Hengzhong's poster, 'A criticism of He Jingfu'. It came as a terrible shock and completely altered the direction of the campaign, turning me into the object of public vilification. Of the posters that followed, I remember only two clearly. Xu Hengzhong's was very emotional; he said that my poster was nothing but rumour and slander, that it made him so angry he couldn't eat or sleep and that he'd spent a whole night weeping bitterly over it. The other one was Sun Yue's. She didn't criticise me directly but said that she had 'departed from the correct stand' in signing my poster: I suspected she'd been reprimanded within the faculty.

I was accused of being a 'rightist'. My crime consisted of opposing the Party's class line with capitalist humanitarianism, attacking class struggle with revisionist humanism and harming Party leaders by spreading rumours. They named me as a Grade One criminal and my diary was seized.

I will never forget that day. Excerpts from my diary were published on posters under the heading 'Look! Evidence of He Jingfu's repulsive immorality!' Sun Yue's name was replaced by X X but everyone knew who was meant. Where I had written of my feelings on performing *Put down your whips*, 'Right now, all I can think about are your fine eyes. Your eloquent eyes', the copyist had underlined it in red and added 'and your coarse skin'. They changed beauty into hideousness; they took love and made it obscene.

Stunned and friendless, I had only one thought: I must explain things to Sun Yue. Finally, I found an opportunity when she was walking in a deserted corner of the grounds. She didn't avoid my approach; nor did she look at me.

'Sun Yue, I'm so sorry; I hope you understand that I wrote only for myself. If it's harmed your reputation, please forgive me.'

I spoke abruptly, and when she turned round her face was streaked with tears.

'I hate you! I hate myself!' she said in a small, unsteady voice, and suddenly I felt a very light kiss on my forehead. By the time I realised what had happened, she had gone.

Was it pity or love, that kiss? An act of charity or a sign of feeling? I asked myself ten thousand times but I never had another chance to ask Sun Yue. Whatever it was, I loved her more than ever; yet I knew that I must stop pursuing her.

In 1962, I was informed that I could return to finish my course at university, but I didn't want to go back. I'd got used to life in the countryside and had been studying philosophy in secret, working out an answer to the problem of how Marxism-Leninism should deal with human feelings. I did, however, write once again to Sun Yue and got a reply from Zhao Zhenhuan, telling me they were married. His letter extinguished a spark of hope.

Suddenly I felt like an orphan and decided to go away. My parents had died in the period of disruption and my only sister was married; I left a note for her and set off. Where I went, not even I could tell you. I set off to learn from the world and the only two books I took with me were *The Dream of the Red Chamber* and the *Selected Works of Marx and Engels*.

I became a real outcast. I had no address, no grain or cotton coupons, nobody looked for me, no letters came for me. Nobody cared who I was or what I was and nobody cared to ask where I'd come from or where I was going. I was known simply as 'Old He, the charcoal burner', 'Old He, the housebuilder', 'Old He, the labourer', 'Old He, the dynamiter', 'Old He, the carter', or even 'Old He, the storyteller'. I worked. I earned my keep. That was all.

Mentally, I was all but frozen, and thought less and less often of Sun Yue until I'd nearly forgotten her. But then once when I was working at a stone quarry and an explosion almost killed me, her image passed across my mind and I was filled with the fear that I might never see her again. I knew then that I still loved her and I revelled in the sensation. If I could still love, I could find the strength to go on living; and so her image helped me to survive the blast. I started to keep a diary again, and in it I wrote letters to Sun Yue. As I remoulded myself, I recreated her as a divine figure with all the most marvellous attributes and qualities. All my hopes went into this creation: I don't know whether I was moved by love for all women or love for all humanity but I do know that love made it possible for me to see my own shadow, to realise that I was still a human being and that I wanted to live.

'Sun Yue, which side are you on? Are you a reactionary or a rebel? I hope you are independent. We must analyse and stick to our analyses; we must preserve things that deserve to be preserved. We have brains in our heads, not tumours: what's a brain for? Thinking, reasoning, analysing. And I hope you can see clearly now what Xi Liu is like; I think he has failed the Party. In 1957, I was prepared to help him in every way I could but he wasn't ready to listen. I hope that you will help him now. Do you agree?'

I wrote this 'letter' in my diary in late 1966. I was indifferent to the 'Cultural Revolutionaries' who called me an unrepentant capitalist; but I worried about Sun Yue, and one day I noticed a news headline which made me give up my job as a carter and come back to Shanghai: 'The Great Proletarian Cultural Revolution is blazing like a fire set to dry tinder in Shanghai university! The capitalist-roader Xi Liu has finally been exposed!' The article described a struggle in the university between the 'rebels' and the 'group protecting Xi Liu'; amongst those described as 'hard-line Xi Liu-ists' was someone called Sun. I feared for you, Sun Yue . . . Would your name always appear like this, half-concealed?

Inside the university, everyone was too busy to recognise me; in any case, I looked just like a peasant from the North. I pushed my way into the auditorium, where a great 'struggle meeting' against Xi Liu was about to begin; and the first thing I saw was a large placard with the words 'Xi Liu's concubine, Sun Yue' written on it.

Her plaits had been chopped off and her hair was dishevelled. Her face was colourless. She stood, bent under the weight of the placard.

'Account for yourself, Sun Yue. How did Xi Liu persuade you to oppose the revolutionary masses?' the chairman asked her severely.

'Xi Liu did not persuade me. I do not understand.' Her voice was very low but even.

'Down with the unrepentant royalist Sun Yue! Down with Xi Liu's concubine Sun Yue!'

'Sun Yue has long maintained a reactionary stance. At the beginning of the Anti-Rightist Movement she ganged up with the extreme rightist He Jingfu. They were lovers, even though she was already engaged to Zhao Zhenhuan. Can anyone deny she's a rightist who slipped through the net the first time? She's a counter-revolutionary whore!'

'Xi Liu is another rightist who should have been caught long ago. His anti-rightist stance was a fake!'

'Down! Down! Down, down, down with . . . !' Sun Yue was being led off stage. It sounded to me as if they were shouting 'Upside down! Upside down!'

So I had not been forgotten, I was still a 'person', a 'tool of class struggle' – at least in the Anti-Rightist Campaign. They cut up history and distorted it and played it for the rabble . . . what kind of drama was this? Should I pity her or despise her? I began to feel confused.

Feelings are reliable; feelings are unreliable. Sometimes it's impossible to know what your feelings are. Past and present, theory and practice, superstition and science, truth and falsehood, you and me, men and animals, all tumbled in a crucible. Stirred. More thrown in. Finally we get a spoonful to taste. Can you tell whether it is sweet or bitter? All you know is that all smells, tastes and colours are there in all their varieties.

Sun Yue was far away, further even than when Xi Liu had fought against me. All I could do to save myself from falling apart in despair was return to my life, drive my cart, read my books, do my research. I didn't mention her again in my diary: to create a spirit you need the right environment, and I had lost it. I buried her and the past. Yet I treasure the past because I want to use it as a gauge against the future. One doesn't know what the future will be like, nor when it will arrive. I didn't expect it when it came.

'He Jingfu, the Party has reinvestigated your case and considers that your punishment in 1957 was incorrect. We have decided to wipe your record clean and find work for you.'

The Chinese Faculty of the university had discovered where

I was, somehow, and recalled me. Sun Yue came to see me on behalf of the Party branch. Her hair was greying at the temples.

I didn't thank her; history had been restored to me, what was there to thank her for? It wasn't a simple question of settling accounts: with whom would I settle them?

'You've suffered over the years,' she said with official concern, sounding like someone in an important position.

'No, I've lived well. And you?' I was cool; I didn't like her new attitude.

'Fine, thank you. What sort of work would you like to do?'

'I'd like to work on the reference collection. I'm writing a book and I need materials and time.'

'What are you writing about?'

'Marxism and humanism.'

'What?'

'Isn't that clear enough? It's an old theme used by capitalists and reactionaries.'

'I don't altogether understand it but I'm sure you'll do it well. I wish you success.'

We were both so cool, almost challenging, but how else could it have been? A series of disasters breaks hearts and relationships. A person has to get to know himself again before he can get to know others.

When I saw how Sun Yue had changed, I realised that the girl I'd loved no longer existed. A different Sun Yue stood in front of me; could I love this one in the same way? I didn't know, but at least I felt a new hope; after all, if she hadn't changed I would be feeling even stranger! It gave me a sense of progress.

She is always very businesslike with me; much more relaxed with other people. When she comes to visit other teachers in the dormitory she never stops to see me; she never invites me to her house. If we meet by chance, we nod . . . it was like that today.

I hadn't progressed far before I hesitated. I don't know why I hesitate when I ought to be moving on. I'm chasing a real person not a divine woman. People are much more difficult to understand. Even though divine women are human creations.

FOUR

XU HENGZHONG

The whole of history can be summarised in two words, 'rising' and 'falling'. In the past I rose and put others down, now I am falling. It's very clear.

Yesterday, I took the little boy to the park. I looked at the other children in their light, bright summer clothes and I looked at Little Kun, still wearing old winter trousers. It was so depressing. On the way home we stopped at several children's clothes shops but the prices were frightening. Then I remembered the sewing machine at home: why not try making him something? I bought two lengths of cloth, borrowed a pattern book, gathered scissors, measuring tape and a piece of chalk, and started on a pair of trousers. The worker and all his tools: something must emerge.

'Your old comrade isn't very pleased with you. Aren't you worried?' Someone had told me about what Xi Liu thought of me and tried to persuade me not to write any more articles. I couldn't really understand why I shouldn't. Nobody was threatening me with legal reprisals for writing about individual liberty, but the friend was a good friend so I agreed with him. The transition from people's power to a legal system must necessarily be slow.

'It's not that simple, you know. Some of the big names have been publishing. They haven't even bothered with pseudonyms.'

Was I supposed to use a pseudonym? Because I'd made mis-

takes? Surely Xi Liu's mistakes were far more serious than mine?
I hadn't accused anybody of being a capitalist or a counter-
revolutionary, but what about him? How many people had he
wrongly accused of rightism? I hadn't had secret affairs with
women, but what about him? Of course fresh shit smells worse
than old dried shit. But what about You Ruoshui? He was fresh
shit, too; he'd been far more active than me in the campaign to
criticise Deng Xiaoping[1]. They didn't need pseudonyms to become
Party secretaries and party officials. Anyway, if I were to change
my name, I'd still be myself. But it's quite the thing to change
your name now. Essays are written on the subject, to the point
where names seem more important than events. Su Qin[2] was
right: 'The poor have no sons but the rich and famous dread their
relatives. Man's life on earth is a struggle for wealth and honour,
what remains if one fails?'

I'll accustom myself to loneliness, study Taoism, seek nothing,
care for nothing. When You Ruoshui got the job in the Party
office, he invited me over for a meal, probably because he was
afraid I'd turn on him. He quoted Zhuangzi, 'The complete man
has no self; the spirit cannot act; the sage has no name.' Very
apt: but if I had no self, who would care for my son? If I couldn't
act, who would pay me a wage? If I had no name, who would
listen to me? I don't want to be famous but I wouldn't mind doing
as well as You Ruoshui. I prefer 'Man's life is a struggle for wealth
and honour, what remains if one fails?' Zhuangzi created Taoism,
he wasn't just a pious follower. Creating and believing aren't
necessarily the same, just like action and knowledge, externality
and internality. Could I pretend to be a sceptical believer?

It's a complicated argument to follow but then everything in
the world is complicated. Crooked lines seem more natural than
straight ones. But when you write things down they tend to be
straight rather than crooked, because it's not easy to describe
complications.

But I must get these complications straightened out: trouser
patterns. Children's trousers must be cut right or they'll be
uncomfortable. He's got a nice little bottom. I've not smacked it
once since his mother died.

'Hengzhong, if I die you must find little Kun a nice new mother.

I'll never stop worrying if you don't. Has Sun Yue . . . got a man friend?' People say odd things when they're very ill. That was what my wife said to me. I was a 'rebel' then, Sun Yue a 'reactionary'. Now the 'reactionary' is Party secretary for the department and the apple of Xi Liu's eye, while the 'rebel' is an ordinary teacher, a pain in Xi Liu's neck. Could these two marry? A stupid idea.

Yet opposites sometimes unite.

Sun Yue is mending Little Kun's shoes. She's never held a grudge against me. She's a Party branch secretary with a heart of gold.

My hand wasn't very steady cutting the trousers. Why can't we go around naked like stone age men? Or wrap a piece of cloth around ourselves like Africans? I'm told it's progress, or culture; actually it's a bloody nuisance. Take some cotton fibres, make them up into a great ball; pull the threads and make them into cloth. Then cut the cloth up. Then join it with thread to make a garment. Heavens, what a process of composition and decomposition just to make a piece of clothing. Call that social progress?

We must use dialectics to analyse everything. One divides into two. Two unite to form one. Separation and unity. This time, I've been 'separated'.

I hadn't been sewing long when someone knocked at the door. It was He Jingfu. Uneasily, I asked him to sit down and gave him some tea. Hearing that he'd come back to the university had made me very nervous: it would be so easy for him to avenge himself on me. I had thought of going and telling him that Xi Liu had instructed me to write that poster; but I was also afraid of provoking Xi Liu any further. So I've avoided him for a long time. I never thought that he might come and see me. I've had enough. Does he want to load another stone on my back? To cover up my nervousness, I picked up the scissors.

He took out a tobacco pouch and looked at me with surprise, as if he couldn't understand what I was doing. 'Are you making clothes? Children's clothes?'

'Yes – what does it look like?' I feared he might derive pleasure from my predicament; on the other hand, it might make him more gentle with me. 'I'm mother and father to the child now, though I don't think I'll win any prizes for sewing.'

He frowned. 'But why are you doing this?'

'Is it wrong for a man to do woman's work?'

He seemed angry. 'It's not a question of man's work or woman's work: but there are too many other things we ought to be studying and thinking about now for you to be wasting your energy on this. Where's your old activism? Is it all dissipated?'

Now he was beginning to dig. I wasn't going to put up with an investigation. 'You don't know what it's like to run a home. Look at little Kun's clothes! I'm his father!' I'd meant to laugh as I said it, but I couldn't. I thought of Little Kun growing out of his clothes.

'I do know. Go and buy him some new things. I amassed a lot of back pay when I was away, and now I live alone. You've not been able to save: I'll help!' His expression was friendly, his eyes were honest; he didn't look as if he bore a grudge. I put the scissors down.

He stood and began to roll up the things on the table; then he threw the bundle onto the bed and looked at me sternly. 'Is it just because you're short of money?'

'No, it's not just the money,' I admitted. 'Haven't you heard? Comrade Xi Liu has just issued an order forbidding me to write any more articles.'

'That's what I've come to ask you about,' he said.

So that was why he was here! To enjoy my difficulties! Faking innocence, I said, 'Comrade Xi Liu is right. I have made errors and my articles have had a bad influence. It shows Comrade Xi Liu's concern.'

His eyebrows looked very fierce and he sucked his pipe. The harsh smoke made me cough. 'You haven't learnt much. Or at least, you haven't learnt enough hypocrisy,' he answered eventually.

I *had* become a hypocrite. I didn't say what I felt. Honest people suffer, even a three-year-old knows that. A lot of people can't distinguish between hypocrisy and honesty: let him try and analyse them, I didn't have to agree or disagree. I'd keep my mouth shut. Let him do the talking.

'I expect you worry whether Xi Liu will ever let you off the hook?' he asked.

He was right – and would *you* ever let me off the hook? I didn't say anything.

'But I don't think you ought to worry what other people think. You've got to free yourself, to take yourself in hand.'

'Are you suggesting that Xi Liu hasn't punished mc enough?' I couldn't stop myself asking, betraying my worry.

'No, I think he's been too hard on you. But you haven't been hard enough on yourself, and look where it's got you. Don't you think you have some responsibility for people, for history? Not for the past, that's over, but for now and for the future.'

They were interesting, these words full of dialectical materialism. I would have to take myself in hand, but what about Xi Liu? You Ruoshui? They weren't wrong because they hadn't made a self-criticism! It might be up to the fool to correct himself, but what capacity do I have for taking on the burden of history? Anyway, what is history? It can be summed up in two words: rising and falling. In the past, I rose and put others down; now my downfall has been brought about by others. It's very simple. They toppled me and now he wants me to 'rectify' myself. I'm no different from anyone else. I won't say anything. Let him talk.

'Why don't you say anything? Don't you agree?' He puffed at his pipe.

'I don't know – it's unfair: you ask me to take on the burden of history but history doesn't have to take care of me. It's been a lot kinder to Xi Liu and You Ruoshui,' I said.

'History is like someone with a very concealed character: it doesn't show its true colours lightly. But you'll see, some day there'll be justice.'

'Highly poetic,' I smiled.

'Poetry can be true.'

'In an ideal world, perhaps.'

'An ideal world isn't so far from the real world.'

'Not at the rate we're going; one step forward, two steps back.'

'You . . .' he gestured with his tobacco pouch, almost as if he wanted to hit me in the chest but changed his mind at the last minute. Then he sighed and said, sadly, 'I don't understand you.

How can you change so much after a single criticism? You're making it into a tragedy!'

'Nobody wants to get hurt,' I answered in a low voice. 'That's what I can't understand about you – how you've managed to remain such an idealist. Hasn't your experience taught you otherwise? I've heard a bit about your years on the road and I can't imagine how you kept going; I admire it, but I can't understand it.'

His pipe was out but he didn't move to light it; just sat looking straight ahead, mouth tightly closed. I was fascinated by his eyes: not large particularly, but clear and gleaming – the kind that express warmth, and tempt you to reveal your innermost thoughts. And as if for the first time I noticed his good looks, his strong features darkened by years of living rough and the fine, high nose which gives him such an air of distinction. People tell me I've got fine eyebrows and good eyes, but beside his they don't amount to much; I wonder if Sun Yue finds him attractive?

He coughed lightly, seemingly to control himself. I was just about to ask his thoughts when there was another knock at the door and Sun Yue came in to deliver Little Kun's shoes. He Jingfu blushed as she took them from her bag: anyone might blush, seeing a ghost from the past.

Suddenly He Jingfu said, 'Branch secretary, do sit down. Our friend here has been talking about his feelings on being readmitted to the Party. We all ought to listen, don't you think?' They went together strangely, his mocking tone and his imploring look, but Sun Yue sat down and I offered her some tea.

He Jingfu began to speak, looking at Sun Yue. She lowered her head. 'Old Xu has just been saying that I'm an idealist, which isn't exactly true. I had faith and ideals when I was eighteen and new to the Party; now I see that I was just deluded because I had no real knowledge of theory or society. If I'd examined my ideals, I couldn't have found any stable basis for them; and I never really had much faith in myself. After I'd been disciplined in the fifties, I became convinced that I'd been wrong – what's more, even my friends thought I was wrong. So in order to understand and rectify my mistakes I started studying Marxism-Leninism; but after a while – what with reading and living with ordinary people – I came to realise that I hadn't been so wrong after all. That gave me something to hold on to, a hope that has kept me going through the years: that one day the Party will acknowledge my truth and even Xi Liu will admit he was wrong. But recently my faith has been shaken again . . .'

Sun Yue glanced at him, then lowered her head again. He cleared his throat as before – whenever he was agitated he cleared his throat – and began to tell his story, the story of a vagrant:

'One year, I joined a group of carters working near the Great Wall. With great difficulty, I'd bought a horse and cart; the horse was bad-tempered so it hadn't cost too much.

'I loved the Great Wall. The first time I climbed to the beacon at the "greatest pass in the world", I forgot my low status. Each brick seemed like a person; the Wall, snaking off into the distance, seemed like an endless mass of people. I felt like a new recruit in an enormous army.

'People had scratched their names on almost every brick in the beacon, as if, like me, they wanted to broadcast the fact that they'd joined this army, as if the Wall was our roll of honour. Nevertheless, I didn't add my name to the list; instead, whenever I was free, I would climb up to the beacon. I wanted to spend my life there, and be buried under the Wall when I died.

'In the group of carters, we were all the same, we were "black", members of the underground. You probably don't realise that outside our normal society there is a "black" society, made up of all sorts of people: those who work on their own, the unemployed, people who have been driven out of the mainstream for all sorts of reasons but who still have to live. We had to band together, otherwise we'd never have been able to get hold of grain coupons or cotton coupons.

'You really have to have been in one of these groups to understand them. They're extraordinarily stable; nobody knows anything about anybody else, nobody looks after anyone else, they exist to make money and that's all that unites them. There's always a leader – never me, I never wanted to be and in any case I'm not serious enough. It takes a very canny sort of bully to hold that kind of group together. Our bully had escaped from a "reform through labour" camp, and it was rumoured that he was a hardened criminal rather than a political detainee. He was pale and thin,

like a scholar except for the wolfish expression on his face and
the huge bags under his eyes which made him look even more
fearsome.

'We were all afraid of him – he was as cruel and rapacious as
he looked – and he forced us to hand over every penny we made.
I was as frightened as the rest, until one day the bastard kept
back eighty yuan of my wages because he said I was "an outsider".
The money didn't bother me much but I couldn't stomach his
attitude any longer. Feeling that all the stones of the Wall, all
those people, could defeat the tyrant, I started to fight back. He
hit me, I hit him, blood started to flow . . . in the end, I was
taken to the Police Station.

'They asked me for my identity papers. Of course, I didn't
have any, so I simply told them my name and proclaimed my
innocence. The policeman was all right – he told me to stick to
the straight and narrow, and let me go – but I could have wept
as I drove my cart away. Identity papers! I had none . . . and
without an identity, what was the point in living? More and more
distressed, I forced the horse to a gallop. I didn't care if I
overturned the cart or crashed into the Great Wall; I'd lost my
identity and I didn't care if I lost my life. By the time I noticed
the cart in front it was too late. We hit the other horse so
hard that it died within a few minutes; and I ended up handing
over the reins to mine. I let the other driver have my cart as
well; it was a relief in a way to think that I now had no ties
at all.

'The carter was a good man, reluctant to leave me destitute.
Before he drove off he insisted on sharing a drink from his hip
flask, and offered me the carcass of the dead horse so I could sell
the flesh. I didn't want it, so he took that away too. I didn't want
anything – just to lie at the foot of the Wall, where if I died no
one would find me and the Wall could slowly absorb my corpse.
Only one question remained: was I really ready to die? And so I
lay there, looking up at the stars filling the sky, and began like
Hamlet to ponder my fate . . .

'I was thirty. In my life I had achieved thirty years of age and
nothing else – no home, no career, no identity papers, nothing.
Nobody needed me. I ate, drank and clothed myself merely to

stay alive. But did I stay alive only to sweat for that gang leader? No! Were my blood and tears meant just to fill the bags under his eyes? *No!*

'I jumped up and began running along the Wall, up to the highest beacon tower. There, by the light of the stars, I took my penknife and scratched three characters on the brick: He Jingfu. My name would stand on the roll of honour. That brick was my identity card, it proved that He Jingfu was a child of China, a descendant of the Yellow Emperor. Leaning against the wall of the tower, it was as if I looked out over all the mountains and rivers of China. I can see it now, so impressive, so varied. Within the pass, all was full and green; beyond lay the flatter carpet of yellow earth. Somehow I was more uplifted by that endless yellow dust: its beauty and strength seemed to lie more rooted in the earth; it stirred my imagination; I wanted to offer it my life.

'A shooting star flew across to the West and fell. The sky was so broad and still, the endless stars like eyes watching the earth. On either side of the Milky Way hung the fixed stars of the Herd Boy and the Spinning Girl, lovers separated and pinned. It seemed as if nothing would ever move. Who in the boundless world notices a falling shooting star? I thought that if I died, I would be to humanity what the shooting star was to the solar system. Unnoticed, silenced. But I was not a shooting star, I was a person with feelings, with love and hate.

'And then I remembered a story my mother used to tell me about the Milky Way: "There is a pearly drop of dew right on top of everyone's head, and that's what symbolises your fortune." She often used to show me the stars and say people were like them; each with his own place and his own power. Nobody needed to prop them up, they still hung in the sky; likewise people could live on the earth without anybody's help or hindrance. Stars shine in the sky and dew sparkles on the ground: that is the philosophy I learned as a child.

'Suddenly I knew that my drop of dew hadn't dried up, that it had brought back this vision of my dead mother and father, of my sister who was so far away, of all the people who had loved me . . .

'I had no cart, no horse, but I still had my hands. So what if I had no identity papers? My worth wasn't something you could register on a piece of paper.

'I sat up all night on the beacon tower and climbed back down early the next morning. I wasn't going back to the carters but I needed work; so I followed the Wall, asking in every village, never with any luck. In the end, I had to leave my beloved Wall and head south, to the banks of the Huai river –

'Sun Yue, what's the matter?'

He Jingfu stopped abruptly. Sun Yue's head was on the table and her shoulders were shaking. 'Don't you feel well?' I asked. Without showing her face, she shook her head and said, 'Go on, you went to the banks of the Huai river . . .'

He Jingfu didn't want to carry on. He finished his story quickly: 'In short, I decided to carry on living and I've not thought about death since then. Life may not have been fair to me but I have to be fair to myself. I can't judge myself against that gang leader; my worth has nothing to do with our relationship. Perhaps flirting with death has turned me into a sort of fossil but I think my bones glow more than his, my phosphorescence is brighter than his.'

Sun Yue got up, rubbed her face and left without a word. He Jingfu watched her. I couldn't stop myself asking, 'Do you still love her?'

'I've never loved anyone else. But being in love and living like a vagrant aren't as similar as they might seem in fiction.'

'I'd like to see you get together with Sun Yue, but you've both changed a lot over the last twenty years. Life has seen too many changes and people's feelings can change, too.'

'True. But to find out how deep our love is, it would have to be tested. It looks to me as if she is avoiding such tests.'

'She might have found someone else. She's not the charming girl she used to be, she's a mature woman. Look, she's made shoes for Little Kun, would she have done that in the past?'

Why did I say that? I still don't know. I despised my cruelty as I said it, but I didn't stop myself.

He stood up and smiled. 'I'm off. I didn't mean to come here and talk about human nature – I meant to talk about other things entirely. But let me just ask you this: it's a question I'm writing on at the moment. Do you think humans have inherent animal instincts? And if so, how do they affect our social life?'

I could have answered without needing to reflect that men *are* animals, and that human life is often a great deal worse than animal life because man can cover up his base desires while he schemes to get what he wants. But I didn't want to think about it, it was too dangerous!

Standing in the doorway, he went on, 'I don't think you can explain human nature simply by applying general rules of social relations. Very basic aspects of human nature like the physiological or animal aspects are still only part of the whole. They influence human nature, but that's not to say that human beings are base; on the contrary, it's what helps them to rise because they've got to overcome their animal instincts. Now that beats hypocrisy, doesn't it?'

I took his shoulder and pushed him out, smiling. 'Okay, you're the expert on human nature. I can't begin to argue about it. But you've got a good grounding in classical literature, why don't you try some literary research?'

'Why? Are human nature and humanism forbidden areas?' he asked, coming back in.

'It's not that they're forbidden areas, no; just that they've got more thorns than roses. And not many people tackle them – why put yourself in a minority? Don't forget, "The tree that stands out in the forest will be blown over, a high river bank will be swept away in a flood and he who stands taller than his fellow men will be opposed." It's better not to draw attention to yourself,' I said.

'You're certainly not an individualist any longer! But you have to remember it's because people like you stand back that the minority stands out.' He shook my hand gravely. At the door, he turned and smiled, 'Tomorrow I'll buy some clothes for Little Kun so you can put your needles away!' I nodded and closed the door behind him. Then I spread the cotton and sewing things out on the table again.

FIVE

SUN HANHAN

For me, history is a torn photograph. I don't like it but I can't forget it.

Ma looks very gloomy these days. She's always scribbling in a little notebook; but when I come in, she stops and locks it away in a drawer. Whenever I look at that drawer I see a barrier between us, an enormous wall.

'Ma!' I put down my satchel and shouted. She just muttered something without turning her head, hurriedly opened the drawer, closed it, locked it.

Should I show her my schoolbook? I'd failed in the physics test – for the first time. And because it was the first time, I was terrified. 'What went wrong? Go home and talk it over with your mother – she has placed all her hopes on you! You mustn't disappoint her,' my teacher had said when she handed back the exercise book. It made me feel even worse.

'Ma.' I forced myself to put the book in front of her.

'Explain yourself,' she said. Her voice sounded hoarse; I didn't dare speak. She turned to me, eyes shining. I looked down. The room was quiet except for the ticking of the clock.

'Ma . . . Don't shout at me. Don't hit me. I can't bear it when I upset you . . .' She didn't move. I looked up to see tears running down her face.

Seeing Ma's tears broke my heart and I began to cry too. Children's hearts can break just as much as grown-ups'.

'Ma!' Why was she so unhappy? Was it because I failed the test?

'Hanhan, you know you're all I've got. If it wasn't for you I wouldn't want to go on living, life is so miserable. But you can't understand,' she whispered.

I can't understand? Then explain it to me! Is it my fault that life is so miserable?

But she didn't say any more. I looked at the locked drawer.

Ma signed my book and handed it back to me. 'Why did you fail? Do you have trouble understanding the lessons?'

I shook my head. I never have any trouble understanding.

'Then why?' she asked rather irritably.

'Well . . . I had an argument that day with someone at school, and when we had the test I was really upset.' I didn't mind admitting it: I wanted her to know how unhappy I'd been.

'What was the argument about?' She raised her eyebrows. Ma is always critical of me; she didn't seem to care who I'd quarrelled with or whether I was right or not.

'This girl was laughing about my name. She kept calling me Hānhān [Stupid] instead of Hanhan [Regret]. Then she wanted to know why I was called Hanhan and she said it was because I haven't got a father . . .' I was almost choking. She bit her lip. 'Ma, please tell me what happened between you and my father.'

Tell me Ma, tell me; I'm fifteen now. I've been wondering about it for ages and at last I've dared to ask.

She waved a hand at me. 'Go and amuse yourself outside. You drive me crazy with your questions.'

I remember Ma being so different, so kind, when I was small. Every day when she came home from work, she'd shout, 'Huanhuan' [Little Ring], which is what I used to be called. She'd swing me onto her shoulders and walk about saying, 'Huanhuan, my little Huanhuan, clever Huanhuan, pretty Huanhuan, sweet-smelling Huanhuan!' She'd say it and I'd repeat it. Sometimes she'd catch me out by adding, 'Smelly Huanhuan!' and I'd be fooled into repeating that too. But whenever that happened I'd jump up and down, shouting 'I'm going to tell Daddy. Mummy's bad, Mummy smells!' Then she'd hug me and laugh, 'Huanhuan doesn't smell. Huanhuan is Mummy's precious, sweet-smelling baby.' In those days, Ma used to dress me in red, fiery red; and everything about her was warm and rosy too.

She changed my name to Hanhan [Regret] when they broke up. Other things changed as well. Ma made sure I ate properly and was well-dressed but she didn't seem to care about herself any more. And she wasn't as warm and close as before; she seemed just to see me as something that ate and needed clothes. I'd stopped being her precious baby, and become her regret.

I was so lonely. If children don't think about death, then I wasn't a child. When I put in my application to join the Youth League my teachers said I wasn't sufficiently positive and optimistic.

Fine, if you're going to lock things up, I'll lock things up too. If you won't let me understand you, then I won't let you understand me.

Ma told me once about a Japanese writer who said that literature was an expression of misery. I agree. Whenever I feel miserable, I write poems; but I don't show them to her. I've got a notebook she gave me, inscribed 'Sun Han, youthful poems', and I've copied quite a few in there – but not the one I wrote on the day of the physics exam. I'm afraid she might see it:

Names

People laugh at my name.
It's a joke.
Don't mock people who should be pitied.
Names, names,
I'm not just a symbol of the inclinations of others,
I can remember certain things
Which echo in the hearts of others.
Though I did not note the date,
I'll never forget that dreadful evening.
Though I was very small,
My memories are still strong.
You can't disappear.

You are still bruising my heart.
My heart will never find peace,
Ever rising and rolling like the waves of the sea.
I do not want to know
The origin of my name.
Let it stay in my heart
And not bruise others.
The light wind; the dancing willows
Told me this, told me everything,
Don't mock my name,
May they forget it entirely.

I haven't got a drawer. My only drawer is my satchel and I keep my poem right at the bottom.

'Huanhuan!' Ma called.

My old name! She must have been thinking of the past too! I ran over and put my arms round her neck: 'Ma, what did you call me just now? Say it again!'

'Hanhan. Didn't I call you Hanhan? Did I get it wrong?'

Her voice was surprised, innocent, and my heart grew cold.

'What did you want?' I asked, disappointed.

'Could you go and fill the thermos flasks? I'm longing for some hot tea.'

'All right.' I deliberately clanged the flasks on the floor, but she took no notice.

Suddenly that man was standing at the door again. 'Good evening, Sun Hanhan. Is your mother at home?'

'Good evening Uncle Xu,' I replied as ungraciously as I could, and told him she was.

He's been such a persistent visitor recently – ever since Ma made some shoes for his little boy. They came over the day she delivered them. He dragged the child in and pointed at Ma: 'Say Mummy, Little Kun! Come on – she made the shoes for you. Thank Mummy!' The boy managed to mutter 'Mummy' and 'Thank you Mummy'. It irritated me so much: why couldn't he have called her 'Auntie'? Why insist on 'Mummy'? I know people use 'Mummy' and 'Granny' pretty loosely in Shanghai, but it really annoyed me when Xu went on like that.

Anyway, he's years older than Ma. He looked like a monkey when he drank the tea I brought him that first time – I made it out of old left-overs, so it all floated dustily in the cup and he had to purse his lips to blow it aside: just like a monkey. I'd started to feel a bit better until Ma began stroking Little Kun on the head, as if he were her own child, and told me, 'Go and fetch some of your sweets for Little Brother.'

Whose little brother? 'They're finished,' I said nastily. Even if I had any sweets, I wasn't about to give them to him. Ma had looked coldly at me, and then at the sweet jar on the sideboard, clearly thinking, 'I've just bought a pound of sweets, how can you have finished them?' But she hadn't said anything. That had made me feel better, too. But now that awful man was here again. How could she stand it? I pretended to do my homework, and listened to the conversation. The last few times he'd come round, I'd gone out and they'd talked until late. What had they got to say?

'What have you been doing recently?' Ma asked.

He looked piteously at her. 'What can I do? I have to clothe the child. I've been teaching myself to sew for him. Old He said I was mad and sent a suit for the boy. But I must learn, he's still growing.'

Ma blushed and turned away. 'Housework is necessary, but you mustn't neglect your own work. We'll find some teaching for you in the faculty.'

'Of course I want to work,' he said, 'but Comrade Xi Liu is still rather wary of me. I don't want to bother you but people said you might put in a good word for me. They weren't sure . . . we were on different sides in the Cultural Revolution and I criticised you . . . I was awful to you . . .' He looked like a devil, leaning over towards Ma, and she shifted her chair back and interrupted him:

'Old Xu, what are you talking about? We are not going to discuss who treated whom badly. If you want me to bear the burden of that particular episode of history in the way some of you people seem to, then we will have to go through it all again. Unfortunately, at the time we didn't have the qualifications to assume the burden of history and history took us on. As for what we have learnt, you've learnt your lesson and I've learnt mine.

On that score, no one can put in a good word for anyone and no one can speak for anyone else.'

Still talking about the Cultural Revolution – still talking about it! From the moment I'd begun to understand anything, that was all I used to hear about. Every day the tannoys would announce, 'The Cultural Revolution is a good thing, a very good thing!' The nurses in kindergarten taught us to shout 'Long live the Cultural Revolution! Long live a unique episode in history!' What was 'a unique episode in history'? I'm only just beginning to understand. Over the last few years, Ma and her friends seem to have spent all their time together discussing the Cultural Revolution: at least today they were reasonably calm. Sometimes they argue, shouting till they're hoarse and red in the face. In the end, there's always someone who says, 'All right, all right, we're just ordinary people! It's not up to us to summarise the lessons of history. Why don't we talk about a wage rise instead? Or vegetable baskets!' Then they all collapse in giggles like children; but the next time they meet, they start shouting about the same thing. I've heard it all so often, I've learnt all the tricks they use. They always refer to their own pasts as 'my previous life' – it's really irritating. And 'history'! 'History has played a trick on us!' There's one man who always says it. Ma says he's just come out of prison. He was serving a limitless sentence for opposing Lin Biao[3].

It didn't take me long to realise they're all intellectuals. I'm a bit of one myself, but cleverer than them: I'll never join a political movement. I want to be a non-Party person. I did apply to join the Youth League, and I suppose that's the Party, but joining the League only shows I want to be a good citizen. Ma often says, 'You must be a sincere person, an upright person and a useful person.'

'Whatever you say, I still apologise. Especially for that time at the criticism meeting when I called you Xi Liu's . . . I never really believed it.' He was still talking. He was pleading.

'Mr Xu!' Ma exclaimed and stood up. Whenever she's upset, she always stands up. Is it to help her agitation sink?

What had Mr Xu called her? I couldn't imagine, but it obviously wasn't anything good! Ma always says to Aunt Yining that one thing she can't stand is slander. People must have been slandering her, even her old classmates; but if she meant that Xu had done it, why was she being so patient with him this evening? Incomprehensible.

After a couple of minutes, she sat down again and said, more calmly, 'Old Xu, from now on we are never going to discuss that episode again.'

'But how can we forget it?' he asked. 'I really admire you. You were subjected to so much but you didn't rebel.'

Ma shook her head. 'You only saw the outside; inside, I was fighting. Especially when I heard about Xi Liu's relationship with Chen Yuli – then I really felt like proclaiming my intention to rebel. But they'd never have accepted a "die-hard royalist" like me, so I kept quiet, for my own self-respect. But secretly I knew I was on the wrong side, involved with the wrong sort; I used to weep in front of Chairman Mao's portrait!'

Ma was really stupid. Nobody nowadays would admit to having been a rebel, not even the real ones. Rebels were wicked, they were counter-revolutionaries – that's what it says in all the novels. What I can't understand is that, then, they were all described as good. Good people, bad people, it's difficult to sort it out; to tell the truth, it doesn't really interest me. If someone is nice to me and Ma, I'll call him a good person, no matter what group he belongs to. But I don't know about this man Xu: does he really admire Ma or is he just sucking up? She's Party branch secretary so people naturally suck up to her. Granny often used to say that if someone was head of something, they could do anything. 'Heads' really frighten people.

'Sun Yue, I wish I understood you.' Xu stood up. He looked very agitated. 'I've seen lots of people who were real activists under the "Gang of Four", who've completely changed their tune now and become heroes of the struggle against the "Gang". Opportunism and covering up one's faults are fundamental to human nature. But you, with all your achievements, never brag about them; and you go on analysing yourself. People like you have suffered; most people just swim with the tide . . .'

'Old Xu, you know all about swimming with the tide – why

don't you go to the Party Committee and make a report? That would help you swimmers recognise your mistakes. If you don't, how can the Party's policies have any power?'

Xu laughed and didn't answer immediately. After a while he said, 'Sun Yue, I know you don't want to go over ancient history again, but has He Jingfu been here?'

Ma seemed surprised by his sudden change of subject. She hesitated, and then came over to me. Putting two yuan in my hand, she said, 'Go out and buy a pound of sweets.'

Was she trying to stop me listening by ordering me out? I ran to the nearest shop and bought the worst sweets I could find. When I got back, they were still talking about He Jingfu. Xu was praising him.

'Old He's a complex character. He suffered terribly that year but it didn't crush him.'

'Yes,' said Ma.

'He's over forty and still unmarried. We old classmates ought to get together and help find him a wife.'

'Yes.'

'As for the past, I doubt that he's forgotten,' said Xu, his head very close to Ma's.

Ma flushed right down her neck and said, 'Hanhan, go and make some supper.'

Obviously they wanted to talk about something important so I washed the rice quickly and put it on the stove. Then I tiptoed back to the door and listened.

'There's not much more to be said about Old He's feelings for you – his diary said it all. He was criticised excessively, but that's all over now and he's grown stronger while you've become more flexible. Have you thought about getting together with him?'

My heart stood still. Was this why Xu kept coming over? And who was He Jingfu? I'd never imagined this. I waited for Ma's reply.

'Have you never thought about it?' Xu insisted.

Ma finally opened her mouth and said, lightly, 'What's the use of dredging things up again? It was nearly twenty years ago. Everyone has their own life to live. We've all changed.'

Bother – the rice was sticking to the pan. Ma smelt it too, and opened the door just as I was racing back to the kitchen.

'It was on too high!' I said nervously. She must have guessed I'd been listening.

Whether it was because of the mysterious He Jingfu or because I'd burnt the rice, Ma's face grew steadily sterner throughout supper. I didn't dare ask about He Jingfu so we ate in silence, cheerlessly, until the nitpicking began –

'Hanhan, sit up straight!'

I hate it. It's worse than silence. When Ma is really upset about something, she always ends up picking on me: I eat too noisily, I don't sit up straight, my head is in my rice bowl, etc etc etc. Sometimes she's so critical I don't know how to carry on with the meal. I sat up and gingerly put a bit of food into my mouth. Am I the cause of all your misery? I wanted to ask; then why did you have me? But I couldn't bear to look at her because I knew her face would show how unhappy she was.

After the meal we both went to our desks. Do other families sit in silence in front of the television? We just sat facing the wall. If only Daddy were here . . .

'Daddy'. Even the word disturbs me. Whenever I talk to anyone, I'm terrified they'll mention my father; with Ma, I just say 'him' or 'that man'. She understands what I mean. I have a father . . . no, it's past history: I had a father. But the word 'Daddy' still has such a strong effect on me. Sometimes I think how wonderful it would be to go to a film with Daddy, or ice-skating; even a game of chess would do. And if the three of us could walk down the street together, I know everyone would envy us and think how happy we must be.

He was very good-looking. I've kept the photograph. Ma tore it up one night, but I collected the pieces when she wasn't looking. That photograph is my history: the faces of the family ripped apart, all three of us. Just like me. Half belongs with Daddy, half with Ma, and I've been torn in two. I look at it often, secretly, and now while Ma was distracted I slipped it quickly out from my satchel. She can't have seen. She's never got time to notice me.

But they've all moved! I was never between them – I was always at one side, looking on. What lively, attractive people!

Huanhuan's arms are outstretched and she's smiling. Huanhuan's mother is laughing gaily, and her father's face, smiling, looks like a young girl's. But a knife is cutting through his face . . . his body is being ripped apart; Huanhuan's mother too, and Huanhuan, and her father, they've all been torn in half, it's too horrible, I can't bear to look, those bitter smiling faces coming towards me, I'm so scared I want to cry out, to run and struggle and escape these three half-people – I wake up. A dream. Ma's hand on my head. Ma stroking my hair. Oh Ma, why is it only in the middle of the night that you are gentle and kind?

I could hear her sobbing. I looked, and in her hand was the photograph, the torn photograph; and I threw myself at her, and she hugged me tightly, whispering between her tears, 'My poor child, I'm so sorry, I'm so sorry!'

'I'm sorry Ma, I'll never upset you again.'

She hugged me more tightly still.

SIX

XI LIU

History has got me by the throat: it's given me a rebel for a son.
There's nothing I can do.

Nanny brought the supper in and the three of us sat down to eat.
I took my place at the head of the table with my wife Chen Yuli
on my left and my son Xi Wang on my right; Nanny sat opposite
me, close to the kitchen.

Xi Wang ate, hunched over his bowl of rice. He's in his second
year at university, studying Chinese literature, and has a place in
one of the student dormitories so he only comes home at weekends. He usually leaves the table when he's finished, but this time
he hesitated: 'Father?' I looked at him.

'I hear that the Party committee isn't going to let people like
Xu Hengzhong completely off the hook, and that you won't let
him publish any articles; is that true?' He sounded angry. The
Cultural Revolution has really destroyed people's common sense:
even Party members can't keep their mouths shut these days.
How can they talk openly about internal matters of principle?
They should be rectified.

'That's an internal Party matter. How did you hear about
it?'

I was trying very hard to keep my temper. Xi Wang is getting
increasingly difficult; he and Chen Yuli are the two people who
have least respect for me as Party Secretary. I'm not afraid of

Yuli, however much she may mock – she's not fundamentally against me. But Xi Wang is different, a complete rebel; he seems determined to destroy everything I've built up.

'What kind of an answer is that? When will you understand that you weren't made Party Secretary just so you could boss people around? And certainly not so you could carry out personal vendettas!' He spoke with such force, spitting out the words like bullets, that I couldn't reply. Let him rant. All I'm worried about is that he might talk like this outside the house and let me down.

'Can't you do anything besides "rectify"? Why don't you "rectify" You Ruoshui? Everybody in the department knows that Xu Hengzhong is only a mouthpiece for You Ruoshui. Who was more active than You Ruoshui in the Campaign to Criticise Deng Xiaoping? Even the old "Gang of Four" supporters call him an ever-flowing stream. But you've got him dammed up and he has to come and flatter you all the time to try and get out of it. You love that, don't you?'

I put my chopsticks down and shouted: 'What do you know about it? You're becoming impossible!'

Xi Wang sneered. 'Impossible! Do you think calling me things like that will stop people talking? I was thinking of you – everyone knows you're my father.'

I was too angry to speak, but Chen Yuli held up her bowl and said, 'Please you two, let's talk about something else. You're so negative these days, Xi Wang – don't you think it's wrong to be so pessimistic?'

Oh, Chen Yuli, why do you have to intervene? He's never had any time for you. Even when he deigns to call you Mrs Chen or Teacher Chen, he makes it sound excessively polite.

'I am by no means totally negative, but there are some things I'm not happy about. Not at all happy.' At least his tone was calm even if his eyes were burning. 'And are *you* happy with everything? Do you really think my father is better than your first husband? Do you really believe he loves you? From what I saw, he was still very much in love with my mother when he was writing all those letters to you saying he wished we were dead so you could be together. Ask Nanny, if you don't believe it. Whatever he wrote, he adored us.'

Nanny brought in some more rice and left the room without a word. If she'd so much as looked at Xi Wang, he'd have calmed down – but she didn't. She brought him up. When I was sent away and my wages were cut, she bought his food with her own money. Chen Yuli has tried to get rid of her by forcing her to retire but Xi Wang always threatens to report her to the authorities. I feel we shouldn't abandon our obligations so I don't support Chen Yuli in this, but I do sometimes think Nanny has a bad influence on Xi Wang. She was very fond of his mother and she doesn't like Chen Yuli.

Once she was out of the room, I stood up and hammered the table: 'How dare you!' The bowls rattled as if in an earthquake. Chen Yuli was standing too, her face blotchy, but she didn't say anything. There was nothing she could do. At times like these, Chen Yuli is much weaker than Sun Yue. And yet times like these had allowed her to marry me.

Xi Wang appeared to be awaiting our reactions with some interest. Of all my children, he is my favourite, not just because he is the youngest but because he's grown to be good-looking, impressive with his deep intelligent eyes. When he was little, I took him everywhere and people always said, 'Look at that child's eyes!' I would never have thought his eyes could make me angry. They stared at me now, as though they were saying, 'What's the matter with you? Have you got something to say? Then say it!' But I couldn't speak.

'All right.' He'd waited for a couple of minutes and we hadn't said a word. 'It's obvious you don't like what I say, so I won't say any more.' He started towards his room but turned back and looked at me. 'Anyway, Dad, if I'm honest, I don't altogether disapprove of your relationship with her. It proves Engels was right when he said, "the fact that man originated in the animal world means that mankind will never be able entirely to shake off its animal origins. The question is how much of the animal remains; the difference is in the balance between human nature and animal nature." I'd hate to think –'

My God! What have I done to deserve such a child? How could he speak to me like this? Man's animal nature! His father's animal nature! Distorting Engels!

'You may insult your father but I won't let you insult Engels. You've gone too far,' I said firmly.

He laughed and swung on the doorframe like a monkey. 'Marxist Father, take a look at page 110, chapter twenty of the *Complete Works of Marx and Engels*. It's easy to find dirt in the collected works. But you're so busy upholding the principles of Marxism you never bother to actually look at them.' He went out, laughing.

Yuli picked up a chair and hurled it down, but I ignored her. Perhaps our marriage has been a mistake. I had hoped to make a peaceful and happy home for my declining years and to make up for what she and I had suffered. Now this seems an impossibility. The older children have little to do with me and don't seem to understand; Xi Wang, on the other hand, seems to understand, but claims that all he recognises is my 'animal nature'.

What a home. I feel lonelier than an orphan. Outside, nobody cares about me and nobody cares about me at home either. All day I'm treated with respect but people's feelings run as shallow as water; nobody cares for officials. Over the last few years I've begun to see this clearly and I've had enough. Everyone says I'm covering up for You Ruoshui. It's not that I can't see that he presents a problem, but he's always worked under me. Even during the 'counter-attack' he was still quite friendly. When the 'Gang of Four' fell, he came to me and confessed his crimes. I can't destroy one of the few people who seem to feel something for me. With so few allies, I'd never maintain my position in Shanghai.

Nobody cares about me, yet I've suffered so much. I'd happily acknowledge the justice of history if I were allowed a happy old age. I never anticipated that history would seize me by the throat and give me a rebel for a son. What can I do?

The terrifying thing is that occasionally I find myself secretly agreeing with some of Xi Wang's ideas. I have to admit that he's more upright and incorruptible than me, with less personal animosity. It's because he hasn't reached my age yet and he hasn't had my experience.

Have I been corrupted?

Was it really from Engels, what he said just now? I went over to the bookcase and took out the volume he'd mentioned. Printers are really careless now; pages 110 and 111 hadn't been cut. But sure enough, there was the passage he'd quoted. I'd never heard of it before; it wasn't included in the *Quotations from Marx and Engels*. But it should be thoroughly researched and upheld as the quintessence of Marxism.

'And have you "thoroughly researched this quintessence"?' I thought I heard my son ask. But he wasn't there. He's often spoken to me like that in the past. I've always maintained that class struggle is the key link [a slogan used a great deal in the late 1970s] and that once the link is grasped, everything will fall into place. I've always held that that is the quintessence of Marxism-Leninism. But students' thinking is so muddled these days it's hard for teachers to get through to them; they've all failed to grasp the key link and forgotten the outcome of line struggle. The Central Committee doesn't seem to see it this way. I can't resolve the question myself. I admit that I haven't read much Marx and Lenin. I've learnt my Marxism-Leninism from Central Committee documents. What's the point in reading a great heap of books? People who have read the complete works of Marx, Lenin, Engels and Stalin say one thing today, another tomorrow. The Central Committee wants us to study theory, but I'm old so it's not worth it. I'd struggle to keep up, muddle myself for a few years and retire. I give up.

The maid came in to tidy up and serve tea. 'Nanny, little Wang's behaviour is getting worse and worse. You might have a word with him,' I said with some despair.

'Everyone's different. I don't think he's too bad. If he's nice to some and nasty to others, that's just him. You can't buy affection.' She hardly looked at me as she spoke and left the room.

I was wasting my time. She was on his side. Still, there was hope: it was all a question of guidance and I hadn't guided him enough. He was only ten when his mother died and Nanny had mothered him. Since then, his head had been filled with all sorts of muddled ideas. He'd had a bad time. I felt sorry for him, but there wasn't much I could say. A father must always remain a father. I can't see things through his eyes.

He was reading. He hadn't got much. Apart from a tape

recorder for learning English and a transistor radio, he had no possessions of any value and spent all his allowance on books. I wanted to give him a bit more but Chen Yuli was against it. She keeps the accounts. Women can be very mean.

I was wearing soft shoes and trod lightly. He only noticed me when I sat down on a chair which creaked slightly. Then he closed his exercise book and said, 'Father?' much more warmly than before. It made me feel better.

I cleared my throat and began: 'I've not had a chance to talk to you much recently. I can see why you resent me. Life isn't easy and it hasn't been for me.' I felt rather emotional and choked slightly; he poured me a cup of hot water. 'I was very sorry about your mother, I certainly haven't forgotten her. We were partners in the struggle . . .' He picked up the photograph of his mother that stood on his desk. Though thin, her hair had stayed black until her death. I sipped some more water. 'I married very late. And you know my health . . .'

Suddenly I felt overwhelmingly sorry for myself. When you grow old, you lose your strength. I felt in need of emotional support and physical care. Could he understand that?

'Father!'

He came out from behind his desk, dragged a chair over and sat beside me. Years ago we used to sit side by side like this. I needed his affection now that I was old. I said, 'Tell me about things, I'd like to understand.'

'All right, Father. I've been looking for a chance to talk. I don't really have any feelings about your marrying Teacher Chen; and I shouldn't have. I love my mother but she's gone. You need someone to look after you. The only thing I regret is that you don't seem to love each other . . .'

'Love – that's a matter for young people. We need to take care of each other.'

'That may be true. Anyway, I don't want to pry into your private life. I wouldn't like anyone to pry into mine.'

'Well, do we understand each other on this point, at least?' I asked hopefully.

'Yes,' he said cheerfully. 'Where we differ is in our approach to history and to current problems.' I listened carefully.

'Father, history has left you with wounds. But you can't just conveniently forget that you have responsibilities. The last few decades have been pretty crazy – don't you feel some sense of responsibility? Take the Anti-Rightist Movement. You were the anti-rightist hero of all the top educational establishments. You uncovered the problem early, attacked instantly and mustered a lot of leftist students to maintain the struggle against the rightists. All these glories are recorded. But have you ever thought what lies behind them?'

Of course I'd thought about it. I'd taken charge of the broadening struggle but all the orders had come from above; I hadn't created anything. I wasn't going to take responsibility for something that I hadn't created.

'What lies behind is people suffering! That Overseas Chinese student, Xie, who couldn't go and visit his mother abroad because he had to uphold Party and country; he finally told his mother why he wasn't allowed to see her after she'd written letter after letter accusing him of being unfilial. He decided that even if he couldn't go he could at least tell her why. When she discovered that she'd been the reason for all the accusations against her son, she had a breakdown. And then there was He Jingfu. He came from such a poor family they all had to skimp to send him to university, but you branded him a rightist and had him expelled. A few generations of people ruined by a rightist "hat" – when I think of it, I want to burst the heavens, I feel so angry! If you weren't my father . . .

'I haven't forgotten the crimes against you either. But I wish you'd think about it. You don't seem to. You spend all day plotting how you can make good your losses of the last few years, but you never think of repaying others for the damage you did to them. Some people have gone through all that and gained great spiritual advantage in the end, but you seem to have lost something precious. Your thinking gets more and more sterile and inflexible . . .'

If someone in a higher position had said this, I might have thought it over. I did reflect that if I looked at myself now, I hadn't gained anything in those ten years apart from sharpening a few character defects it would have been better to lose. Yet the person criticising me was my son, who was about a third of my age. I felt my face reddening and my ears burning and it was hard to contain myself. I raised the teacup to my lips but it was empty. He must have seen my discomfiture, for he took the cup from me and filled it with water.

'I don't think we can look at history emotionally. There are special circumstances in every period and these require special policies.' It seemed to be the most appropriate and dignified answer. But my son was still very emotional. He seized my hand and said:

'I do hope that you will keep up with the changes.' I wondered silently which changes he meant. 'Can't you feel it? It's only recently come to me – and all because of one person. All that suffering, all the difficulties of life are what create individuals. Have you ever thought of that, Father?'

Was this my son? I hardly recognised him. In front of me stood an impassioned poet and I was quite moved by his words. I looked at him, a good-looking boy, strong, healthy and optimistic. When I was his age, I joined the revolution. Something might come of him if he stopped writing poetry and worrying about huge philosophical questions.

And who was the 'one person' who had awakened him? Who did he go around with? What use were their ideas to him? 'Tell me about this individual that you so admire,' I said, smiling.

'It's He Jingfu, you know him quite well. You branded him a rightist, but he doesn't bear a personal grudge. He's been studying history and society. He's only an archivist in the Department but he's more popular with the students than any of the lecturers.' His admiration for the man was clear.

During the Anti-Rightist Movement, some ten per cent of the students at Shanghai University had been branded rightists. I can't remember many of them now, but I'll never forget He Jingfu. It was because of him that I quarrelled with Zhang Yuanyuan. She practically accused me of executing students. I went to visit her when she was very ill, but she dismissed me: 'If you *have* got a kind heart, then bring those students back to me.' I knew that some of them couldn't come back; would never come back. On her death Zhang Yuanyuan left only one instruction: that I should not go to her memorial meeting. She was a very tough woman. Perhaps we had overdone it a bit. Some young people have rightist thoughts, some are emotionally unstable, but these are all merely internal contradictions and should be cured by education. We had attacked them as 'enemies'. The results had been bad, but was it all my fault? I, too, was only carrying out orders!

'No, it's because you are ambitious and you want to get on!' That's what Zhang Yuanyuan would have said. But on what grounds?

Unfortunately I had once said to her, 'We come from the same liberated area. Your abilities and educational levels are pretty much the same as mine, but you'll never rise very far because of your rightist ideology. If you were to change, I might be able to help you; I've often thought of proposing you for deputy Party Secretary.' All I'd been trying to do was advance her career but she never saw that.

'He Jingfu is very stimulating,' I said now, calmly and seriously. 'But remember that according to dialectical materialism everything divides into two. We treated him badly – that's one side, but the other view is that he certainly made mistakes. He was biased and emotionally unstable. If he's learnt from his experiences then we will be happy to hear it. Party policy has always been to learn from past mistakes and to cure the disease by saving the patient. Now our task is to inspire activists and to unite all those who can be united in order to carry out the four modernisations!'[4]

Xi Wang's eyes had begun to gleam again. 'Policy statements. You know them by heart,' he said.

'It's my Party work,' I replied.

'It's a pity. You remember texts but you don't remember people. And policy is directed at people.' He went back to his desk and fiddled with the notebook he'd been reading.

'Do you see He Jingtu often?' I asked tentatively.

'Yes, we talk every couple of days,' he replied, defiantly.

'What do you talk about?'

'Are you compiling a dossier on him so you can put a rightist "hat" on him again?' he asked, more defiantly.

'I just want you to choose your friends with care. Young people go to extremes. If they like someone, they put him on a pedestal. He Jingfu was on the road for so long; do you know what he was doing then?' I became sterner. No good could come from Xi Wang associating with He Jingfu. I could already see the signs.

I hadn't realised how angry the boy was. He stood in front of me and said in a great fury, 'Of course the Party Secretary is concerned and wants me to tell him what He Jingfu did! He travelled halfway across China and took all sorts of menial jobs. Naturally he didn't exactly participate in the socialist economy! He took the small capitalist's road. He even had to resort to lying. Once when he couldn't find work and had nothing to eat, the head of a brigade asked him if he knew anything about brick kilns. He didn't, but he said he did. He slipped off by night to another kiln to see what it was like. He took measurements and made drawings and when he went back they built a kiln according to his sketches. Wasn't that fraudulent? But you couldn't do anything like that. And he can accept his mistakes, too. Twenty years ago he decided to research into humanism and he's never forgotten that decision. He researched the whole of China and learned from the masses, looking for answers. He's just finished a book on Marxism and humanism.'

He picked up the notebook. 'Here it is. Are you interested?'

'Marxism and humanism? What is he trying to say?'

'He's trying to show that Marxism and humanism aren't incompatible. Humanism is one of the fundamental points in Marxism; basic, revolutionary humanism.'

It was wild talk. Capitalist ideology running wild. Though it had been criticised for decades, it seemed that there was still a place for landlord humanism. But I did not dare to discuss it in front of my son, I was afraid he'd catch me out again. I needed to look at the evidence.

'All right,' I said, trying to pacify him. 'Let's wait till he's finished it and then we'll discuss it. Nonetheless, even if a hundred schools of thought may contend, there's no place for capitalist libertarianism. You must raise your critical level; new ideas aren't necessarily revolutionary.' I used the last phrase deliberately, and repeated it . . .

'You don't know anything about new ideas. I suppose you're the most revolutionary person around?' he interrupted.

'I won't discuss it with you! Go your own way; I take no responsibility.' I stood up and put the teacup on the table as I spoke.

'I never wanted you to take any responsibility! But I warn you, Father, you ought to think of retiring. The Party would let you. It would be best for you. You don't see that your power is way beyond your abilities. You've risen too high.'

'No doubt. You clearly don't think I've even got the capacity to be your father! Get out of my sight!'

I couldn't stand it any longer. Was this what fatherhood had become? I didn't want a child like that. Let him live alone. Xi Wang looked at the photograph of his mother and his eyes softened. Would he admit to me that he was wrong? I waited.

'Okay, Dad. Anyway, there doesn't seem to be much left to hold us together. I stayed here for my mother's sake. Just before she died she asked me to try and understand you and never to leave you. I promised I would. But now it looks as if it would be better if I left. I'll move all my things to the university tomorrow and I won't come back for weekends.'

'You –' my voice failed.

He looked away and said, 'There is just one thing – will you still give me thirty yuan a month? Otherwise I'll ask for a bursary.'

'I'll give you the money to live on,' I answered weakly.

'Tell the wages office and I'll go and collect it there. Then I won't have to annoy you by coming here,' he said calmly.

I nodded, and left his room.

'Well, have you been teaching the baby some manners?' Yuli asked, unpleasantly sarcastic.

'Don't talk rubbish!'

She began to cry. Let her cry. 'You've deceived me,' she spluttered. 'If I'd known what it would be like, I'd never have married you. Now even the children don't pay any attention to me, I'll . . .'

'You'll what? Only you know,' I said coldly. 'It's not too late. If you want to leave, then leave. I can manage alone.'

She began to cry harder but said no more. Poor woman! I spoke more warmly: 'Don't cry, don't. Xi Wang is moving out tomorrow so there'll only be the two of us left. Enough of cheating and deceiving, let's face things together. We don't want to make ourselves a laughing stock a second time.'

She stopped crying and leant against me.

That night, I didn't dream.

PART TWO

Each heart is looking for a home.
Each one is different.

SEVEN

HE JINGFU

Hanhan, let's be friends.

'I've left home!' Xi Wang announced, throwing his bag down on my bed, both happy and angry.

I didn't immediately understand what he meant, so I made him sit down and tell me slowly. After hearing about his argument with his father, I was silent for a long time.

'Teacher He, I think it's better this way. Now, I'm free. What's the point of having a family?' I didn't answer. I was too confused by what he'd done.

'From now on, the only connection between me and my father is the thirty yuan!'

That sentence shook me. I didn't look at him. I liked him. We were both of the 'lost generations'.

I was deep in a book in the dormitory one day, when a boy came in and said directly, 'Teacher He, could we talk?' I looked at him suspiciously. 'My name's Xi Wang. I'm Xi Liu's son. But don't worry, I'm not like my father.'

His unusual approach made me laugh and I said, 'You *are* like your father. Is there anything else I ought to worry about?'

'You're quite right to worry. Ruining you was only one of my father's many activities. Even now he's still proud of being the anti-rightist hero. If I'm like him, you'd better prepare the poison.'

I wasn't used to young people talking about their fathers in such a way, even if this particular father was the man I disliked most in the world. 'We don't have to discuss your father,' I said. 'What else shall we talk about?'

He said, 'I wanted to ask you something. You've been through a lot. How come you're still an activist? Do you still believe in what you used to believe in? Or have you seen through it all? Are you like Zhuangzi, looking for your own liberty in your own objective world?'

I began to look seriously at the boy who sat in front of me. He had eyes that didn't seem to belong in his young face; they looked older and more experienced, deep and full of warmth. I trusted them, they showed his true nature. We became friends.

'How have you managed to create so many problems in your short life?' I asked him.

His answer surprised me. 'Only animals would judge the world purely on their own experiences. I'm a man and I am also a child of my country and people. The history of my country and its people is also my history. Any problems thrown up by that history automatically involve me. That's my burden. And my strength.'

I was very fond of him, yet today his actions upset me. Was there really only thirty yuan between him and his father? What kind of relationship was that?

I know there are all sorts of fathers and all sorts of sons in the world, all sorts of families and theories of morality. But I've never been able to accept that so-called class struggles and line struggles should be waged in the home; I've never been able to understand how parents, children, husbands and wives and brothers and sisters can renounce their relationships and cut themselves off from each other. Haven't we learnt anything from the past? Thank heavens my family had not been like that.

What should I say about Xi Wang's decision? I couldn't say he'd acted totally out of selfishness because even if he didn't love his father, he still loved his country. But I'm sure that if Xi Liu had been *my* father I couldn't have abandoned him.

'We're from different generations, you and I,' I said after a long time, and with some ambiguity.

'You don't approve?' He didn't like ambiguity.

'It's not that. It's that I couldn't behave as you have done.' I knew that I was still being rather vague but I couldn't make myself express a clearer opinion.

'You don't approve,' he said, decisively. 'It's because our fathers are different.'

That was true, our fathers were different. My father was an old peasant who sold bananas. He didn't know what a world view was, and he couldn't have explained morality, but he worked hard for others all his life and sacrificed himself for his children. I learnt about people from his example. I wouldn't have exchanged him for Xi Liu; I wouldn't have exchanged him for ten Xi Lius.

'Nevertheless, a father is still a father. And, anyway, why do you accept his money?' I asked.

He laughed. 'That's how you can tell we're from different generations! If I don't take his money, I'll have to ask the university for a grant. Why should I take money that other people need badly when my father can easily afford it? He gets quite enough money, it wouldn't be right.'

'You look at things in an odd way. I'd have hoped that you'd have some sense of obligation towards your father. He's not a bad man.'

'It depends on how you look at it. If you look at it from a historical standpoint, then he ought to have been eliminated. I've been trying to get him to retire but he won't listen. I can't do anything about it, let history take its course.'

I looked at him, shocked. I'd never seen this side of him before, a cold, extremely cold side. How could he be both so warm and so very cold; did one give rise to the other? What did he really believe in? What was important to him?

'I know you believe in *fair play* [in English in the original] but it just doesn't work in China today. Old customs die hard,' he said. He seemed to have guessed what I was thinking.

'But must we go on believing like the "Gang of Four" that revolution has to explode in every home and every heart?' I asked.

'I'm not saying that. Everybody faces history, let history decide. Otherwise we'd have no sense of responsibility. Perhaps I don't value blood relations. I didn't think that someone like you who has no family links would value them.'

His last sentence was mocking; he thought a solitary person like me shouldn't have any family ties. But I didn't have to reject mine: memories of them had kept me warm, even when I was so alone. And I still looked forward to having a family of my own and looking after it as my father had.

'Of course, family relations and class relations are totally different. But family relations are a very basic form of social relations; the family is the fundamental social unit. If we can't manage family relationships, how can we expect to manage society?' I asked.

'Manage family relationships? That's one of your illusions. Just look around you! It's just that sort of feudal stress on family relationships that leads to high cadres favouring their children over everyone else, even if it's illegal or harmful to others. I can't stand that kind of attitude!' He was getting angry.

'But don't forget that we've created a new kind of family relationship, another sort of morality. Take Mencius' ideas on age . . .' Without noticing it, I'd begun gesturing with my tobacco pouch. I'd have liked to tell him about the tobacco pouch and about my father and my family but he was looking at me too critically. He was critical of people and society but there was a lot he didn't understand. He didn't know much about the darker side of life.

He laughed. 'Let's stop fighting. I can see you are much more muddled than I am – you've probably got good reason to be. I've got to move my things today, we'll talk again later. Can I leave some things here for a while?' I nodded and he left. But he came back an instant later and said in a low voice, 'It's Sunday. Why don't you go and see Teacher Sun? It's clear you need a family!' I almost pinched his ear but something stopped me, he obviously wasn't entirely joking.

Sun Yue. Once after a meeting, she had handed a needle and thread to one comrade and said, 'Your button is coming off.' I had looked down at my jacket. I had a button dangling too, but she'd just given me a look.

Sun Yue. I met her yesterday when we were all watering newly planted trees. I watched her going backwards and forwards with her bucket, carefully watering the small trees. I went over to her and she gave me a nod and then walked off. Had she forgotten? Sun Yue. All my intentions of locking myself up in my room to write had disappeared but I didn't want to go to her house. I couldn't face another cool reception.

I left the key in the door for Xi Wang and went out. Where was I going? I didn't know. Might she come back to water the trees again? Sun Yue, do you want a family? Can't we even talk amicably? Whenever I hear you speak in a meeting I always think how close our ideas are, but whenever I meet you I am aware of the distance between us. Why is it? I bumped into you yesterday after class. You said, 'It's Saturday night, are you going out?' What did you mean?

'Who wants my mother?' A young girl suddenly looked out of a doorway. She came over; it was Sun Yue's daughter, Hanhan. Had I said her name aloud? Had I knocked on her door?

'You came once before, didn't you? Aren't you He Jingfu?' she asked.

I nodded.

'Ma, He Jingfu's come over,' she shouted through the doorway, and very politely invited me in.

I followed her, furious with myself for being so out of control. Teacups. Hot water. Tea. Sun Yue was extremely polite. It was a warning: keep your distance. I wanted to leave straight away.

'Xi Liu's son has quarrelled with his father. He's moved his things over to my room. I came to talk about it.' What was this? A confession? A report on Xi Wang? Why couldn't I say I'd just dropped by? Why couldn't I behave naturally?

'Young people today are lucky, they have the freedom to break all sorts of barriers,' she said, without looking at me.

I was surprised. 'You mean you approve?'

'Approve of what?' she asked.

'Of Xi Wang breaking with his father.'

'I wish I was as brave as him.'

'What do you mean?'

She blushed and paused before replying. 'I was probably thinking of something else. I've been trying recently to get more confident about speaking in public and sometimes I say things without really thinking what I mean.' She didn't look at me.

We are so similar – I've been trying to become a more confident speaker too. I don't quite know when I first started. But everyone has several 'me's' inside them and sometimes they get muddled. Solitary people have the most 'me's'. What did she just say? That she envied young people their chance to take power into their own hands? She meant that for herself. She feels she has no independence; she feels held back, that's certain. She's trying to decide. But what does it mean? What is she trying to decide? What's holding her back?

On the table was a novel, one I'd read several times. I picked it up and flipped through the pages. One section was underlined in red with a question mark and an exclamation mark in the margin.

'What do you think about the part where the battalion leader sets the counter-revolutionaries free?' I asked.

'I don't know. I've made a break with capitalist humanism. I don't want to sacrifice myself again for anything similar.'

'Doesn't proletarian humanism exist?'

She looked at me suddenly. My heart beat faster and I couldn't stop myself getting up and going over to her. 'It does exist, Sun Yue,' I said. 'You've read Marx and Engels. Read some again. They were great men and they had hearts, they wrote about MAN. In capital letters. Their theory and their revolutionary practice were all for the realisation of that kind of humanity. They wanted to destroy everything that prevents man from being human. Unfortunately we've got some self-styled Marxists who only think of tactics; they've abandoned or forgotten their aim. They make it seem as if revolution means the destruction of the individual, of families; they've built walls to separate people. We've destroyed the feudal economic class and have set up other political classes instead. I'm one of the eight black groups[5] and you're an intellectual, a "stinking number nine". But our children can learn to be better. Now, people are given "hats" even before they're born. Is that materialism?'

She stood up, crossed the room and picked up the teapot to

pour me more tea. Then she said, 'Do sit down, Comrade He Jingfu.'

It was like a bucketful of cold water. I looked at her, confused. Her face was pink. Had I said something wrong? Why didn't she say so? Why did she ask me to sit down? Was I too close to her? She'd learnt to conceal her thoughts from others. She certainly wasn't the Sun Yue I'd known. Not knowing whether to sit or stand, I took out my tobacco pouch.

'Uncle He.' I'd forgotten Hanhan, sitting there all the time, watching us and listening. Did she speak in order to help me? I pulled my chair over to her and asked, 'What are you doing here? Why don't you go out?' But instead of answering, she said, 'Were you at University with my mother?'

'Yes.'

'In the same class?'

'No, I was one year above her.'

'Then how do you know her? I don't even know everyone in my class.'

'It was the same with us.'

'But you were a friend of Ma's, weren't you?'

I felt uncomfortable and Sun Yue looked tense. Well, I'd tell the truth: 'I've always been a friend of your mother's.'

'And Ma? Has she always been a friend of yours?' There was an even greater danger in this question, because Hanhan's face was grim and her tone aggressive.

Sun Yue went pale and said 'Hanhan!'

Hanhan turned on her mother. 'Why shouldn't I ask? It's what you ask my friends.' Sun Yue looked at me unhappily, got up and went out. Hanhan bit her lip.

'Sun Yue!' I shouted. 'This is your home, I'll leave!'

She came back in carrying a bag and said with an effort at calmness, 'I must just go and buy a few things. You two entertain each other.' She left without looking back.

I felt deeply uncomfortable. What did she mean? Was she deliberately trying to hurt me? In front of the child?

Hanhan was crying quietly. I stood up, but she said, 'Don't go.'

'Why did you ask such a question? It was hardly polite, was it?' I felt cross with her, and that she had been rude. Should a child behave like that? She bit her lip again but wouldn't be put off. 'Won't you answer the question?'

I didn't know what was making the child so miserable, and had even less idea why she was being so aggressive. Not wanting to make her more unhappy, I decided to be honest. 'I liked your mother but she didn't like me. She preferred your father.'

'Are you married now?'

'No. I'm not married.'

'Do you know that my parents are divorced?' She sounded even more forceful.

'I didn't know. I've only just found out. I was thrown out of University before I graduated, for being a rightist. I hadn't seen your mother since then, until the other day.'

Hanhan seemed calmer. She had very pretty eyes. Very like her mother's.

'Were you on the opposite side from my mother?'

I nodded. The tension faded.

'And have you been rehabilitated?'

'Yes.'

'What's the point? You're old now.'

'What do you mean, what's the point? You don't reason like a child, Hanhan.'

'I'm not a child. When you left University, did you go back home?'

'Yes.'

'What did you do?'

'Planted vegetables.'

'That's why you smoke home grown tobacco!' She picked up my tobacco pouch and sniffed it. 'Did you grow vegetables for twenty years?'

'No. I was on the road for about ten years.'

Hanhan's eyes widened. Just as her mother had been baffled by the city when she first arrived, so Hanhan was baffled by my life. 'On the road? A gentleman of the road?'

'Sort of.'

She laughed. 'Did you beg?'

'No, I worked. I travelled over half the country and I had seventeen different jobs.'

'Why did you travel? Did you want to be like Gorky?' What an innocent child! Want to be like Gorky! She couldn't imagine that even Gorky wouldn't have taken to the road if there had been any alternative. But I didn't want to say so.

'Let's not talk about it. You're young. You wouldn't understand.'

'I do, I do understand. I understand everything. Tell me!'

You understand everything? What if I were to tell you that I travelled for my life, in quest, that I travelled for love? Would you understand? You couldn't. How is it that a wounded and persecuted heart doesn't bleed to death or stop and give up? It needs nourishment, above all spiritual nourishment. Where is this to be found? Only from a mother, from people. You, who have lost your father's love, have a greater need for your mother. When I was travelling, with the wind for food and the dew for shelter, I never felt that I was far from my mother. I drank from her and leant on her breast. I saw her face, unadorned. I saw her beauty; I also saw the white hairs at her temples, the callouses on her shoulders. She has borne a thousand million children, loving them all equally. Their different fates tear at her heart, she knows joy and bitterness; sometimes she sings, sometimes she moans. My mother gave me tenderness but she also whipped me. Can you understand all this, child?

'No, you shouldn't have to understand things like that,' I said.

'You want me to grow up stupid,' she said, crossly.

No, I just don't want to burden you. 'We'll talk about it some other time, all right? Now you tell me where you've been. Has your mother taken you to the Great Wall? If you haven't seen it, I'll take you there some day. Every Chinese ought to see the Great Wall. If you've seen the wall, you can achieve greatness!'

'Why?' Hanhan was more cheerful now.

'Because it's so old and it's so impressive and it's so tortuous. It's tortuous, just like our history. When you stand on the wall, it's almost as if you can hear someone whisper, "The Wall isn't finished. It'll never be finished. Every boy and girl in China must add one brick. Have you added yours?" When you hear it, you'll forget your own sorrows and shout, "I'll add a brick! I'll fire my heart and make a brick!" That's the moment when you'll understand what happiness is and what misery is. You can't know it yet because you don't really know China, do you?'

Hanhan looked at me. At that moment, I felt love for her. Her heart was transparent, as clear as crystal and full of feeling. I seemed to be looking at the young Sun Yue again.

'Were people bad to you? There seem to be more bad people than good people in the world now!'

'No, Hanhan. It doesn't matter whether it's China or anywhere in the world; there are more decent people than bad people. Otherwise there'd be no progress and no hope.'

The more I looked at her, the more like her mother she seemed, especially her eyes. I don't know how such eyes, not very large eyes, could be so full of feeling. Sun Yue had never looked at me as sweetly as Hanhan – she either glanced quickly or stared at me angrily. She had devoted herself entirely to Zhao Zhenhuan. He was a fool to have left a wife like her.

'Was my father a "good man"?'

What sort of answer did she want? I knew nothing of the divorce, though my sympathies were with Sun Yue. Still, I didn't want to hurt the child. I could only say, 'What does your mother say? What do you remember of him yourself?'

She rummaged in her satchel and handed me a photograph which had been torn and stuck together again. Apart from the child, it was just as I remembered the young pair I'd first seen in the tricycle rickshaw: Sun Yue and Zhao Zhenhuan.

'All I can remember is this photograph. Ma tore it up. I asked her why and all she said was that from now on, Dad couldn't come and see us. Hanhan and Ma are on their own.'

'She didn't want to upset you. You shouldn't really ask about these things.' I felt sorry for her. I didn't know what to say.

'I'm in the photo too. I don't see why I shouldn't ask why she tore it up.' She was like Sun Yue in her stubbornness. But what could I say? How could she understand?

'Who do you think was to blame? Dad or Ma?' she asked.

'Your mother is a good woman,' I answered.

'And Dad?'

'He's good, too,' I said. I don't think I said it quite right.

'But not like Ma. So it was his fault?'

It was very hard to bear her insistence. All I could do was try and change the subject once again. 'Hanhan, please let's talk about something else. How's school?'

She didn't answer.

'Hanhan, it's the first time we've talked to each other. We can't get to the bottom of everything at once, can we? Later on, when we know each other better, I'll tell you everything I can. I'm a bit muddled today, forgive me.' Trying to escape the emotional depths, I added, 'You ought to be out with your friends on a Sunday!'

'I haven't got any friends. Nobody cares about me. Ma doesn't care about me either. I'm so lonely.'

It appalled me to think that a fifteen-year-old child could feel lonely. Almost more upsetting, she was like a world-weary adult. I was so much more lively than her when I was fifteen. How could we let this child carry such an emotional burden?

'You must love your mother, Hanhan; she deserves your love.'

'But she doesn't love me! If I try to be friends with her, she treats me like a baby and won't talk about things that matter. Do you think it's because she quarrelled with my father that she doesn't like me? I can't bear it!'

Tears began to roll down her cheeks. I tried to comfort her by stroking her small head but she pulled away, her face red. Then she looked at me, and her eyes were full of trust, not accusation. She so much needed a father; it was as if I had become one to her.

When Sun Yue returned Hanhan asked, 'Can Uncle He stay for supper?'

I looked at Sun Yue. She avoided my eyes and said, 'There's nothing much to eat.' Hanhan pouted. I smiled at her, nodded to Sun Yue and left. I thought I'd never get back home. The distance seemed elastic and increasing, like the distance between me and Sun Yue.

'Teacher He! Where are you going? Off for supper?' Xi Wang was shouting at me. His arms were full of belongings and he was still in the morning's excited mood. I said nothing but helped him carry his things.

'You seem a bit low,' he said, concerned. I nodded and he went on, 'Emotions can really wear you down. But I'm totally liberated now. I'm like you; I'd like to see everyone getting along wonderfully, everyone with a happy home, but life just doesn't live up to our ideals. Personal relationships have been all but destroyed. Everywhere there are divorces and broken hearts. We can't put the bits back together all at once. The generations, and people, too, have been sucked into all sorts of contradictions which all pull in different directions. It's enough to make you give up! Sometimes I really feel depressed, as well . . .' But he was still excited, although it wasn't because he was happy.

'What did your father say?' I asked him.

'Not a word. Nanny told me he didn't have any breakfast. Even though I loathe him, I'm sorry for him. But it was better to get out, even though Nanny cried.'

We walked on in silence. The sun was sinking and our shadows were long and slanted.

EIGHT

ZHAO ZHENHUAN

Sun Yue, I want you to forgive me.

I want to write to the editor-in-chief. I want to write a letter of complaint. The editor-in-chief has been interfering with Wang Panzi's party rectification.

Before the Cultural Revolution, a group of our reporters wrote a book called *The Development of Revolutionary Journalism*. The year before last they began to revise it for a new edition. One of the writers was Wang Panzi. He wasn't the principal editor but he'd done quite a lot of research. Now that the book is ready for the press, a problem has arisen over the list of authors' names. The editor-in-chief wants Wang Panzi's name removed because he was a 'rebel'. What's more, the editor-in-chief wants to add his own name as an 'advisor'. I think this is wrong. Wang Panzi made mistakes but he's been rehabilitated. Is it right to interfere with people's freedom to publish? As for calling himself an advisor, he's just advertising himself. He didn't advise at all, all he did was make a few phone calls and set up a few 'connections' when we were doing the research. If that deserves editorial credit then the cook in the canteen should be credited, he's made a far greater contribution.

When it was discussed by the editorial group, the principle of the matter was ignored. We talked for hours and everyone praised the editor-in-chief. It began to seem as if the 'advisor' had written

most of the book. At the same time, everyone attacked Wang
Panzi. Did he still have the nerve to consider himself one of the
authors? For the last few years he'd been saying the book was a
'poisonous weed'. That was true. But as I remembered it, if
everyone who'd attacked the book was to lose credit as an author,
then nobody would be credited, not even me. And certainly not
the 'advisor'. Everyone knew what he had constantly said in public
meetings – hadn't he attacked that 'big poisonous weed'? At the
beginning of the Cultural Revolution he'd been the leader of the
movement and he was the first to criticise the book.

But who would dare to cross the editor-in-chief? I didn't want
to.

Wang Panzi came to see me because I was head of the small
editorial group for the book, and because I got on quite well with
the editor-in-chief. Lanxiang also pleaded for him and reminded
me that Wang Panzi had been very good to us – he'd even bought
her a nylon blouse and hadn't wanted any money. We could pay
him back sometime later, he'd said. And he hadn't asked for it in
months. Yesterday's 'good turn', today's 'friendship'; I didn't
worry much about it. But I did want to change the way that I
always skirted round difficulties. Sun Yue used to criticise me for
it. So I went to see the editor-in-chief and explained my feelings.
I said that Wang Panzi's name ought to stay. If I achieved
that then I was prepared to compromise and let the 'advisor'
stay.

He said, 'Wang Panzi was rehabilitated because that was in
accordance with proletarian policy; but should we also allow him
to write and address meetings and achieve personal success? No.
The dictatorship of the proletariat isn't infinitely lenient. On this
question, Wang Panzi will just have to submit. Think of how he
ordered people about a few years ago!'

He added a friendly warning: 'We know that you used to be
friendly with Wang Panzi and we've had to explain that to people.
When you were chosen as head of the reporting section, we
couldn't announce it immediately because of your connection with
him. You ought to think about that. We'd like to make more use
of you – so you should try and work with us, not against us!

It was maddening. Why was I so feeble? Would I just agree for the sake of promotion? I didn't want to carry on being docile and obedient.

So I wrote a 'letter of complaint from the masses' to the Propaganda Department of the Provincial Party Committee. The head of the Propaganda Department reacted quickly, 'If what Zhao Zhenhuan says is right, then this matter must be taken very seriously.'

The editor-in-chief called me to see him today, and told me about the reprimand from the Propaganda Department. He was respectful. But suddenly his expression changed and he said, 'But you didn't tell the whole story. This whole business of removing Wang Panzi's name was brought up by your editorial group. The leadership has not expressed an opinion. How can you thrust the responsibility onto your superiors? We must go into the matter. We can settle it according to Party policy.' The mother hen had become the cock. His problem had become my problem. The accuser and the accused had changed position. The thief had shouted, 'Stop thief!' I was being forced into the role of the rat. I knew there was no point in arguing with him so I decided to write again to the Provincial Propaganda Department and explain the problem. I'd never seen things through before but I was determined to do it this time and get things sorted out properly.

I began a draft. I had to be serious. I had to get the details clear. I had to make my position clear. I had to sharpen my views. And then suddenly Wang Panzi walked in, smiling, holding some papers in his hand.

'Zhao Zhenhuan, this is a report I've written. I showed it to the chief editor and he says it can go out. I've also got a memo for you from him.'

Another miraculous transformation! I looked at the smiling miracle-worker in front of me. It was a smile with its own peculiar character, cheap and durable, a mixture of treachery, flattery and stupidity. A lot could be made out of little capital. I couldn't smile like that. If I pretend, it's obvious.

He gave me the memo. The flying dragon and dancing phoenix writing of the chief editor ran across the sheet: 'Zhao Zhenhuan, I've made some investigations amongst the masses and also talked to Wang Panzi. I realise that he does have a correct attitude to his mistakes and feel that his name need not be removed from *The Development of Revolutionary Journalism*. Would your editorial committee please discuss the matter again, firmly uphold the party's policy and let me know the results of your discussions.'

The memo was perfect. I held it out to Wang Panzi. 'I'm not having any more to do with this. Tell him to deal with it. I think I'll resign from the committee.'

Wang Panzi thrust the paper back into my hand. 'Come on, can't you take it on the chin? We're close friends. I never thought it was you who wanted my name scratched out. You're a friend.'

I smiled coldly. 'And are you my friend? Did you just take it on the chin from the chief editor?'

'I'm not that hypocritical, don't worry. But, of course, I wasn't as highhanded as you are.'

Me highhanded?

'Look, the idea was to stop our names being removed from the list. What's wrong with abasing oneself a bit to regain self-respect? Why the sudden purity?'

So now I was being pure. I'd have liked to punch his face to put a stop to his smile. I couldn't bear it. I pushed him out of the room.

I despised myself for getting involved in such a tiresome business. It's not that I don't understand people like Wang Panzi, so why did I defend him? And now he was backing down! It's true: the roads in the Taihang mountains can break carts but they are smoother than a man's heart; the water in the Wu gorges can dash a boat to bits but it is calmer than a man's heart. Sun Yue would no doubt have found me weak, yet again.

All right, Wang Panzi. I've never really considered us friends; from now on, I'm not going to get myself entangled in your problems.

I'd filled the house with cigarette smoke by the time Lanxiang and Huanhuan came home. Lanxiang said, 'There's enough smoke in here to kill us! Why didn't you open a window?'

She went to open one but I wouldn't let her. 'I like it like this.'

She looked at the ashtray and said, suddenly, 'So Wang Panzi's been over. What did you talk about? What's the matter?'

She must be very fond of Wang Panzi if she knows even his

cigarette stubs. What is their relationship? I never noticed it before.

'He's written an article and the editor-in-chief has approved it. His luck has turned.'

To see her delight, you'd think she was Wang Panzi's wife, not mine. Before I met her, she was known as 'General Mistress of the Rebel Headquarters'. I never believed it; now I have my doubts. Why had Wang Panzi been so keen to get us together?

'Huanhuan, did you remember to bring the toy Uncle Wang gave you?' she asked.

Does Huanhuan look like me? Lanxiang got pregnant soon after I met her, and the very day after she'd told me, Wang Panzi came round and winked at me, asking for a red-dyed egg to eat. [Red-dyed eggs are offered at the birth of a baby.] Had I fallen into a trap? I was very confused at the time.

Huanhuan does look like me, everyone says so. Her eyebrows and features are like mine. But what does that prove?

'What are you writing? Can I tidy up? We should eat.'

What was I writing? A letter of complaint on behalf of your Wang Panzi! I ought to write a complaint about him.

Right at the start he came to see me to tell me that people knew about me and Lanxiang. If we didn't resolve our position, things might not be so easy. All I had to do was ask for a divorce. Sun Yue refused.

He went to see a 'rebel comrade-in-arms' who worked in the law court, and got two letters of witness to the divorce, stamped them with the seal of the rebel brigade and that was it. I'd cheated on Sun Yue. I felt awful about the child.

My second daughter is definitely mine, I know because I feel so attached to her. 'Huanhuan, come here! Give daddy a hug!' I've got another daughter, with Sun Yue in Shanghai. What is that daughter like now?

'How nice. You're really close in this photograph.' With a cold smile, Lanxiang threw something at me. It was a small plastic frame with a photograph in it, the photograph of the former three of us.

'You've been in my drawer!' I was angry.

'I was looking for something. You always lock it. You said there

were manuscripts in there but that was what you were hiding!'
She was almost hysterical. Sun Yue would never have been like
that.

When she received my letter about the divorce, Sun Yue came
here to see me. I left her shut up in a small room and I didn't see
her. I was frightened of seeing her, of hearing her speak. She
didn't make any fuss at all, nor did she seek out any of my friends
or say anything. She stayed in the room all day, crouched over
the table, writing. All the persuasive words she had she wrote
down in a notebook, and she left it in my drawer.

'This is a special diary, Zhenhuan, read it! Read it for our
marvellous friendship, read it for our daughter's sake. "Flowing
water and falling blossom have no feelings but those who were
childhood friends always care." One false step brings ever-
lasting grief, Zhenhuan! Even if you insist on divorcing me, don't
marry Feng Lanxiang. You won't be happy, you can't. Please,
please!'

I easily agreed to have nothing more to do with Feng Lanxiang.
At first, Sun Yue believed me and began a serious self-criticism
in her diary. But then one day she found a photograph of Lanxiang
and me together, and a plait of Lanxiang's hair and a sickening
letter. If Sun Yue had told anybody about these I would have lost
all face. Instead, she locked them away, in front of me. Lanxiang
said she was just trying to win me back.

It was then that the Worker-Soldier Propaganda Team of her
university sent a group of people to take her back. They said that
her 'restorationist crimes' had been uncovered at last . . .

I took advantage of that opportunity, with Wang Panzi's help.

Sun Yue, I'm sorry.

Huanhuan wanted to see the photograph and started to cry
when I wouldn't give it to her. With a terrific effort, I tried to
keep calm. The child shouldn't see us fighting; I mustn't hurt
another child.

Lanxiang wouldn't leave it. She grabbed the girl and shouted,
'Huanhuan, you tell him to go off and find Sun Yue!'

Huanhuan asked innocently who was Sun Yue.

Lanxiang said contemptuously, 'The only person your father
cares about!'

I was so angry that I began to shake, and between my teeth I said, 'If you really want me to leave, I'll leave! I just don't want you to regret what you've said. I've never regretted anything. If Huanhuan tells me to go, I'll go willingly.'

That did it. Lanxiang began to cry. She pushed Huanhuan towards me and sat down, crying. It was stupid and shameless of me to bully a woman who didn't understand about principles. I was behaving in a very traditional way, putting the blame on a weak woman. Lanxiang wasn't wicked; I didn't really think she was. I just irritated her by constantly comparing her with Sun Yue. This maddening woman, why did she have to get involved with me?

'Come on, don't cry. Let's have something to eat and then Huanhuan can go to bed early for once.'

Lanxiang went off obediently and busied herself in the kitchen, returning to give me a glass of spirits. She is frightened of me – with any other husband, she'd be domineering. We're an ill-matched couple. We're also on the wrong side and following the wrong line!

I drank a few glasses of warm spirits; she was my wife and I was her husband. It's always been like this. She works on my weak points. Can alcohol make me forget Sun Yue and my other daughter? She's dreaming a pathetic dream.

I've really had enough of living like this. I so much long to tell Sun Yue how miserable I am and beg her forgiveness. I often think of walking arm-in-arm with her, beside a river, along a road, talking about ideals, art, current events, love, hate. I'd love to read her letters, beautifully written and full of interest, letters expressing honest emotions. Close to the edge of the sky, a river; the utmost effort, one's heart's blood, an exchange of letters. I've burnt all her letters. I wish I could burn events, forget everything. I'm mentally castrated: at work we just talk about work, at home we just talk about food and drink.

Sun Yue won't be able to forgive me. She shouldn't forgive me. I behaved too vilely.

No, tonight I don't feel like sleeping. I'll sit a while. And another while. Thinking about it is good, it's calming.

I only just started the letter on behalf of Wang Panzi. I'll tear it up now, of course; it's a waste of time. The writing paper from the press is very nice, thin, smooth and lightly ruled. I used to write to Sun Yue on paper like this sometimes and she used to say that in reading such a letter one had to apply the skills of a critic of calligraphy. My father taught me to write well with a brush.

Let's try a few characters on a clean sheet of paper: Sun Yue, I want you to forgive me . . . The paper was snatched away. Lanxiang had crept up behind me. Her cheeks moved; she wanted to say something but did not dare. I pitied her.

'What are you going to do about us? I know I did some awful things to you, but not since we were married. I've put everything into our marriage. What more do you want of me?' Getting one's misery out, confessing, can make quite ordinary people shine with spirit. Lanxiang looked like a Leonardo Madonna, worldly beauty and piety combined. She was very moving. I'd never been as moved by her before. I thought that if one thing was changed, Lanxiang could become a beautiful, noble and well-bred woman; like Sun Yue. Naturally, a woman who was exactly the same as Sun Yue wouldn't have enticed me into divorcing Sun Yue. It was the doing of ghosts and spirits.

I took her hand and made her sit down. I had to talk to her. Cheating and pretending were doing us no good.

'Lanxiang, I've never really loved you,' I said.

She pouted. She didn't believe me. She's never understood the difference between play-acting and real love. Is that surprising? She never got beyond the first grade of lower-middle school, and had a pretty strange education from society.

'I can't divorce you and I'm certainly not going to set up some irregular relationship with another woman behind your back. I've caused enough regret by doing it before.' Knowing I was referring to her, she blushed. She isn't totally stupid.

'We were thrown together by chance in the Cultural Revolution and we've stayed together by chance. But I've never given you my heart and now, more than ever, you can't expect it of me.'

Her eyes were vague, agitated, frightened, angry . . .

It was strange, I felt slightly happier, as if I'd got rid of some of my anger over Sun Yue.

When she received the letter announcing the divorce, how had her eyes looked? 'Broken-winged, knowing the hardships of life, licking the blood, soothing the wound, where is the pain?' A wounded person, a wounded heart. Let everyone lick their own wounds! Let everyone lick away the traces of their own blood! Her eyes must have been pained and angry.

My slight feeling of happiness changed into the pleasure of revenge. Where was it directed, my revenge? Against Feng Lanxiang and against myself. Sun Yue, we're punishing ourselves. You must feel a bit better.

'Why don't we draw up a three-point treaty,' I said, very coldly.

'What?' She didn't understand.

'I mean, we should draw up some mutually agreed conditions, in order to keep the family together,' I explained in simpler language.

'What conditions?' she asked nervously.

'First, that we don't talk about our disagreements to others. To the outside world we are blissfully happy.'

'I can do that. I'll smile at everybody,' she said, happily.

'Second: In front of Huanhuan, nobody mentions Sun Yue. We don't want the child to know about the past,' I said.

'You think I want to talk about her? I wish she'd never existed!' she said, quite cheerfully.

'Fine. Now we come to the third. Being honest with each other, but also not interfering.'

'What do you mean?' She didn't really understand.

'In our actions we'll be honest with each other, but as for feelings and ideas, we leave each other alone,' I translated.

'You'll think about Sun Yue all day and I'm not supposed to mind, is that it?' She spoke sharply. 'I won't let you write to Sun Yue.'

I didn't reply. I must write to Sun Yue to ask her forgiveness. And there's my other daughter, the crystallisation of our love.

Lanxiang's face suddenly puckered and she began to cry. I pulled her up from the stool. 'You ought to go to sleep.' She leant against me, pathetically.

Sun Yue, please forgive me!

NINE

SUN YUE

Xu Hengzhong, I'd never thought about it.

I've had rotten luck.

'Sun Yue, please forgive me!' Zhao Zhenhuan's letter threw me into more confusion. I've always known it would come some day. The scars have reopened and begun to bleed again. He wanted to reopen the scars.

Hanhan was going on a school outing so I had to get her things ready in a hurry. She made me feel even more pressed.

'Ma, if Uncle He comes for me today, will you ask him to come over next Sunday?' she said, just before she left.

'Who is Uncle He?'

'He Jingfu.'

So he's been back. Since he came to the house, she's asked me about him every couple of days. And he stopped me himself yesterday just as I was leaving the office, to ask me about my divorce with Zhao Zhenhuan. Finally, he said, 'You shouldn't have agreed to a divorce. You should have thought of Hanhan.' I was surprised that he should talk like that to me. For my own self-respect, I hadn't told him exactly what Zhao Zhenhuan had done; but he still didn't have to blame me. It's true, I shouldn't have agreed – but who asked for my consent?

Forgiveness! It's easy for you to ask, Zhao Zhenhuan. When I was being attacked for the second time, you added to my troubles by forcing the divorce on me. 'Even her husband wants to drop her!' That was what they said in the University. 'Dropped', 'abandoned', strange to hear such words associated with the Party member Sun Yue. Yet it was true. You didn't only want to drop me; you wanted to ruin my reputation, too. 'I can't take the slander! They say you're Xi Liu's mistress; I don't want anybody's mistress!' 'You misled me, you never loved me!' 'Why did you enslave me? I don't want you!' Letters like that, day after day. After a day of being attacked as a 'cow ghost' and a 'snake spirit', I would come home to find nothing, just Hanhan and your letters.

'Mummy, there's a letter from Daddy!' Hanhan used to say cheerfully. I couldn't read them in front of her because she always asked if you said anything about her, if you missed her. 'Write back to Daddy!' I'd wait till she was asleep before I read them. It was as if they were basins full of blood that you were forcing me to swallow.

I had to invent things for the child. 'Give me a little time, let me go and talk to him again,' I begged the Worker-Soldier Propaganda Team.

'Don't try and change the direction of the struggle for personal reasons!'

I tried to talk about it with friends. Immediately, a big-character poster went up: 'Sun Yue has started her counter-revolutionary clique-formation again!'

Some sympathetic people used to ask me how things were, surreptitiously. I told them. So I was accused of another crime: stirring up public opinion, deceiving the masses in order to gain sympathy.

When I received your letter announcing the divorce, I could only cry alone.

Forgive you? How can I efface the memories?

'Don't take your troubles out on the child. Don't you realise, she feels very lonely?'

Am I a mother? Do I love my child? You are a single man, He Jingfu, how can you possibly understand?

That day, the Worker-Soldier Propaganda Team gave me the letter announcing the divorce. No words of comfort; they positively enjoyed my predicament. Without really looking at it,

I put the letter in my bag and went to the kindergarten to collect the child. As soon as I saw her, I began to cry. She started to cry, too. 'What's the matter, Ma? Do you miss Daddy?' All the way home, she asked endless questions. I could only shake my head and cry. What could I say? The legal authorities have the power to protect women and children but on my divorce notice it said that the child would stay with the mother and the father had no financial responsibilities for the child. From then on, the child was mine alone. I didn't know how I'd manage to bring her up under the circumstances. I really couldn't take the accusations and attacks. I put her to bed early and sat alone, thinking. I longed to leave the world. I tidied up a bit, tore up photographs and went to sit by her. She must have known what was going on because she wasn't asleep. 'Ma,' she said, 'come and sleep here, I'm frightened!'

'Hanhan, my good little Hanhan. If Ma wasn't here, how would you manage?' I hugged her tightly and cried.

She put out a little hand and wiped away my tears and said, comfortingly, 'If you've got to go off, don't worry. Your relatives in the countryside will look after me.' She'd seen the opera, *The White-haired Girl* the day before and she'd learnt the phrase 'your relatives in the countryside' and now she used it. Clever child! Darling child! Poor child! I hugged her tight and cried all night.

For the child, I've struggled to survive. Do I take my misery out on her? I'd like to swallow all my sorrows but it isn't easy and when I'm especially unhappy, it must show on my face. It has an effect on her . . . I've worried about it, blamed myself for it. Do you know that? Yet you still reproach me. I don't think we'll ever understand each other, you and I. You always seem to think that life has been kind to me whilst it's been very hard on you.

What an ear-splitting noise! The campus is a long way out of town but it's still very noisy. In the buildings near the main road, it's very difficult: if you close the windows it's chilly and dark, if you open them the noise is deafening. It's enough to drive you crazy. It's better to shut the windows and go out. Hanhan won't be back for lunch, so what's the point in staying in alone? I'll go and find a dumpling stall and eat something.

The weather is surprisingly fine. In the park, the peach blossom is pink and the willows green. As the seasons change, we change, like flowers that open in the spring, like the brightly dressed students walking in the park. Flowers open and then drop. People are young and then old. The transformation happens once in a lifetime.

Here, this is the most out-of-the-way corner of the park. Shrubs grow low and thick. It is a place for lovers to meet. It was here that He Jingfu and I . . . what did I feel then?

I found him attractive on our first meeting. He wasn't as good-looking as Zhao Zhenhuan but in some ways his looks were more brilliant. Even the stupidest person could see that his eyes really were expressive and they used to follow me about, like spotlights. I couldn't avoid him. I compared him increasingly with Zhao Zhenhuan. He Jingfu loved me but his affection was a bit exaggerated; he wanted constantly to talk about love. He would bring it into everything. In the reference room, he used to pass me books, telling me to read them. And they affected me. If I was moved by something, I'd feel him looking at me. I read all the books he read. He read all the books I read. Without any particular plan, everything got muddled up. Without my realising it, we became friends. Then, that time when we were acting in *Put Down your Whips*, in the bright glare of the spotlights, I understood what was happening. I had to struggle to behave normally. I was afraid of him and stayed away – I found him too attractive, he could have led me away from my childhood friends. So I publicly announced that I was in love with Zhao Zhenhuan; I deliberately took Zhao Zhenhuan's arm in front of him, I used Zhao Zhenhuan's charm and popularity to calm myself and give myself courage. I deliberately set out to resist his attraction.

His diaries were made public. Who thought up this weapon of class struggle? Driving someone to the execution ground on the strength of his private feelings? Because of that example, I burnt my diary at the very beginning of the Cultural Revolution; it still upsets me to think about it. But was there any comparison between my diary and He Jingfu's? No one had ever loved me as he did. At the time, I longed to copy down his diary, sentence by sentence!

Every evening, I would escape from Zhao Zhenhuan and come here amongst the shrubs to wait for him. We'd never made any arrangement to meet but I firmly believed that I'd find him. I wanted to tell him: let people laugh, let them say what they like, you gave me your love. I want you to accept mine. Then one day, he was there, standing in front of me. Traitor! Double traitor! You've betrayed your love! You've betrayed the Party! I ran away.

When I was 'telling my heart to the Party', I told them all about it. The league leaders were very serious but they helped me and said I'd 'learnt the lesson of class struggle'.

The shrubs haven't changed in twenty years. They are still bushy and still low, but my memories are broken and grown old. I've tried hard to forget him. He was a 'rightist' and I was a 'leftist'. Left and right, how could they fall in love? Hadn't I finally forgotten him? I'm not sure. It was as if I'd shut the genie up in a jar but never dared take the lid off again. I've never dared to question myself too closely, either.

Does he understand all this? What does he think of me?

Forgiveness! It's easy to say. In order to protect my innocent love for you, Zhao Zhenhuan, what sort of price did I have to pay? How much sacrifice did I have to make? I had to shut my eyes, lock my soul against every pleasant temptation. In order to be faithful to you, I had to betray myself. I gave myself to you completely. Naturally I had regrets but I thought I could find comfort in fidelity. You repaid my fidelity and honesty by abandoning me.

No, I've no longer the strength to forgive anybody. All I can do is ask him, He Jingfu, to forgive me. No, I don't want to do that. I just want to forget it all.

'Sun Yue, I wish so much that you were still the Sun Yue that I remember. Why do you struggle on with such a burden? You must know that you can't carry it forever, it's too much.'

He Jingfu! The Sun Yue you remember is the Sun Yue you created so lovingly. She never existed. The real Sun Yue also had her 'past', but that 'past' had already died. Died and could not live again. Then, she had solid faith, ideals, beautiful hopes and

high spirits: she thought that if one gave one's heart, one got the
same in return. With all her heart she built an image, nourished
and loved it, until a cruel storm destroyed it, toppled it, washed
it away. Then what she saw and felt lost all its colour. She began
to suspect that her flourishing flowers and rainbows were soap
bubbles she had blown through a straw out into the world. There
was nothing left to believe in. Jingfu, didn't you hear her weeping?
If one day a nun discovers that God is of her own making, doesn't
she feel betrayed?

Sometimes I thought I'd go mad. When night fell and all was
peaceful, I would cry and scream inside.

The weather is marvellous today. The storms are long past.
But when will everything regain its original colour? You can't just
paint things over, patch things up. The bones need to mend, the
sinews need to be toughened, the blood needs to be renewed.
Sun Yue's grey hairs will never grow black again. He Jingfu, love
the illusory Sun Yue that you created. I don't want to destroy her
with reality.

'Teacher Sun!' A pair of sweethearts emerged from the trees,
giving me a start.

They were an intriguing pair. The girl had quite often snivelled
in front of me, but each time, before I'd found the boy to tick him
off, they'd gone off hand in hand into the park. Her tears were
part of being in love and I could never take them terribly seriously.

'You haven't gone into town?' I asked.

'There's singing practice this afternoon. We're going in for the
competition,' the girl answered.

'Oh, fine. It's good for young people to sing revolutionary
songs. They stir you up.' I said, smiling. But I blushed, for the
word 'revolutionary'. It was a habit, I knew perfectly well that
good songs weren't all 'revolutionary'.

'We've heard that you were a cultural activist when you were
a student. Why don't you come and sing with us this afternoon?'
the girl asked. They were just like me and Zhao Zhenhuan. I was
always the one who talked but he was really in charge.

'Fine, I'll come!' I said cheerfully, surprising even myself. The
boy looked at me, the girl said, 'Goodbye,' and they walked off
together.

I couldn't go and walk amongst the trees again. Goodness knows how many young couples I might bump into!

I went back along the stream that ran through the University park. Would I really go and sing with them? The faculty Party secretary couldn't promise things lightly. But for the last ten years, apart from a few songs based on Mao's quotations, I hadn't sung a thing. Had I forgotten all the songs I used to know? Let's see. 'The sky over the Liberated Areas is bright, the people of the Liberated Areas enjoy it . . .' I used to sing that when we were dancing the yangge[6]. Once the red satin sash was pulled too tightly round my waist and I couldn't stop myself crying in front of the teacher. All I can remember now is the bit that goes, 'The cockerel, the cockerel, crows with all his might, calling to the sun, the sun, the red sun; how can the young strong boy stay in bed like a lazy bug?' It was one of the boy's songs from *Little Brothers and Sisters Cultivate the Wilderness*. We didn't have a loudspeaker when we performed it, and the teacher got four 'brothers and sisters' to sing together so that the audience could hear. There weren't many boys who could sing and the teacher said I was a tomboy, so I was asked to take one of the boy's parts. I had a white towel on my head. Zhao Zhenhuan helped me tie it on. He also played one of the 'brothers'.

'The millet leaves were green, the Japanese soldiers came on the 18th of September . . .' That was one of the songs from *Put down your whips*. When He Jingfu sang, I think the people in the back row could hear every word. It sounded like thunder to me, it shook me so that I could hardly see. But I can't remember all the words . . .

'What's made you so happy that you're singing?'

It gave me such a fright! My terrible habit of talking to myself! Xu Hengzhong came up behind me carrying a basket. He'd probably been behind me for some time.

'Doing the errands on a Sunday?' I asked, for the sake of saying something.

'What can I do? I've got to feed the child. I'm father and mother so I've got to be a housewife,' he said, smiling.

I felt sorry for him.

'Where's Hanhan?' he asked.

'She's gone on a school outing.'

'Where are you going?'

'Nowhere in particular.'

'I'm making some clothes for Little Kun. I must have cut them out wrong, I can't seem to fit the pieces together.' He seemed to be asking for something from me though he didn't look at me.

'I'll help you.'

People are strange! A few years ago, no one could have imagined that he and I would walk together, I was so repugnant to him. Originally, he'd been another 'protector of Xi Liu', but he joined the rebels just before the 'January storm'[7]. He also sent his wife to see me to try to get me to change my position. I decided to have no more to do with them because I despised the way he changed with the wind; as for his joining the rebels, I could never understand it. He'd been a real flag-bearer for Xi Liu, an anti-rightist hero. At the great meeting, he'd been very upset when Xi Liu was attacked. The papers at the time were full of his exploits! He was normally someone who took the lead or spoke up first. How could he have joined the minority group when the 'conservatives' were still in power?

'Xu Hengzhong.' I smiled before I opened my mouth. 'There's a question I've been wanting to ask you for years.' He looked at me, waiting.

'You've always been a cautious person, how did you come to join the rebels?' He blushed. He was a good-looking, elegant man. When he was a student he'd been very popular amongst the girls, but there'd been something about him I found unattractive, something indefinable. It was as if his heart was wrapped in oiled paper so it couldn't be seen clearly and it couldn't be touched. Would he tell me the truth?

'I've often asked myself the same question. The answer is partly out of self-interest, partly out of stupidity.'

It almost amounted to a confession. Life certainly teaches people lessons.

'Do you remember that big-character poster I put up about He Jingfu during the Anti-Rightist Campaign?' he asked. I nodded. 'You only know the half of it!'

I remember being shocked that a 'model' activist could resort to such slanderous tricks. In 1957, when the campaign began, Xu Hengzhong, like everyone else, had seriously wanted to help the Party rectification. On the poster He Jingfu put up, he'd signed his name but he'd scrawled it, in small characters which were difficult to read. One evening, he noticed Xi Liu and some other Party leaders looking at the poster. He stood to one side, listening. He'd been upset by the Xie affair and hoped that the boy would be allowed to leave the country to see his mother, but he was also afraid that Xi Liu would want revenge on He Jingfu. Xi Liu's face was distorted by anger.

'Party morale is low; trouble will erupt any day,' he said to his companions.

Xu Hengzhong was scared. When they left, he searched for his name on the poster, and though it was very inconspicuous he decided to scratch it out. Just as he was finishing, a man came over with a camera; Xu Hengzhong recognised him as the editor of the University journal. The man asked, 'Which department are you from? What are you doing here?' and he could only babble that he'd been unable to sleep. The man was suddenly very interested and asked, 'Because of the poster? What's your opinion of it?' Again, he could only stammer that he didn't know the real facts of the case. The journalist said, 'Comrade Xi Liu didn't actually say those things about the Party not admitting the existence of feelings, he was just talking about class sentiments. What he actually said was that we admit the existence of human feelings but that all emotions have class content. Don't you think that He Jingfu has been spreading slander and making a poisonous attack on the Party leadership?'

'I couldn't really see the difference,' Xu Hengzhong said. 'But what he said about a poisonous attack on Party leadership made me break out in a cold sweat. So I nodded in agreement.' As he was talking to me he seemed small and weak.

The next day, Xi Liu had summoned Xu Hengzhong.

'I hear you're not happy about He Jingfu's poster, so much so that you can't sleep at nights?' was Xi Liu's opening remark.

Xu Hengzhong neither affirmed nor denied it. 'I've been sleeping very badly recently.'

'What's your class background?'

'Poor peasant.' He didn't dare admit that his grandfather had been a landlord. His father had been born of a prostitute and managed to have himself classified as a poor peasant. He had in fact been poor. When Xu Hengzhong was small he never even had any trousers and all the villagers used to call him 'Bare Bum'. We called him 'Bare Bum' too, though it didn't fit very well with his rather refined air.

'Good. Your class sentiments are definitely reliable. It's a refreshing change from He Jingfu's humanism. You're a good example – throw yourself into the struggle, dare to defy the reactionary slander of the rightists. We'll back you up.' Xi Liu's expression was serious but quite friendly.

'So you wrote your big-character poster?' I asked.

'I was really confused at the time. I had nothing against He Jingfu and couldn't see that He Jingfu's poster was anti-Party, but Xi Liu's opinion was that of the Central Committee and I was frightened of implicating myself.'

I repeated my question.

'The editor of the University journal sketched it out. I copied his draft,' he replied.

So that was what had happened. I once went to the Arts factory and saw lots of wooden puppets. Some were sitting, some standing. Somebody would move the head of one or the hands of another. They laughed. They cried. They were brave, they were frightened. It all depended upon the person operating them. If a child had been to the factory, would it have responded innocently to the hero on-stage and shouted at the villain? It probably would. The world of the stage is different from reality.

'What do you think?' Xu Hengzhong asked me nervously.

'I've always taken every political struggle very seriously. I always wanted to throw myself heart and soul into each struggle, but I never thought . . .' I couldn't really say what I thought.

He understood. 'You're right, I didn't really think . . . I'd got myself into an undreamt-of position. I entered the Party, I was famous. I finally understood that the rights and wrongs of struggle were fortuitous; they didn't depend upon honesty.'

'So becoming a rebel was also fortuitous?' I asked. I felt as if

rap. Not because of Xu Hengzhong
houghts were leading me.
nd in the know that the rightists in
ed,' he said, ashamed.
He didn't say anything else. What
more could be said? We were both
een through these things are fated.
all our own? Not necessarily. Who
thought? We've all asked 'why?',
And like tragic actors acting out a
who ought to be the villain and who

s from the path and threw them into
ake patterns in the water but they all
made ripples.
stones from my hand and threw them.

m lightly so they skim the surface,' he

'I can't do it,' I said. He blushed.

Little Kun saw me and shouted, 'Aunty Sun!' He was a pretty child but he was timid. He seemed to implore people, 'Love me! Don't tease me! Pity me!'

At the house I took up the pieces of cloth that Xu Hengzhong had cut out, and began to sew. Little Kun stood so close he was in the way.

'Don't be a nuisance, Little Kun! Don't distract Aunty Sun!'

The tannoy outside started up. The song they were playing made me think of He Jingfu.

Xu Hengzhong stopped washing vegetables and asked, 'Can you do anything with it? Is it possible?'

I nodded but didn't reply.

'The revolution sent me far away, far away . . .' the song continued. Had his travels frustrated He Jingfu? Or brought him beauty? I couldn't bring beauty into his life. It was a sad song. There was blood in He Jingfu's song. A shooting star by the Great Wall. And the pearl on the top of *my* head? I didn't need his pity or sympathy. What had gone wrong had gone wrong. If something can't be repaired, it can't be repaired.

I made the clothes and tried them on Little Kun. There was something slightly ingratiating in his smile but there couldn't really have been – a child wouldn't know how. Xu Hengzhong came up to cuddle the boy. He was too close to me; I wanted to go home.

Xu Hengzhong said, 'Tell Mama Sun she must have a meal with us, tell her not to go home.' So the child repeated the words three times. On the third, his mouth twisted and he began to cry. I felt I had to stay.

If the three of us sat down to eat together, what would other people think? Xu Hengzhong must be really desperate to try and court me after what happened before.

'Little Sun, it's rarely as cheerful as this at home. Is it the same for you?' he asked suddenly, putting down the chopsticks. I didn't like to say anything.

'I hope you'll come often, like today,' he said. I didn't reply. 'We've known each other for over twenty years, through thick and thin.' He came closer. 'When we were students, there was one girl I really wanted to chase but Zhao Zhenhuan got there first.' I looked at him in surprise. 'Hanhan wants a father. Haven't you thought of marrying again to make her happy?'

He Jingfu had asked me and I'd replied, 'No, I haven't thought of it. And I don't want to think of it.' Perhaps I'll think about it if I have to. Not for the child but for myself. To break free from Zhao Zhenhuan's betrayal. To avoid He Jingfu's compassion. To destroy my illusions. All I feel for Xu Hengzhong is sympathy. Sympathy isn't love. Li Yining is quite right, ninety-five per cent of couples just make the best of it but some of them manage it so that no cracks appear to the outside world.

Making do is something. But it's colourless, it doesn't amount to reaching one's full potential. How could I answer Xu Hengzhong? He looked pleadingly at me. The colour had drained from his face. I smiled and said, 'Xu Hengzhong, I've never thought of it.'

'I know, I'm not much of a partner. I'm weak. And now my market value is even lower than my real worth. Nobody respects me. I've got no illusions.' He sounded bitter. He seemed to have aged ten years.

Suddenly I saw that our fates were similar. We seemed to be following the same path but we were at different points on it. Our 'market values' had been determined by this tortuous path and yet they had no relation to our real worth. Did we have to continue like this? When would we be accorded our full worth and be able to discard our 'market value'? We'd both been through uncertain years, been buffeted a couple of times, but we ought to be able to discard the past.

I told him what I'd been thinking and his face regained some of its colour. He was so easily influenced, it was as if his fate lay in the hands of others. He was so different from He Jingfu. People could face the same difficulties but an over-sensitive person could lose himself. I didn't like excessively sensitive people.

I thought I ought to go.

'Please forgive me for what I said just now. I shouldn't have.' He sounded dispirited again.

I was rather annoyed and said sharply, 'If you knew you shouldn't say it, then why did you?'

He was upset, he was a very unmasculine man. I didn't need people like him. I left.

I walked very fast to try to dispel the effect. When I reached the isolated shrubbery, I thought of what I'd said to the students about going singing. Go! Join the young people and these confused thoughts will disappear. Young people like Xi Wang are lucky. They carry a light burden, not the burden of history. Can we ever be like them? Or will they become like us?

TEN

SUN HANHAN

Ma, I must have a serious talk with you.

It's really annoying, Xu Hengzhong keeps coming round. He's taken to coming every Sunday with his revolting little boy. I feel sick at the sight of him. Small eyes, small nose, he's a miserable, feeble little thing. But Ma seems to like him and always hugs him, as if he was her own. It's depressing.

'We've come to spend Sunday with you!' He stands in the doorway, smiling. He brings a plastic string bag filled with vegetables. They probably get bored eating on their own and want a change. Most peculiar. I asked Ma why they were always coming round. She said he'd only just been 'rehabilitated' and not many people had anything to do with him so we had to be nice.

Today, I really wanted Ma to send them away. It wouldn't hurt. But she said nothing and gave no sign of whether she wanted them to stay or not. It was just as usual, Ma's face was calm, her eyes pained. Physically, eyes don't vary but their expressions do. I like studying Ma's eyes but sometimes those 'windows of the soul' aren't much use. You look in through the window but you can't see what's in the room.

Xu Hengzhong took the vegetables out of his string bag, one by one, and little Kun helped him. Ma didn't move and didn't speak.

I didn't want to join in the meal. Some of my school friends had already asked what relationship he had with us. One even said, 'My Dad knows him. He says he's a "Gang of Four-ist".'

Ma didn't worry about me. I'd go out. I wasn't going to eat at home. 'Ma, I'm going over to a friend's house,' I called from the door.

Xu Hengzhong smiled and said, 'Don't forget to come back for lunch!' So you are in charge in my home are you? Who do you think you are? I paid no attention to him and left. Ma came to the door and looked at me sadly. 'Whose house are you going to?'

'I won't go far, I can find my own way back.'

I ran, feeling like crying, and when I looked back at the flats Ma was still standing at the doorway. She has a hard time. She has to be branch secretary, and teach and do everything at home. She doesn't get a very high salary but she certainly earns every penny. The last time they raised the salaries, they would have given her a rise but she made them give it to someone else. When it comes to raising wages she seems like a real communist, but not in anything else. Do Party members conceal their feelings? I can't work her out. She always says one ought to be clear and straightforward. She isn't. Is He Jingfu? I'm not sure.

He's never been over since the day Ma wouldn't let him stay and eat with us. I was furious with her. He agreed to be my friend and she was very impolite to him. If she doesn't like him, why does she always talk about him? The day before yesterday she told me I wasn't frugal enough, and said, 'If you had to rely on your own labour in order to eat, like He Jingfu, you'd understand how you ought to live.'

I asked, 'Will He Jingfu come over on Sunday?'

She looked angry. 'Don't be stupid! Whatever for? Sunday is for going out with your sweetheart!'

'Who is his sweetheart?'

'You drive me mad! Mind your own business. How should I know?'

All right, all right, we won't talk about it. But you brought him up in the first place, didn't you?

Did I know which building he lived in? I wandered from block to block, wondering whether I should ask or not.

A boy wearing the university badge looked at me, and suddenly held out his hand and grabbed one of my pigtails. 'Aren't you Little Hanhan?'

Why can't he just call me Hanhan? Why the 'little'? And grabbing my pigtail! At school, none of the boys even speak to the girls and none of them would dream of grabbing a girl's pigtail.

'Whoops! Somebody pulled your hair! I love pulling girls' pigtails!' he laughed. 'I haven't got a little sister so I had to pull yours instead!' He stretched out a hand and tried to grab it again. I dodged and began to run; then I thought, why not ask him where Uncle He lives? He caught me up and patted my head, saying, 'Don't be cross, I was only teasing! Where are you off to?' I softened and smiled at him and told him I was looking for He Jingfu.

'He's ill. He's in hospital. I was just going to pick up a few of his things for him. Come along!' He led me into a building and explained that he was Xi Wang and that he guessed from my face that I must be Sun Yue's daughter.

I asked him how He Jingfu was. He said, 'I'll just get his things and then I'll tell you.'

He opened the door of a small room on the second floor next to the lavatories. It was very bare. Apart from a battered wooden trunk and a few bookcases, there wasn't really anything that could be called furniture. There were two beds. He Jingfu slept on one and there were a few things scattered on the other. Xi Wang explained that teachers whose families lived far away would sometimes get him to put their relatives up for a couple of nights. His quilt was a real peasant's one; the red flowered cotton had faded to a greyish colour and the cotton quilting was visible through a few holes. The pillow was small and hard, with a plain woollen scarf spread over it.

'So this is how he lives!' I was surprised and upset.

Xi Wang was gathering up a bowl and a few other things and bundling them into a bag. When I spoke, he turned and sighed, 'Little Hanhan, there are too many things in the world that one regrets. If I hadn't come over to see him today, he could have died in here and nobody would have known! He was already delirious when I came in. He's got acute pneumonia. If it hadn't been treated, it could have killed him. Right! I'm ready, let's go.'

'You haven't forgotten anything?' I asked as I shut the door.

'You're right! His tobacco pouch!'

It was hanging at the head of the bed. I took it down and carried it, walking beside Xi Wang.

'Why does he smoke a pipe? Only old people smoke pipes.' I looked at the pipe, which was very ordinary, and at the pouch made of a piece of blue peasant cloth, old and tattered.

'It was left to him by his father. When he's better you must get him to tell you about it. His father was a good man.'

'You tell me about it first!'

'No, I must get to the hospital. Anyway, I'm no good at stories.'

I was very worried about He Jingfu. Who would look after him in hospital? Did his sweetheart know he was ill? Xi Wang must know who she was. 'Have you told his girlfriend?' I asked.

'What girlfriend?'

'I don't know. Ma said he must be busy with a girlfriend.'

'Aha.' He was very interested and asked me rather confidentially, 'Does your mother often talk about He Jingfu? Does she think well of him?'

'I don't know. She often mentions him but she wouldn't let him stay to eat with us.' I looked at him. 'On the other hand, that Xu Hengzhong is always coming round. And he stays to eat. It's really annoying.' I didn't want to say anything bad about Ma but I didn't want to lie to He Jingfu's friend.

'Really?' He didn't say any more. What was he thinking? After a while, he asked, 'Which is the better person, He Jingfu or Xu Hengzhong?'

'He Jingfu, of course,' I answered truthfully.

He was so pleased he couldn't resist tweaking my pigtail again. 'I absolutely agree with you. He Jingfu is very strong-minded. Do you know what I mean?'

'Yes. They say at school that I'm strong-minded.' To tell the truth, I didn't really know what he meant but I was too embarrassed to admit it.

Xi Wang shook his head and smiled, 'No, Little Hanhan. You and He Jingfu are quite different. You are a wilful child, right?' I nodded, not quite following him. 'But He Jingfu has his own independent opinions on life and things. To know what is right and what is beautiful and to go all out for it isn't easy. He Jingfu understands people and he values humanity. He has tremendous self-respect.'

'My teacher said that too much self-respect leads to "humanitarianism",' I said, though I didn't know whether it was true or not.

'Oh, Little Hanhan! If people don't respect themselves, they're no better than animals! You can't understand it yet. But if you stick around with people like He Jingfu, you'll learn a lot, things that no one else could teach you.'

That was what I really liked about He Jingfu, and I was glad that Ma had been a friend of his. How did he compare with my father? My father was much better-looking, but was he independent-minded? I couldn't tell from the photograph. Ma never wants to talk to me about my father. And now she's talking to Xu Hengzhong. Blast him!

Ow! I bumped into a branch of one of the willows bordering the road.

'What gloomy thoughts were you thinking?'

Xi Wang must have second sight if he could tell what I was thinking. He must be pretty clever. Ma used to say that it would take a lot for me to admire anyone. It's true. I don't admire a lot of admirable people because all they talk about is the need to struggle for communism and the common good, but what do they actually do? They all put themselves first. It's the same at school. Xi Wang seemed different.

'Do you like He Jingfu?' I asked. I knew he must but I wanted to hear him praise him.

'Of course I like him. At first, I felt sorry for him because my father had punished him and I wanted to understand him, to help him. Later I got to like him. Do you know my father? He's Xi Liu, the Party Secretary of the University. He was the one who branded He Jingfu a rightist.'

'He must be a wicked man,' I said without thinking.

He blushed. 'No, he's not a bad man. He did that, but he did it under peculiar historical circumstances.'

'So you defend your father,' I said, crossly; I was defending He Jingfu.

'No, Hanhan, you're wrong. I want to be fair to people. I'm not favouring my father. I don't respect him.'

'I can't say that about my father.' How could I say that? How had I suddenly lost my guard, let down my defences? I hoped he hadn't heard it. I'd said it very quietly. And there was a truck passing at that moment, wasn't there?

He turned and looked at me. He looked amused and not amused. He must have heard. 'Tell me about your father!' he said.

I bit my lip and didn't say anything. I wasn't going to let my guard down again.

'I've heard he's very good-looking. I'd like to see him,' he said.

I couldn't bear it. I really couldn't stand it. I took the torn photograph out of my bag and showed it to him. My father was good-looking. I was pleased.

He looked at it carefully. 'He really is handsome. Your mother must have taken a real fancy to him.'

'What do you mean?'

'All I meant was that people are always attracted by good looks. But what's far more important than looks is the soul. He Jingfu has a beautiful soul. Do you understand?'

'Are you saying that my father doesn't have a beautiful soul? You don't know him! He's not like your father. He hasn't attacked anyone as a rightist.'

He pulled my pigtail again. 'You still love your father! Your mother hasn't told you anything. You're not that young. Your mother ought to tell you about the family, otherwise she'll create a rift between you both.'

He was quite a complex character. He seemed to know everything. Ma oughtn't to hide things from me. I must have a serious talk with her today; I want to get everything straight. But will Xu Hengzhong ever leave? That un-independent, unrefined man! And his pathetic child!

'Right, here's where I get the bus. You ought to go back home.

I'll tell He Jingfu you came over today, all right? He often talks about you.'

We shook hands and I set off home. Oh no! I still had the tobacco pouch!

Xu Hengzhong and his child were still there, of course, sitting round the table drinking tea. I don't know why, but I suddenly felt furious. I put Uncle He's tobacco pouch on my desk, dragged a stool into the middle of the room and sat down.

Ma looked at me, and then at Xu Hengzhong. She seemed rather cross but she spoke to me nicely: 'We've kept some food for you. I'll go and warm it up.'

'I've eaten.'

'Where did you eat?' she asked, still pleasantly.

'At a friend's house. From now on I'm going to eat at a friend's house every Sunday. That way I'll save you money, I'll eat less and I'll be less trouble,' I snorted and turned my back on her.

'We'll go back home. Goodbye, Hanhan.'

At least he had some sense. I turned and watched him. His face was expressionless. There was nothing in his heart and nothing in his face. I knew what my language teacher meant about internal and external expressions now. He was so insensitive it was a joke.

Ma said goodbye to them at the door and came in, clearly angry. 'Don't you have any manners? Aren't I your mother? Don't I deserve some respect?'

When she's angry, Ma never raises her voice. If anything, her voice is lower than usual, with every word like an arrow, hitting its target.

I couldn't seem to calm myself down and I kicked the stool over.

Thump, thump! She hit me hard on the back, twice. It hurt.

'Hit me! You can kill me if you like, I don't want to go on living!' I began to cry noisily. I'd never cried and shouted like this before. Ma didn't often hit me and never hard, and she usually cried if she did, as if she was hitting herself. Today, she hit me really hard so she must have been terribly angry. I felt very sorry for what I'd done. She seemed to be angrier than ever.

I leant my head on the back of the chair and prepared for further blows.

Nothing moved. I looked up. Ma was sitting on the bed, staring ahead. She looked very unhappy and very surprised.

'Why did you say that? Where did you hear things like that? That you don't want to go on living. Did you think that up, Hanhan?'

She was talking to me but she didn't look at me. 'Is there nothing nice about me? Do you hate living with me? Go and find him, then! Go and find your father!'

I was appalled. It was worse than being hit. I really felt she didn't love me. I'd been beastly to her but she was still my mother! If I didn't have her, if I had to go away from her, then I really would die.

I got up and went over to her, and stood beside her, crying. 'Ma, I'm sorry. I'll never say it again. I don't know what's wrong with me today, I'm really fed up and I can't think about anything else.'

'Where did you go just now?' She stroked my head . . . and my back, where she'd just hit me.

'I went to see Uncle He. But he's very ill and he's in hospital.'

Ma's hand was still on my back, 'What's the matter with him?'

'He's got acute pneumonia. Xi Wang told me.'

Ma took her hand away and stood up. I took her hand and said, 'I'm sorry.'

'It's all right, Hanhan. Have something to eat.' She walked over to the bookcase and pulled out a medical dictionary. She read for a while and her expression altered. 'How is he?' she asked anxiously.

'He's out of danger, Xi Wang said.'

'Good. Come and eat, Hanhan. I'll warm it up for you, okay?' She was still looking at the book.

'Don't bother. I'm not hungry. Please, will you tell me about you and Dad. I'm old enough now.'

Ma's back shook slightly. She put the book down. She didn't say she would but she didn't say she wouldn't. She went over to her desk and opened the drawer that she always kept locked, took out a letter and handed it to me. Then she went into the kitchen.

As soon as I saw it came from Zhao Zhenhuan in Guangzhou, my hands began to shake and my heart beat faster.

'Sun Yue, please forgive me!' That first sentence made it all clear, it was like a bucket of cold water poured over me. I thought of what Xi Wang had said, that the beauty of a person's soul was the most important thing. Could someone with a beautiful soul do something so awful that he had to beg for forgiveness? Did my father have a beautiful soul?

'How did I get together with Feng Lanxiang? In sum, it was because I'm cynical . . . I played with my emotions, I played games with my individuality . . .'

So that was it! There was a woman – a bad woman! He was so good-looking. Now his face was indistinct in my memory, so indistinct that I couldn't really see it at all.

'What I really can't get over is that I resorted to unscrupulous methods to get a divorce from you. I feel I destroyed you psychologically. Sun Yue, am I really human? Am I still fit to be a father to the child?'

Huh! His fine straight nose and his full lips. He hurt Ma. He destroyed her. Unscrupulous methods! What sort of people use unscrupulous methods? Bad people; wicked people!

'I've been punished for it now. My hair is quite white.'

He should be punished. A heartless person like that ought to be punished.

I'd held on to such strong feelings for him. They'd made me dissatisfied with Ma and given me such mistaken ideas. I'd stuck the photograph together so carefully and always kept it close to me. I'd always hoped that one day . . . No. Now I had no hope. I must tear up the photograph.

The photograph no longer exists. I tore it into tiny pieces and threw it in the dustbin. If he were dead, I might feel a bit calmer. I could never tell anyone at school what sort of a father I had.

Forgiveness? Never! Ma, don't forgive him! I'll never forgive him!

I lay on the bed and cried, cried so painfully. I felt as if I'd suddenly been thrown into a cold and cruel world, frightened, miserable, angry. I wanted to destroy everything, even myself.

Ma lay down beside me. Over and over, she said, 'Hanhan,' and I could feel her tears on my face.

I hugged her. 'Ma, I'll never marry anyone. I'll never leave you.' She cried even harder. 'Why didn't you tell me before, Ma?'

'I didn't want to destroy your beautiful illusions. I was afraid you'd find it difficult with your schoolfriends. I was wrong. I was emotionally weak. When I found it difficult to bear I used to take it out on you. That made me feel even worse, but I couldn't help myself. From now on, we'll help each other, we'll manage fine.'

I lay there with her for a long time. I felt that I'd grown up in her eyes at last. The locked drawer no longer existed.

'Do eat something. You must be hungry,' she said to me, sweetly. I ate to please her.

She gathered up the bowls and chopsticks but I insisted on washing up. She smiled at me and her smile made me both happy and miserable. She had suffered so much, and she'd concealed it for my sake. And me? Had I thought of her? I'd always been terrified she'd remarry. Was that right?

I looked at her. She was very pretty. And very young.

'Ma, if He Jingfu is in hospital, who will take his food in to him?' I suddenly thought of him. Didn't he like Ma? I liked him, too.

'Nobody, Hanhan,' said Ma.

'Would it be all right if I took him something?' I asked tentatively.

'Fine! Leave the dishes, I'll do them,' she said, blushing slightly.

I was pleased, but a little sad too. Ma used to like He Jingfu. I almost told her, 'You go!' So as not to let her know that I felt sad, I smiled and said, 'He Jingfu is a really good man. Xi Wang says he's an independent spirit. I would like to be independent, too.'

Ma said, 'That's good.'

'When he comes out of hospital, can we ask him over for a meal? Last time you were quite rude to him.'

Ma was evasive. 'Off you go, we'll talk about it later.'

'Can I ask him today?'

She looked serious and said, 'Don't be silly!'

Partly because I was unsatisfied, and partly out of petulance, I said, 'You don't mind asking your friend Xu Hengzhong for a meal, why can't I ask my friend He Jingfu over?'

Her eyebrows rose. 'Children shouldn't meddle in grown-up affairs.'

She'd turned the key in the lock again. I bit my lip and got ready to go out. Suddenly I remembered the tobacco pouch. 'Will you pass me the tobacco pouch on the table, Ma? It's He Jingfu's heirloom!'

She went over and looked at it for a while. Then she waved me off, saying, 'Out you go! He shouldn't smoke with pneumonia. Give it to him when he's better.'

That was thoughtful of her. Does she like He Jingfu or not?

ELEVEN

LI YINING

Why don't you live like me, my friend?

We middle-school teachers never have any free time except when we're ill. In fact, we don't even have much then. There's still the housework. I've had flu for three days with a temperature of 39°, and the doctor's told me to take a few days off. Today, it's down to 37.5°. My head is stuffed up and I've got no energy, not even for knitting a jumper for my daughter. My husband has done most of the cooking and cleaning; if I asked him to learn to knit, he'd agree quite cheerfully. But how can I ask him to do even more of the housewifely chores? The other workers in his factory already tease him for being hen-pecked. He never has time to relax and he's only in his early thirties!

Sun Yue dropped in earlier. She rarely comes over during the day – she spends most of her time in the faculty office, and the rest at home, preparing lessons. She teaches foreign literature, she's read all the famous writers innumerable times, but has to keep up for her lectures. Recently she's been fascinated by modern Western writing; she says it repays study and there are things we can learn from it, and that it should be introduced to the students. I don't understand her. She's suffered, and she's preoccupied with her problems, full of contradictions and doubts, but she works like a Trojan, much harder than any man. No matter what there is to do, ask her and you know it'll be done.

Sometimes I can't help reproaching her, 'You've been struggling all your life, you've sacrificed yourself for the revolution and you've never had any help from anybody. What are you searching for now? Who acknowledges that you've made the greatest sacrifice for the revolution? Who gives you any credit? You've given away your youth, romance and your family and you haven't got anything in return. Haven't you learnt anything? Have you not got used to being alone?'

She never gets cross, she never denies it, just sighs and says, 'There's nothing I can do about it. Working hard has become a habit. Living means trying to do something for people.'

'Do people need you?' I often ask her, cynically. I know she takes it hard but I still say it. I want to wake her from her dreams. I don't want her to be fooled again. Whenever we talk like this, she falls silent or else responds by quoting a poem: 'Those who know me, ask me why I am worried; those who do not know me, ask me what I seek. Where is man in the remote blue sky?' It makes me unhappy to hear it. I understand her, I do understand her. We are of the same generation, we've been through the same experience.

Why did she come over today? Did she know I was ill?

'I didn't know you were ill. I was feeling miserable and I had to get out. I passed your house and thought I'd just knock and see what happened. I really didn't think you'd be at home,' she explained as she came in.

I told her to make herself some tea and come and sit on the bed and tell me what was making her miserable. Bit by bit it all came out: Zhao Zhenhuan's plea for forgiveness, Xu Hengzhong's supplication, He Jingfu's attitude, and Hanhan's precocity.

When she'd finished she raised her head and looked at me. 'Yining, I meant to keep it to myself but I couldn't. It was stifling me. I would have suffocated if I hadn't been able to tell someone. But who could I tell? Hanhan is too young and nearly all my colleagues and friends are men. What do you think I should do? All I want is a quiet life like everyone else, but I can't seem to find it. I can't believe I'm so awful that I don't deserve peace and quiet. Women who are much much worse than me seem to achieve it!'

That was the problem. She saw things far more clearly than I did, yet she would still ask my advice. She probably wanted to hear me say what she'd already worked out for herself. I could say it, to calm her. What I said next I'd said countless times before, but I said it again today:

'It's because you're not prepared to lower your standards and because you place too much emphasis on spirituality. It's terribly unrealistic. If you could only separate spiritual existence from daily life, you'd be much happier. Come down to earth and join the rest of us!'

'What do you mean? Separate spiritual existence from ordinary life? Wouldn't we become just like animals?' As always, she seemed shocked.

She always wants me to play her alter ego and argue with her: I don't mind the role because I often see her as *my* alter ego. The difference is that the ego that has taken the leading role for me is the one that's still being opposed and suppressed on her side. That's why she still suffers and why I'm basically content. But today I didn't want to have a philosophical argument with her. Although I've studied philosophy and I teach politics, I dislike that sort of argument as much as anyone. Of course I know that without a soul a man would be an animal. I'm terrified that man might descend to the level of animals. I used to look at the monkeys in the zoo when I was small. The adults cradled the babies so tenderly, I found it hard to bear. Why were monkeys so like people? People were supposed to be more precious! Gradually I came to realise that people can't shake off their animal origins. There are laws in the animal kingdom which might usefully be applied to human society. It's hard to know whether people shouldn't be like monkeys or monkeys shouldn't be like people.

Poor Sun Yue! I wanted to cut her open and take out the part that was so confused – otherwise she would torture herself forever. 'Don't let's talk abstractions. I like talking about concrete things. There's no practical point in discussing whether or not you should forgive Zhao Zhenhuan. You can't remarry him, and anyway he doesn't live here so why don't you forget him? It's obvious that he's in a bad way and he's thought of you. So what?

Think no more of him. Now, tell me honestly, where have you got to with Xu Hengzhong? I've heard whispers!'

'I won't see him again. Hanhan doesn't like him.'

'And you? Do you like him?'

'I'm sorry for him, that's all; he's going through a bad time and I can't ignore him.'

'Plenty of people are worse off than him. Do you want me to introduce them to you?'

'What do you mean by that? I've already decided not to see him again. But if he wants to come round, can I just throw him out?'

'If you made your decision clear enough, he wouldn't come round again. But tell me truthfully, weren't you thinking of marrying him?'

'Never!' She leapt to her feet. 'How could I? How could I? I pity him. I've tried quite hard to find something lovable about him – for example, he's good at making a home nice. But it's no use, as soon as I find the slightest good point in him, I immediately feel disgust. He said he pinned his hopes on my kindness but I told him it wouldn't work, it couldn't work, it would never work!'

'Well then, just cut him out. There's nothing between you so don't worry about him. If you're really determined he'll pin his hopes on someone else soon enough. He wants a wife and he'll have to lower his sights. I can easily find someone for him.'

She laughed. 'You sound like a representative from the Marriage Bureau!'

'I don't care what I sound like. It wouldn't be a bad idea to open a bureau. I've done better than some in my "introductions".' I pressed her, 'Tell me what you think of He Jingfu!'

'I used to like him.'

'And now?'

'Now? I don't know. I respect him and I trust him, but I certainly don't want to marry him. I broke up with him years ago. If I chased after him now, what would it look like? People would despise me and I might well despise myself.'

'But is he chasing you? Do you think he might?'

'I don't know. I don't want anybody's sympathy or pity. And I certainly don't want charity. What I've done, I chose to do. Some of the choices were made against my will, sometimes very much so, but in the end I suppose they reflect my ideas about life. I don't want to forget everything that happened, even if it still causes me regret. I treasure memories because of that. I couldn't live with him . . .'

'Fine, then give up He Jingfu!' I said straight away. I knew one thing, that she was in love with him. But I didn't want to encourage it. I didn't think Sun Yue could take many more jolts and if she got together with He Jingfu, she wouldn't be able to avoid them. I don't know him personally but people say that some of his opinions are a bit extreme. Who can tell how China will change in the future? Who can tell whether or not there'll be another anti-rightist struggle? No more political movements, that's what the people want. But it's not easy to achieve.

Sun Yue was still thinking about He Jingfu. 'He ought to have a family. And a settled life. But he can't fall in love with just anybody. He wants . . .'

'Why don't you forget your self-respect and go after him? Bandage his wounds!' I said rather aggressively.

'I know it's difficult to distinguish between self-respect and vanity. Perhaps what I call self-respect is only vanity. But I'd find it hard to forget,' she said to herself.

'Well, go and talk to him!'

'But he's ill in hospital. Should I go and see him?'

I replied with deliberate coolness: 'The Party branch secretary ought to be concerned with the daily life of the masses. It would be better if you did go and see him.'

'No, I shan't go.' She shook her head, as if I'd ordered her to visit him.

I very much wanted to see this He Jingfu – anyone who could have such an effect on Sun Yue must be pretty unusual. But it can be hard to tell: the eyes may be the windows of the soul but they may also betray it. Hadn't Sun Yue respected Zhao Zhenhuan? And me . . . but that was all forgotten now!

'What do you think I should do?' she asked again.

What could I say, apart from wanting her to be happy? Suddenly I thought of telling her about myself. I haven't told anyone about my past for years – I'm satisfied with my present life and I've tried to bury it for the sake of my husband and children. But telling Sun Yue would help because I've been through what she's going through. And if she wants to, she can escape, as I have.

Li Yining's story

Life has taught me two unforgettable lessons.

When I was at university, I fell very much in love with a fellow-student who was seven years older than me. We decided that when we graduated, we'd apply to go to the border regions and marry and live happily ever after. But in the term before graduation, the Party organisation suddenly summoned me to read two letters which accused my boyfriend of abandoning the wife 'who had shared his misfortunes'. One was from the wife, a village woman, the other was from his father, a highly respected veteran of the revolution. For me, it was a bolt from the blue. He'd never mentioned anything about this. I only knew that he was the son of a revolutionary veteran and that because his mother died when he was born, he'd been brought up by a family in the village. After liberation his father returned for him, but he didn't get on with his stepmother so he stayed in the village until coming to university. He'd always seemed a bit worried about our future but he'd never explained why.

I went straight off to find him and have it out but he found me first. After he'd explained, I didn't know what to do. But I didn't blame him.

In the family which brought him up, there was a girl, a couple of years older than him, who'd always taken care of him. Her parents arranged an engagement between them when they were very young, according to local custom. He was fond of the girl, and respected her, but he didn't love her. For him, she'd always been an elder sister and mother-substitute. She was illiterate and he loved reading. When he was about to go off to university, she was afraid he'd break off with her so her father 'regularised' the marriage by obtaining a marriage licence.

'But why did you agree to the marriage?' I asked.

'At the time, I didn't know what love was. I thought it was the right thing to do. I was willing to spend my life with her. I didn't realise that I'd soon fall properly in love. When you've met the real thing, you forget everything else.'

She'd grown to be a distant memory for him, increasingly distant. Wrongly, he'd thought it would all work out because they weren't really married. But he soon realised that he was in a trap. Every time he went back to the village he begged her to let him go so that they could find their own happiness separately. Every time she refused to break with him. She would rather have a *marriage blanc* than agree to a divorce.

'You should have told me. Why did you keep it from me?'

'I didn't intend to. I just didn't have the courage to tell you. I deliberately stayed at university all through the holidays, hoping she might get fed up . . . I didn't think my father would do anything.'

The 'child bride' had got someone to write to his father to tell him that her 'husband' hadn't been back, and the father had immediately contacted the university to find out what was going on. When he learnt that his son had a new girlfriend, he went straight to the village and scolded the 'child bride' for being so weak and accommodating towards her 'husband'. The poor girl didn't realise that her husband had fallen in love with someone else. Apparently she was so distraught that she tried to hang herself but, fortunately, she was saved. That only made matters worse, nobody in the village talked of anything else, and the person who seemed most determined to maintain the proprieties was his father. He did everything he could to coerce his son, including writing to the university authorities.

'What are you going to do?' I asked. 'Will you spend your life with the village girl?'

'What can I do? I don't see what alternative I have . . .'

'But how can you? And what about me? If you are that weak I must have made the wrong choice.'

That was what I wanted to say to him, but I didn't. It was true; what could we do? In the early 1920s, our love might have been praised as 'anti-feudal'. Was it necessary to marry to repay kindness? But we'd been through the anti-feudal period and the

New Democracy movement and were living under socialism. The
Marriage Law gave men and women equal rights in marriage. For
that reason, our love was seen as immoral, an 'outbreak of
capitalist ideology'. What was more, I was from a capitalist family
and had relatives overseas so my position was already suspect.

Of course, if my boyfriend had come from a high cadre family
the affair might have been settled amicably. But he was an
ordinary student and had no one to act for him. His father wasn't
prepared to let his son off, he wanted him to learn a lesson. And
the university respected his father.

We were both criticised, him by the Party committee and me
by the Youth League. Finally we broke up. After graduation, he
was sent back to the village to stay with the wife who 'had shared
his misfortune'. As for me, I resolved to apply for a posting in
the border areas, and I got it. When I set off, my fellow-students
carried me on their shoulders. He stood in the distance, watching.

I worked in Tibet for two years but came back to Shanghai
because I was ill. Soon after, I fell in love with a colleague. Having
learnt something from my previous experience, I made enquiries
as to his political position and his family background. Fortunately,
he had no political background to speak of and was one social
grade above me – he came from a petty bourgeois background.
I told him about my political history and insisted he think about it
carefully. He said there wasn't anything to think about and we
got married.

Our home wasn't bad. He was a music teacher and would sing
at home every evening. I loved music, so it was wonderful. I
thanked the Supreme Emperor for finding me such a happy
home.

We couldn't know that in the second year of our marriage, the
Cultural Revolution would hit us. Politics are like a flood that
dashes against everything. Seeps into everything and sweeps
everything away. Our happy home became the 'Petöfi headquarters'[8] of the school and my husband and I were both 'cow
ghosts and snake spirits'. Because of my class background and
overseas connections, I was more seriously attacked than him –
he'd made the error of marrying a 'divider and demoraliser'. In
less than a year, no doubt under the influence of the 'divider and

demoraliser', the one with 'ways and means', he found his own way out. Then he attacked me, claiming that for the last three years, during the bad harvests, I'd been secretly plotting to betray the nation to the enemy abroad. The fact was that in 1962 one of my relatives abroad had died and left me an inheritance. I never received it, but is there any better evidence than that of a husband? I was sent to the lower depths while he achieved 'liberation' through chastisement.

My heart froze. My country, the people, the Party, my friends, all felt alien. I began to think that there was nothing lovable or inspiring in humanity, nothing between people but a battle to survive. The only difference between men and beasts was that animals didn't have to listen to propaganda or make excuses, and that people could think up devious ways of pushing themselves forward and cheating others. I began to believe what Sun Zi[9] said about human nature being basically evil.

I often considered suicide. One of my girl students saved me in the end. She looked after me very seriously and persuaded me to carry on.

I longed to be 'rehabilitated'. The first things I wanted were a divorce and a transfer from my old school. I got both. I came to the place I teach in now and lived in the school. One day, the student who had helped me so much invited me to her home, where I met her elder brother. He is now my husband. The first time we met he called me 'Aunty Li', which was what his mother had told him to say. I didn't object; he was eight years younger than me.

Meeting that family helped warm my frozen heart. I began to trust people a little and feel for them – but I never thought I'd fall in love again, or that anyone would love me. What brought us together was his mother, a very good-hearted widow, now dead. She tried her hardest to find me a new husband so that I could start a new life; she said she knew how hard it was to be alone. But all her efforts failed – who wanted to marry someone with my political background, a woman already twice married? In the end her eyes turned on her son and she said, 'Marry Teacher Li! She's a good woman!' She encouraged him to take pity on me and to think of me as a wife and mother. Dutifully, he complied. He stopped calling me 'Aunty' and started calling me 'Teacher Li'. Later it changed to 'Elder sister' and, finally, Yining.

He'd only got as far as lower middle school when he went to work in a factory to help support his mother. At the beginning of the Cultural Revolution, he was an apprentice. I didn't know how I could love a young man eight years younger than me, whose educational background and interests were so different to mine. The first time he called me 'Yining' and muttered that his mother wanted us to marry, I was really shocked. I dragged him over to the mirror and forced him to look at the difference between us. He stared into the mirror with terror in his eyes and said, 'Mother says you look younger and I look old, so from our appearance there's not much difference.' I asked him if he thought we would suit each other. 'I've no education,' he replied. 'You'll have to answer the questions and make me understand.'

His innocence touched me and I tried to feel differently about him. I'd been through political struggle and class struggle and I'd had enough; I desperately wanted a rest. Offered a shelter from the storm, I crept into it. I remembered being in middle school, where the literature teacher was always trying to make me read Bing Xin's poems, something like 'The wind and rain has come, the birds hide in their nests. When the storm rises amongst people, I want to hide in my mother's breast.' My mother had died long ago but I wanted to hide, no matter how simple the shelter.

I married Yixin. My life grew calm, because I'd escaped the political furnace. Yixin wasn't bothered by politics. For him, I was his wife, the mother of his daughter, an essential mainstay of his home. He loves his home, his daughter and me. He'd give everything for us and I am happy.

Yixin can't appreciate music but he'll come with me to any concert. Even if he's fighting sleep, what does it matter? He's very tired. He doesn't like reading novels or poetry, but if I tell him stories from books, he listens. He doesn't really take them in, because if I try and discuss them with him he doesn't know what to say. But what does that matter? He cares about the home and he looks at me and I know he's thinking I ought to buy a new jacket.

I said that you ought to separate life and spirituality, but that's not because I reject spirituality. I know that the spiritual life can be lived on different levels. I've just lowered my level. At the same time, I've achieved spiritual satisfaction because I know that in this world there is one person who is always with me, who would sacrifice anything to make me happy. And that this has created a spiritual need for me: I must repay him, I must sacrifice for him.

To make him happy, I'd forget music and literature; I'd forget philosophy and ideology, all the things that Hegel said were so important for the development of the spirit. I've bought cookery books and sewing patterns. I've learnt to cut my husband's and daughter's hair. So as not to make my husband conscious of the fact that I'm older than him, I try and dress a little younger. You could say that I've learnt to dress up my soul.

That is how we live. I'm happy. I suspect that I could have lived differently, but life ought to be like this.

All we lack now is a television. If we only wanted a nine-inch screen, we'd already have enough money. But Yixin says that twelve-inch screens are very popular and our daughter backs him up. We'll struggle on and we'll get one in the end.

After we've bought the television, we'll struggle for a washing machine. Yixin says that my health is not good and that I ought to be liberated from household tasks. 'The task of the working class is to liberate the women at home from their household chores – isn't that wonderful?' he sometimes teases me and my daughter. She always shouts, 'Dad's great! Long live Dad!' And he hugs her.

She's growing up. She needs more and more things. After the washing machine, we ought to get a tape recorder, to help her learn foreign languages.

Life means more and more things. Material needs have gradually invaded my soul. Wants are endless and each desire becomes the object of struggle, so that you can't think of anything else.

Philosophy produces philosophers, politics creates politicians. I'm an expert in life and I research daily life. I feel happy and I feel contented. That's what life does.

That's my story. It's not an exciting life but it's quiet. If you want excitement, you often get storms, too. If people notice you they may want to destroy you; if nobody notices you, you'll probably live a calm life.

It's a choice you have to make.

Sun Yue clasped my hand tightly. Her hand felt cold and moist.

'If I'd been one of your fellow-students, I'd probably have criticised you. And if I'd been one of your colleagues, I'd probably have encouraged your husband to attack you. It's frightening, Yining. All the things that used to be normal are tragedies now, unnoticed tragedies.'

'It's all past, Sun Yue. Don't think about tragedies and comedies. I've forgotten it all. It's the debris of the past, throw it in a corner and forget it! It's like knitting. If you get it wrong, unpick it and make something else. Nobody will ever know what it was meant to be like originally.'

My comparisons made her laugh, but she suddenly checked herself and said, 'In knitting, it's just one stitch, but people's lives are made up of thousands of threads.'

'You don't need to stare at the pattern, just cut it out. Cut it out and it's over.'

'It's not as easy as that, Yining; tell me, don't you have any regrets?' She took my hand again.

My heart missed a beat. Things that I ought to have sought and didn't get, those are things I ought to regret. But she was talking about illusions, impossibilities; if you can't get those, what is there to regret? The boyfriend who broke off with me is quite happy now. He was good at avoiding trouble, good at avoiding danger. Should I regret what I might have had from him and didn't get? Is he the only person on earth to have got away scot-free? There are greater escapists than him in the world, should I spend my life regretting them? And will the world change because of my regrets?

'No, I don't have regrets,' I said.

She looked at me searchingly for a while and, seeing that I was telling the truth, sighed and said, 'Perhaps I ought to be like you . . .'

'Then tell Zhao Zhenhuan, Xu Hengzhong and He Jingfu to drop dead!' She smiled. 'Find yourself another honest man and set up house. That man I told you about isn't bad.' I stroked her hair. She seemed to be miles away. 'Honestly, look at you! You ask me for advice and you don't listen to a word. Sun Yue, be like me, forget your dreams!'

Just then my daughter came home from school. She threw her arms round my neck and said, 'Daddy bought you such lovely fruit on the way to work. He said you must rest and I must take care of you for him . . .'

'Enough, enough!' I was a bit embarrassed and looked at Sun Yue. Her face was pale. 'Didn't you see Aunty Sun?' I said. 'Give her a kiss!' But as my daughter leapt on her she turned her head and two tears dropped from the corner of her eyes. I felt terrible. I didn't know what she was thinking, why she was so unhappy.

'Aunty, what's the matter?' Sun Yue shook her head and hugged the child. Suddenly, like an adult, my daughter said, 'Aunty, let me tell you something. You shouldn't worry too much about other people, you should take good care of yourself. When you're old you must go to the park and do gentle exercises and eat nourishing food, all right?'

Sun Yue laughed, but her tears continued to flow. Then she let the child go and said, very seriously, 'I'm afraid I'll never manage it.'

'Then you'll have to face the storms,' I sighed.

'Let's put our trust in heaven!' And she stood up.

TWELVE

CHEN YULI

Sun Yue, don't forget, talk should be taken seriously.

Xi Liu started to pick a quarrel as soon as he got home. He'd really been provoked by Sun Yue at the Party meeting and he took it out on me. You'd think it was me that had upset him and not Sun Yue.

It wasn't the first time. But I still told him what some of the teachers in the Chinese Department said about her; that she was too casual and she shouldn't be so friendly with Xu Hengzhong and He Jingfu at the same time. Xu Hengzhong was always going over to her place to eat, and since He Jingfu had gone into hospital she was forever sending her daughter there with food for him. The people in the hospital thought Hanhan was his daughter! And yet you're so superior, Sun Yue. Whenever you see me, you look at me slyly as if you're trying to suggest something. Are you any better than me? I can't stand people who pretend to be virtuous. But Xi Liu respects her. He's always thought her more capable than me and he made her departmental Party secretary. She's got responsibility whilst I'm just a worker in the Party office.

I'd thought I'd be letting Xi Liu see her real face and hadn't realised that he'd make it into a question of line struggle. He thought he could disentangle himself by using slogans. When he talked about 'everything', he didn't say whether the 'everything'

he was referring to was just the university, or the whole Party
or the whole country. I don't think he just meant the university.
He said that if people went on talking like that, it would be
disastrous for the country, the Party would be purged and it
would be just like after Stalin died. He was sure the Central
Committee would take it up some day.

'And the intellectuals will get it in the neck. Every time we try
to rectify mistakes or follow the correct line, the intellectuals leap
out from their rightist positions and stir things up. Of course
there are two very different problems. There are a few real
rightists who want to set the country on a different course once
again, but most people are simply muddled by now. Sun Yue is
one of them, she's very confused. We should warn her. Otherwise
she'll make mistakes the next time we rectify rightists.'

I didn't give a damn about the next campaign to rectify rightists,
I didn't think it would ever happen. Xi Liu was at home all day,
he hadn't the faintest idea about what people were thinking. I did
agree we ought to warn Sun Yue. 'Yes, I'm worried about Sun
Yue too,' I said to him. I hoped he'd warn her soon and squash
her.

He called a meeting today, a meeting of all the departmental
Party secretaries. Apart from talking about general things, he
cautioned Sun Yue. He did it carefully and thoughtfully – he didn't
want to make it too hard for her. Honestly! He wasn't very
specific, all he did was criticise the direction of work in the
Chinese Department; he said their politics weren't very good,
they'd been neglecting the elimination of bourgeois ideology, and
the ideology of both teachers and students was a mess. He
gave two examples: first, that He Jingfu's influence was growing
amongst the students and quite a few of them were taking him
as a model. Even our own son Xi Wang had been encouraged by
He Jingfu to leave the family home. Perhaps we'd been too hard
on the man in the past, but could we forget the anti-rightist
struggle? Was he a hero or not? Was his influence amongst the
students positive or not? Had the Chinese Department discussed
it or not? The second point was that Xi Liu had recently criticised
the students for writing love poems on the blackboards, and some
of them had responded with an anonymous letter saying Xi Liu

was a feudal Taoist and a cartoon of him as a priest. What did all this mean?

Finally, he said to Sun Yue, 'Why don't you go and talk to He Jingfu and tell him to be careful of his influence amongst the students?'

He also told her to take the anonymous letter and look at it, see if she could work out who had written it and correct them. Then she should report back to the Party.

He said it kindly. He's always like that in meetings, and people get the impression of a considerate, serious and trustworthy man. That was my first impression of him and I always wanted to hear what he had to say. I was still impressionable then and I told him everything, even my childish loves. I thought of him as immensely pure, without an evil thought in his head; I never dreamt that that day when his wife was out . . . What's the point in thinking about it? The wood has been made into a boat. What's done can't be undone.

I thought Sun Yue agreed with Xi Liu. But she proceeded to oppose every point he'd made:

'I've discussed very seriously the current ideological trends and the political situation. Don't we all accept that practice is the sole criterion for determining the truth? I do. It's been difficult for me to accept and it's meant denying a lot of things I used to believe, but I do accept it. Because it's right.

'As for trends amongst the teachers and students in the Chinese Department, I can't agree with Comrade Xi Liu. Everyone has participated very actively in discussions we've been having on truth and they've come up with some new ideas on cultural theory. Isn't that good? I can't believe you want us all to be dumb.

'I understand exactly what you mean about He Jingfu. He's completely different from most of us, he's made what he can out of his ordeals, he doesn't think he's a hero. He's fond of the students and gets on with them well. If we Party workers could understand young people half as well as He Jingfu, if we cared about them like him, then they'd respond. But some of us don't want to, we only rely on our power to demonstrate our force.

'And the anonymous letter is just a common phenomenon of

mass criticism. The masses' opinions are correct. But Xi Liu wants to make an issue out of it . . .'

I was terrified that she was going to bring up the old business of me and Xi Liu, but all she did was glance at me. After a pause, she went on, 'I'd like the Party Committee to think about it carefully. Do we really want to find out who wrote the letter?'

All Xi Liu could say was, 'All right, we'll discuss it.'

The letter really wasn't worth discussing; it only attacked Xi Liu, it wasn't anti-Party or anti-socialist. Anyway, there'd already been a lot of articles in the papers condemning the suppression of popular opinion. Of course, in order to save Xi Liu's face, the Party members were all very tactful: 'Comrade Xi Liu's warning is necessary. Any criticism must be made openly, we don't want people being afraid of reprisals. We're all against revenge. We must make our attitude clear to the masses but we don't need investigations.'

Oh Xi Liu! Perhaps now you can appreciate what Sun Yue is really like. The people you elevated don't listen to you. I saw him sucking his cheeks and knew he was about to get really angry. Let her see it! Let her realise that she's not Heaven's favourite. She's not inviolate. Let everyone see she's lost your confidence.

'What are you doing? Bring my slippers!'

Xi Liu was shouting. He can only exercise power at home. At the meeting, he'd just sucked his cheeks at Sun Yue, tightened his lips and swallowed his fury. Paper tiger! He's even lost confidence in himself. Things aren't going his way. He thinks he's a politician but who knows what goes on in his head?

I put the slippers in front of him, and waited for him to change his shoes. I was really fed up. If I had the choice again, would I choose him?

I'd have made a good psychologist. I studied it, but because of him I had to give it up. He got me into the Party and made me secretary of the Party committee. Though I never rose very high in the hierarchy, people were careful of me. When they elected Xi Liu, they elected me. People who were afraid of him were afraid of me: it was most gratifying. What the hero feared, the beauty controlled – how could psychologists explain that? I wanted our relationship to be a great secret but of course people got to know about it and talked behind our backs. And there were others, like that old Zhang Yuanyuan woman who even criticised Xi Liu after she'd been sent away, saying that 'some party leaders take young girls as their playthings; this is the rotten ideology of feudal emperors and it is corrupting the Party'. She had no evidence so we let her talk, who listened to her? Those letters! Those poisonous letters! I should have burnt them! But I was afraid he'd take a fancy to someone else . . . It happened and it can't be undone. Xi Wang is right; he doesn't love me, he just found me attractive.

But Xi Wang had gone and there were only the two of us left at home; we might as well lean on each other. He'd got as thin as a stick but surprisingly he wasn't bent or round-shouldered so it wasn't obvious. When I looked at him, I cared. Of course, I'm his wife and we were in love so naturally I care. If I didn't, what would people think of me?

Sun Yue is cleverer than me. I often think that Xi Liu would rather have had her as a lover. But she's thornily protected her chosen position. And people still pursue her now . . .

'Sun Yue is far too full of herself, she thinks she's better than anyone,' I said.

'She's not proud. It's just a question of political vacillation. Get me the *Quotations from Marx, Engels, Lenin and Stalin*.' I got it without another word. 'Read this section,' he said, passing me the opened book.

'"One of the characteristics of the special group of intellectuals in today's capitalist society is that they express individual opinions, and are not disciplined or organised . . . In this they are different from the proletariat, and this is why they are dispirited, their ideology is unstable and frequently harmful to the proletariat . . ."'

I read aloud until he waved his hand for me to stop. With a victorious smile, he said, 'Lenin was absolutely right! And some of today's intellectuals think that Marxism-Leninism is outdated!'

'But Lenin was talking about intellectuals before the Russian Revolution,' I pointed out.

'Marxism-Leninism is universally applicable truth. You ought to remember that, too,' he said, severely.

I wasn't going to argue about it with him. I knew he didn't like intellectuals, not because of Lenin's argument but because he didn't like intellect. He once saw an essay entitled 'Knowledge is Power' in a magazine and roared with laughter: 'Knowledge is power, how very original! This writer doesn't begin to understand the basics. What is it that impels history forward? It's people! It's class struggle! And the Party! If knowledge is power then we have to leave everything in the hands of the intellectuals. And where would that leave the working class? Where would that leave the masses? And the Party?'

I told him it was a quotation from an English philosopher and he responded even more forcefully, 'Well, that makes it perfectly clear. Should we listen to the slogans of capitalists?' I can never work out whether he's full of self-confidence or secretly full of doubt. He certainly views intellect as the enemy. The more power it gets, the less he has; he understands that much.

Why should he and I argue about it? My fate is inextricably linked with his. But I couldn't forget Sun Yue, so I took up the argument and said, 'The position of intellectuals has changed and our policy towards them has to change too. Nonetheless, Sun Yue is far too much of a rightist.'

'She's too much of a sentimentalist. She was very deeply influenced by Western literature when she was a student and she didn't try to transform her world view. It's hardly surprising that she's taking a rightist direction now that conditions have changed again.'

We agreed on something. I leant closer to him.

'But you still promoted her!' I pouted. If only he were ten years younger.

'What do you know about anything? Sun Yue's mass base is better than yours. I can't forget the people who supported me in the past.'

'But aren't I the one who's given you the most support?' I said, flirtatiously.

'You?' He looked at me, almost laughing. 'It's different. You had your reasons, didn't you?'

Was this how he expressed his feelings?

'So you mean Sun Yue didn't have any personal reason for supporting you?' I asked bitterly.

'Unlike you, she doesn't put much stress on personal feelings.'

I flared up inside. He was always bringing in Sun Yue. I'd given him everything and my reputation had sunk. People bully the weak and fear the strong. Sun Yue doesn't put much stress on personal feelings? Huh.

'Then why did she repulse He Jingfu? Why does she chase him now? It's a scandal! Do you want to shield her from scandal? You heard what she said today! She's really thick-skinned. "As for He Jingfu, I understand exactly what you mean." She certainly "understands" He Jingfu, and she "understands" Xu Hengzhong too!'

I stifled a laugh when I saw Xi Liu's cheeks start working.

'I'm really worried about her,' I went on. 'Both Xu Hengzhong and He Jingfu have political problems. If they aren't resolved, she may well make mistakes and create a bad impression in the Party.'

I had succeeded. Xi Liu's cheekbones became less pinched and his mouth opened in a smile. That was the one pleasure in being with him, you could study the reasons for his changes of mood and their manifestations and sometimes you could conduct scientific experiments. It was only at times like these that I remembered what a good student of psychology I used to be.

'Go and talk to Sun Yue again. Talk to her in private, she's very conscious of face and she might accept what you say if there's no one around. If you don't go, shouldn't I?'

I was trying to build on the new mood. To Xi Liu, I was a woman with no definite views of my own, which was true. But all people must have some cunning and they must have some secrets from others – otherwise there'd be no need for psychology. Of course, the Cultural Revolution abolished psychology, but you can't abolish the varieties of human feeling and that was something Xi Liu couldn't understand. All he wanted was for people to praise him and obey him. On that basis he was very satisfied with me, and the corners of his mouth twitched as the smile moved up his face and he looked at me with almost a gleam in his eyes.

'I won't talk to her for a bit,' he said, stroking my shoulder. 'Why don't you go and have a chat with her? There are some things that you women comrades can say more easily. Tell her we don't want to intrude in her private life, but that we can't help being concerned about her political life.'

Could I go? I hadn't talked to Sun Yue on my own for years. We're well water and river water, each flowing on our own course. In Party meetings, she always sits far away from me. Whenever she comes here, she never meets my eye. Had Xi Liu made a psychological error? Had he forgotten what happened? I said nothing, and looked at him doubtfully.

'I know you don't talk to her much. Women's preoccupations are restricted, but the ten years of the Cultural Revolution taught me that it is very important to unite with our comrades. If I didn't have people to protect me, I couldn't survive. You and Sun Yue have both suffered on my account so you must face her as if she was a member of the family, a sister. Don't bother with petty things, try and achieve understanding on the big questions.'

I made my interpretation of his words: a Party leader needs a group of people under him, ostensibly acting as assistants but also serving as bodyguards in a way. The family of such a leader has to act as the mortar, gluing the group together. Now Xi Liu was placing his trust in me which proved, finally, that I was the person closest to him. I decided to go. Let Sun Yue see how tolerant I am.

Sun Yue was just about to go out with her daughter, but she told her to go on alone. Hanhan gave me a very unfriendly look and said deliberately to her mother, 'Uncle He is always talking about you. Xi Liu said you ought to go and see him. And now you won't.'

Sun Yue smiled at her. 'You tell Uncle He that I'd meant to come and see him today. Tell him to relax and get well. I'll definitely get to the hospital tomorrow.'

Very politely, she invited me into the room, and asked me to sit down. Then she waited for me to speak. She didn't look at me directly but stared out of the window so all I could see was her profile. She looked very beautiful. Though she had a lot of grey hairs, she still looked far younger than her age. On her head, grey hairs seem evidence of strength rather than years. I don't think I'm much worse-looking than her but I can't match her poise. She used to act and she's always been concerned about appearances.

I broke the silence. 'I hope the Party meeting didn't upset you today? Xi Liu meant well.'

'It was quite normal for a Party meeting. We never talk about anything else,' she said without emotion and without turning her head.

She really was proud! I was representing Xi Liu, however, so I continued, 'Little Sun, I expect you realise that Comrade Xi Liu is very fond of you.' I won't call him 'Old Xi' in front of you; that way, madam, perhaps you'll realise that I didn't come just to be insulted. 'Comrade Xi Liu did not really make the masses' opinion of you clear at the meeting, do you know why?' I thought I was being friendly enough.

Had that sentence struck her? She turned her head and looked me in the eye. Her eyes weren't large but they were fine and gave an impression of warmth. But were they really warm? Just listen to what she said.

'Comrade Xi Liu's concern is quite unnecessary. I'd very much like to know what people in the Chinese Department think of me. Did he send you to talk about it? Then talk! Don't be shy!'

Xi Liu, it's your concern that's misplaced. Well, you asked me to talk, so I'll talk. I'd like to see just how thick your skin is. 'Comrade Xi Liu certainly didn't send me to talk about that. He doesn't believe what people say. He considers you to be a person of principle in your political and private life, and that you couldn't possibly behave like that.'

'What do they say I've been doing?' she asked. There was a line between her brows as if a dot had been drawn there. She was obviously agitated.

'Doesn't Xu Hengzhong come here often to eat? I'm just asking, I don't want to worry you.'

'I'm not worried. Xu Hengzhong comes here more often than other people,' she answered coldly.

'Didn't I warn you about that? Though his problem has been resolved, there are still repercussions. Of course we understand that there's nothing between you, but other people . . .' I deliberately didn't finish.

She smiled coldly and picked up my sentence: 'Why don't you think there's anything between us? Believe! It's entirely possible.'

'We only think well of you.' I smiled at her. I'd lost all my determination.

'Thank you for your concern. I'll look after myself. If Comrade Xi Liu doesn't want to intrude in my private life then you shouldn't bring up Xu Hengzhong's relations with me!' She was pale but she managed to smile to show that she was calm. 'And as for Xu Hengzhong's mistakes, I know they've already been dealt with; you don't think he's in league with plotters and you haven't restricted his movements and you can't interfere in his private life. You mentioned repercussions: well, I think we've all made mistakes, but if the Party did things right there wouldn't be any repercussions. And if there are, we ought to deal with them.'

That's Sun Yue for you. She always wants to demonstrate that she's purer than others. Look, she's so important and she's only concerned about the Party! This is how we should all be! But she was avoiding the key question, whether her relationship with Xu Hengzhong was improper. Or was I being stupid?

'No, no, no, Sun Yue! I don't want to talk about such big problems. I'm only concerned about your relations with Xu Hengzhong.'

'If I won't talk about it with you, what crime will you accuse me of?'

Her face grew paler and paler, her eyebrows seemed thicker and her eyes blacker. I was half-pleased, half-confused. I thought for a moment and said, 'What has that got to do with it? All I mean is that if you are having a relationship with Xu Hengzhong, then you ought to be a little more careful about He Jingfu. I hear you send your daughter to the hospital every day with food for him. The people there all think she's his daughter.'

Now she blushed; even the whites of her eyes reddened. I thought I'd found her weak spot. It looked as if she really cared about He Jingfu – he was just the type to attract Sun Yue. And hadn't they had an affair before?

She seemed to want to say something but didn't. Resting her face on her hands, she stared out of the window, presenting me with her profile. 'Have you thought about that?' I went on. 'With two people at once . . . And both of them with political problems! What's more, everyone knows about you and He Jingfu when you were students. So what are they going to think now? You gave him up and now you've picked him up again. Sun Yue, we both went through it together, you ought to take what people say seriously.'

She shook, but quickly stilled the movement and continued to stare out of the window. She seemed to be speaking to herself but the words were clear: 'Yes, I ought to take it seriously. Here, everyone thinks they've got the right to interfere in other people's lives because they think that private lives are full of class struggle. Some people use that to create all sorts of gossip, just to thwart others. When will it ever end?'

'So, take care! Old Xi and I are truly worried about you. If there's ever another uprising, who knows what will happen to China? You ought to be more careful.' I really meant it. I don't know why, but I'm frightened of the future – who can tell whether there'll be another Cultural Revolution? If there ever is, I hope there'll be lots of people standing together with me. After all, Sun Yue used to be in the 'protect Xi Liu clique'!

She stood up and shook her hair. 'Let's not talk about it any more, Comrade Chen Yuli. Please tell Comrade Xi Liu that in future matters concerning the Chinese Department will have to be discussed in Party meetings, but that I can't conceal my opinions, nor do I want to cling to my faults. As for my life, I'll deal with it myself. I have to take responsibility for my own actions. And if people think that I've opposed the Party or broken the law, perhaps they could address themselves to the legal authorities; there's no need to shield me.'

At her door I almost bumped into Xi Wang. He just nodded at me, went into the room and said, 'Teacher Sun, I've come to talk to you about He Jingfu.' They stood together, and they looked very close. I felt vaguely – I don't know what I felt.

'You're back?' Xi Liu greeted me with a smile.

I nodded and sighed. 'Sun Yue has changed so much, it's frightening. Government policies, Party regulations, they mean nothing to her. All she can think about are her own feelings. He Jingfu has had too strong an influence on her, and our Xi Wang. I just saw him going off with her to see He Jingfu. Your confidants, your son, they're all being sucked in by that man. They're forming new alliances.'

Xi Liu looked at me in surprise. I told him every detail of my conversation with Sun Yue; naturally I laid stress on some parts and underplayed others. When I'd finished, all he could say was, 'It's incredible! It's incredible!'

THIRTEEN

HE JINGFU

Sun Yue, let's build our lives together, don't let's wait.

I didn't think Sun Yue would come to the hospital to see me. I suspect it was arranged by Xi Wang and Hanhan.

Yesterday, Xi Wang said, 'I'm going to see Teacher Sun to ask her why she won't come to see you.' I asked him not to but he must have gone anyway – otherwise why would Sun Yue have come to see me today? What's more, she came with Xi Wang.

Xi Wang and Hanhan went away, giggling, leaving Sun Yue sitting by my bed. Fortunately, I wasn't wearing the hospital pyjamas and sitting on the bed at the time, or I'd have been fearfully embarrassed! I didn't want her to see me as an invalid, lying down. I didn't want to appear in the least bit pitiful in front of her. What I wanted from her was love, not pity.

But I was afraid that I'd already become an object of pity. Hanhan told me that Xu Hengzhong was always going to their house to eat and that he was very close to Sun Yue. More than once, she asked me, 'Will my mother marry Xu Hengzhong? Do you think they ought to get married?' And more than once I warned Xi Wang, 'Don't talk about adults' affairs to Hanhan, she's already got too much on her mind!' His answer was straightforward: 'We don't want idiots in charge of the nation's affairs, so we ought to teach children not to be childish. Your generation was like a blank sheet of paper; as soon as you met any colour, you were dyed. You all banged your heads till the blood flowed, some became stupid, some became dumb and some died. What's the difference between a blank sheet of paper and an idiot? People like Sun Yue are still hesitating today: she's hesitating between you and Xu Hengzhong. What do you think that says about her?'

I didn't know what to say; perhaps we should teach children differently. Was Sun Yue hesitating between me and Xu Hengzhong? Was she really? It seemed possible, and yet it was unthinkable. Could she really like Xu Hengzhong? Hanhan herself had said they were very close. And that day at Xu Hengzhong's house, he had given me a hint when he showed me the shoes she embroidered for Little Kun.

The cupboard beside my hospital bed was stuffed with things sent by Sun Yue: jars of fruit, fresh fruit, biscuits and milk . . . I used to love receiving them but now I began to fear her gifts. I told Hanhan, 'Don't bring any more or I'll have to settle up with your mother and return the money!'

She took no notice – 'We're just feeding you, what's wrong with that?' Sometimes, she's so edgy she's on the point of tears. I find her sorrow very upsetting.

Sun Yue, you are laying two tracks at once: which one leads to love?

She sat by my bed for five minutes and apart from asking straight away if I was better, didn't say another word. I longed to ask her, but ask her what? How could I ask?

'If I were you, I'd ask her, "Do you love me?" And I'd tell her, "Only I can make you happy, only you can make me happy,"' Xi Wang had advised me. He knew I couldn't talk about love. I laughed at his abruptness – he couldn't understand that questions like 'Do you love me?' have no interest for people of our age and experience. We no longer need, no longer believe in, words and statements; we only believe in what we see and what we feel. Love comes from feeling, not from talking. I feel that there is a distance between us, a distance created by our experience and our characters. I'm trying to shorten the distance but is she? What is there between her and Xu Hengzhong?

Clearly ill at ease, she said nothing and let her eyes wander over the other patients. Did she want to say something but feared they would hear? There were eight other patients in the ward. I could see them all winking at each other; they obviously thought Sun Yue was my girlfriend. I'd already told them I wasn't married and that I hadn't got a girlfriend, but they didn't believe me. They asked me whose child Hanhan was and I said she was the daughter of a friend. They then asked if it was a man friend or a woman friend. To stop them talking, I told them it was a man friend. When Sun Yue came today it was instantly clear to them all that she was Hanhan's mother. In order to stop them saying anything improper, I immediately introduced her, 'This is the Party Branch Secretary of the Chinese Department, Comrade Sun Yue.' She blushed.

'I should have come to see you earlier. Other Party members have been already, it's only me . . . I was very busy.' As she spoke, she looked at the other patients, as if she wanted to warn them not to misinterpret her position.

Miserably, I replied, 'Thank you, Party Branch Secretary, for your concern. I'll be out of hospital soon, so you needn't have bothered.' I was thinking of the old, straightforward Sun Yue, and didn't so much like the new, artificial one I saw in front of me. I knew that there were all sorts of reasons for people behaving in artificial ways, to make things easier, to conceal the truth . . . But I've always disliked artifice, it's unhealthy.

'Did you come on behalf of the Party Branch?' I asked coldly.

She blushed, like a child that's been caught out, like the Sun Yue of long ago. Still she said nothing. I felt torn between wanting to tell her to go home early and wanting to keep her, for when she did look at me her eyes were full of warmth. She examined the medicines beside my bed, more carefully than a nurse, as if she understood what each drug was for.

'You aren't taking anything for fever now? Is your temperature back to normal? Are you nearly better?' she asked, with pleasure on her face. Had she been studying pharmacy because of my illness? I opened the bedside cupboard, took out one of the apples she'd sent, and offered it to her. She took out a knife, cut it in half, and gave me a bit.

It was very quiet in the hospital, and we went out to the garden. After all these years, it was the first time I'd sat on a bench with her; close, yet both staring at the shrubs.

'They've got the same sort of bushes here,' she said, feeling the leaves one by one, her voice low.

My heart began to beat faster and I said, 'They're my favourite.' She glanced at me quickly but immediately turned her head. When she turned back, her expression was serious.

She asked me about falling ill and the treatment I'd received and I told her about it, in the same way that I'd told other people.

'Is it very difficult, living alone? If anything happens, nobody knows. We didn't look after you well enough.'

The official speaks! 'We', 'we'! That's one of the advantages of Chinese – a simple noun can mean all sorts of things. It can mean oneself as part of a group or it can be a humble way of simply referring to oneself. The individual can hide behind it.

'No, I'm used to a solitary life, and have no thought of changing. You needn't worry,' I said rather ungraciously. The 'you' was deliberately ambiguous. It could have been taken as singular or plural.

She was quiet for a long time; then, no doubt to fill the silence, she asked who'd been to see me. I listed them one by one, as if I was reporting to a superior.

'Those who have come most often are Xi Wang and Hanhan,' I said, finally.

'What do you think of Hanhan?'

'She's easier to love than you,' I replied.

She blushed down to her neck and I realised what I'd said; I regretted it and would have liked to explain. But how could I? Should I say she wasn't easy to love, or say that she was lovable, but not as lovable as Hanhan? I gave it up, better not even to try and explain. Let her make what she liked of it.

'I ought to go back,' she said.

'Fine,' I replied, and stood up. Her reason for coming was clear: she was representing the Party and demonstrating its concern for me. If a tiny bit of emotion had been evident, it must have been a leftover from years ago. I wanted her to go. If she could behave calmly with me, I would behave calmly with her.

She still didn't leave, but took a letter from her bag and gave it to me, saying, 'I almost forgot. Wu Chun sent a letter to all of us. Do you remember him? He was sent to Tibet when he graduated.'

I took the letter. A long, pale face with eloquent eyes appeared in my mind.

'You pedantic scholars!' he wrote. 'Have you forgotten the wine-lover? I'll have to keep reminding you, you wine-and-meat friends. [10] The wine-lover loved wine but meat is better.'

I seemed to see that long pale face change into a coarse, common face and those eloquent, dream-filled eyes turn into a huge shouting mouth. I had to laugh, Sun Yue too.

'Wu Chun has really changed!' she said.

'We've all changed; we had to. We've turned from half-finished products into real people. Different lives create different people. Different people lead different lives. There are people on every path and behind each person is a path, whether crooked or straight. People go up and down; sometimes they choose the wrong path. People bump into each other; that's life.'

Sun Yue was obviously pleased by my words. Smiling, she said, 'You sound like a metaphysicist!'

I smiled back, 'Metaphysicist? I think it's the concrete truth. Do you want me to translate?'

She nodded, but as I searched for words she leapt in: 'He Jingfu, I've been wanting to talk to you – really talk. But I haven't got the energy. I don't know how to make myself clear.'

I began to tense. Had she come today to try and clarify things? I waited.

'My thoughts have never been as muddled as they are now. Lots of things I've never dared or been able to think of before are spinning around in my head. I can't get rid of them.'

So that's what we're to talk about. I was both relieved and disappointed. That she was in a muddle was quite clear – why get upset about it? Being muddled isn't necessarily bad. People's thoughts are like society, now ordered, now confused, now very disordered, now carefully controlled. And if society has been stirred up, then people's ideology will also be shaken. It's quite natural. On the one hand, social disorder can provoke a useful and illuminating self-examination; on the other, perhaps only when society is finally at peace can people decide which way they should be going. Was that what Sun Yue was doing?

'Sun Yue, if a person's ideas aren't stirred up at least once in his life, all we can say is that he didn't really live or think, or he was an idiot.'

'Yes, but I'm frighteningly confused.'

'Tell me what's so frightening.'

'I can't explain . . . When the Gang of Four were in power, I felt terrible. I suffered; every day I hoped they'd be toppled from power. When they did fall, I went out on the streets with tens of thousands of people, shouting and singing. I couldn't stop myself crying as I watched the workers banging drums. They banged at my heart and drove winter away. Spring had come, and I revelled in the warmth and had no time for reflection.

'But my elation didn't last. I began to think about what we'd been through and then I felt more miserable than ever. It wasn't the results of those ten years of struggle that made me miserable so much as their origin. What's more, the results and the origin are still present today. I used to weep about it: I felt I'd been wounded and cheated. At night, when everything was quiet and Hanhan was asleep, I used to ask myself, "What do you see? What do you think? Has your confidence been shaken? Are you chasing after illusions?" Oh, it's really frightening!'

She began to cry. Let her cry. If she hadn't devoutly believed, if she hadn't ardently pursued, if she hadn't seriously thought, she wouldn't be able to cry. It's only shallow people who feel nothing but joy at victory. A victory often makes people unhappy. I'd felt it, when I realised how unjustly I'd been treated . . .

I was almost gratified by Sun Yue's suffering.

'I felt as if some hand had removed a prop from my soul, the most important prop, I felt like Jia Baoyu[11] when he lost his magic piece of jade, I couldn't decide anything . . .' She rubbed her eyes as she spoke.

'You're worried, you're upset and you're searching,' I said. 'But either you won't find what you're looking for or you fear it will turn out to be an ordinary, soulless stone, isn't that right?'

She looked at me, startled, and nodded.

'It's very common, Sun Yue.' I longed to take her hand. But I didn't. Instead I reached into my pocket, looking for my tobacco, and remembered what Hanhan had told me – 'Ma has taken custody of your tobacco pouch!' So I clasped my hands in front of my chest. She was watching me, I didn't look at her. Why had she 'taken custody' of it?

'Here!' She handed me the pouch and said gently, 'But you shouldn't smoke!'

How did she know I was thinking about it? The jade mouthpiece was polished clean and the pouch itself had been mended with a patch of blue cloth, and I understood why she'd kept it. She couldn't love Xu Hengzhong. But even now that love was in front of my eyes, I still doubted. Old fellow-students talking, eating together, what was so surprising about that?

I couldn't restrain myself from moving closer to her. She seemed surprised, and coloured slightly.

'Sun Yue!' I said softly, and took her hand. Her eyes were shining. There's so much I want to say to you, Sun Yue. 'Where did you find that bit of blue cloth?'

As soon as I'd spoken, I regretted it. Why did I say that? It wasn't what I wanted to say.

She smiled. Was she smiling at my clumsiness?

'Don't you know that Mao said "Nothing is impossible in this world"?' she answered quietly, freeing her hand from mine.

'Sun Yue,' I said again. Saying her name was like a talisman. She turned her face to me, waiting for me to speak. I packed up the tobacco pouch and gave it to her, 'I'll give up smoking, you keep it.' She took it and looked at me for a long time. Your eyes are so beautiful, so full of feeling and idealism. Oh, Sun Yue, do you remember what I wrote in my diary twenty years ago? 'I've so often thought of your eyes, your eloquent eyes!'

I said it again today, but wordlessly, with my eyes.

She understood. She shivered and shifted a little further from me.

'Have I changed a lot?' she asked, gently.

I nodded.

'Do you think that's normal?' – even more gently.

'Very, Sun Yue,' I answered.

'But I don't think I'm suitable to be a Party member.'

'Why not?' I asked, surprised.

'My belief is wavering,' she murmured.

'You mean you think you used to be a definite Marxist, a hundred-per-cent Bolshevist?' When it comes to sarcasm, I'm exactly like Xi Liu. I'd like to change but I can't.

She didn't answer.

Oh, Sun Yue, I can see you don't really understand. You've muddled blindness and confusion and you also think that doubt and certainty are irreconcilable opposites. Where did you and I get our belief from? In the classroom, from books. With no effort at all we became 'Communist fighters'. Yet Marx and Engels battled for half a century to establish their beliefs. They researched into the culture of all humanity and the development of European capitalism, they critically absorbed the riches of the progressive spirit and participated in the real struggle of the workers of Europe and America. Belief has never been lightly established and lightly established belief can never be firm. Only those who have faced danger or learned to dissemble can wear their belief like a badge.

'But then, perhaps my original belief was just blind,' she said to herself. She'd obviously thought about it.

Suddenly, she began to laugh. 'I was just thinking of the time after Liberation,' she said. She had been at primary school and the teacher used to take the children into the fields to explain the principles of revolution. One teacher used to take them to eat their lunch next to a dung heap in order to instil 'proletarian feelings'. They ate, with the dung and the maggots as topics of conversation.

'I used to believe that if I had "proletarian feelings" the smell of shit would be like incense. I tried very hard to improve myself but I was a very bad person because I couldn't bring myself to look at the maggots. When another child said, "Sun Yue, a maggot is climbing into your rice!" I leapt up and threw the bowl away. They all laughed and I was terribly embarrassed. I determined to overcome my revulsion and sat close to the shit, eating furiously and forcing myself to look at it. All the time I told myself, "I haven't seen anything, I haven't seen anything . . ." and I finally finished my bowl. I was congratulated by the teacher.'

'And what does that explain?' I asked.

'That the teachers who were trying to instil proletarian feelings in us didn't know what proletarian feelings were. If we are blind, it's because we were taught by blind people, we mistook bronze for gold and gold for bronze. Though I haven't met quite such incredible muddles since then, similar things keep happening,' she said.

'And do you still rely on your incantation, "I haven't seen anything"?' I asked, smiling.

She nodded and laughed. 'Yes, always. But it's lost its power because I've seen too much. Maggots aren't very likely to climb into bowls so they don't matter, but life, that does matter, doesn't it?'

'So doubt is very often self-created, but knowledge that has been achieved through doubt is fairly reliable,' I said.

I was very happy because I felt that the gap between us was shrinking. I looked at her beautiful profile and remembered what had happened twenty years ago in a corner of the garden amongst the low shrubs. Sun Yue, there's no one around, I could give you . . .

'There's something I want to tell you . . .' She suddenly turned her face towards me and spoke hesitantly.

'Tell me.'

'Xu Hengzhong has been coming to my house a lot recently; he . . .'

It was like a clap of thunder in my brain; my happiness vanished. No, I didn't want to hear her talk about Xu Hengzhong, not when the distance between us had narrowed. So I cut her off by saying, 'I know all about that. You must take care of Old Xu, help him to find a fiancée.' I knew I sounded harsh, but I hadn't the strength to say it nicely.

'What?' she glanced at me. 'You mean I ought to introduce someone to him?'

'Yes. You aren't what he needs and he can't give you what you need,' I said, looking straight at her.

She lowered her head again. 'Do you know what I need? Even I don't know . . .'

'Give me my tobacco pouch,' I said, holding out my hand. She hesitated and then gave it to me. I filled the pipe and smoked, without looking at her. I wanted to turn her face, to compel her to answer the question, 'When did you learn to pretend? Do you really not know what you want?' But I said nothing, just smoked. Fine, if that's how you are, can I force you? I've never tried to force anyone or anything.

The smoke made her cough. 'You really shouldn't smoke.'

I paid no attention and answered, 'You alone know what you really want. How can I know? I don't believe that a person really doesn't know what he wants. It can only mean that he or she is doubtful or afraid of what he wants, or lacks confidence.'

'You are very hard.'

'Yes, I don't tell people what they want to hear. You are too soft.'

'Yes, but that doesn't please people either.'

What sort of psychological stage had we reached? She lifted her head and stared at me, as if none of our conversation had actually taken place.

I'd hoped for a real clash of souls but her eyes told me: it can't happen today. She'd just covered up the heart that had leapt into sight and she'd buried it deep. And I remembered that she was also my departmental Party secretary. People's hearts aren't made of iron but they can be hardened by external forces. I would have to wait and let things take their course. Force wouldn't help. Anyway, what need had I to force things? I'd waited long enough. Today, she had opened the window to her heart; perhaps tomorrow she'd open the door.

I changed the subject. 'Now that Wu Chun is here, where will everybody meet?'

'At my place, of course. I'm going to buy lots of meat, fat meat. It wouldn't do if he didn't get enough to eat,' she said.

'I'll buy the wine.'

'Will you be allowed out of hospital?' she asked.

'I'll be there. As long as you don't play the typical hostess and say there's nothing to eat!'

She laughed. I stood up and held out my hand: 'It's late, Comrade Party Secretary, you ought to be getting back home.' She shook my hand lightly and started to leave. But she turned back almost immediately and said, 'You shouldn't smoke. Smoking causes pneumonia.' Her eyes were animated.

I gave her the tobacco pouch. 'All right, I'll give up, you take care of this.' She smiled, took the pouch and walked away.

I watched her back and two Sun Yues appeared before my eyes: one warm and spontaneous, the natural young Sun Yue, and the other the silent, mature and slightly artificial Sun Yue. Which did I prefer?

'Is that your girlfriend?' one of the patients asked. They all know I'm single. 'She's not bad, she looks like an official!'

I didn't like her 'looking like an official'. That was the artificial aspect.

'No, she's not my girlfriend, nor is she an official. We were fellow-students,' I replied and walked back to the ward. If the old warm and spontaneous Sun Yue could join with the new silent and mature Sun Yue . . . Could that happen? I thought so. We all start off as spontaneous children, and the events of life in society change us and curb our nature. That's normal, necessary. But the curbs and changes have to work together, to form a person's consciousness, desires and behaviour; otherwise they can force people to feel oppressed, to hide their true nature and even force them into artifice. If artifice becomes dominant in a society, then spontaneity is seen as abnormal – which can give rise to many silent tragedies. I like spontaneous purity and I am sure that Sun Yue can regain her spontaneity and purity. She's already discovered her true self but she's still not used to that self and still doubts it. It'll get better, Sun Yue, it'll get better.

You are a flesh and blood mortal and you used to have a heart that could leap. You've got brains in your skull and you can think; out of the things that you want to dwell on, you can create your ideology, make your judgements. You've got a mouth, you can proclaim your feelings and not just parrot. In the past, you forgot all this, and you've really never thought about it till now. Today, you've stood up, you've discovered that you have this potential, this need. You're afraid, you're doubtful, even ashamed. What's so strange about that?

It'll get better, Sun Yue, it'll get better; but how I long to say to you, 'Let's build our lives together now, don't let's wait!'

FOURTEEN

SUN YUE

Hanhan, I've had a strange dream.

When I got back from the hospital, Hanhan greeted me excitedly and watched my face carefully, no doubt wanting to see what effect the visit had had on me.

The day before yesterday, I read her diary. It happened by accident: I wanted to look at her schoolbooks after she'd gone to sleep, and a small notebook fell out of her satchel. Curiosity made me read it. Most of what she recorded was to do with school, problems she'd had in lessons, squabbles with school friends, what she thought about certain teachers and so on. She'd told me most of it at the time. But some things she'd kept secret and these were the things that interested and moved me. It was a mirror to myself; sometimes it made me laugh, sometimes I nearly wept.

'Everybody has their troubles, the pity is that there is no one to tell them to. Who knows how I suffer? Who pities my solitude?' She wrote that after seeing the film *The Fifth Girl with a Basket*. The predicament of the mother and daughter in the film had aroused her sympathy; I remember that when the girl said to her instructor, 'I'd love to have a father just like you!', Hanhan said she had a headache and left. She must have been thinking of He Jingfu. She wrote, 'I love Uncle He, I love him as a father. Why isn't Ma friends with him? Why does she prefer Xu Hengzhong?'

Had reading her diary finally convinced me to go and see He Jingfu in hospital? I was secretly grateful to her, but under her watchful eyes I felt I must retain my calm. 'It's late. You've finished your homework so go to sleep, Hanhan,' I said quietly. She mumbled something but didn't move, her eyes still on me. She'd grown up but not quite enough. She wanted to share too much of my life. It was a desire that she hadn't expressed in words but she was quite definite about it and I couldn't ignore it, though I didn't want to think about it today. I was full of my impressions after visiting the hospital, his every sentence, every glance, every movement; he'd been so agitated he'd clasped his hands in front of his chest . . .

'I'm tired, Hanhan, go to sleep.'

I undressed and climbed into bed. Hanhan was disappointed. She took her clothes off, muttering as she threw them one by one on to the stool and some fell on the floor. I paid no attention to her, I was wrapped up in my own thoughts.

He Jingfu hadn't despised my ideas at all; I'd worried too much that he might. He's rapidly becoming a philosopher. Now he's forty he's reached the age of doubt. He's right, doubt isn't a bad thing, but when will I pass through the stage of doubting and reach certainty? I just can't decide whether I'd be happy if I got together with him, or not. He's touched me deeply but I still feel that the differences in our natures are very strong. I remember a quotation, 'An old tree touches the sky, straight and tall and you say it is unthinking; it curls and winds in a hundred twists and turns and I suspect that it is impractical. If natures are similar, habits are different.' Where did I see that? Was it in his diary? No, but it's very like the two of us for we've influenced each other a lot . . . He gave me his tobacco pouch to look after. Is it a symbol of love? He didn't say.

I couldn't sleep so I thought I might as well get up. I took the tobacco pouch out of my bag. Hanhan had said it was his only family heirloom, hadn't she? It must have some story. I must ask him to tell me. I don't know enough about him. We've never had a chance to talk alone.

'Ma!' Hanhan suddenly sat up. She gave me a fright. I quickly hid the pouch.

'Did you mend the tobacco pouch?'

Heavens! She wasn't asleep! She must have seen me.

'Go to sleep and don't worry about other people's affairs. You'll never wake up tomorrow!' I said, pretending to be very serious.

'Okay, okay, I won't. Ma, he shouldn't smoke, he'll get cancer.' She smiled at me secretly and settled down again. I locked the tobacco pouch in my drawer and got back into bed.

That night, the horseman in my dream seemed to be him, I think. I could only see his back. And the person who called out to him also seemed familiar. Who was it? Who was it? . . . My eyelids pricked and I felt dizzy, I tried to stop thinking about it. But that figure on horseback appeared before my eyes and strange things took place. It was only when I woke up that I realised I'd been dreaming.

I've never had the slightest belief in fortunetelling but every time I dream, especially strange dreams, I think about them for a long, long time afterwards. I want to understand what they mean and to know what they foretell. I'm like my grandfather; he used to predict the fate of the family according to changes in nature. The dreams I told people about were all fairly complete, not like the fragmentary dreams Freud analysed which had no beginning or end. I worked on my dreams and when I was still half-asleep, I'd remember them bit by bit. I'd make the misty parts clear and where there were abrupt breaks, I'd link them and patch them up.

I thought about last night's dream even longer than usual and it became more complete and more strange. It would make a good story:

My Dream

A strange epidemic has suddenly started in the town where he and I live. The sick seem like madmen, they throw the furniture around and turn their homes upside down, throwing all their possessions to the floor, one by one, some even set fire to their houses. After they've destroyed all their possessions, they begin to tear at their chests, and like surgeons they examine their own viscera. It's really shocking, some of them take their hearts in their hands and weep piteously over them or scold them; some of them cut out their intestines so that the food they eat drops straight to the anus and they say that this avoids lots of twists and turns; some tear out their heart, lungs and liver and throw them away for dogs to eat. They get plastic hearts in exchange. They throng the streets, absolutely delighted, eating whatever they see, although a lot of it is shit, and they all shout, 'Today at last I've eaten my fill!'

The city's specialists in infectious diseases all got together to study this epidemic and discovered it was an infectious mental illness that arose because the weather suddenly turned warm. A lot of frozen nerves were resuscitated and savagely attacked people's minds. Healthy people were concerned and upset; they burnt incense and prayed: 'Heavens, freeze over again! Don't destroy our city!' We had got used to the cold.

Prayers and medicine were both useless; the epidemic spread.

He and I (I don't know who he is, nor what our relationship is; all I know is that we have lived together for some years and that I obey him in everything) have so far managed to avoid the plague. To keep out the contagion, we have shut the doors and windows and cut ourselves off for ten days or so. One day he forced me to pray three times, chanting, 'Freeze earth, congeal sky, so that the diseases die. When ice from the warm earth has fled, then the plaguey germs will spread. Heavens freeze, earth freeze! Amen.' He insisted that I kneel or it wouldn't work. I hated doing it. When I was small, I used to like kneeling in front of grown-ups and kowtowing to receive a little red envelope with money in it, or hear them praise me. But one year at Spring Festival, I had to kowtow so much I got to loathe it. Several generations of the family were seated in the main hall, my paternal great-grandfather, my paternal great-grandmother, grandfather, grandmother, great-uncles, great-aunts, father, mother, uncles, aunts, elder brothers and elder sisters. I was the youngest. Each generation in turn had to bow and offer congratulations. One after the other, they knelt and said, 'Happy New Year to Father, Happy New Year to Mother, Happy New Year to . . .' It had already been going on for half a day, and I was last. I would have to kowtow most often and nobody would kowtow to me.

I remember that hall full of men and women, young and old, all waiting for me to bang my head in front of them. I was already getting nervous. I bent my knees and crouched down:. 'Happy New Year to Great-Grandfather, Happy New Year to Great-Grandmother, Happy New Year to Grandfather . . .' I knelt, I stood up, I bowed with my hands clasped in front of my chest, I knelt, I stood up again, I bowed again. 'Happy New Year to Uncle, Happy New Year to Aunt . . .' My knees were beginning to feel like jelly but there were still many relatives waiting for me to kowtow. Then I thought of a way out: copying the way men greeted each other politely, I put my two fists together and wished the remainder a collective 'Happy New Year to my cousins, brothers and sisters'.

Everybody laughed, but my father was furious: 'It won't do, Little Yue! You must do it properly.' So I had to greet them each and every one separately, my father's sisters, then my elder brothers, then my elder sisters. I had four elder sisters, the youngest only a year older than me. She spent all her time pinching my sweets but today I even had to kowtow to her. When I saw her self-satisfied expression, I only wanted to scratch her face and tell her she was shameless. She began to bawl, and my father scolded me again, 'You're very disobedient, Little Yue, kowtow to your elder sister!' Crying, I knelt down. When I stood up, I was wailing.

I've hated kowtowing ever since. Fortunately the custom was abolished after Liberation. But he was always trying different ways of making me kneel and pray. I had to accept.

I felt I was suffocating; he wouldn't let me take off my clothes because he said I'd catch cold. I opened the windows to create a draught but he shut them again. I pressed my face against the cool glass and looked into the street.

'There are things strewn all over the place. What are they throwing out now? Do let's go and look,' I said.

'No, we mustn't,' he said decisively.

I rolled my eyes, trying to think of a plan. 'Look, look over there, that looks like a leather coat. They used to be impossible to find. It would be a pity to waste it, I'll get it for you.'

'What?' He looked unwillingly. 'Yes, you're right – it's bound to get cold again. Those lunatics! You go and get it. If there's anything else, we'll think about it. Go quickly, and come back immediately – and don't go near anybody.'

'Fine!' I replied cheerfully and went out with two of his huge suitcases.

Outside it was bright and warm and I wanted to throw off my clothes and enjoy it. But he was watching, his face pressed against the window, so I didn't dare disobey. I picked up all the things within reach and in no time at all had filled the two cases. I went back; he locked the door tightly behind me.

We examined all the things I'd brought. Hats of all sorts and sizes, some for us, some for others to wear. Sticks of all kinds, made of different materials, some for climbing mountains, some for beating people. Leather coats, long gowns, overcoats, night-clothes, cloaks, the sorts of clothes that people here wore when the weather was cold. Wooden fish [drums used in Buddhist temples], books, steamed maize bread, malt extract, pairs of narrow leather shoes, coloured glass mirrors . . .

I felt in the pocket of an overcoat and found something hard, like a walnut. I took it out to look at it and it made me jump! It was a human heart! I shouted, 'A heart! You, look, a heart!' I always called him 'you'.

He was startled, too, and took it from my hand. He examined it carefully and smiled. 'Coward! Can't you see it's dead? It's already withered and discoloured.'

I hadn't been upset because the heart was dead, I just wanted to know whose heart it was and what my finding it meant. I looked at the overcoat and suddenly I threw it away as if I'd had an electric shock. I recognised it. It was He Jingfu's – he'd been wearing it when he came to our house to look for me.

'It's He Jingfu's overcoat and He Jingfu's heart!' I said to him, terribly upset.

He picked up the overcoat and looked at it closely; then his expression changed and he nodded, 'It's He Jingfu's all right.' He knew how I felt about He Jingfu.

I can still remember, that year, that month, that evening when

He Jingfu came to our house, to see me. But he wouldn't let him, he said He Jingfu was a monster who wanted to eat me. He pushed me into the back room and hid me while he told He Jingfu that I wasn't at home and that I wouldn't want to see him. I looked through a crack and saw He Jingfu's eyes fill with sorrow and disappointment and he shouted at the wall that divided us, 'Sun Yue, do you really not want to see me? Will you at least accept a present from me?' I wanted to reply but I heard two thumps on the wall, a secret sign telling me to keep quiet, and I didn't dare say a word. He brandished a walking stick at He Jingfu and said, 'Why don't you clear off? If I hit you with this, it'll send you down to the eighteenth hell!' He drove He Jingfu away and I did nothing to stop him. Remembering all that, I asked, 'You, what was it that He Jingfu wanted to give me that time?'

He hesitated before replying. 'It was this heart. But it was alive then. At the door, he pressed it into my hand but I managed to stuff it into his overcoat pocket. I don't know where he is now, nor why his overcoat has been thrown out.'

'He Jingfu must be dead! His heart has died, too, and it's all my fault!' I cupped the heart in my hands and wept as I spoke. My tears fell onto it and I felt it move slightly in my hands, and my own heart shook as if I'd had an electric shock. I looked at the heart. Strange, it had been blackened and withered a minute ago, now it was glistening. My heart was beating wildly, as if it wanted to burst from my mouth. I pressed the heart close to mine.

He looked at me. I held out my hand to him; the colour drained from his face until he was yellow. He shouted, 'Sun Yue, quickly, throw it out of the window! That heart may well carry the plague! It will harm us, it hates us!'

I didn't want to listen but I cupped the heart in my hands again. Suddenly, it sparkled as if it was a transmitter and the message it wanted to transmit was only to be heard by me: 'No, I don't hate you. I don't hate anyone. Sun Yue, swallow me! I belong to you.'

I put the heart in my mouth. He saw me and threw himself on me like a madman, trying to snatch it away. He was too late. I swallowed it.

'Sun Yue has caught the plague!' he shouted, holding me away from him.

My strength suddenly grew and I struggled free. I went towards my room to fetch a small knife I used for cutting fruit. It was stainless steel. I began to cut my chest open.

'Sun Yue has caught the plague!' he shouted again. I could see that he was ill, his nerves were in turmoil. I examined my heart. What was the fuss about?

There was a bit missing from my heart and it was covered with dust. I washed it under the tap and dried it. 'What can I do about the missing part?' I wondered. 'Put it back, it'll grow again,' said He Jingfu's heart. I put it back into my chest and it left no mark.

I looked at him in triumph. 'There! I'm fine now. Come, let me wash your heart!' I pointed the knife at him.

He looked at me with horror. 'What? Do you want everyone to know that I haven't got a heart? Have you no sense of comradeship?'

I was shocked. 'What happened to your heart?'

'That day when He Jingfu's heart was dripping blood, I felt terrible. I was sick that evening and I threw up half my heart,' he muttered.

'But you've still got the other half,' I said, pitying him. 'There was another half, but when I had diarrhoea I shat it out.' His voice was so low, I could hardly hear.

'Why was that?' I asked.

'I'd eaten too much,' he replied. His expression was anxious. In all these years, it was the first time he'd ever looked worried. I felt even more sorry for him.

'But don't you feel strangely empty?'

'No. I've filled the space with other things. If you don't believe me, feel it.'

I felt, and it was solid, hard. All these years I'd been with a man with no heart! How had I managed to live with him?

'We must split up! I can't live with a man with no heart! Or shall I spit out He Jingfu's heart for you?'

'You're mad! How can you get at his heart?'

As he said that, it was as if he was possessed by demons. He looked at me, wide-eyed, and his mouth grew enormous till his lips touched his nose. I felt as if something strange was happening to my body. I went to the mirror; my face had changed! My white hairs had gone, so had the wrinkles around my eyes, spring had returned to my body. Strangest of all was that my heart gleamed, as if I was wearing a flashing badge. Was it because I'd swallowed He Jingfu's heart?

I stood there, dumbstruck.

'Sun Yue has got the plague!' he shouted as if he'd woken from a dream. Quickly I covered my hair. I was afraid that if people saw it, they'd think I'd dyed it.

'Sun Yue has got the plague!' Who was shouting? It sounded like a woman. I ran to get a face-mask and put it on; I was afraid that if people saw my face, they'd think I was wearing make-up.

'Sun Yue has got the plague!' 'She's got the plague!' Lots of voices were shouting together, and I could hear footsteps. I was frightened and covered my shining heart with my hands.

People thronged at the window, looking at me as I used to look at the village idiot when I was a child, mocking and pitying, frightened and watchful.

He was telling them how I caught the disease, but I couldn't hear what he said. Suddenly he pointed at me and said with hate, 'It's all because she swallowed that heart. We must dig it out!'

They began to pour in through the window and door: 'Tear it out! Tear that heart out! We can make a badge of it! I want a badge!'

A stainless steel fruit knife stabbed at me. Was it my knife? I dodged. I leapt upwards through the ceiling and stood on the roof. They followed. Some of them wanted to lift the roof off.

I said to myself, 'Fly!' kicked at the roof and flew. I could fly. I'd learnt it from fairy stories. But today I was flying too low, my feet kept banging against buildings. I was flying in circles and I was flying too slowly.

I was tired. It was harder and harder to stay in the air, and my feet brushed the earth. Dispirited, I said to myself, 'That's it. I'll have to let them tear the heart out.' Suddenly, however, I understood that it was a dream and that people can do what they want to do in dreams. So I said to myself, 'Fly high! Fly past everything, up to the ninth heaven!' It didn't work, my feet kicked at the ground but I couldn't take off.

I was resigned to being caught when I heard a voice say, 'Sun Yue has arrived!'

I was overjoyed, my feet kicked the air and I flew. The front of my chest shone more brightly than ever. I thought to myself that I'd become a tiny star, travelling round the earth. One day I might be like the stars He Jingfu saw above the Great Wall, I might fall to earth, who knows where. The universe is vast and boundless, the earth forever tranquil . . .

When I woke up, I thought very seriously about two things. First, who was 'he'? Was it Xu Hengzhong? Zhao Zhenhuan? Xi Liu? Wu Chun? . . . I enumerated all the people I knew and none of them fitted. However hard I tried, I couldn't work out how old he was, what he did or what he looked like. Very odd! Secondly, I wondered what the dream meant. Did it mean that I would be happy with He Jingfu, or not? It appeared to say that I would, but according to my grandfather's method of dream interpretation, dreams were the exact opposite of reality. So if you dreamed of a birth it meant a death, and if you dreamed of a death it foretold a birth. And as the dream suggested we unite, in reality we'd break up.

I began to sweat, though I hadn't sweated in the dream.

'Ma, I just had a dream.' Hanhan lay close to me and she sounded happy. 'Uncle He left the hospital and he came here!'

The same sort of dream. I closed my eyes and pretended to sleep. I didn't want to talk to Hanhan. She loves analysing my dreams. But some dreams can't be interpreted.

PART THREE

It happens every day. A heart meets a heart; there may be fireworks, or just an echo.

FIFTEEN

THE WRITER

They don't all take the same path; they reach the same goal by
different routes.

Introduction: On the X day of X month in X year, the graduates
of the classes of fifty-nine and sixty from Shanghai University's
Chinese Department, He Jingfu, Sun Yue, Xu Hengzhong, Wu
Chun, Li Jie, Su Xiuzhen and I, the 'writer', all met in Sun Yue's
flat. It was quite an historic meeting, worthy of record. Each
person was a type and each one's experience could have furnished
material for a novel. But there must be millions of people like
them in China. If everyone were to write a novel, an extra ten
thousand publishing houses would not be enough to cope. And
how long would it take to read them? What a task it would set
future historians! Literature strives for the broad outline, history
values conciseness. They asked me to write a summary of their
meeting. They wanted me to follow certain principles scrupu-
lously: to use my novelist's descriptive skill; they wanted it to be
original, they wanted it to be sharp; of course I could express my
own views and praise or criticise, but I had to be truthful and
honest and not hide behind the traditional historical style.

They call me 'the writer' but I'm a hen without chicks, for
though I'm over forty I've only published one novel. Fortunately,
it made my name and I was admitted to the Writer's Association.
Whether or not you are a novelist, whether or not you actually

write, once you're a member of the Association, you've arrived, you've made it.

I don't feel very confident about my writing but I couldn't refuse them. There are limits to my skill and I won't be able to avoid mistakes. I take responsibility myself. Let this serve as an introduction.

The Writers' Account

It began at nine in the morning. We all gathered at Sun Yue's flat. Some of the women arrived first to help prepare the food, and by ten-thirty everyone was sitting at the table.

Sun Yue's flat is by no means large, 14.2 square metres. It contains a double bed, a table for writing, a table for eating, a chest of drawers and a bookcase. For the two of them it's not cramped, but it was far too small for all of us. There weren't enough stools so some had to sit on the bed, packed close. The two tables were pushed together. Somebody suggested we move the chest of drawers outside to create more space but Sun Yue didn't want to. There was a green narrow-necked vase on the chest with a few fresh flowers which she'd put out specially for the party. If we moved the chest, where would the flowers go? And if the flowers went, the party would lose some of its special atmosphere.

Xu Hengzhong agreed. 'We can't do without flowers! This party was difficult to organise; though we almost all work in the same city, we're all of us busy with our own affairs so we meet very rarely. This time we're lucky to have Wu Chun, Su Xiuzhen and Li Jie as "guests from afar".'

Wu Chun had been in He Jingfu's year and had lived in the same dormitory. As soon as he came in today, he kicked off his shoes and threw them under the bed. Immediately the food arrived, he picked up a pair of chopsticks and popped a bit of fat meat into his mouth, so that it was full before the rest of us started eating. After a moment, he put down his chopsticks and said, 'I've been really lonely in the countryside and I was longing for relief from boredom. I never thought you'd all be so welcoming, I'm very touched. Yesterday I talked all night with He Jingfu and I said I wanted to give everyone a present, so I've written a rather terrible poem . . .'

Xu Hengzhong shouted cheerfully, 'Great, Wu Chun! You used to be known as a "boudoir poet".'

Everyone laughed, even Li Jie, and Sun Yue said, 'You're making exhibitions of yourselves. Thank goodness Hanhan is having lunch at school. When the mother cat is away, the kittens all get out of the basket. Today the kitten is away and the mother cats are really creating havoc.'

He Jingfu pushed at Wu Chun's shoulder and said, 'Take no notice of the big cats and small cats, get out your poem.'

Wu Chun nodded and pulled a crumpled piece of paper out of his pocket, opening it slowly. He gave it to Sun Yue and said, 'Show us your performing talents again.' Sun Yue read it through and refused: 'It's too silly! What sort of crazy poem is this? I can't read it.'

Some of the others struggled for a look, but Wu Chun grabbed it back, shouting, 'You aren't prepared to struggle for glory, nor will you tolerate hardships; I'll read it myself!' He was from Zhejiang province and his pronounced southern accent made 'I' sound so funny that everyone burst into laughter again. He waited till we'd stopped, stood up and assumed a very proper stance, just like the teacher we all knew who'd taught us Yuan drama. With a grimace, he closed his eyes, puffed out his chest and began: 'I've heard . . .'

We all tried to stifle our laughter as he intoned. We listened and laughed but by the time he got to the end, no one was laughing. When he read about hoarfrost and worrying about the next generation, his throat was dry and he coughed several times. Two of the softer-hearted women had tears in their eyes. By the end, everyone was sunk in their own painful thoughts. We looked at each other without speaking. Wu Chun drank a glass of wine and his eyes began to sparkle again.

Xu Hengzhong was baffled. 'Wu Chun!' – Wu Chun turned his head – 'Wu Chun, what was your poem about?'

Wu Chun opened his eyes wide and said, 'It's rather like our lives, there's no limit to the meaning. Who would have thought, twenty years ago, how different our lives would be? Can any of us explain the meaning of his life? If you take me, I willingly volunteered to go to Tibet. I was willing to give up my life for my

Tibetan brothers but I didn't imagine I'd end up as a soldier. I ride a horse and I carry a gun, I face danger and I've been doing it for ten years. The bullets must have eyes, for none of them have got me yet. I love the place but my health isn't up to it and I've had to go back to a life of semi-retirement in the village.'

One person said, 'I'd heard you hadn't done too badly.'

'Not badly!' Wu Chun slapped his leg and then reassumed his casual air: 'Do you want to hear about my great romance?'

It really was extremely romantic. When Wu Chun came back sick from Tibet, he was still a bachelor and his poverty-stricken mother had already died. His unit in Tibet feared that his new life would be very difficult when he returned and sent a special letter of introduction: 'Today Comrade Wu Chun is returning to his village because of illness, please try very hard to find him light work and try equally hard to resolve the marriage problem . . .'

Quite straightforwardly, Wu Chun handed the letter to the Party headquarters in the commune when he got back. It all went according to their request, he was assigned office work in the commune where he could do as much as he wanted or stay at home and rest if he wanted. What's more, within a week the women staff members of the commune had helped him set up a family home.

'In a week!' Some friends were quite shocked. Sun Yue didn't believe him and asked He Jingfu, 'Is it true?' He Jingfu smiled and nodded. She wanted to ask more, but noticing how he was looking at her she turned away and said nothing. I found their relationship interesting.

'That's just like you, Wu Chun! And is your wife pretty? Was it love at first sight?' Su Xiuzhen asked.

Wu Chun laughed. 'Little Su, I'm no longer an intellectual. I know nothing about love. All my life, except for my mother, I've never loved anyone and no one has loved me. I wanted someone to look after me. Though I'm not well, I saved quite a lot of money in Tibet, and my wages aren't low. She knew what she was coming to. Her family is in economic difficulties, she's got lots of brothers and sisters, so what's wrong with marrying a bit of money? As for feelings, her looks are all right and she seems to be able to stand the sight of me and that's enough. It may not have been love at first sight but it's certainly going to last.'

The company listened, nobody laughed.

'Do you get on?' Sun Yue asked, mustering her courage.

'What's getting on? She's a nurse in the commune hospital, she works all day and comes home at night. She busies herself about the house and I drink. She doesn't like me to drink and says it'll kill me. I'm not afraid, if the bullets couldn't harm me, why should I fear wine? I tell her, "Lay out the wood for the coffin in front of the bed, you can hold the funeral tomorrow but tonight I want to drink, don't bother about me!" and she doesn't. We're not like you intellectuals, sitting together amongst the flowers, looking at the moon and discussing love. But I'm content. And I think if I can leave a son and a daughter behind in this world, I won't have lived in vain.'

Sun Yue sighed and asked, 'How are you now? If you're not well, you ought to ask to go back to intellectual work.'

Wu Chun clapped his hands and laughed, 'Back to intellectual work? I've forgotten everything I ever learnt at university so it's quite appropriate for me to stay in the countryside. I can't think of taking a real job. I know I'm no use to the nation and I'm not very happy. I'm bored, so I came to see you . . .' He wiped his face and fell silent.

I said, 'He's right. It's all very well for us to talk about going back to intellectual work. It would be hard for him, everybody's circumstances are different.'

I'd never really had to consider what learning was worth. When I graduated, I was assigned to the Cultural Office as a secretary. I prepared notices, corrected essays and wrote up meetings . . . I was so busy I hadn't time to think. That's no exaggeration, I was busier than the head of the office. I did sometimes think that if he and I were to rationalise our work, I'd be better off and he'd have a nasty surprise. But it was a fantasy; he'd joined the revolution in 1938 and I wasn't born till 1940. I wrote a short story called 'Who is the head of the office?' but the only person who read it was me, I didn't dare publish it. I was afraid I'd be accused of attacking the leadership and if I was unlucky, of being branded 'excessively ambitious' – though I knew I was quite without ambition. My working principle was that since we had to

work together, I would submit to his orders. But when there are
so many talented people in the world, why is it that all we need
is 'capital' or family connections, not wisdom or ability?

Su Xiuzhen suddenly pointed her chopsticks at me and interrupted my thoughts. 'Little Writer, you're quite right. We say that
intellectuals ought to go back to intellectual work but we can't
stir things up too much, there's still the task of revolution!'

She's wonderful with her high-sounding words. She certainly
doesn't want to go back to intellectual work as she was never
interested in it in the first place.

She came from quite a good background but she wasn't keen
on studying. She was the worst in the class and spent all her
energy on dressing well. When we graduated, they wanted to
send her to an army unit but she cried and howled and refused
to go and said she'd never tolerate 'iron discipline'. She requested
permission to go back to her old family home in Shandong, saying
that she had a fiancé there. Her sudden acquisition of a fiancé
surprised everyone – she'd apparently met the county Propaganda
Head when she was at home for the spring festival and it had
been 'love at first sight'. Her request was approved and she went
home and married immediately. She was found a 'special job' in
the Propaganda Department and soon joined the Communist
Party. She told us all about these happy events.

I remembered her coming to see me in 1971. She looked as if
she was prospering, she was elegantly dressed and getting stout.
I told her that Sun Yue had divorced and was having a bad time.
I told her she ought to try and help her.

'But I can't do anything with her! I went to see her as soon as
I got here. That woman! How did she get to be so poor and
proud? And she's anti-social.'

I couldn't work out what she meant by anti-social, so I asked
her.

'For heavens' sake, can't you see? We've all got to accept
society as it comes. Little Zhang, I'll tell you something; the lower
orders are already totally corrupted, totally! And if we don't keep
up with them, we'll get the worst of it. I don't care, whatever
they do, I'll do. You've been to my house; it's comfortable isn't
it? But Sun Yue would rather die than give up her principles! In

all good faith I introduced her to two friends in Shanghai but she takes no notice.'

'Well, you're very social,' I teased her.

To say something like that to her face was unusually acid for me. But, as usual, she misunderstood and answered cheerfully, 'I've learnt to be! My husband is hopeless; if he'd been any good, he'd have managed his promotion years ago. And he doesn't make any use of me. These days who doesn't use his wife quite openly to make a few connections?'

What an extraordinary woman, I thought when she left. Had she really got a higher degree?

'You're the girl in my poem who's gone into commerce!' Wu Chun said, half-joking, half-serious.

'Right! And you've moved from internal to external commerce. It's much more interesting!' I added. She was now a true merchant. Her odour of scholarship had completely disappeared.

Her chopsticks pointed at me again. 'Don't be mean, you inky pen! Do you think I don't know about you? There's nothing so marvellous in being a secretary!'

I wanted to reply but I couldn't think what to say. I watched her angrily waving chopsticks.

Sun Yue saw we were both quite cross and said, soothingly, 'What's the matter? We've all had a hard time.'

Then I thought of what I ought to have said: 'It's better to be an inky pen than a straw. A straw is always yellow, it can't turn black.' But before I could open my mouth, Su Xiuzhen said, 'That's right, we're all old classmates, I've come a long way to see you all . . .'

My ideas sharpened and I responded quickly, 'You came to pull teeth! Didn't you want to see if all the women were wearing dresses? And if dances are held every week?'

Some people began to laugh. Su Xiuzhen pointed her chopsticks at me a third time. I was getting ready to stab her back but He Jingfu used his chopsticks to prevent me. He smiled at Su Xiuzhen and said, 'All right, Little Su! As for the different courses our lives have taken, all we can do is understand each other, not influence each other. We certainly mustn't fight. We've heard your opinion, now let's see what the others have to say.'

Wu Chun applauded him: 'There's another country person like me here. Little Li, you've combined being a graduate with being a peasant. What do you have to say?'

Little Li was Li Jie. After we graduated, she asked to go back to her village as a teacher, and when that happened her boyfriend broke up with her. In 1964, we read about her in the local newspaper: she'd been named a 'model teacher' and praised by the peasants. Since then, there'd been little news of her. It was only by chance that she was in Shanghai to attend a meeting for middle school literature teachers, and we'd just learnt from her that she'd married an illiterate peasant. Naturally that hadn't been published in the papers because at the time she was a 'Black Guard'.[12]

She'd never talked much. When we were students, no one paid any attention to her. People only discovered her, with surprise, when she asked to be sent to the countryside. She got up on the stage, took the microphone and said three or four times, 'I want to go to the countryside and be a teacher!' Her boyfriend had graduated from another institute in Shanghai. He wrote a letter to the leadership of our department asking that Li Jie be kept in Shanghai. She was called to see them and she said the same thing, 'I want to go to the countryside, to be a teacher. We've talked it over. He'll change his mind, I won't change mine.'

Today she was pretty and dressed simply and neatly, and as soon as you saw her you thought she was made to be a teacher. When she noticed that we were all looking at her, she became a little uncomfortable and pushed her hair behind her ears, not knowing what to say. Taking advantage of this, Su Xiuzhen couldn't resist interjecting, 'Little Li also got things wrong.'

Sun Yue tugged at her sleeve and she stopped. Nevertheless Su Xiuzhen's words paved the way for Li Jie. Gently and candidly she looked at us all and said, 'I didn't get it wrong. I'm from a peasant family. I studied in order to serve the peasants. I know how difficult it is for peasant children to study and I wanted to do something for them. I'd always meant to take that course and I never wavered. I'm content with myself.'

'You don't have to marry a peasant to serve the peasants! What common language is there between you and your husband?' It was Su Xiuzhen again. She was really irritating; she knew perfectly well why Li Jie had made her choice. In 1964, when she was well-known, she'd been hotly pursued by a young local army official. They fell in love, but just as they were about to marry the Cultural Revolution began and Li Jie was called a 'snake ghost and cow spirit'. Because he was afraid that her reputation would damage his career, the fiancé broke off with her. After that, Li Jie decided she would marry an illiterate peasant, not an official. Su Xiuzhen seemed to have failed to understand.

Sun Yue looked angrily at Su Xiuzhen and the others showed their disapproval in their own way. Li Jie remained calm and said, smiling, 'I chose him myself. He'd always wanted to serve under my army officer, but after what happened he changed his mind. When my officer returned to the village for his wedding, he asked my husband to join the party. He refused. Instead, he came and sat silently in my school for half a day. I thought that was kind.'

Su Xiuzhen didn't dare say anything, but she pursed her lips and shook her head, looking tragic. Li Jie noticed and, looking at her, added, 'Of course there are some things missing in our marriage. I sometimes find it hard.'

Interested, Su Xiuzhen opened her eyes wide.

'Our intellectual life is dull. My children can't watch television or go to the theatre. When my son was five, I took him to town to see a film for the first time. I'd already explained to him what a film was but the first time he saw a close-up he was so frightened he asked to go home. I kept telling him to look, but he cried and said he wanted to go to the lavatory. I had to take him home halfway through so as not to annoy the rest of the audience.'

Su Xiuzhen laughed and said, 'Country children are all like that!'

Li Jie's eyes flared. 'You think it's funny? When we were going home that day, I really wanted to cry. I held his hand very tight; I felt sorry for him. I wanted to say to him, "Child, you are ignorant but that should be no surprise to you, nor to me. I came to the countryside to help you throw off your ignorance and I don't regret it. Truly I don't regret it."'

She stopped and lowered her head like a shy girl. Sun Yue looked at her, her eyes full of tears.

'If someone knows what they're doing, even if life is hard, the spirit is strong and that's a form of happiness,' someone said.

'The price is too high,' Xu Hengzhong sighed.

'If you know that what you are trying to achieve is right, what does the price matter?' Sun Yue said quietly.

He Jingfu looked at the speakers one by one and said, with a slight smile, 'It's very interesting. When we talked about ideals as students, we were confident and passionate, eyebrows dancing and faces gleaming; but look at us now! Gloomy and doubting. Have ideals depreciated or have we?'

'Everything has depreciated,' Xu Hengzhong replied immediately.

Sun Yue looked at Xu Hengzhong unwillingly and said, 'I don't see it like that. Real ideals can't lose their value. Otherwise they'd be illusory. We can't lose our value either, not unless we remove our bones.'

He Jingfu smiled at her. He didn't say whether he agreed or disagreed. Sun Yue reddened.

Xu Hengzhong looked at Sun Yue and laughed. 'Little Sun, you've forgotten that there's always something illusory about ideals, they are inevitably empty dreams. And as for our own value, we don't determine that ourselves.'

Sun Yue shook her head firmly. 'I don't agree.' But she didn't seem to have an argument to present to Xu Hengzhong. She glanced quickly at He Jingfu, apparently imploring him to help her.

He Jingfu immediately put down the wine glass that he'd raised to his lips and carried on: 'Old Xu has a point. If we compare ideals with reality, they go beyond perfection and therefore necessarily contain an element of illusion. But ideals aren't therefore illusions. There's a scientific basis for ideals, they can be realised, and that means they can give people real strength. I've always believed in communism.'

'And how do you look at communism now?' Xu Hengzhong asked with a sneer.

'It exists. Despite what happened to me in the fifties, if you look at it from the point of view of the whole country, there are quite a few things that happened in the fifties and sixties that ought to be remembered. For us as cadres, and for everyone, there were new growths of idealism, that can't be denied.'

Gaining confidence from He Jingfu, Sun Yue said, 'We all grew up in that atmosphere.'

'And now?' Xu Hengzhong seemed displeased with He Jingfu and Sun Yue; his sneer had moved up from his mouth to his eyebrows.

I didn't altogether like Xu Hengzhong's attitude and went to the rescue of He Jingfu and Sun Yue. 'Now we've discovered some problems and we're going to deal with them. You can't say that we're any further away from our ideals.'

Smiling, Sun Yue stabbed at me with a chopstick and said, 'You get the prize!'

Seeing that Xu Hengzhong was discouraged, He Jingfu poured him a glass of wine. 'Come on Old Xu, drink up! Ideals aren't illusions. Today I've seen idealism in Li Jie's quest and in your present dissatisfaction. What ideals really are is a constant search to improve reality, to elevate it. If we abandon that, then what is generally accepted as idealism becomes an illusion. We must destroy fantasies.'

Xu Hengzhong laughed and raised his glass to He Jingfu.

Xu Hengzhong was a mixture of the elegant scholar and the pedant; some people admired him, others couldn't stand him. Those who admired him said he was good, those that didn't said he was bad. Both sides expressed their own views and often the examples they used were the same.

Wu Chun didn't seem to like this sort of argument and kept on eating and drinking. The others had put down their bowls and chopsticks but he still held a glass of wine. Remembering that he was the guest of honour, I said to the rest, 'We should drink a last toast to Wu Chun, no more talk!'

To my surprise, Wu Chun put down his glass and said, 'No, keep talking. Old He, I'd like to put something to you: do you think we can determine our own worth or not? I think that it is up to us to decide whether to be human or devil.'

'You're talking about our moral worth,' He Jingfu commented.

'What sort of worth are you talking about? If a person doesn't take moral worth into account, what sort of person is he? These last few years I haven't really done much, but as far as being a human being is concerned, I don't think I've lost or lowered my value.'

'One has to demonstrate one's worth, it has to be acknowledged by others,' Xu Hengzhong contradicted him.

'Yes!' shouted Wu Chun. We all thought he was going to get furious so we raised our glasses and said 'Drink, drink!' but he waved us away, smiling. 'Don't worry, I'm not raving drunk. I just thought of something . . .

'One year, there was a drought. The wheat never came up; we were all desperately worried. On the day after New Year, there was a terrific snowfall. I was at my father-in-law's. Because of the drought, the village cadres made a radio announcement: Get down to the fields quickly and put the snow from the banks and ditches on to the wheatfields! Everyone rushed out, and my father-in-law opened his door. There were people in the fields already, but not one of them had gone to the communal wheatfield. They were all piling snow on to their own private plots. The 'overfulfilling of the norms'[13] policy had made things very hard for the peasants, and the only grain that belonged to them and that they could actually eat came from their private plots. It wasn't the tail-end of capitalism amongst the peasants, it was the stomach of peasant humanism. My father-in-law said, 'You are a commune cadre and a Party member, let's go to the big field.' But I said, 'No. Let's go to the private plot.' Later I was criticised by the commune leadership but the peasants all congratulated my father-in-law for choosing a good son-in-law. Now you tell me, was I demonstrating my worth, letting others see it?'

'What's the point of letting mere peasants see your real worth? Didn't you get criticised by the commune leadership?' answered Xu Hengzhong.

Wu Chun was going to say something but He Jingfu overtook him: 'Your views of worth are different. Wu Chun is talking about the value of an individual human being but Xu Hengzhong is talking about market value. We certainly can't determine the latter, but then we shouldn't be searching for market values.'

Wu Chun slapped his fat thighs, shouted 'Right!' and drained his glass.

Xu Hengzhong saw He Jingfu, Wu Chun and Sun Yue lined up in battle against him and knew he couldn't resist, so he hastened to retreat. He clasped his hands and said, 'Brothers, I admit defeat. I proclaim that from being an idealist, I've become a realist and the rot has entered deeply into my bones. I fear it's incurable.'

Sun Yue had a parting shot: 'There must be a difference between a realist and a super-Confucianist.'

Xu Hengzhong clasped his hands again. 'Then perhaps I'm a super-Confucianist.'

Wu Chun laughed and clapped Xu Hengzhong on the shoulder. 'Hero of the Anti-Rightist Movement, how come you're so humble?'

Xu Hengzhong blushed and explained himself: 'On page 263 of the *Quotations from Chairman Mao* it says that circumstances are always changing. Isn't every humble person a transformed hero?'

He Jingfu probably didn't want to make Xu Hengzhong uncomfortable by talking about the Anti-Rightist Movement so he rescued him from his predicament by saying, 'Old Xu has had things hard these last few years. We've all gone our different ways but there have been some painful lessons to learn. In that we're all the same.'

Su Xiuzhen hadn't been able to last out the battle. She'd begun by glaring at people as they spoke, but after a while her eyes had closed. She was sleeping with her head on the table and woke suddenly to pick up what He Jingfu had just said: 'Very true. It's awful that Old Xu has been bringing up a child on his own. We must find him a new wife. Do you want me to help?'

I'd offended her just now so I only teased her gently. 'Sister Su wants to help out? We've got three single men and women here!'

He Jingfu and Sun Yue looked uncomfortable.

Su Xiuzhen was suddenly full of energy; she clapped her hands and cried, 'Leave it all to me. I may not be a local but I know more people than you do!'

Wu Chun shook his head. 'This isn't commerce. Don't take too much on. Worry about Old Xu, don't waste your energy on Sun Yue and He Jingfu.'

Su Xiuzhen seemed very surprised and confused. She looked from He Jingfu to Sun Yue and back again, and then said, 'You mean you two haven't "put down your whips"?'

It was a crude joke and it fractured the mood. Sun Yue paled and He Jingfu said nothing. Li Jie stood up. 'We've finished the meal a long time ago, we must clear up.' Everyone began to busy themselves, but Li Jie stopped us again: 'The men can sweep up and drink some tea, we women will do the washing up.' With that, the women went off to the kitchen.

When we'd swept the floor, we sat down and started talking. Wu Chun said to He Jingfu, 'I'm anxiously awaiting the announcement!' and I added, 'The past is behind us now; I think Sun Yue still cares for you very much.'

He Jingfu smiled but didn't say anything. Xu Hengzhong looked at his watch, stood up and announced, 'It's late. The boy is on his own at home and I'm a bit anxious so I'll go. If anyone wants to come over to my house for a while, they're very welcome.' But when he got to the door, he rushed back in and said excitedly, 'It looks as if Zhao Zhenhuan has come too!' We all ran to look.

He was right – Zhao Zhenhuan had come!

SIXTEEN

ZHAO ZHENHUAN

I've come to be tried, to help me find myself.

It shook me to see so many old faces. I think of you often. Whenever I think of Sun Yue, I think of you by extension. Especially you, He Jingfu. In 1962 I wrote you a letter on behalf of myself and Sun Yue: 'We are married and very happy. We hope that you will soon be able to change your job and that you will be happy.'

I've thought about it a lot recently. It was a callous, proud and unpleasant letter. At the time you were my rival in love and a 'class enemy'; I was particularly concerned about the former. I was very happy about my victory, and anxious, because I knew in my heart of hearts that you were more powerful than me. At the time, Sun Yue was still young and she didn't understand much; she was receptive to your influence but wouldn't marry you. I used emotional arguments to draw her to me and to break her relationship with you. I didn't know then that I would eventually break the red cord myself and sink deep into the stinking mud . . . And now are you getting together with Sun Yue?

I looked at you all one by one, and you looked at me. I longed to stretch out my arms and hug you all but your eyes stopped me. Is it my sudden appearance that startles you? Is it my white hair? Or do you despise me? Why are your eyes cold, suspicious, hostile? Why is there not one friendly face?

He Jingfu wouldn't let me in. Was he the head of the household?

None of them would let me in so I let them lead me away from Sun Yue's, muttering, 'I just came to see Sun Yue and the child, nothing else . . .', but no one took any notice.

Finally they stopped. I couldn't see Sun Yue's house. He Jingfu held out his hand and said, 'Do you still remember me?' I shook it, doubtfully.

'I didn't know you'd come back to the university,' I said. I wanted to ask him if he was married or not but I didn't dare, I was afraid of his reply. Xu Hengzhong also held out his hand; he was thinner than before, but he still had style. I shook hands with them all, except for Wu Chun who stood aside, looking at me with enmity. 'Wu Chun!' I said.

He stepped aside. 'I won't shake hands with you,' he replied. 'I've got something to say to you. I don't want you to upset Sun Yue, you've hurt her enough. Old He, I'm going to go back and tell Sun Yue we've gone. You take him to your place.'

So He Jingfu doesn't live there? Has he got a home somewhere else? Wu Chun went off and He Jingfu took my arm warmly: 'Come on, we won't eat you!'

I followed them, feeling very miserable. How many times had we wandered through these grounds hand in hand? I was surprised how fresh the memory was. Ever since I'd left Sun Yue, I'd wondered how my old fellow-students would treat me if we met. I was afraid of it and yet I wanted it. I'd done everything I could to get news of them, yet I'd avoided meeting them. Bumping into them today . . . I'd brought it on myself. It was painful, the scenery was the same, the people were different. But there was some comfort: in the midst of their reproaches, I felt the wall between us being gradually demolished.

'Have you just arrived?' Xu Hengzhong asked in a friendly way. I nodded. I'd just got off the train. I thought Sun Yue probably wouldn't have moved house. That warm and fragrant room used to be my home. The three of us lived there.

'Have you come on business or is it just a visit?' He Jingfu asked, looking at me.

I nodded, then shook my head. I couldn't answer. I'd never be able to explain. I'd come on business and on a visit. But you could also say I'd come here for a special reason.

I broke up with Feng Lanxiang over a month ago. I was the first to break the three-point treaty; to be honest, I couldn't stand it any longer.

It had quite a lot to do with Wang Panzi. The editor wanted me to write a piece criticising a play. I thought the play was good so I refused. He got angry and said, 'Then I'll find someone else to do it. But I think you ought to strengthen your sense of organisation. You work here, can't I ask you to do something for the paper?' What did he mean? Hadn't I done everything I was supposed to do? We didn't have to behave like slaves to the newspaper, did we? And give up all our independence? Whenever he wanted to slander someone, he referred to a 'sense of organisation'.

I faced him and said, 'It's not my job. I'm a reporter, not a theatre critic.'

He smiled coldly. 'It's a fine distinction. Up till now you've always been very obliging.'

Let him report to the government, I don't care. I said, 'In a world where ghosts have power, I can't demand my rights as a human being, but in a world of people I want to be a person.' I left him a bit of 'face', because I didn't point out that he'd been very 'obliging' too, over the last few years. He'd been prepared to sell his soul but nobody had wanted to buy it. He should wash the dust from his own soul, first.

The editor didn't force me to do it but he gave me a new 'hat': democratic individualist. I thought about it but I couldn't see why I should wear it. Let him call me any sort of '-ist', I wasn't going to write any more pieces I didn't want to write. I'd had enough.

How many times had I done it? Writing today's piece to criticise yesterday's, and tomorrow's to criticise today's. People who knew me used to ask, 'How many voices have you got? You change your position so quickly.' 'I've only got one,' I would say lightly, 'but my range is extensive. I've been practising voice production so I can pitch it anywhere.'

It depressed me. Some day the reckoning would come. Confess my selfish motives, examine my objectives, dig out the roots of my ideology, promise to correct my mistakes . . . it was always the same in every political movement. But every time, I knew I couldn't change, I'd never change; even before the investigator's ink was dry I'd have committed another crime. I'd buried the reporter's sense of responsibility and feelings, and with them my self-confidence and self-esteem. I'd become a soulless instrument, I'd completely lost myself.

Enough was enough. Pieces I didn't want to write, I wouldn't write. Is a 'hat' always heavier than a good heart?

Three days later, the newspaper published an article criticising the play. It was signed by Wang Panzi. Two days previously he had told me that he'd been given the assignment and that he'd refused it. He was shameless, I never wanted to see him again.

A good play has a long run. Three days after his article appeared, the editor sent out a memorandum: 'Wang Panzi's position is very good, he's been making concrete efforts to overcome his mistakes. In accordance with Party policy I want him back in the newsroom and back in his position as head of the newsroom.' He was my boss once again.

Feng Lanxiang was at me all day. 'People have to take good assignments if they're offered. Why aren't you more like Wang Panzi?'

'I don't like being the boss. Of course, if we discuss pay in future the boss will get more than the other reporters, but I don't regret the money, I wouldn't touch it.'

I told her again and again but it went in one ear and out the other. But what she should never have done was to buy wine and food and invite Wang Panzi to the house to beg him to ask the editor to make me deputy head of the newsroom.

That day, I had a terrific argument with Feng Lanxiang in front of Wang Panzi, and was also very rude to him. I moved into the dormitory at the newspaper.

All sorts of opinions about me immediately sprang up at the paper; I was stuck up, I was an individualist, I was envious of Wang Panzi, I wanted to get rid of my wife because she was only a worker. I took no notice but buried myself in work and, when I was free, I did research. Perhaps I'd leave the newspaper and go back to the university to teach. I could teach journalism.

Wang Panzi was certainly thick-skinned. He maintained the

dignity of a boss. Whenever he saw me, he'd clap me on the shoulders and say, 'Old Zhao, don't bother about what people say. I've never had anything personal against you, I admire your spirit. You intellectuals are a bit different. Petty officials like myself don't have your freedom!' I could have spat in his face but there was a notice up in the office, 'Please don't spit'.

Then yesterday he came to see me in the dormitory. He smiled and said, 'I've got a nice assignment for you. I want you to go to Hangzhou. It's a beautiful spot and you can relax for a bit. It's not far from Shanghai, so you can take the opportunity to visit your old university. I'll pay for the trip!'

A nice assignment? It was clear to me that the editor wanted me out of the way. Still, it gave me a chance to go to Shanghai and that was exciting. I said, 'I'll think about it.'

'What's there to think about? Zhao Zhenhuan, you're our winged steed, you've got to go!'

What was the assignment? No doubt some fruitless investigation. I'd been a reporter long enough to guess. I avoided his hand before it fell on my shoulder, and said, 'Winged steed or not, a horse is always a horse. It exists for men to ride.'

'Very original! That's a new slant on the relationship between the "ten thousand mile horse" and the horse trainer; the horse trainer knows horses, cares for them, loves them, lives for his carthorses. But if you've got a horse that can run ten thousand miles in a day but won't accept a rider, nobody wants it. It's an interesting subject for an essay – why don't you write it? I'll send it to the editor.' His spit flew like stars.

I thought about 'Please don't spit' again but I kept my patience. 'Mr Wang, you misunderstand me. I'd rather be a lame man with a heart than a brainless horse that can gallop fast.'

He looked blank, and then smiled and slapped me on the shoulder. 'Fine, fine, that's an individual opinion. I like people with their own opinions. Well, are you going to Hangzhou or not?'

'I'll go,' I replied and yesterday evening I set off. I didn't go directly to Hangzhou; I got off the train at Shanghai. I told no one that that was how I was going to do it and I didn't tell Wang Panzi so he could pay less for the train fare.

* * *

Seeing that I wouldn't give him a direct answer, He Jingfu didn't
ask me any more.

We all arrived at the teachers' dormitory. He Jingfu must still
be single; I didn't need to ask, I knew as soon as I saw the sort
of room he had. My heart began to beat fast, anxiously. I don't
know what ghosts I feared.

'Do sit down.' He pulled out a stool for me. I'd just settled
down when Wu Chun arrived. Immediately, the atmosphere in
the room became more tense, because of the way he looked at
me, his eyes sharp and slightly wild. My heart closed up. What
did he want? He Jingfu pulled at his sleeve and said, 'Come on, if
you want to talk, sit down. Don't just glare.' I relaxed and smiled
slightly, remembering Wu Chun as he used to be; we were
fellow-students, friends, and we often used to talk openly to each
other.

'You still have the face to smile? How did it all happen? Your
solemn pledges of love were just so much piss? Face us and tell
us!'

His loud voice made me jump. I looked at him with my mouth
open and couldn't say anything.

Xu Hengzhong pushed a stool over to Wu Chun and forced him
to sit down, saying, 'It all happened a long time ago. What's
the point of bringing it up now? Let's talk about other things
first.'

'It all happened a long time ago.' True, it was a long time ago.
'Why bring it up now?' No, I do want to bring it up. I came
because I wanted to bring it up. I can't think of anything else, I
can't talk about anything else. 'Damn you, Wu Chun,' I said, 'I've
got no good explanation. It's because nobody swore at me before
that I've become what I am today. I really want you to judge me.
Curse me, Wu Chun! You're right to want to hit me; I can't return
the blows.'

Wu Chun slapped his knee and released his breath heavily and
said nothing.

I wanted to talk, I had a stomach full of words, and I pulled my
stool over to him. 'Do you remember, Wu Chun, when we were
getting our work assignments after graduation? There were a
few of us together and you pulled my ear and said, "If you don't

remember to send me parcels of sweets, I'll beat you up!"'

Wu Chun muttered something and I went on, 'You often said you envied me my happy love affair. You said, "When will the star of love shine over my head? Will I find my love in the Himalayas?" We were always talking about love. You talked of your hopes and I talked of my infatuation.'

He looked at me briefly, said 'Hm,' and breathed out heavily again.

'Did you get the sweets I sent?' I asked.

'Yes, I got them!' he burst out. Suddenly his voice lowered: 'I received your packages of sweets when I was in the border regions and I felt as happy as if it had been my wedding. Perhaps you don't realise that I derived my sense of purpose in life and work from your happiness and that of thousands and thousands of others. I often used to think that though I'd thrown away my academic career and left my home, I was protecting my country, my friends and relatives. I didn't want to see the country at war again, I didn't want to see more widows and orphans. I was the only child of a widow and my mother endured a lot to bring me up. But I learned that apart from disease and war there are plenty of other ways of creating widows and orphans, and the most common is the despicable act of abandoning your wife and children.

'Sun Yue could have chosen someone better than you. But you left her, you bastard! You bastard! Whenever I see her, I think of my mother, and when I see Hanhan, I think of myself as a child. I could weep!'

And Wu Chun did cry, loudly. He Jingfu leapt to his feet and handed him a towel. I would have liked to hug Wu Chun and cry with him, just as we used to laugh together in the old days, but I couldn't cry. I just felt hurt inside. His words were like a great hammer, breaking up the frozen river of my heart; the ice floes began to move and their sharp edges hurt. Yet with the pain came a first, slight sense of relief, for clean water was flowing beneath the ice.

Wu Chun had upset everyone. For a long time, no one spoke. One by one they left until there were only four of us: myself, He Jingfu, Wu Chun and Xu Hengzhong.

Xu Hengzhong turned to me. 'How are things now?'

I answered simply. 'I have received the punishment I deserved.'

The three of them all exclaimed at once, for different reasons, I think.

'If you're perfectly happy now, you probably don't think often of Sun Yue and the child,' said Wu Chun, staring at me again.

It was a reasonable supposition, but the problem was that I couldn't be happy because of what had happened. I can't remember a time when I haven't thought of Sun Yue and the child with great clarity, and that is the reason for my unhappiness. If I were happy with my life, it would mean that my original self was completely dead and gone, and that the problem of Sun Yue and the child no longer existed. How on earth could I explain this tortuous reasoning? They understood my silence.

'What are you going to do? Are you going to get divorced again? Or has something else changed?' Xu Hengzhong asked, looking anxious.

I've certainly thought of divorce; though I don't hate her, I couldn't stay another day with Feng Lanxiang. But I can't decide because of little Huanhuan. Over the last month, I've gone to collect her from kindergarten every Saturday, kept her for the night in the dormitory at the newspaper office and sent her back to the kindergarten on Sunday morning. Each time, I've asked her, 'Who do you like best, Mummy or Daddy?' She's always replied, 'I like Daddy and I like Mummy,' which is understandable. Feng Lanxiang might not be a good wife but she is a good mother to Huanhuan. Like almost all mothers, she devotes herself entirely to her daughter. Whatever she eats has to be nourishing, whatever she wears has to be pretty. She's always looking for dancing classes for her and such things. She was certainly more absorbed in Huanhuan than me. Huanhuan was the only link between us.

Yesterday before I left, I made a special visit to Huanhuan and took her out to the Tianjin Restaurant to eat dumplings. She loves dumplings but yesterday she didn't seem very happy and ate hardly any. I asked her what the matter was and she said, 'When will you come home, Daddy? I want you to come home!' I told her I was busy at the newspaper. She said, 'Mummy told me you're deceitful. She said you didn't want Mummy any more. Is that true?'

I felt awful; I seemed to see another Huanhuan, my first. Now, that Huanhuan is called Hanhan [Regret]. Was I about to create another 'Regret'? But how could I go on? Piteously, she said, 'Daddy, don't leave Mummy. I want Daddy and I want Mummy.' I agreed I wouldn't and she pressed her face against mine, happily. I can still feel the closeness.

'Anyway, we've got a daughter and I'm very fond of her,' I said, finally.

'Then why have you come to see Sun Yue?' Wu Chun asked harshly. 'To beg her forgiveness? Do you want to get together again?'

'Get together again? No. I just wanted to let her know how things are now and to ask her to let me see the child,' I replied after thinking carefully. Of course, it wasn't that simple. I wanted to find myself again. I thought that I would only be able to glimpse my past 'self' through Sun Yue. If a broken mirror could be mended[14] how I would treasure the mirror! Unfortunately, it can't be done, can it?

'Is Sun Yue still single?' I asked timidly, looking at He Jingfu. His eyebrows shot up, but before he could say anything Wu Chun said, 'She's single now but she won't be for long.'

'What? Who is her new boyfriend?' I didn't know quite what I felt.

'Why do you need to ask? Anyway, he's far better than you. So do you still think you ought to upset Sun Yue?' Wu Chun said.

I fell silent. Ought? What ought I to do? Perhaps my coming here, my wanting to come here was all unnecessary? And yet I did have a family here, though I could have no control over it. Perhaps I didn't need to let Sun Yue know how I felt about her now. But I had to see her and tell her everything. Knowing that she was going to marry again soon only made my need more urgent. I never, never, never wanted to lose her . . .

Wu Chun stood up, came over to me and locked his arm around my neck. 'Old Zhao, I can quite understand how you feel but we have to think of others. Why don't you come and stay with me for a few days? There are mountains and streams, fish and shrimps, and there's my friendship as an old fellow-student. Why don't you come with me this evening?'

Xu Hengzhong said, 'That's a wonderful idea, Old Zhao! Why don't you go and enjoy yourself. Let's leave the past alone.'

I nodded with difficulty. 'I'll go.' But I didn't want to go to Wu Chun's village, I'd rather have gone to Hangzhou. Let's bury all the past deep underground. From today, I'll never see another of my fellow-students, nor will I think of them.

'No!' It was He Jingfu, who hadn't spoken for a while. Suddenly he stood up and said to Wu Chun, 'You've already got your ticket, there's no need to change your plans. I'll look after Old Zhao.' Then he turned to me. 'Meeting at this moment after all these years, we ought to have a good talk!'

Wu Chun and Xu Hengzhong said no more. I stayed. I didn't know why He Jingfu wanted me to stay, but I wanted to stay too.

SEVENTEEN

HE JINGFU

I can't keep calm.

Now there were only the two of us, Zhao Zhenhuan and me, left in the room. I thought I ought first to offer him something to eat but he said he didn't want anything; neither did I. I got out some soda biscuits and made two cups of tea.

'Have something to eat,' I said, putting the biscuit tin in front of him.

He shook his head. 'Have you any cigarettes?'

I pointed to the notice on the door behind him: 'The inhabitant has given up smoking, so please don't bring tobacco here'. I wrote it when I got back from the hospital. I told Hanhan I'd decided to give up smoking and she whispered happily in my ear, 'I've discovered a secret! Ma is very fond of your tobacco pouch. She often gets it out and looks at it. She thinks I'm asleep but I'm only pretending.' Hanhan was there when I pinned up my notice and she said she'd tell her mother . . .

'I've given up several times too, but when I'm upset, I always want to smoke.' Zhao Zhenhuan looked at the notice and smiled rather bitterly.

'Give it up again. You don't look terribly well,' I encouraged him.

'Yes, I ought to. You seem to have made up your mind. You haven't got any at all?'

'No. Anyway, I smoked a pipe,' I said.

'Pipe tobacco would do. Let me smoke a pipe.'

'But my tobacco pouch . . .' I hadn't meant to say that.

'Have you burnt it? That wasn't necessary,' he said, sympathetically.

'I didn't burn it; someone else is looking after it.' I don't know why but I didn't want to tell him the reason, though I thought I should give him some explanation.

'A girlfriend?'

I hesitated. What could I say?

'Is it?'

'It's a small friend. Hanhan.' That seemed the best sort of answer.

'Hanhan?' The corners of his mouth quivered as if he didn't know whether to laugh or cry; it broke his regular features. He'd aged so much, I couldn't believe he was the same Zhao Zhenhuan who'd arrived in the tricycle cart with the beautiful Sun Yue.

'Hanhan, your and Sun Yue's daughter. She sometimes comes over. She's a charming child,' I said, trying to be calm.

His eyes lit up briefly. 'Does she look like Sun Yue now?'

'She's very like Sun Yue but there's a bit of you in her.'

'Really? Has she ever talked about me? She must have a very bad impression.'

'She never wants to talk about her father with other people.' My reply was almost rude but the subject was upsetting. The unusual friendship that had grown up between me and Hanhan made me more uncomfortable. I'd already privately begun to consider myself her father and here was her real father, her proper father. And to be sitting here with him, discussing such things: it was hard to take. Yet I'd asked him to stay – wasn't it because I wanted to talk about them?

I'd been flustered from the moment I saw Zhao Zhenhuan. Just as the distance between me and Sun Yue was narrowing, just as our hearts were getting closer, he arrived. My first thought was: 'Don't let her see him!' That was why I'd led him away from her door. Yet now I'd asked him to stay.

He was carefully examining me and my room. I thought I'd

warm the atmosphere a little, and said, 'You look at me as if you didn't recognise me!'

'You're both familiar and strange,' he replied, unconsciously smoothing his white hair. He'd aged awfully.

'That's very dialectical. I feel the same about you,' I smiled.

'You're still single?' His eyes rested momentarily on my bed.

'I'm afraid I seem to have become president of a bachelors' club.'

'You ought to get married.'

'There are a lot of things I ought to do, but I can't do them all, for a variety of reasons.' I couldn't explain everything to him. I saw his arrival as one of the reasons.

He seemed to understand and changed the subject: 'Where can we get a couple of cigarettes? Would anyone in the dormitory have any?'

He had that same expression around the mouth, as if he might suddenly smile or cry. Then I realised that it had become almost habitual with him, and felt sorry. 'I'll go and find some,' I said.

I went to the shop and bought him a packet of cigarettes. He took one greedily: 'Have one yourself! The odd one can't do any harm.'

'No, I won't.' I was determined.

'I haven't got your willpower. That's why I'm on the slippery slope,' he said, blowing a thick cloud of smoke at me.

'Willpower comes with practice; one isn't born with it,' I replied.

'Even with practice, I'd never acquire your iron determination.'

'You haven't been through the same things as me.'

'That's it. I've been wondering about my life: was it easy? I don't know. People say I've been lucky but I think I've been very unlucky.' He smoked cigarette after cigarette.

What had his life been like? For years he'd taken no part in any political movement and seemed to have no impetus to activism. He'd always seemed like an onlooker; he'd rolled along like a smooth pebble in the flow of mud, never thinking of finding a place to lodge himself. In 1957, during the Anti-Rightist Movement, he'd had plenty of opportunity to attack me and thereby demonstrate his political stance or vent his personal anger, but he hadn't. He'd never said anything in the meetings criticising me, or put up a poster to blacken my name. He'd become a riddle to me, though he left quite a good impression. Yet he felt he'd been unlucky. I felt it too, but who had caused his misfortune?

'My father was a poverty-stricken intellectual who spent his life teaching in the village school. When I was small he taught me that cultured people shouldn't take political sides; politics were dirty and to be feared. I took his advice to heart. But there is no Peach Blossom Land and even my father couldn't avoid political attacks. In the Cultural Revolution he was accused of being a feudal remnant. He was dragged through the streets, terrorised and humiliated, and he died soon afterwards. I was deeper into the political maelstrom and I felt even more strongly than my father the terrors and dirt of politics, but where could I hide? At home? I no longer really had a home. So I numbed myself and sought comfort in dissipation. I feel I've mortgaged my soul to the devil.'

I was shocked by his words. They reminded me of Goethe's poem, in which Faust mortgages his soul to the devil in order to achieve the greatest happiness. I hadn't thought that people these days made such pacts in order to escape political storms. Faust had managed to redeem his soul, but what about Zhao Zhenhuan?

'Devils may be running out of bottles to store souls in. Perhaps you can buy yours back. I have the feeling you've already started.'

'Is that how you see me?' he asked, agitatedly stubbing out his cigarette.

'Yes. There can't be any other interpretation,' I replied firmly.

He walked up and down saying over and over again, 'People need other people to understand them, they so much want other people to understand them. Just now I was on my guard against you, trying to work you out. I thought you might reproach me and mock me and then throw me out. You've got the right to do it. You know, I've thought hundreds and thousands of times that you understood Sun Yue better than me. I never really understood her.'

I've thought the same thing thousands of times. Of the two of us, I understood Sun Yue better than you, and because of that I loved her more than you did. That's why I keep pursuing her. But now, as always, you've turned up. Do I want to send you away? No, I can't: I can't forget that we were students together, I can't send you away, disappointed. Have you worked that out? I hope so. I was using all my strength to overcome my desire for a cigarette.

'All I loved was Sun Yue's beauty, intelligence and warmth. I was pleased that she belonged to me, proud. But as for the most precious thing about her, her spirit of sacrifice for the highest ideals, her passionate search for a better future, I didn't like it and I tried to squash it. Yet if she hadn't had that spirit, she wouldn't have been Sun Yue. I've often thought it was lucky that we all lived in different places after our marriage, otherwise she might have come to regret her choice. What do you think, old He?'

I thought it highly likely. And now? He'd understood her soul and begun to love it – I ought to have been pleased. But the feelings that leapt in me were quite the opposite because now Zhao Zhenhuan was a real 'rival in love'. Should I have asked him to stay? Wu Chun had been thinking of me. While he's here, I can't but treat him as an old friend going through bad times, as a prodigal who wants to reform. I thought he might throw Sun Yue into an emotional confusion but I hadn't realised he would constitute a threat to me. Can love come and go? Ought I to send him away?

'Why did you ask me to stay?' He suddenly stood still in front of me.

'I thought you ought to see Sun Yue and Hanhan,' I replied.

'Thought? What do you think now?' He looked at me, the corners of his mouth moving.

I said nothing. I wanted to say that I'd had second thoughts, but the twitching corners of his mouth made me sad and I didn't know what I could say.

'Tell me honestly, what are your relations with Sun Yue?' he asked, clutching my shoulders. He seemed confused, expectant, anxious, earnest . . .

'What does it matter to you? Go and see Sun Yue. She must still be at home,' I said, shaking him off.

'No. I've told you so much, you must answer.' He was insistent and pressed his hands on my shoulders.

'Leave me alone. When I was on the road I learned to fight,' I said, freeing myself again.

'So you still love her?'

He looked at me with dread. I didn't answer, but I met his eyes.

'What about her? She must love you. She was always under your influence. And you just mentioned Hanhan. It looks as if you're already fairly intimate. I shouldn't disturb you. Did you want me to stay so you could tell me? It's as it was when I wrote you that letter in 1962 . . . you've got a chance to get your own back.'

That hurt. Did I really want to get my own back? I honestly hadn't thought about it. I don't approve of revenge and don't think I could pursue it. Why didn't he go?

'I'd better leave. Please tell Sun Yue that I wish you both all the best.'

The blood rushed to my face and I felt hot all over. I wanted to plunge into an icy river; it was as if I'd been hit on the head. Had Zhao Zhenhuan hit me? Yes! He hadn't considered Sun Yue's feelings in the past, yet now he was thinking about what was best for both of us. And me? God might have given me the power to love others but he hadn't given me the right to deprive other people of love. I knew that Hanhan loved me and I felt that Sun Yue loved me, but they hadn't authorised me to decide their fate.

He held out his hand and I grasped it with all my strength till he almost gasped with pain. Then I made him sit down on the bed, where he rubbed his hand and looked at me with incomprehension.

'You can't just leave like this. You really ought to go and see Sun Yue and Hanhan,' I muttered.

'Would that be convenient?' he asked. Judging from his tone and expression, he seemed to be sincere.

'It's not a question of convenience. We were students together and we're from the same county. In other words, there's no special agreement between Sun Yue and me. That should be a relief to you.'

'In fact, all I wanted to do was to let her know that I think at last I understand her and that I hope she'll understand me. I know

I've got no grounds for asking anything from her, it's all over between us, it's all in the past. If she does get together with you then I do wish you both well. Naturally, it will be hard for me . . .'

He choked; his face was not only tense, but twitching. People lose the things they love; suddenly they discover they are no longer theirs. I know how it feels. I held up my hand to stop him saying any more, gave him a cigarette and said kindly, 'You've smoked too much, this is the last for this evening. You can have the rest tomorrow.' I put the packet away in my pocket and told him to rest a while: I thought I'd go out.

He stopped me and asked, 'Will Sun Yue see me?' He was afraid she might refuse. When he'd got off the train today and gone to her house, he'd been in a very emotional state. Now he was calmer and glad he hadn't gone in then, as he didn't know what would have happened.

I hadn't thought about whether Sun Yue would be willing to see him or not. At first, when I got to know her again, she didn't mention him and I, of course, didn't want to bring up the past. I hoped that she might have forgotten it all. But talking to Hanhan that time had made me think about Zhao Zhenhuan. She didn't understand anything of what had happened between her parents; what did that suggest? That Sun Yue didn't want to poison the child's image of her father because she still cared and still hoped? The thought made me die a little, and desperate to find out more I called at Sun Yue's office one day after classes.

'What did happen between you and Zhao Zhenhuan? I thought you got on very well,' I said.

'Why are you so interested in that? It was extremely banal; he fell in love with somebody else,' she said, coldly.

'And you divorced for that? Once married, you can't divorce very easily, especially if there's a child,' I said.

'You've got no right to ask me about it!' She was angry and upset.

'I'm not blaming you,' I explained hurriedly. 'It's because of Hanhan. "Regret"! Why on earth did you give the child a name like that? Don't you think it's something of a millstone?'

That made her even angrier. 'What on earth do you know about it? You know nothing! You don't understand anything and you think you can blame me for everything. You wait till you're married and you've got a child and then if what happened to me happens to you . . .' She stopped, no doubt realising that her final sentence would have been full of obscenities!

I'd realised that this was not a string to be plucked, though I still didn't know why. I didn't want to ask the third party. What impression had her life with Zhao Zhenhuan left on her? Did she miss him or hate him? I really needed to know. I thought that the reason for the distance between us probably lay there. But would that distance now grow greater or smaller? What changes would there be in her feelings after she'd seen Zhao Zhenhuan? What choice would she make? She was so difficult to predict.

But I must help Zhao Zhenhuan to see her. For him, for her, for Hanhan and for myself. Sun Yue was the only one who could decide everything.

'I'll go and let Sun Yue know you're here,' I said decisively.

'You?' He was doubtful.

'Yes, it had better be me. Whether you trust me or not, I'm going to tell her you're here in my room, and that I hope she'll come and see you.'

'All right.' He didn't argue. How did he feel about my decision? Did he think I was going to say nasty things about him? Why was he so negative? It was his fault. I'd already had enough, I couldn't take care of everything. I told him to rest and said, 'I'll be back later.'

It was already nine in the evening. Sun Yue had had a tiring day; would she be asleep already? Perhaps I shouldn't go. It was late, we all ought to sleep. And I didn't go to her place very often. Perhaps after today I wouldn't be able to go again.

I looked for her windows from a distance to see whether there was a light on. But I couldn't work out which were hers, so I just had to go to door number 201 and knock in order to discover whether she was asleep or not.

I only knocked once and the door was opened immediately. She wasn't asleep and didn't seem surprised to see me. Picking up a stool, she said, 'Take it, let's talk outside. Hanhan is asleep.'

I followed her out and we sat by the wall. She waited for me to speak.

'You must be tired today. Haven't you had a rest yet?' I said, trying to sort my ideas out.

'I am tired. I would have gone to bed but I was waiting for you to come round.'

'How did you know I'd come?' I asked, surprised.

'Isn't Zhao Zhenhuan in your room? I saw it all. And Xu Hengzhong came and told me you'd asked him to stay. In fact, even if he hadn't told me, I'd have guessed. I knew you'd encourage him to stay and I knew you'd come over to encourage me to see him.' She seemed very composed.

'Why should I encourage you to see him?' My heart began to thump and I knew that my voice had changed, it sounded low and hoarse. She knew me, she understood me completely! I longed to tell her everything I'd been thinking.

'Because of your humanist stance!' she said, looking at me quickly before she lowered her head.

'Is that all?' I couldn't stop myself asking, my voice shaking.

'What other reason could there be?' she replied in a low voice.

I wanted to say that it was because I loved her. I love you! Don't you know that? For twenty years, I've never loved anyone else. But I couldn't say it. Today I must carry out my duty, albeit unwillingly: I must plead for my rival in love. I didn't reply to her question or look at her; just gazed at the sky, at the moon and stars. The building and its surrounding walls cut off the view; they squeezed it in so that the moon looked as if it had been hung high up in a picture frame; the walls made me feel pressed in.

'Jingfu!' A pair of warm hands touched my knee. I held them lightly, then tighter. I held them close to my chest.

'Though I've loved for twenty years, my love is still a blank sheet of paper. You've just traced the first mark on the paper!' I burst out.

She shivered and withdrew her hands. They suddenly seemed cold.

'Jingfu, it's because you are a clean sheet of paper that I don't want to live with you.' Her hands hovered in front of me, near the third button of my shirt. That was the button that had been loose. The day she'd sewn on a button for someone else, I'd sewn it on tightly myself. She seemed to remember.

What? I was baffled by what she'd just said, I really didn't understand.

'I can't live with you because you are a clean sheet of paper, and I don't have a clean sheet of paper to offer you. I used to be clean, but life has coloured me grey. I can never wash myself clean. Zhao Zhenhuan's arrival makes it all the more apparent, and I hate it!'

A cold shiver ran through me. Had life hurt her so much? I tried to comfort her: 'Sun Yue, life is a whole, love is just a part. If you take the whole of anybody's life, no one is clean. I'm far more stained than you.'

'No. Your colour may be dark but it's not grey, it can't make you feel ashamed. I'm different. Every time I think of what has happened between us, I feel I owe you something. So how can I love you as an equal?'

I was stupefied. I had no idea that that was how she saw our relationship. Did she think I owed her nothing? No, Sun Yue, it's not like that at all. All I want from you is love. But she went on:

'I've thought about it so much but I can't live with you. My self-respect won't allow it. I'm not deceiving myself, I love you, I love you very much. I call out to you in dreams and I've imagined our life together. But then another image appears: history's accounts are being settled, people's failures to understand, mockery . . .

'There's only one way for me, and that's to live alone. Li Yining is always telling me to separate life and thought. I think that's what I'm going to do: I'm choosing thought. Forget me, Jingfu! I'm emotionally weak and excessively proud and I can't do anything about the contradiction. If only . . .'

She buried her face in her hands. Sun Yue, I want to take your face gently in my hands and lift it up and look at you carefully. You kissed me once, I've never kissed you. Now, we are so close. There's no one here but the moon and stars pinned in their frame . . .

Her shoulders shook and I could hear her crying. My heart broke. I put my arms around her shoulders and said fervently, 'No, Sun Yue. I'll never forget you, never, never.'

'But I've decided!' she said, calmly, firmly, and shook herself free of my arms.

Could I cry? Could I shout? I felt like roaring and weeping. Why had I come rushing here this evening for the final judgment? It was really as if our fates were being manipulated, it was the work of ghosts, they'd created this terrible misunderstanding.

In the end I didn't cry and I didn't shout. I stood up suddenly, knocking over the stool, and struck at a tree trunk.

'Jingfu!' she said, in a low voice.

I turned to her and held out my hand, saying, 'Let me have my tobacco.'

She went silently and fetched the pouch, which was filled with fresh tobacco leaves. I didn't ask her: why and where did you find such good tobacco? I just filled my pipe and sucked furiously.

'Please forgive me,' she said, not daring to look at me.

'It's not a question of forgiving or not forgiving, I respect your decision. Anyway, it doesn't matter to me whether I marry or not, I'm used to living alone,' I answered, not daring to look at her.

'You should get married. There are lots of nicer women than me . . .'

'Fine, I'll go out looking . . . Don't let's talk about it. Zhao Zhenhuan is very conscious of his past mistakes. You really ought to see him.'

'Ought?' she said, with a smile that was both cold and bitter. I didn't see it but I could feel it.

'Ought. Whatever you think, he's an old friend and he's Hanhan's father. And if he's repentant, it's our responsibility to help him. His hair is quite white like an old man's . . .'

'All right. Please tell him that I'll wait for him here tomorrow morning.'

I held out my hand to her and said, 'Goodbye. Take care of yourself.'

She shook it tightly and said, 'Thank you,' three times, her voice getting lower.

I left. She stood, waving to me, as if she were seeing me off. I walked a few steps and turned to look. She was still standing there. I could make out her shadowy figure.

I walked over to a tree and stood under it, looking towards her building. I could no longer see whether she was still standing there. But I could see the light at her window. Now I remembered it clearly. Now I'd never be able to forget it.

I didn't want to go straight back to the dormitory and I wandered from path to path. Everyone was asleep. The dim lights in the grounds gave off a feeble glow, but without any lights at all I'd still have been able to find the corner of the grounds with the low shrubs.

'I call out to you in dreams and I've imagined our life together.' Sun Yue, did you say that, or did I?

'There's only one way for me now and that's to live alone.' Yes, alone. When I was on the road, when I was going through political attacks, I never thought that I'd live all my life alone. Now it's clear that that is my fate: to live alone.

Zhao Zhenhuan wasn't asleep. When he saw me come in, smoking my pipe, he asked anxiously: 'Why are you so late? Was it a good talk?' I didn't want to reply. 'You've brought back your tobacco pouch?' he asked.

'You ask too many questions!' I shouted and lay on my bed.

I heard him punching his mattress and sighing.

'Tomorrow morning, Sun Yue will be waiting for you at home,' I said, my voice muffled.

'Was that her idea or did you persuade her?'

'If you're going to keep talking, I'll throw you out!' I snapped the light off and paid no more attention to him.

That night, neither of us slept, but neither said another word.

EIGHTEEN

SUN YUE

Reconciliation?
Forgiveness? Is it that easy?

Zhao Zhenhuan has arrived.

Yesterday Xu Hengzhong, very tense, said, 'I've got something extraordinary to tell you. Don't get upset.' Anything that's been through his head gets changed, what was there to get upset about? I'd seen him. I was just about to go back into the room for something, when I saw them all leading someone away. I recognised Zhao Zhenhuan immediately. But I didn't feel like telling Xu Hengzhong.

'Zhao Zhenhuan is here. He wants to see you.'

Really? Is that so extraordinary? I've always thought that some day we'd meet again. He would act repentant and I'd act martyred. But now he's arrived and he's arrived at the wrong time. I was trying hard to forget, and becoming closer to He Jingfu.

'I won't see him,' I said to Xu Hengzhong.

'You're right. You shouldn't see him. He's remarried and had a child. He's probably come looking for some emotional comfort, but he ought to know that in China now the rule is that a man can only have one wife and he's got no right to look for any consolation from you.'

His words were quite reasonable but his attitude irritated me.

There was something unconvincing about his special concern for me and I cut him off:

'I know. Please tell him I won't see him.'

'Wu Chun wanted to send him away immediately but old He insisted he stay with him.' He spoke with anger in his voice.

'What?'

'Zhao Zhenhuan is still at He Jingfu's place. It was He Jingfu's idea.'

I couldn't see my face and I don't know if my colour changed but what he said made me feel quite faint. He Jingfu had made Zhao Zhenhuan stay and he'd persuade me to see him, I knew it. But I couldn't imagine Zhao Zhenhuan staying with He Jingfu. Zhao Zhenhuan is like a many-faceted mirror placed between me and He Jingfu. Through him we see ourselves and the other, and we see past events that we ought to forget. We all need mirrors, but not that sort. Over the last few days, I've been doing everything I can to avoid the reflection and to stand together with He Jingfu, facing a plain glass in which all we can see is today and the future. Now He Jingfu wants to keep that old mirror and hold it between us. Zhao Zhenhuan is at He Jingfu's place! My past is living with my present. The past and the present have a stomach in common and now that stomach has grown a great mouth ready to swallow me up. I hate it. Who do I hate? Zhao Zhenhuan? He Jingfu? Or do I hate that tell-tale Xu Hengzhong? Do I hate myself? My thoughts come too fast and I can't get things straight; but I will see Zhao Zhenhuan. Because of what he once gave me, I'll see him. For his present happiness, I have to see him.

'No, please tell Zhao Zhenhuan that I will see him.'

Xu Hengzhong couldn't understand my sudden change of mind and tried to discourage me: 'You must remain calm. You're still young, don't let him drag you down.'

I didn't think a person could be dragged down by another, so I said, 'I am calm. Oh, and there's something I ought to tell you: I asked my friend Li Yining to look for a wife for you. She rang up yesterday.'

He blushed.

'She knows a woman who's over thirty and has never married.

She's good-looking and her family is very well off. When would you like Li Yining to arrange a meeting?'

He blushed down to his neck. Coy, he hesitated for a while and then opened his mouth, and said, 'Next Sunday in the park.'

That was marvellous. I congratulated him sincerely, and then told him to leave: 'He Jingfu will probably come round to talk about all this. You've got a child at home, you'd better get back.'

He stood up, and as he left, he said, 'It still doesn't seem right!'

Then Zhao Zhenhuan was here. Timidly, he stretched out his hand to me. I didn't move, and he withdrew it. I stared at him openly; it was like looking at an ancient and faded picture.

His hair was quite white, entirely white, though it was still thick. He'd always been proud of his hair, thick, shiny and black; he'd always taken care of it. Now it was unkempt.

His face used to be drawn in a single smooth line, but now he'd grown thin it was angular. And there were so many lines at the corners of his mouth and eyes.

'Screw up your eyes! Harder! Do it again! I want to draw some lines above your cheekbones.' Was it in the fifth year of primary school? We were going to do a propaganda play and he and I were to be an elderly couple. He was very worried about us looking old because we didn't have any wrinkles. We couldn't screw up our eyes enough. Disappointed but kind, the teacher could only pat our smooth faces and sigh, 'That's enough. We'll just draw a couple of lines here. It's not in the least convincing.' He poured flour on our heads so they were completely white, and we tottered along the street, singing and making faces. Grown-ups pointed at the two of us and said: 'Look at them! Aren't they killing!' His father was cross with him and said it was unseemly, children pretending to be married couples.

Life is the best make-up artist. We don't have to screw our eyes up now, the lines have come of their own accord and are clearly drawn.

'Do sit down!' I showed him a chair and poured him a cup of tea. He doesn't like it too strong.

He was weighing things up, cautiously. He looked round the room: there are a few more books than there used to be; the wall is peeling. Once he chalked a picture for our daughter on it and there are still faint marks left. I ought to have the walls white-washed again.

We bought the cot for Hanhan: now it is pushed into a corner and piled with things. That was where we'd both looked in wonder at the tiny girl, only a few days old, with a round face like his and eyes like mine. As soon as she was born I sent him a telegram, 'We've got a daughter; come quickly,' and he came. But within two days he got a call from the newspaper: 'Urgent task; return immediately.' He kissed the baby and me, and he left. Before he had even got through the door, I was in tears. I suddenly felt that I needed support; how could I look after this tiny little life on my own? He stopped and came back and sat down on the bed beside me: 'I won't go! There's nothing that they can't do without me.' I rubbed my eyes and pushed him away:

'Go, go, I can manage!'

When he reached the door, he sighed and turned back. I bit back my tears. But when I heard his footsteps going down the stairs, I hugged the baby and wept bitterly. The baby increased my reliance on Zhao Zhenhuan and I felt that I could hardly bear to live apart from him.

The vase on the chest of drawers is new. There used to be a big red glass vase there, a wedding present from our classmates. We used to keep some pretty plastic flowers in it. On the day we divorced I smashed it. I didn't want any souvenirs.

He turned to me and looked me up and down.

'You haven't changed much, you still look very young,' he said after he'd finished scrutinising.

He said it so lightly, that I hadn't changed much. Did he want me to be like him, did he want my black hair changed to white? Did he think he hadn't hurt me enough?

'I've managed to survive this far, thank heavens,' I said.

'I know you hate me.'

Hate? It was more like contempt. With a cold smile I answered, 'If that's what you think, there was no need to come.'

'I wouldn't dare ask anything of you but I would like us to be friends. After all we were childhood friends.' As he spoke his eyes caught mine.

Yes, we were, and that was a precious time. I stared at him and he turned away. I'm the only person who can stare him out like that.

'I can't ask you to marry me again. But we grew up together, we were best friends when we were children. Don't be too hard on me, don't drop stones on me now I've fallen in the well.'

Silently I begged him to stop. I was exhausted by fighting, I couldn't bear to go through it again. What the bloody hell have you come here for? What's all this childhood friends rubbish! Don't be so pathetic, I thought.

I shivered. It was as though I had heard the words aloud. I looked at him; he hadn't spoken. He didn't look like the sort of person who could say such things. But how could I ignore all that had been said in the past?

'I've forgotten what our relationship used to be. I haven't got your powers of recall,' I said coldly.

He was silent. The corners of his mouth moved up and down, as if he was about to smile and cry at once. He'd never done that before.

'*You are bound to regret it,*' I had written to him.

'*Now that I've left you, nothing can make me regret it. I'll never see you again,*' he'd replied.

I could still see the words. Was it the same person in front of me?

'How have you got the face to come and see me again?' I said, contemptuously. I wanted him to understand how I felt. Could I forget what had been said and written?

His mouth quivered. He said, 'You ought to ask me how I summoned the courage to come and see you. May I smoke?'

I handed him an ash tray. All my friends have taken up smoking. When they are depressed, tea or wine aren't as effective as tobacco. Are they all so fed up?

'Everybody has regrets, but when I consider the misery I've caused you, I really think I ought to kill myself!' He lit a cigarette and puffed furiously.

Would he ever hurt himself physically? I've done it. The day I came back from the terrible meeting at the university with the letter forcing me to accept the divorce – 'You are pure! You shouldn't have married me, a coarse person like me, it was all your idea' – I banged my head against the wall, I beat my shoulders till they were purple and green with bruises. I couldn't let my daughter see them.

'Enough! I don't want to hear any more about how repentant you are. I'm not a saint, I'm not God. I can't forget and I won't forget!' I smashed my fist down on the glass top of the desk and it broke, and my hand began to bleed. He saw it and reached out, but I avoided his hand and sucked the cut myself.

He looked at me, first with surprise, then with sadness. He seemed disappointed. After a long pause, a bitter smile appeared on his face.

'Sun Yue, I know I deserve to suffer. But you won't even let me say how sorry I am. You aren't being fair.' He'd calmed himself, his voice was steady.

'Fair? You want me to be fair? Were you fair to me?' I asked furiously. My hand still hurt a lot.

'Sun Yue.' He sounded like an animal in pain, angry and upset. I watched him steadily and he said, more firmly: 'I didn't come to be forgiven but I wanted you to understand. I think we ought to understand each other. I think we can. Because we don't just have each other to consider, there's our past and our future. Our marriage no longer exists, but we were fellow-students, friends and the parents of the same child. You don't have to consider me, but you ought to consider the child.'

'Did you ever think of the child? That time . . .' When he mentioned Hanhan I could have spat a stomachful of bile all over him.

'Ma, when will Daddy come back?'

'Daddy's busy, darling. Be my precious baby and don't keep asking about him, all right?'

'Everyone at kindergarten has got an army uniform. I want one.'

'I'll get you one.'

'Their Daddies all bought theirs, I want Daddy to buy it.'

'All right, I'll write to Daddy and tell him to buy you one.'

I wrote a 'letter' and pretended to post it. Three days later I bought a little soldier's uniform and gave it to her.

'Lovely Daddy! Will you write and thank him? I'll write to him, too.'

You write, darling, you write. How many characters do you know? You know enough to write 'Little Ring says thank you to Daddy.' Stroke by stroke, all crooked. I 'posted' it for you.

He wants me to consider the child?

'Sun Yue, I beg you, don't say it!' His eyes and voice implored me not to go on. I turned away.

'I've felt terrible about Hanhan. I want to make it up to her from now on. Won't you even give me that chance? Look at me, I've gone white. And . . .' He pulled out a wallet and held up a photograph. 'I've always kept this on me . . .'

It was the photograph of the three of us, on Hanhan's first birthday. He looked at it with tears in his eyes, and wiped his eyes with his sleeve. I handed him a handkerchief. My anger was subsiding, and I began to feel sad instead.

'Sun Yue, you must believe me, life's lessons have left even deeper impressions than your condemnation. I know now that I never really loved you, or rather that I didn't love the whole you. The only person who loves you like that . . . is He Jingfu. You're right for each other. You need dreams, you need to keep looking for the aim and meaning of life. I just came to tell you that. Oh, Sun Yue, if only life could begin over again . . .'

I stopped him. 'Don't talk like that. You've already got a new family. You've got to keep going, for your wife and child, you've got to keep on!'

'Yes, I've already got a new family.' His mouth began twitching again; I couldn't bear to watch it. If he wanted to cry, why didn't he cry? If he wanted to laugh, why didn't he laugh? Why did he do it?

'Let me see my daughter once! I can imagine her . . .' He got up and went over to the desk, and lowered his head to look at the photographs under the glass. They were all photos of Hanhan, from birth to now, most of them taken by me, here. He looked at them one by one, touched them and kept saying, 'Hanhan, Hanhan!'

I felt like crying but I didn't want to cry in front of him. I was afraid I wouldn't be able to stop myself so I got up and walked up and down.

He sat down on my chair. In the old days, when he came to see us, I used to give him that chair. He used to pull me over to sit on it with him: 'I want to get transferred so we can be together! For years heaven has been in the south and earth in the north, both worried about the other. Separation can produce some beautiful poetry but poetry isn't as good as life!' I always replied, 'Let's wait until they arrange it. They must be concerned about us. We shouldn't make requests to the leadership; we're party members.'

'My arrival hasn't affected how you feel about him, has it?' The question came suddenly and made me break out in a cold sweat. If I'd chosen He Jingfu, if I'd married him and lived with him, if there hadn't been that unspeakable and unthinkable storm, would this tragedy ever have happened?

He laid his head on the desk and his shoulders shook. I couldn't bear him to cry. When we were students, if I just spoke coldly to him, he'd cry, he'd get ill.

I went and stood beside him. This was what we used to do, ten years ago. He'd sit and I'd stand beside him. His shoulders were still shaking. Unwillingly I put my hand on his white hair and said, 'Don't cry! I'll let you see Hanhan.'

He turned suddenly and seized my hand and pressed it against his face. His tears fell wet along my fingers, warm tears. They ran into my cut and it began to hurt again.

I shivered. What was I doing? Understanding? Forgiving? Was it that easy? Was that why they said, 'Frailty thy name is woman?' Could a few tears wash away the humiliation I'd suffered? Could a few kind words close the wounds? No, tears made wounds more painful.

But what could I do with him? I didn't know how to take revenge.

'Is she a good student?' he asked.

'Very good. She works hard,' I replied, freeing my hand.

'If you let me repay my debt to the child, I'll be so grateful, Sun Yue!' His eyes were soft, beseeching.

I looked at my watch: it was almost lunch time. Hanhan had no classes that afternoon, so she was coming home for lunch. Should I let them meet?

'Come on Hanhan, this is your father!' I pulled Hanhan and pushed her in front of him. Was it a scene from a film? Yes, a foreign film: the father come to see his illegitimate daughter and the abandoned woman acknowledging him, for the sake of the child. He was still single and there was a great reconciliation. Could I act the part today? 'Hanhan, this is your father. Call him Daddy.' Hanhan would call him 'Daddy' and then turn to me and call me 'Ma'. What connection would that imply? What would people think? Would they say I was magnanimous or weak?

'It's late, you'd better go. I'll talk to Hanhan about seeing you,' I said finally.

His face grew tense. 'Will she see me? Have you taught her to hate me?'

'I don't know whether or not she'll see you. She hasn't had a father for a long time. If you turn up suddenly . . . I think she may well not want to see you,' I said coldly, controlling a feeling of sympathy for him.

'Please, Sun Yue, don't destroy my hope! Your future is brighter than mine, you've got He Jingfu . . .' His mouth trembled again.

I've got He Jingfu! I felt suddenly full of blazing anger and picked up a chair to throw it to the ground, screaming at the top of my voice, 'I hate you! I'll never forgive you!'

His face twitched and my heart hardened. We stood facing each other, staring, for a long, long time. He turned his eyes away first and said gently, 'All right, I'll go. One day you may regret your behaviour. Because of the child, you're bound to regret it.'

He left. I stood still and didn't say goodbye. Would I regret it? Because of the child? Had I not done the right thing? Ever since she was born, I've put up with hardships, skimped my food and clothing and borne the burdens; wasn't that all for the child? Now she's grown up, friends and colleagues are all happy for me: 'Sun

Yue, the hard years are over!' People who haven't been through it don't know what it's like. For years, one thought has sustained me – I must bring the child up, I must bring her up well. She's been my entire life. Because of her, I could say to life, 'I must go on living!' Because of her, I could face him, Zhao Zhenhuan, with a clear conscience and say, 'I'm the one who was abandoned, not you!' Wasn't it right that the child belonged to me alone? Any impartial person would say she was mine, mine alone; did I now have to offer her up, to give away my own flesh for someone else's peace of mind, for the very person who had abandoned us? Would I regret it? Were things so unfair?

I heard footsteps on the stairs, thump, thump, as if someone wanted to kick the building down. It was Hanhan: she always came upstairs like that. Each time I told her to tread more lightly, she promised she would; but the next time she came upstairs, thump, thump, thump.

I tried hard to calm myself; I didn't want her to feel there was anything strange going on. In my everyday way, I said, 'You're back . . .'

'Ma! Guess what!' She stood in front of me, her face shining. One hand was clenched in front of her chest.

I pulled at her hand and with my head on one side said, 'It's your Youth League badge, right?' Happily, she unclenched her fist, and there it was, gleaming. Comrade Sun Hanhan was a member of the Communist Youth League. I was pleased too, and smiled as she hugged me.

'Ma, how old were you when you got into the Youth League?'

'Fourteen.'

'I'm older than you were.'

'Not much – but you know a lot more than I did then.'

Her eyes were shining, just like mine when I got into the League. But I didn't know anything then, and I believed everything. Hanhan wasn't like that.

'Ma, it's not a good thing to know too much, is it? They say my ideology isn't stable and that I'm too up and down. But that's how it is – when I read about good people and good things in the paper I'm excited, and when I meet bad people or bad things, I get depressed. I'll try and improve. You'll help, Ma?'

I patted her head, smiling. I can't really supervise her behaviour. When I was young, my emotions were stable and I simply progressed in a straight line. But now? Is it a good thing or a bad thing to be emotionally stable? Doesn't it have something to do with being cheerfully unaware, stupid, simple in one's reactions? I don't know, I really don't know. As I've grown older, I've lost the self-confidence that Hanhan's friends have. So all I could do was pat her head.

'Ma, do you think we are like your generation?' She was excited, thinking, asking endless questions.

'How do you mean?'

'Complex.'

'What do you think?'

'Do you think our lives will run more smoothly?'

Our lives will run more smoothly! That was just a child's hope. Was it possible? I wouldn't like to guarantee it. When I was at school, teachers and grown-ups were constantly telling us: 'You're not like us! Everything's smooth, milk and honey now!' But the bitter taste had finally come. Was that what we had to teach the next generation? No. For Hanhan, the beginning had not gone smoothly. She'd had to put up with misery that other children hadn't had to bear. And that was what our life had brought her: it was her first inheritance from her parents. What other things had she inherited from us? And what would she make of herself?

I began to feel unhappy, and sorry for the child. I'd just been thinking that I'd made the supreme sacrifice for her, and now I began to feel that it was she who had made great sacrifices for me. I was the one who was emotionally unstable.

'Hanhan!' I raised her head and looked at her with love: 'There's something I must talk to you about.'

'What?' She was still cheerful, and looked at me with eyes wide.

'Your father's arrived. He'd like to see you.'

The smile left her face. 'Where is he?'

'He's at He Jingfu's,' I replied.

'Why is he there?' She seemed surprised. What was she thinking?

'He Jingfu asked him to stay,' I said, as calmly as I could.

'Have you seen him?' She looked at me.

'Yes. Will you see him?' I asked her. 'You must decide yourself,' I added. 'As for me, I can't forgive him. I can't forget the past. But I can't force you to do anything.'

My heart began to race. I didn't know what answer I wanted to hear. I hoped that she would understand how I felt, but I didn't want her to feel I was laying an extra burden on her. It was a dilemma, I knew. It is my dilemma. I am that dilemma.

I waited for her to answer. She was still looking at me, holding my eyes as if her answer lay in them. I waited and waited, and she finally said, 'I won't see him, Ma.'

'Hanhan!' I hugged her. 'We need each other, we need each other.' She nodded and stayed close, not raising her head. My heart grew calmer.

Perhaps I should have said, 'Go, Hanhan, I don't want you to make sacrifices for me!' Perhaps I should have said, 'Forgive him, Hanhan; I'm wrong!'

But all I said was, 'Let's leave it like that, Hanhan. Now let's eat.'

NINETEEN

SUN HANHAN

Why is it that the first thing history loads on my shoulders is a burden?

The simple noun 'Daddy' has become a possessive, 'my Daddy'. Ever since Ma showed me the letter, I've been hating him inside. He left Ma and he left me and I hate him. He's with some woman that I don't know and I hate him. He's made it so that whenever I think of him I go red, and I never dare talk about him in front of my classmates. I hate him.

He says his hair has gone white, it serves him right. But what does his white hair look like? Does it look like an old person's? I'll call him the old person. If he's become an old person, is he still good-looking?

He says he's got a daughter called Huanhuan [Little Ring]. That used to be my name. Why didn't he call her something else? He says he thinks about me every day but I don't believe it; if he misses me why hasn't he come to see me?

In the section meeting today when I was admitted into the Youth League, the teacher said, 'Sun Hanhan has made rapid progress recently which has a great deal to do with her home background.' It's right, Ma does teach me. Ma is the head of the household, the old person doesn't figure. If he knew I was now a member of the League, what would he think? Would he be as happy as Ma? 'I've got a daughter in Shanghai and she's a Youth

League member!' he could tell other people. 'It's all thanks to her mother. I haven't been able to be a proper father to her, I'm ashamed to say,' he could tell his friends. No, I'm just making it up, he won't know. Ma won't tell him and nor can I. We've paid no attention to him for so long, it's as if we never knew him. He might get angry, and he might make me angry. Anyway, he's got another Huanhuan. Is she like me? I'd love to know. I hope she isn't like that wicked woman! I blame that woman for everything.

Today, 'my Daddy' has suddenly arrived.

Should I see him? This Daddy? This sort of Daddy. Of course I shouldn't see him. But I'd love to see if his hair is really white. And I'd like to ask him why he's come.

Ma said it was up to me to decide. Why does she want me to decide? Can't she take charge? 'I can't forgive him' – she's made her position clear. Should I forgive him? She doesn't want to force me. But what does she want? I wanted to look at her eyes but she turned away. I don't suppose I ought to take a different attitude from hers: she brought me up, I have to stand by her. And he's got a wicked woman.

'I won't see him, Ma.' That was how I finally answered. Her eyes shone suddenly, as if she was pleased. She didn't want me to see him, I was right. Otherwise she would have been hurt.

After lunch, she made me sit by her and hugged me. I knew she wanted to comfort me.

I stayed there for a long time. Her heart beat so fast. She didn't say anything, just stroked my head, lightly, lightly; perhaps she sighed. If we had gone on like that I might have cried, but it wouldn't do, I had to be strong. I left her and opened my satchel. I had so much homework! Languages, geometry, physics, the teachers seemed to be competing in giving us as much homework as possible. I hadn't watched television for ages, or read a novel and I was getting short-sighted. They said I was doing well but I was using all my free time and sacrificing my sight. Was it worth it?

'*Aujourd'hui tout s'est bien passé. Aujourd'hui tout s'est bien passé.*' Had it been a good day? I got into the Youth League. And my father arrived.

'Hanhan! Why do you keep repeating that sentence?' Ma asked.

'Sorry, I'm tired after the meeting,' I said. *'Aujourd'hui tout s'est bien passé'*. My father is waiting for me at He Jingfu's. If I don't go, will he mind? *'Aujourd'hui . . .'*

'Hanhan, don't read any more if you're tired. Go out and amuse yourself,' Ma said.

'But I've got so much homework today . . .'

'Don't worry, today has been rather unusual. I won't blame you if you don't finish it all.'

Her voice was low and she was obviously upset. I was, too. Today had been unusual all right, too unusual.

'Hanhan, you don't blame me, do you?' she asked, suddenly. She must have been looking at me all this time, following my every movement. I want to finish my homework, Ma.

'Blame you for what?' I asked, pretending not to understand. I picked up my French book again.

'Do you really not want to see him? Did you refuse to see him just to spare my feelings. You do blame me, don't you?'

She suddenly seemed old, like an annoying old lady. I wanted to say, 'Just don't ask! You're driving me mad!' but after looking at her face, I couldn't. I did some geometry; I drew a triangle; I covered my exercise book with triangles. One dot, then another dot, then join up the two dots; that's me and Ma. But if you draw another dot, just one more, then two lines appear mysteriously to form a triangle. It's complicated. Perhaps I should rub out the last dot? But I can't rub out my father. That's how complicated things are in life. Suspecting . . . looking for proof . . . driving people crazy. I suspected my father was at He Jingfu's, should I prove it by going to see him? No, I didn't want to go. I just wanted to go out and see where I ended up. I stood up, opened the door . . .

'Hanhan, where are you going?'

'I'm going over to a friend's house.'

'Tell me which number it is and I'll come and collect you later.'

'Don't bother, I'll come back by myself.'

When had it started to rain? A fine drizzle, Ma always said that was 'bad rain'. 'A light rain soaks through clothes; people who don't say much get up my nose.' I'd have to get soaked, I didn't want to go back for an umbrella.

Where was I going?

My father was at He Jingfu's. He Jingfu had asked him to stay. Why? Does he like him? No, he can't possibly. Xi Wang told me in confidence that He Jingfu was in love with Ma. He asked me if I approved or not.

'I knew it anyway,' I said.

'You're a deep one! How did you know?' he asked, smiling.

'It's obvious!'

'So little Hanhan knows all about love!'

He rolled his eyes at me, mocking. Furious, I said, 'Of course I do.'

'All right, all right, so you know all about it. But do you approve?'

I couldn't answer his question. How could I judge adults' business? And if I did, I wasn't going to tell him; who did he think he was? If Ma or Uncle He had asked me, I'd have said: 'Yes! I think it's wonderful!' I really like He Jingfu very much.

But now my father is here, can I still approve? It's very difficult. What is he really like? Is he bad or is it just that He Jingfu is really good? But would He Jingfu ask a really bad person to stay? Surely not. But he must hate my father, he must be jealous, like Othello. Othello killed Desdemona. Love must be terrifying! I think I'd rather be a nun.

Isn't this the way to He Jingfu's? I'll go and ask him why he asked my father to stay. And if I bump into . . . Well, then I'll meet him. I won't have deliberately sought him out, I can't deceive Ma.

I knocked.

'Who is it? Are you trying to knock the door down?'

As soon as I heard the voice, I knew it was Xi Wang. I shouted, 'It's me, Hanhan. Is He Jingfu out?'

The door opened. I looked all round the room. There were only two people there, He Jingfu and Xi Wang. The quilt had been rolled down but it was flat; there was no one underneath it. Had he gone? My nose prickled but I wasn't going to cry. I wasn't going to let Xi Wang laugh at me.

He Jingfu pulled me into the room and tugged at one of my pigtails in a friendly way. There were dark rings round his eyes and he looked very tired.

Was it because of all this? What was up with him today? He was looking at me very carefully. Just like Ma looked at me, as if there were words written all over my forehead. I didn't like him staring at me, I couldn't hold my tears back any longer. He Jingfu didn't say anything, just stroked my head and wiped my face with his hand. Xi Wang didn't say anything either. He gave me He Jingfu's towel and I wiped my eyes but the tears didn't stop.

'Come on, Hanhan, you've had good news today!' Xi Wang said suddenly, smiling. He was always teasing. But he was gentler than usual. I didn't know what he meant; what good things had happened to me?

'You've got your Youth League badge! Congratulations!' he said, pointing to my chest. It was true, I'd forgotten about it. I ought to have told He Jingfu.

Did Xi Wang think that being admitted into the Youth League was good news? He wasn't a member. 'I've got a beard, I don't want to join any youth organisations,' he'd said to me.

'Have you asked to be admitted to the Party?' I asked.

'We'll have to wait and see,' he said.

'See what? Whether you've got all the qualifications?'

'All the qualifications? What qualifications? If I'm compared with my father, which of us is better qualified to be a Party member? You tell me.'

'Your father, of course.'

'On that score, Hanhan, you'll have to accept that you don't understand as much as me.' He was a tease. But today he'd congratulated me, and he seemed to be sincere.

'Hanhan, I hadn't noticed!' He Jingfu looked at my badge. 'Let me offer my congratulations too. Now tell me, what have you been thinking today?' He made me sit down in front of his desk and put a jar of sweets beside me, and then he sat on the bed.

What had I been thinking about today? Wearing a red scarf, getting into the League, getting into the Party, becoming a heroine? Step by step, onwards and upwards? There was a mountain in front of me, steep and without footholds. It would take too much energy to climb it and it wouldn't necessarily make me a heroine.

Could I say that to Uncle He? No. He asked me again: 'Tell me what you've been thinking today. Does it seem like a great mountain ahead of you? Do you wonder why you've got to climb it? You could go round the bottom.'

'Why don't you say something?' asked Xi Wang.

I shook my head. 'I haven't thought anything. Uncle He, it's such a miserable wet day, I can't bear it!' When I said I couldn't bear it, I began to cry again. Didn't Xi Wang mind about anything? He must get fed up sometimes. Had he never cried?

'Has your mother told you about your father?' He Jingfu asked quietly. I nodded. 'What do you think about it?' I shrugged.

Xi Wang seemed to be desperate to say something. He took off his glasses and said, like a wise old man, 'Hanhan, you can talk in front of us. To be honest, if it had been my father, I would have seen him. You ought to see him.'

I looked at him in surprise. He wasn't in the least close to his father, why was he speaking up for mine? Did he mean it? I looked at He Jingfu who nodded and said, 'You should see him, Hanhan. Your mother's attitude is hysterical.'

I felt as if I'd swallowed an ice lolly; I went cold inside, yet full of sweetness. He Jingfu was speaking up for my father as well, so he couldn't be bad. He Jingfu is a good man, he can't be jealous. Perhaps Xi Wang is wrong, perhaps I've guessed wrong? But then why is Ma so fond of He Jingfu's tobacco pouch? I tried to be honest with He Jingfu: 'I knew my father was here and I came to see him.' Where is he? I looked round the room again, looking for traces of my father's presence . . .

'He thought it might be too hurtful for your mother so he decided not to see you. He's left a letter for you.'

He Jingfu seemed to read my thoughts. As he spoke he took a letter from the drawer and handed it to me. On it was written: 'To be forwarded by He Jingfu: Zhao Zhenhuan'. Unfamiliar writing, an unfamiliar name, seeming to hook up from the bottom of my mind things I'd forgotten. He used to hold me high up in the air, frightening me. 'I'm going to drop you! I'm going to drop you!' I would regain my courage and yell, 'You dare! You dare!' and he wouldn't dare. I used to frighten him by shouting, 'I'll jump, I'll jump,' kicking at the air. He would put me down gently and hug me – 'You're as obstinate as your mother!' It all seemed so long ago. I was still his daughter and he was still my father. I was fifteen and it was the first time I'd had a letter addressed only to me, written by my father.

I opened it, turned to the wall and read:

Hanhan, I'm very upset to have missed the chance of seeing you. Your mother doesn't want you to meet me, I know that. Do you want to see me? I've brought a lot of unhappiness to you and your mother and I'll always regret it. I've never really been a proper father to you, and I'm sorry. From now on, I want to make up for what you've missed; I want to be a father to you.

Hanhan, don't forget me. I've been bad to you; you may be angry with me, you may hate me, but please don't forget me. The things I did have torn me in two and I need strength, my dear daughter! I can't believe you won't help me!

Oh Hanhan! My hair is quite white, just as you are beginning to understand life. Every day, I hope that you are happy and that you and your friends will be able to lead a different life and not be as confused as my generation. Your future is bright, work hard!

Tell your mother, anyone can take the wrong path, but they don't have to go down it a second time, they can change. Life has created so much anger and hatred between people and created so many wounds that now we must try and soothe and comfort them, in friendship and reconciliation. I do believe that one day she will come round to my point of view.

I must leave, but we will meet one day.

Your father.

'Daddy!' I whispered. I had said it so often to myself through the years. Today I wanted to say it to him but he'd already gone.

A white-haired man walks towards me, holding out his hands, faltering: 'Hanhan, Hanhan, help me, I'm failing, I'm growing old. But I have to say goodbye to the past and climb the mountain.' Poor Daddy! Hanhan is coming to help you, to help you climb the mountain.

A white-haired woman is coming towards me, trembling, holding out her hands: 'Hanhan, Hanhan, help me! I think the mountain
ahead is going to fall, it's going to crush me!' Dear Ma, I'm
coming! I'll take you away, so you don't have to see the mountain
again.

Two pairs of hands dragging on my shoulders. I'm being torn
in half! My heart is breaking. Ma, Daddy, why can't you go
together, in the same direction? Why do you want to break me
in half? I wish I'd been there to stop you. If you hadn't got married
you wouldn't have given birth to poor Huanhuan-Hanhan. It would
have been better.

My tears dropped down one by one like a broken string of
pearls. He Jingfu kept wiping them away with his fingers. I
grabbed his hand and cried harder.

He sighed, and leaned on the back of the bed, pulling something
out from under the pillow. I turned to see what it was; it was his
tobacco pouch.

Had Ma given it back to him? Why? Was it because of Daddy?
Did she still care about him? No, she couldn't; she'd said she'd
never forgive him. Had she? He Jingfu is a good man. He's the
best and nicest man I've ever met.

'I really don't understand Teacher Sun. It's a simple matter
and this is how she deals with it. She's suffering, the child is
suffering and Zhao Zhenhuan is suffering – and so are you!'

'Xi Wang, don't talk like that!' He Jingfu said furiously.

'But that's how it is! She's too wrapped up in herself. She's
selfish!' Xi Wang said, unable to restrain himself.

Was Ma selfish? 'Ma has sacrificed everything for me! You're
selfish! What's it got to do with you?' I shouted angrily. I wanted
to protect her.

Shaking his head and sighing like an adult tolerant of children's
failings, Xi Wang said, 'Hanhan, you don't understand. It's a social
duty of parents to give everything for their children. When we
have children you and I will do the same. It's a duty, not a
sacrifice; but if you consider a duty to be a sacrifice, then you are
selfish.'

I don't know anything about duty and responsibility. All I know
is that Ma loves me and that no one forced her into it. If it's a

duty then why don't all parents do their duty? I don't believe a word of it. He's just inventing a theory to criticise my mother. She's already been criticised enough, why does Xi Wang want to add to it? I won't let him; I want him to feel hurt enough to cry out and not to say any more. So I said, 'I know you love arguing. But I want to ask you something: do children have any duties to their parents? When I think of how you've treated your father! And you still call yourself a human being?'

The fire in Xi Wang's eyes died, and he sighed. After a long silence, he pushed his glasses up his nose and said amicably: 'Strong stuff, Hanhan. I've hurt you and now you've hurt me, right?'

He'd understood. How much older is he than me?

'If my father said to me, "Little Wang, I was wrong, but now I want to change. Help me!" then I'd leap up cheerfully. I wouldn't just hold out my hands – I'd kneel down and offer to carry him on my back! But my father never recognises that he's made any mistakes. I tell you, he never feels sorry for his family, only for the Party, the people, history. History! He never thinks he's done anything wrong himself. Even at the worst times, when he was washed up on a sandbank at the mercy of the tide, he still dreamed he was a hero and fought against the stream, saying it was the tide that was wrong. People who saw it found him frightening and pitiful. If I could, I'd give him a good push into the stream of history so he could swallow a bit of it in and swim with it, not against it. Or else, I suppose, I'd like to haul him out for a rest; but I haven't got that kind of strength . . .'

His words seemed poetic to me, to burrow straight to the heart. I'd never seen his father, but I thought I knew what he must be like. A dried up old man with his cheeks puffed out, standing on the seashore addressing the waves: 'Go back! You're wrong, go back!' The waves were choking him, filling his mouth with water till he could no longer shout. Ideological rigidity. Xi Wang's father isn't like mine; he seems to realise that now. He isn't that bad, I was too fierce with him just then.

Embarrassed, I smiled at him and he smiled back.

Why couldn't Ma see Daddy as Xi Wang did?

'Do you think my mother is selfish?' I asked He Jingfu.

He Jingfu was examining his tobacco pouch; he turned to me and said: 'You must forgive your mother. She's been through a lot.'

I was relieved that he hadn't criticised her. I hoped that all of them, Daddy, Ma and He Jingfu would think well of each other.

Xi Wang didn't seem to agree with He Jingfu. He seemed to want to say something, but when He Jingfu looked at him he just shook his head. He Jingfu smiled. 'You get over-excited, Xi Wang. You've got to look at history's leftover problems from a historical perspective.'

'But who, in the end, is going to shoulder history's burden? The next generation?' Xi Wang asked. He was like a fighting cock, his spirits rose when he could argue.

'There is already a heavy load on the back of the next generation. If we want the wheels of history to turn, you'll have to help push!' He Jingfu replied.

'But right now, my generation, and Hanhan's, are already sharing our parents' suffering. All we ever hear is: you must make allowances for the previous generation, you must make allowances for your parents. Does the previous generation make allowances for us? Do parents make allowances for their children?'

Why was he so agitated? He made me part of a different generation from his. I think what he said was right, though. Being children, we have to suffer for being children. 'You're too young' is what Ma always says to me. But when she was fifteen, had she already met with the kind of things I've had to deal with? In books it says that if you plant melons, you'll harvest melons; if you plant beans, you'll harvest beans. What have I planted? Nothing. But my basket is already full of bitter melons, so heavy I can't pick it up; they were all planted by grown-ups. There's that torn photograph and now this letter. They'd say it was history. What is history? I've never seen it, I've never had anything to do with it, yet it has heaped this load onto my back as if I'd done something wrong! Is that fair?

'Xi Wang, you're always in too much of a hurry to get things clear,' He Jingfu spoke again. I wanted to hear how he was going to refute Xi Wang. 'You must distinguish between knowledge and practice, between theory and reality, and see them as opposites in a system where they are both opposed and part of a unity.' He pushed the pouch back under his pillow. 'But you're not prepared to accept the existence of opposites.'

'I am, but I think we ought to act to reconcile contradictions. You always want me to wait,' Xi Wang argued. 'Waiting and sticking to the well worn path are practically the same thing.' He looked at He Jingfu, pleased with himself.

He Jingfu just smiled. 'If you don't want to wait, that's fine. Who doesn't want to eat a peach straight away? If the peaches are ripe on the trees, why wait? Why wait till they'll drop straight into your mouth?'

I smiled, and Xi Wang smiled. What He Jingfu had to say was more interesting than Xi Wang's opinions.

'And yet you have to wait,' he continued. 'History is a very abstract term. But what makes history, what pushes it along? Lots of things, but mainly people. That means that it's concrete, but it's muddled and varied. The people like us who are shouldering the burden of history, why shouldn't we wait? The history of a nation, of a period, is made up of thousands and millions of people's contributions. And all the individual contributors want to go their own way, to the very end; won't you let them? Do you want to pull the cart all by yourself?'

'You can't do it all by yourself, Xi Wang!' I said. I was fascinated. His eyes shone behind his glasses but he didn't say anything. He Jingfu was quite a formidable opponent.

'But . . . oh!' Xi Wang's expression and tone softened. What was he going to say? Why did he stop?

'I'm not trying to put you down, Xi Wang. I admire your generation, you're braver than us, more alert, more ready to create and transform. You haven't been through the same tortuous changes that we have, which were what woke us up. Once we woke, we had to take the burden on. Yet because you aren't so intimately connected with history, you can't really grasp its true significance, and you tend to dismiss it. I like your broad view of the world, the past, the present and the future; I just hope that when you put your knowledge into practice, you'll pay attention to others; that you'll think it all out very carefully and never forget that you are an ordinary human being. That way, you'll never feel isolated.'

'Perhaps I can't wait till I can put it into practice!' Xi Wang sighed.

'I think you can. How old are you?' He Jingfu asked.

I scratched my nose and looked at Xi Wang. He was going to pull my pigtails.

'All right! Hanhan and I will wait. So what do you think our future will be like? Will it be a wide smooth tarmacked highway?'

He Jingfu laughed. 'That's enough of that. Hanhan isn't interested, are you Hanhan?'

'Yes, I am interested, Uncle He, and I agree with you. I have to wait till Ma has gone her own way, to the end, don't I?' I said.

'Right!' He seemed very pleased with me, though he put his hand back under the pillow and took out the pouch again. Can you overcome a craving for tobacco just by looking at a tobacco pouch? I doubt it. He must be very anxious.

'But, Uncle He . . .' I wanted to ask what would happen when Ma had finished going along her own historical road? Remembering that Xi Wang was listening, I stopped.

I looked at Xi Wang. Why didn't he go? He came before me. I wanted to talk to Uncle He alone.

TWENTY

HE JINGFU

My father's influence came from his heart.

When he realised that Hanhan was glaring at him for a reason, Xi Wang winked at me and said, 'I've got lots to do; Hanhan, you stay.' He got up and left. Hanhan followed him to the door and shut it behind him.

I let her sit next to me and waited for her to speak, but she said nothing for so long that I finally asked, 'Is there something you want to talk about?'

'No.' She shook her head but I could see from her eyes that there was. Her eyes were like Sun Yue's, fine and bright. They were normally gentle and lovely, but when she was worried they seemed to dart about. She looked at the letter in her hand and then at me.

'Hanhan, is it something you feel you should tell me?' I tried to make her relax, to tell me what was worrying her. Children shouldn't worry too much.

She bit her lip and seemed to be making up her mind.

'I feel very sorry for Daddy,' she said, looking at the letter.

'Yes. I feel very sorry about his present problems,' I answered.

'Uncle He, do you think Ma will ever . . .' She looked at me doubtfully.

'Is it that you want to see your parents reunited?' I forced a smile and tried to repress my own agitation.

She looked at me and shook her head. 'That's not possible –
he's got that other woman. Uncle He, don't they get on? Do you
think they will divorce?'

'It's possible,' I replied.

'Then what about their Huanhuan?'

'She'll stay with her father or her mother.'

'I'd love to have brothers and sisters. It's lonely on your own,'
she said.

I understood what she meant: the logic was clear. If the family
of three could be reconciled and the new little Huanhuan added,
mightn't that make a happy family? But what about me? What
would be my position? Would I be hidden behind the family
photograph, or coloured in and added to it? My heart is in the
hands of others. I wanted to look at the tobacco pouch again but
restrained myself; Hanhan is a sensitive child.

'Uncle He!' she said suddenly, giving me a start. I was worried
in case she'd guessed what I was thinking.

'Did Ma give you the tobacco pouch back or did you take it
back?'

She was still interested in that. How should I answer? What
did she want to hear? Sometimes it's difficult to work children
out. I didn't want my reply to hurt her and I wanted to know what
she meant, so I smiled and said: 'Guess.'

She scanned my face and said, tentatively, 'Ma gave it back to
you, didn't she? She said she'd give it back when you came out
of hospital.'

I nodded. I knew what she wanted to hear and I didn't want to
disappoint her or make things worse for her.

'Uncle He, don't worry.' She shifted closer to me.

'Why should I worry?' I asked, confused by the child. I
was sure my voice betrayed me and I couldn't look directly at
her.

'I know you're worried. Xi Wang told me you love my mother,'
she said, so softly it seemed she didn't want anyone to hear. I
heard every word, her concern, worry and sympathy. What a
strange child. 'Isn't that right?'

Why ask me? If you've already detected love in the confusion,
then you know. Didn't you come and happily tell me all about your

mother? Weren't you encouraging me to fall in love with her? Today you want to know if you're right. I know that if I say 'no', you'll be hurt or suspicious, you'll think I'm concealing things from you. And if I say 'yes', how will you feel? All I can do is play at being a child with you.

'Yes, Hanhan,' I said, looking at her.

She crumpled up the letter in her hand, threw herself on the bed and cried.

Why are you crying? Have I hurt you? Have I made it worse? I know what it is: you love me, almost as much as your mother. You want me to be happy but there is a problem between the people you love . . .

Don't cry! People are always like this, life is always like this. Everybody's heart gets broken, it can't be avoided. You're still young. Your web of social relations only consists of a few strands. It'll get more densely woven, more tangled. Perhaps then you won't cry, as I've learnt not to.

I lifted up her head and tried to wipe her face to stop her crying. 'Hanhan, I can't bear to see people cry.'

'Will we still be friends?' She hung on to my hand.

'Of course. We're very good friends. Come on, link little fingers and we'll be friends forever.' I linked fingers and she smiled through her tears.

'You're so good! I'll come and see you often.'

'Lovely, you're always welcome.'

She grew calmer and started leafing through the papers on the bookshelf.

'You ought to go home. Your mother will be worried.' I thought Sun Yue probably didn't know Hanhan had come to my place.

She took my wrist and looked at my watch and stuck out her tongue. 'Oops, it's supper time, I must run.'

I picked up my rice bowl. 'I'm going to the canteen, we'll go together.'

'Should I show Ma the letter?' she asked.

'Yes, Hanhan. From now on you must be more sympathetic to your mother and slowly let her know your point of view. She'll listen, she loves you very much.' My throat tightened as I said this, but fortunately we arrived at the canteen. 'I'm going to eat,'

I said, 'you go home,' and she reluctantly said goodbye and went
off.

I waited until she had disappeared and then went back to my
room. I wanted to sleep; the last two days had been exhausting.

I locked the door; I wasn't going to let anyone in. I wanted to
lie down peacefully on my own.

So this was the end of my twenty-year plan. I'd started with
nothing and I'd ended with nothing. A boy lay down and turned
into an old man. That long when he lay down, that tall when he
stood up. With no ties.

I'd never known the pleasure of love but I knew the pain. From
nothing to nothing? I felt for my tobacco pouch under the pillow.
The new cloth patch was 'something', it had changed. It was the
only trace of love in my whole life. Sewn by hand, stitch by stitch,
finely. What were you thinking Sun Yue, as you sewed each
stitch? I can't believe that you weren't showing your love as the
needle pierced and opened the cloth. I can't believe that you
didn't want the seeds that you'd sewn to sprout, to flower and
fruit.

'*My pride won't let me*,' she said. Is that how it really is? I
thought about it all last night but came up with no solution. Zhao
Zhenhuan was tossing and turning. I longed to ask him what
happened when you met. I longed to know what impression
remained. But I said nothing. Hanhan showed me her torn photograph and it still hangs in front of my eyes. The torn parts mend
themselves, the forms of three people become whole, close.

'*If there's a future life . . .*' Sun Yue, would you then think
of marrying me? If it really is that your pride won't let you,
then it's real pride. But were you really just telling me to wait?
Perhaps I don't have to wait for the next world, just for the
future . . .

'Did Ma give back your tobacco pouch or did you ask for it?'
That really made me think. I think I asked for it. Yes, I did. 'Let
me smoke,' I said, holding out my hand. She gave it to me. When
I left, I didn't ask if she still wanted to keep it for me, I just took
it though it was a token of love. Why am I so inattentive? Even
Hanhan noticed; I never notice anything.

I ought to go and tell her that my feelings won't change. I'll wait, I'll wait forever. I want to give the tobacco pouch back and tell her to look after it forever.

I got up and went outside into the courtyard. The sky was hung with stars. I walked on until I could see the lights at her window, shining brighter than the stars. I stood, staring.

Sun Yue, if you are standing at the window, are you looking towards me? If you're a star, can you shine through the window and illuminate me? See into me? *You're really good*, I could hear Hanhan saying. 'Good' can mean a lot of things. *I feel sorry for Daddy*; I agree, I feel it too. *I wish Ma and Daddy could get on again.* I feel the same. *I know it's been hard for you*; she meant she approved of my sacrificing myself for the happiness of her family. Today Hanhan made her estimate of me, not on an emotional basis but on a moral one.

Is it a moral problem?

If a person just lives for himself, he's not even worth as much as an animal. Even pigs and dogs love their young.

My father told me that. I mustn't be that way, no matter how hard it is. I turned round. Sun Yue, might you suddenly notice me and come flying after me? Asking for my tobacco pouch? I hurried back to the dormitory, locked the door behind me, and lay down. Sun Yue didn't follow me, she hadn't seen me. Or perhaps she didn't want to run after me. Fine.

This was the end of my twenty-year plan. Starting from nothing and ending with nothing. No, there was one tiny trace, one memento, the tobacco pouch.

In my life I've loved two people, my father and her. Together they've left me with one memento, the tobacco pouch. Is it coincidence?

From now on it will be more precious to me. I see two hearts in it, my father's and my lover's, one a peasant, one born of books, so different and yet both loving, both suffering, both ready to sacrifice. Sun Yue; my father.

Weeping over the body of his brother, my father had cried:

'Oh my brother! We grew up together as orphans, begged for food. One winter we failed to find anything to eat and we couldn't bear the hunger. Hand in hand we went to the river, hand in hand we waded out into the middle, me in front, you behind. The water rose up to my stomach, and up to your chest. You couldn't stand up and cried, "Elder brother, don't let's die! The water's too cold . . ."; so hand in hand we went back, you in front and me behind. We sold ourselves to two big houses as servant boys. With Liberation, we became brothers again. You even became a cadre; who ever thought you would throw yourself in the river again? Brother, are you still afraid of the cold water? Why don't you speak?'

It was probably the longest speech he ever made. I can still remember every word because that was when I learnt things about my father that I'd never known before.

My uncle killed himself 'to escape punishment'. His crime was 'violently opposing the three red banners of the General Line for Socialist Construction, the Great Leap Forward and the Peoples Communes'. Though people were dying of hunger, the newspapers still talked of supporting the 'Great Leap Forward' and urging peasants to sell their 'surplus grain' to the state. And my uncle, the deputy head of the commune, couldn't understand how such things could happen under the leadership of the Party. 'Many of the Party leaders are from peasant backgrounds, surely they must know you simply can't produce ten thousand kilos of grain from a sixteenth of an acre? Why do they let journalists boast so groundlessly? If they go on much longer, people will die of starvation!' He wrote a letter to the Central Committee to send people to investigate. His letter was sent back.

One day, a meeting was called in the commune, to oppose counter-revolutionary elements. The country public security chief presided. I went with my father. We didn't know that the object of struggle was my uncle . . .

At the end, he was dragged off to prison. On the way, struggling like a madman, he managed to escape and threw himself into the river. His hands were tied so he couldn't move and he hadn't the energy to struggle . . .

The body of the counter-revolutionary who had committed suicide to escape punishment was dragged out of the river and became the object of struggle once more. It was easier when he was dead. Was he allowed a proper burial? No. Throw him into a pit and have done with it. He certainly wasn't to be allowed a coffin.

What could we do? My aunt was pregnant, but in front of the crowd she changed his clothes and buried him. He wasn't quite forty.

'I want to get uncle's body home, even if it means going to prison.' When my father came back from the river, he smoked pipe after pipe, all night. 'Speaking out on behalf of the peasants, is that a crime?' he said to himself over and over again. The second night, we took up some floorboards and made a box. We went to the riverside in the dark and dug my uncle up. We carried his body back and buried it in the box in the field at the back of the house.

Maybe people in the village knew, maybe they didn't, but no one told tales.

'After you died, your family lived with us and shared everything. If we ate well, then they ate well. If we were hungry, they were hungry, too, just like when we two brothers were both alive.'

My father's thoughts and feelings hadn't been in the least influenced by 'class struggle'. He'd never wanted to become a 'tool of class struggle', probably because he was too ordinary, too insignificant. He was of no particular use to anyone and he had nothing to lose in 'class struggle'. Year after year, month after month, day after day, he was out in the wind and rain. A group, a family, can rise and fall. A person can belong to a different class yesterday, today and tomorrow. Some people have learnt how to adjust their emotional position and change their slogans according to the 'needs of class struggle'. They've learnt to change direction, to know the right 'line', to unite or divide, to consolidate. My father could never do that. He was too ordinary, too insignificant. What use would he have been in 'class struggle'?

On the other hand, 'class struggle' was of considerable use to him. It oppressed him but it also gave him the opportunity to demonstrate his spiritual worth. That spirit gave me a rare upbringing; I drank from it . . .

My aunt brought the child and came to live with us. All we had at home were people and mouths, there was no grain, no livestock. We ate what we could find, we sold everything we could.

The grown-ups could bear it, stoically, but the children? My little brother was only seven and my aunt's son was even smaller. And there was also the baby in her belly that would want feeding . . .

My father and I, the two breadwinners, dug in the fields every day. My mother, who had bound feet, took my sister out every day looking for sweet potatoes that had been missed. So as not to be caught stealing and become 'black marks on the face of the commune', they sewed lots of pockets inside their trousers and slipped the sweet potatoes inside. How many could they bring back that way? Sometimes they would dig a hole in the field, make a little fire, roast a few and then slip them into their trousers.

My mother gave my father a hot sweet potato. He gave it to his nephew. My little brother burst into tears. My mother dragged him away, wiping his face.

That went on for years. My brother was the first to go. Then my mother fell ill . . .

'Kowtow to your uncle!' My aunt dragged my little cousin in front of my father saying, 'I can't bear to see your whole family dragged down because of us! I'll take the children and see if we can do better somewhere else. If we can hold out for a few years then we'll come back.'

My father sighed and sighed and smoked pipe after pipe. His pouch contained dry cassia leaves. Finally he said, 'If you think you can manage, then go. I'm so sorry . . .'

Not long afterwards, my mother went the same way as my little starved brother. There were only three of us left; my father, my sister and me. Soon my father and sister couldn't leave their beds. I was the only one who could get up and scratch about for food, and even I had appalling dropsy. Like my mother, I concealed bags and pockets in my clothes and went out to look for sweet potatoes still buried in the fields. If there weren't any close by, I had to go further. My fingers tore as I felt amongst the brambles for treasures to take home.

My father got worse. Every day he grew thinner. Every evening, I would sit by his bed and stuff dry leaves into his pipe. I watched the leaves burning and my heart burned, unwilling to bear it any longer. If I could have turned my heart, my blood and love into tobacco . . . 'Dad, don't smoke it,' I'd say filling his pipe.

'It's the only pleasure I've had in my life, let me smoke!'

Where did Sun Yue find that good tobacco? She can't possibly know that you can smoke cassia leaves.

One day, my father called me over to his bed. I gave him a pipe, but he hadn't got the strength to smoke. Tears rolled down my face. The corners of my father's mouth twitched – was he laughing at me? He was crying. I wiped the tears away for him and he clutched at my hand. He looked and looked at me as the tears ran down the deep creases in his face, and he said, 'There's half a sweet potato left over . . . I'm dying but you mustn't die, if you die no one will know what sort of person you are. And there's your aunt, you must look for your aunt . . .'

He didn't finish what he had to say. He didn't smoke his 'tobacco'. I knelt by his bed. I didn't move for a long time.

When I rose, I picked up the pipe and the tobacco pouch and inhaled my first 'tobacco': cassia leaves. My father had left it to me.

My uncle was rehabilitated, and my aunt came back with her son and the little girl who was born in the middle of the trouble. 'If only your father was still alive . . .' she was always saying to me.

I always replied, 'I'm sure he'd be relieved that you're all right.' I knew that my father would have been pleased, because he never thought about himself. But how could I not think of him?

Whenever I pick up the tobacco pouch, I think of you. I breathe in your influence just as I sucked at my mother's breast. My mother's milk was made from blood, my father's influence came from his heart.

Apart from the tobacco pouch, my father left nothing to remember him by and nobody thought to commemorate him or hold a memorial service. He was too ordinary, too insignificant. The huge sacrifices that he had made, what did they have to do with history? History only records the actions and fate of great men. People like my father can only get in under the umbrella of 'the masses'. Many people say that it is people who create history; but if you read or write history, how many real examples are there of people with feelings and individuality under that blanket heading of 'the people'?

I remember my father, and I mourn him. My funeral oration is the book I've written, *Marxism and Humanism*. It is essential, great and honourable to wipe out class exploitation; but it is wicked to make class struggle, to create classes and divide and split people and families. Our predecessors liberated the people, their successors have harmed the people. Our predecessors treated people as people, their successors just treat people as tools that can talk.

Sun Yue hasn't seen my manuscript. I've often thought of showing it to her but her manner has stopped me. The day before yesterday, I bumped into one of the editors from the publishing house and he said they were going to publish it.

I'll send her a copy and I'll write on it: 'To the one I've longed for and sought for twenty years'.

No, that's inappropriate. It might be misinterpreted. I ought to write something like 'Comrade Sun Yue, please correct and criticise'.

Comrade! We used to sing, 'The proudest name is comrade, it is more glorious than any other.' Yet now, if you use it, people think you're unfriendly and sarcastic. Why?

Comrade Sun Yue! Are my twenty years of longing to be expressed in that form of address? No, it's too cold. Yet that's how it is and that's how it ought to be. The diary that has accompanied me everywhere still has a little yellow flower pressed between the pages. A paper flower.

This is how the twenty-year plan ends. I started from nothing and I've ended up with nothing. A boy lay down and turned into an old man. With no ties.

'There's only one way for me and that's to remain single.' No, Sun Yue, I hope that doesn't happen to you. I'll make that sacrifice.

I'll always treasure my tobacco pouch. It was my father's. The tobacco in it is Sun Yue's. And that fine, fine stitching.

TWENTY-ONE

SUN YUE

I've gained through loss.
From now on, I'm going to build a life for myself.

Hanhan finally came home, very late, her face puffy and her eyes red. I didn't dare ask where she'd been or what she'd been doing. I suspected she'd been to look for him.

'Let's eat!' I said, trying to be casual, bringing in a nice supper that I'd prepared for her.

'I've eaten, Ma.'

'Where did you eat?'

'At . . . at Uncle He's.' She hesitated before answering.

'Were you looking for *him*?' I wanted to be more direct; I wanted to say, 'for your father', but I thought it would upset her.

'I didn't go to look for him. On the way back from a friend's house, I bumped into Uncle He. He took me to the canteen and he gave me a letter.' Her answer was a bit confused. I didn't believe she'd just bumped into He Jingfu, but I didn't want to challenge her. I felt anxious and sorry for her.

She held a letter out to me and as soon as I saw the handwriting, I said, 'It was written to you, I won't read it.' Disappointment crossed her face and she went to her desk. She read the letter through, drew two lines on it with her fountain pen and ran out, leaving it behind. She said she wanted to ask one of her friends about a maths problem.

Had she seen her father? Why had Zhao Zhenhuan written to her and why had he asked He Jingfu to give her the letter? The questions dragged at my heart but how would I find the answers?

The letter lay on the table. I'd said I wouldn't read it but she'd left it there and deliberately underlined two parts. I was sure she wanted me to read it: the underlinings were for me. I already realised that Zhao Zhenhuan had gone, but Hanhan's red eyes preyed on my mind. Had she cried in front of He Jingfu? What must he think of my behaviour? I've refused to repent and I've forbidden them to meet. He must think I'm selfish; yet does he realise that it was all because of him?

'Ma!' Hanhan shouted before she came in, and I left her desk quickly. I didn't tell her about reading the letter and she didn't ask.

'Ma, do you think Sun Zi was right about man being inherently bad?' I hadn't expected a question like that. I didn't know where she'd learned about the philosopher Sun Zi, nor why she was interested in such questions.

'Where did you think that up?'

'I was looking at a book of Uncle He's, on ancient Chinese philosophy. It said that Sun Zi thought human nature was essentially evil but Mencius said it was basically good. I think Sun Zi is right . . .'

Her answer shocked me. She was so young, how could she think human nature was evil? Had I shown her the blacker side of human nature? I didn't know how to answer.

'Did you ask He Jingfu? He's the expert in these things,' I said. I deliberately mentioned He Jingfu because I wanted to talk about him to everybody. He Jingfu, He Jingfu, He Jingfu . . .

'No, I didn't. But anyway, I've changed my mind. I think Mencius was right, too. Some peoples' natures are good, some bad. Don't you agree?'

Though I was a university teacher and had often discussed the question of human nature and humanism in class, I didn't know how to explain it to a fifteen-year-old. Anyway, I didn't want to argue from a theoretical standpoint, I wanted to know what she felt.

'Hanhan, it's a very confused philosophical problem. You tell me first why you think Mencius was also right.'

'Because I know a good person. A very good person.'

'Who?' Surely she couldn't mean her father?

'Uncle He. Ma, he's really good. He told me I ought to see Daddy. He told me to tell you . . .' She looked me straight in the eye. Had I paled? She said no more.

I understand, Jingfu. You've decided to give up your pursuit. That was what I asked you to do yesterday, and yet today I hope you won't! Your 'twenty-year plan' – is it going to end like this? We both began by losing and we are going to end by losing. What a terrible waste!

I pushed the window open. The sky was full of stars. In the city, stars always seem fainter, they don't stir the imagination; they make you feel that the universe is dark and constricted.

Was it this time yesterday that He Jingfu came? Will he come again today? I'd so love to see him and talk to him. For over twenty years we haven't really talked in a proper way, like friends. We've always been so tense that it hasn't been possible.

Now, everything has passed, really passed. Now, we can really talk, like friends, close friends.

He Jingfu, when I was with Zhao Zhenhuan and when I was trying to extricate myself from Xu Hengzhong, did you misunderstand me? You could well have thought that all I wanted was a home. But it wasn't like that. I think I'm searching for something noble, pure. And that's why I suffer so many setbacks and miseries. I feel sorry for myself and worried about my future, but I do fundamentally believe in myself. I don't resent what's happened in my life, or mistrust life, but what I do resent are the simple-minded and childish views society has of me, and what I mistrust are my own attitude and my understanding of life. Mistrust can mean loss of hope; or it can bring about decisions.

Life hasn't been as lovely as I'd imagined it would. But it hasn't been as frightening, either. Life is life and its strength lies in its being full of contradictions and uncertainties. It both swallows and forges spirits. I've tasted the bitterness of life, but in the midst of bitterness I've tasted sweetness.

Have you read Shakespeare's *The Tempest*? Shakespeare saw

life as full of the struggle between beauty and ugliness, good and evil; and out of that struggle come all sorts of beautiful spirits and hideous and evil demons. The greatest of all creations is the master of all human and magical skills: he symbolises human perfection. In the conflict between good and evil, he demonstrates man's strength and faith. He can stir up a storm, wrecking the king's ship; and he can quell the storm in a second. All the beautiful things on the earth cluster round him. He keeps a grasp on history, controls the present and creates the future, he fosters good and suppresses evil, he destroys hate and nourishes love.

In sum this symbolic figure teaches humanity one thing: Man decides the destiny of everything. That is the crystallisation of Shakespeare's lifelong quest. Only those who've spent a lifetime in search of something can understand it.

I understand it because I've always been searching. I've stumbled time after time, but I've learnt how to think.

The power of destiny seems enormously strong; it can do what it likes with people. How many brilliant people, famous people, have been tossed about by it? It has caused many to be forgotten, wiped out. But isn't that because they lacked self-awareness and self-confidence? If we were to take power into our hands, wouldn't we regain control of our destinies?

I'm not going to look at my shadow and lament my fate any more, or blame everything and everybody except myself. I'm going to make the past into nourishment for the present, and make my misery a source of wisdom. I don't want to cover up my wounds with ointment and I don't want to forget the past or treat it lightly. But I know that misery is like all other feelings, it can be elevated. It can become art, philosophy or faith. Though I've lost my youth and I've lost my love, I haven't lost everything. I've held on to the ashes of my enthusiasm and they still glow enough to warm me and light the way.

Jingfu, you always said that a person shouldn't wait but should act and create. You're right. Now I want to create, I want to create with you. I've lived, I've thought, and there must be a harvest. Even if it's only weeds or brambles, at least I will have made it. I've always wanted to be a writer, but for the first half of my life I've just been a student and teacher of literature. I've always ridiculed myself, thought my ambitions greater than my ability, my ideas beyond my capabilities. Now I finally see that I never really lived, thought, suffered or enjoyed anything independently. I've paid the price for it, and what a price! But the future harvest could be great, too – it can and it should. As long as I still breathe I shall continue to demand things of life. Jingfu, life has oppressed us – can we live with this oppression?

Is there someone out there? Is it you? You haven't come back to encourage me to forgive Zhao Zhenhuan, have you? Do you want us to reconcile our differences? Don't come, don't talk about that again. I myself can forget what needs to be forgotten and remember what needs to be remembered. You must see that the more you try to persuade me, the harder it is for me to forgive.

When I stop being miserable about losing you, then I'll be able to forgive Zhao Zhenhuan. You may be able to separate the two, I can't.

But when *will* I stop being miserable about losing you? My love for you has gone way beyond what I intended because it's not just the simple love between a man and a woman, it's the crystallisation of all the suffering I went through before and what I learnt from it. That makes it very precious, and I don't want people to ridicule it or trample on it. Did Zhao Zhenhuan think of that? All he wants is to recover his soul, he doesn't realise that you and I need spiritual tranquility. All he seemed to want to do was to remove himself from my life and leave you and me with a 'pure land'[15]. You took his repentance seriously but I can't forgive his selfishness. He needs understanding and friendship; did he ever give them to me?

Poor Hanhan, what is she doing? Writing a letter?

You seem to be standing not far away from our window. The light of the stars is so faint, I can't see your face clearly. I'd love to rush out to you and tell you that your love is buried forever in my heart. Buried love is the most free. It has cast off formality, whereas marriage is nothing but a formality uniting men and women.

We'll be real friends from now on; I'll never feel uncomfortable in your presence again. From now on I can help you and support you without fear, because we'll simply be friends.

Jingfu! Have you gone back home? If I could become a star, I'd shoot through the window, follow you and lodge myself in your chest.

He's gone. I can't see him any more. Was it him?

'Ma, can I have an envelope?'

So she was writing a letter. To whom? Unwillingly, I left the window to give her an envelope.

'Can I have a stamp?'

If she won't tell me who she's writing to, it must be Zhao Zhenhuan. Let her have a stamp.

From now on, a faint line will be drawn between us. The more it is drawn, the stronger it becomes. Hanhan will draw. Zhao Zhenhuan will draw too and there's He Jingfu, he can help. There are two things I'll have to hide: my fury against Zhao Zhenhuan and my love for He Jingfu. Hanhan, I do understand. And I hope you understand me.

PART FOUR

The sun comes out in the east, it rains in the west; clear here, not so clear there.

TWENTY-TWO

XI LIU

Now that it's all come out in the open, things are getting more and more uncertain.

I'm sure this sort of thing will bring about another anti-rightist struggle. It's all because of this book, *Marxism and Humanism*.

Humanism! Humanism! It's been criticised again and again over the last thirty years but it hasn't been defeated. Is it surprising? This He Jingfu became a rightist twenty years ago when he preached humanism and opposed the Party line on class struggle. He still hasn't learnt, he's got worse. If we hadn't found out about the book in time, it would have been published. It's all thanks to Yuli. She told me about it. All I knew was that he was writing a book, because Xi Wang had said so. I hadn't realised it would be ready for publication so soon. The publishing house has moved very fast. I wonder if the editor has some connection with He Jingfu?

'Where's the editor from?' I asked Chen Yuli.

'I think he's from Hebei province.'

Then he probably doesn't know He Jingfu. He Jingfu certainly isn't from the north.

'Is there anyone in the publishing house who knows He Jingfu?'

'I don't think so,' she said. 'No, there is. The person editing his book is a graduate of the university. He was criticised in 1957, I don't know what for.'

They always find each other, people like that. But what is the

Party committee in the publishing house thinking of? Why don't they do something?

You Ruoshui is a very quick worker. I asked him to write a report on the book the day before yesterday and he's already finished. According to his report, *Marxism and Humanism* is clearly revisionist:

'He denies that class struggle in socialist society is of long duration, acute and complex; he opposes the fact that class struggle is a key link. Surely this is the fundamental question? If we aren't going to grasp class struggle as a key link, what are we Party members supposed to do?'

'I can't read his writing, Yuli. You read it to me. How does he oppose class struggle?'

Chen Yuli can be terribly annoying. As soon as I get home, she fills me with tonics, silver wood-ear fungus and deer horn. Her revolutionary determination is weak. If we don't grasp class struggle, will we still be able to afford to eat wood-ear fungus and deer horn?

She read a quotation from He Jingfu's book:

What are the class conditions in socialist society? It's time we ana-lysed them by 'seeking truth from facts'. Broadening class struggle, saying that every contradiction is a 'class contradiction', deliber-ately creating class struggle, all of these have greatly harmed our country. Peasants can't understand how, thirty years after liber-ation, the enemy can still be increasing in numbers!

What kind of talk is this? He's negating all the political movements since Liberation! What he's saying is that not only have we done nothing good these last thirty years, we've actually been doing harm. Was the campaign against counter-revolutionaries wrong? Was the Anti-Rightist Movement wrong? Was it wrong to expel the 'Gang of Four' from the Party? The essence of Marxist doctrine is class struggle. Are we supposed to reject that?

'Underline that bit in red for me. I'll read it at the Party meeting tomorrow. Let everyone hear it and see if they still want it published!' I ordered Chen Yuli.

'Father!'

Is that Xi Wang? What has brought him back here? Didn't he say he wanted nothing more to do with me? I gave him a cold look and paid him no attention. Chen Yuli looked at him.

'Nanny said you hadn't been terribly well, Father.' His attitude was different, much friendlier. Had he realised that he'd been wrong? That would be fine. It's hard to condemn your own flesh and blood. I pointed at the sofa, indicating that he should sit down, and said:

'You know all those beatings I got; whenever the weather is damp, the scars give me trouble. It's been worse recently.'

'I know. I've brought you some medicinal herbs. He Jingfu says they're very good. When he was away he learnt a bit about it – he's almost as good as a doctor.'

What a 'humanist' He Jingfu is! How kind he is to do a little bit of good to humanity! But he's writing books on the sly. Xi Wang can talk about 'humanism' but I don't see He Jingfu's poisonous medicine as 'humanism'. It's up to me to deal with this.

'Are you still friendly with He Jingfu?' I asked him.

He looked at me, hesitated and said, 'I suppose so.'

'Did you know the book he wrote is due to appear soon?'

He looked at me, still hesitant, 'I heard something about it. I don't know any details.'

Was he protecting He Jingfu? He had more faith in He Jingfu than in me. Though ours wasn't the Confucian ideal of a father-son relationship, I still thought I'd encourage him to see less of the man. He's the sort who seems good, but when the circumstances are right he can stir up trouble. I held out You Ruoshui's report to Xi Wang but Chen Yuli stopped me and put it in her handbag.

'Xi Wang, your father's health is getting worse and we've been relying on these expensive tonics.' Chen Yuli got out box after box to show him and he took them with a slightly mocking smile, his eyes never leaving her face as if he was watching her perform conjuring tricks. She kept on chattering: 'We spend almost all our joint salaries on them, but we could spare you a little more pocket money. Students are different nowadays, they want new clothes and more books, they're more extravagant than we wage-earners. That's why people are having smaller families.'

'Don't worry, I've got enough money,' Xi Wang said after she'd put all the tonics away.

I frowned at her, to make her stop fussing. Xi Wang was being more polite to her today, she ought to respond in kind.

'Have you read He Jingfu's manuscript? Did you see any problems in it?' I asked carefully. Why was Chen Yuli wrinkling her nose at me? Women comrades are complicated. She doesn't really care much about him because he's not her own child.

'I haven't read all of it. What I saw, I thought was all right. I'm not really sure what humanism is so I can't say whether I approve or disapprove. Do you find problems in it?'

His attitude had changed, he seemed to have learnt something. Had he been rebuffed? Had he thought it out himself? The young need guidance, especially when their ideology wavers. I have to admit that Chen Yuli hinders me in my attempts to teach the boy. It's the father's fault if the child won't learn.

'You're right,' I said to him with satisfaction. 'Chairman Mao taught us: "Party members ought to question everything and think things out for themselves; consider whether things are right or wrong, whether they are moral; they mustn't follow blindly and they mustn't uphold slave mentality." To approve of humanism while not knowing what it is is ridiculous. But young people tend to follow blindly. You're beginning to realise that, which is good.'

Xi Wang listened patiently and then said, 'You're right. I tend to think I know everything, to think I understand Marxism-Leninism, but I don't. I haven't really learnt from you and Chen Yuli. What is humanism anyway? Tell me.'

What is humanism? We've criticised it for so long, don't you students know what it is? But I could see he really didn't know, and wanted me to explain. I couldn't.

What is humanism? I thought about how to answer him. I could usually remember, why couldn't I think of an answer now? Did it say in the book? I couldn't think. Xi Wang was watching me, waiting. Ah, I suddenly thought –

'Chen Yuli, give me You Ruoshui's material. It explains it very clearly.'

She looked at me doubtfully, and glanced at Xi Wang. I waved my hand impatiently and she gave me the papers.

You Ruoshui was very clear. He Jingfu praised humanism: 'First he negates the doctrine of class and class struggle, and proposes class reconciliation. Second, he proposes abstract freedom, equality and brotherhood, which in practice means he wants us to love our enemies. Thirdly, he talks about human nature and human feelings in the abstract, opposing the class analysis of individuals. Fourthly, he praises individualism and the liberation of the individual.' I read out each point and Xi Wang listened carefully, writing it all down in a small notebook.

'You can see how dangerous it is. We've criticised it all before,' I said.

As I spoke, he nodded. 'It didn't seem like that when I read it. Has it been changed? I thought it only criticised the broadening of class struggle. How has it changed into an attack on the doctrine of class struggle?'

I gave him the bit that Chen Yuli had just read out to me and he noted it down. He flipped through the material and stopped at one point to ask me, 'Have you read all this?'

'No, I've only got to the fourth point. You read out the important bits,' I said.

He read:

We must respect people, respect their individuality and cultivate and strengthen their dignity.

I consider that in our society today, people's self-esteem is too weak. Thousands of years of feudal ideology have gradually forced us to be the sort of people who don't value thinkers, who can't appreciate individual opinions, who don't want to develop their own individuality. It seems as if the value of an individual's life does not lie in that which he can offer, as an individual, to society, but rather in what he doesn't offer, in the submersion of his individuality into the general. Yet life is so bland without individuality. Fortunately, there have been people who weren't happy under those circumstances, who didn't succumb to that outworn attitude. They stood out, they became individuals, innovative and independent. They moved people, stirred things up and pushed history forward. Wasn't the generation of revolutionaries made up of individuals like that? They command our respect, and isn't it because under the circumstances in which they found themselves, they most notably demonstrated man's worth? Because of them, we must give our unqualified approval to individuality. We must encourage our friends to value individuality, to cultivate it.

At this point, Xi Wang stopped reading and looked at me. I just couldn't believe a Party member could have written this. Value individuality? Party members must be the tools of the Party. If everybody wanted his own point of view, his own individuality, how could we carry out the Party line? Each blowing his own bugle and singing his own tune? And at the worst time . . .

'Read it again!'

Xi Wang read it again and I listened carefully. It was stirring up anarchy and counter-revolution.

'Isn't this confused ideology the corruption of the bourgeoisie?' I asked him.

'During the Bourgeois Revolutionary period, ideas of individual liberation were often raised to counteract feudalism,' Xi Wang replied.

'And does He Jingfu approve of individual liberation?'

'That's what it says.'

Humph! Making socialism into feudalism, making Yan'an into Xi'an. So what's new about that? Does the problem of individual liberation still exist in socialist society?

'And how far does He Jingfu want our individual liberties to go? Does he want to turn us into bourgeois?' I asked, unable to keep my voice down.

'Father! I've only read one passage,' Xi Wang said, and went on reading:

As I wrote that, I seemed to hear a voice saying, 'Watch out! You've reached a danger point. You've become a mouthpiece of the bourgeoisie.'

So he can see it himself. Let's see what he says next. 'Read on!'

Friends, wait a moment. I know that I've been influenced by

bourgeois humanism. But I'm going to hand that bourgeois humanism back to you. Bourgeois humanism only allows for the liberation of a few; the majority have to sacrifice themselves for the few and lead the life of animals. Of course this is sham humanism. But there is another humanism, Marxist humanism, which wants to liberate all mankind, which wants each person to become a free individual. Re-read Marx and Engels: 'In socialist society, nobody is circumscribed, everyone can develop in whatever field they like. Society regulates production, so we are all free to follow our inclinations, to do this today, that tomorrow; to hunt in the morning, fish in the afternoon. In the evening, after supper, you can debate. None of this makes a person a hunter, a fisherman or a debator.' What a wonderful world! There, every man is the master of his own destiny. Friends, don't you see that Marxism gives humanism its most fundamental, most revolutionary significance? Don't you see that in order to achieve the ideal state of communism, we must destroy everything that oppresses human nature, that we must sweep away the feudal remnants that stifle individualism? You can't believe that it's beneficial, or that it's too difficult to get rid of it?

Xi Wang laughed and said, 'That's interesting!' I don't know what he meant. I could see that arrogant He Jingfu cocking a snook at me. He says he's a bourgeois and then he puts a feudalist's hat on me. Anti-feudalism becomes fashionable. When we attacked the gentry, wasn't that anti-feudal? Does he mean that in our sacrifice of an entire generation, we didn't even destroy feudalism? He's mad!

'Father, what are you going to do? Are you going to forbid publication?' Xi Wang flipped through the pages again and handed them back to me.

'Something will have to be done,' I replied, though I had no concrete ideas. All I would do was take it to the Party meeting for discussion and see what the Party view was.

'I think it would be better to let them publish. When it's published, you can criticise it. If you're right, you've nothing to fear!'

He was still a child. Could we allow such things to be published? That would be like a child firing a gun, creating havoc for fun. The policy of 'letting a hundred flowers bloom and a thousand schools of thought contend' was a proletarian policy, it didn't mean allowing bourgeois freedom. If it was published and created a bad impression, it wouldn't just be He Jingfu's problem, it would be a problem for the whole university and the responsibility would be placed with the Party committee. I shook my head and said to Xi Wang, 'How could that work?'

Chen Yuli had been sitting and listening to us. She was looking at Xi Wang as if he was a complete stranger, probably because his attitude today made her think he had changed. Now she smiled and joined the conversation:

'Xi Wang, did you know that this book has provoked fierce arguments in the publishing house? One friend who works there said to me, "Heavens, it's a very brave book! If he'd published it twenty years ago, he'd have been branded a rightist." A lot of people don't think it ought to be published, though the chief editor wants to do it. He approves of the person who's editing it, but then he's also a rightist.'

Xi Wang smiled at her, and she went on, more excitedly, 'My friend said that if he'd received the manuscript, he'd have rejected it; otherwise, he'd have been held responsible if any problems had arisen. When I heard that, I thought I ought to ask a few other people in the university about it. It's a very serious problem.'

Xi Wang nodded at her and then turned to me, and said, 'Father, don't you think it's the publishing house's problem?'

It had never occurred before. In the past, the publishing house had always asked the opinion of the Party committee in the relevant department. This time, they hadn't asked our view, nor had they carried out any political investigation into the author. It was a real muddle. Still . . .

'We can take the initiative and tell the publishing house what we think. They'll have to take us seriously. Yuli, ring up the editor, I'd like to have a talk with him first.'

Chen Yuli shook her head and said, 'Do you think it's wise? You shouldn't act on this sort of matter on your own. Leave it to the collective leadership of the Party committee.'

She was right, I ought to rely on the collective. The lessons of recent years had been painful. Things got stirred up, people fought; then there was trouble and everybody retreated. Sometimes they turned on those they'd sided with. Hadn't You Ruoshui's slogan been 'Be prepared to attack former allies according to the circumstances'? It was difficult to resist the first blow. If I was to turn on former allies, whom would I attack? This time, I must let the Party discuss it, let everybody express an opinion.

'Let's wait till it's been discussed. Xi Wang, tell me what your fellow students are thinking these days. Are they still as confused as ever? Are they still covering the blackboards with love poems?'

'From your point of view, of course they're muddle-headed. But there aren't that many love poems. And of course I've got my ideas but I can't discuss them with you. We're too far apart. Though your slogans are Marxist, you seem to me to be wearing a long gown and mandarin jacket with peacock feathers swaying on your hat. It's pathetic.'

'So your sudden concern was just put on?' I said, surprised and angry. Xi Wang looked at me, leapt up and made for the door. I was furious. 'Where did you learn to be so two-faced?'

'I learn to be two-faced! You ought to consider your own actions! You'll put your hand to anything to stop the movement of history. You don't just meddle, you use your own power to accuse others and to use them. Is your behaviour open and above board? I hope you aren't going to meddle any further, you'll only make a fool of yourself!'

'Get the bloody hell out of here!' I shouted.

'Okay, Father. I did in fact only come here today to see how you were. He Jingfu is always telling me to come and see you. But obviously my ideas are of no use to you. Still, it wasn't a wasted visit: I've heard your enlightened views and I've seen your material. Without meaning to, I've been acting like a KGB agent – thanks!'

He left. My peace of mind was shattered. He Jingfu wanted him to see me, to help me? What kind of man does he think I am? Backward? Pitiful? They have an inflated view of themselves, those two!

'I tried to tell you not to give him the material! You always trust your precious baby boy! He's obviously going to tell He Jingfu. If He Jingfu gets panicky, he may well withdraw his manuscript himself, and all our efforts will have been in vain!' Chen Yuli chattered on at me, her mouth working.

That's a real woman's opinion. If He Jingfu did get in a panic and withdraw his manuscript, I'd be overjoyed. I was afraid he'd find some other method of joining battle with me. Those young people have all become very crafty. They've all become politicians, even Xi Wang.

'Don't worry, it'll all be settled tomorrow at the Party meeting. Isn't the food ready yet?'

'Not quite. Nanny is getting old and slow. We waste such a lot of money on her, nobody else would.'

'We are practising revolutionary humanism. She's got no one else.'

'I don't believe in this humanism. I'm just like the young people, I believe mutual usefulness is the basis for human relations. She's only here because she's got no one else. If she had, she'd have left us long ago.'

Humanism! Humanism! Though we've criticised it so often, people still want to talk about it. Everybody loves everybody else, everyone is equal, they don't want too much class struggle, they want everything to be harmonious. I don't want to attack people but they want to attack me. People! People! That's how they all are! They fight all day and get nowhere, but if they don't fight, they aren't happy!

Nanny brought the food in eventually. She certainly is old. She can't really manage the housework, it's no wonder Chen Yuli complains. But it's not really my business.

'From now on, you run the house. But you must take care of Nanny. She worked for years for no wages; we ought to repay her.'

Chen Yuli nodded and smiled. Nanny had no children, where would she go? My back aches, I can't look after everything. Let Chen Yuli take care of things.

TWENTY-THREE

SUN YUE

Why did it have to come to this?

I never imagined that the first time I went to his home, it would be to talk about this.

'Jingfu, you can't publish your book; that's a Party committee decision.' What would he think? What would he say? I knew he hadn't written it to make a name for himself. He'd written it out of idealism, he'd written about what he'd learnt of humanity during the past twenty years.

Because of my own pride, I'd never asked about the book and its publication, but I knew a little. I had two voluntary informants; one was Xu Hengzhong. He was always trying to get me to tell He Jingfu not to do such a rash thing: 'Old He doesn't know about the struggles during those years, it's blind enthusiasm on his part. I know there'll be a time when things change and when the interpretation of the past is altered.'

There was another, 'the writer'. He isn't very dynamic but he's the best informed source amongst our fellow-students, particularly about the world of culture and publishing. He's often told me about the arguments and the effect on the publishing house of this particular book. When the manuscript was sent to the compositor, he came rushing to see me with great glee – 'Sun Yue, let's have a drink! I've got good news!' – just as if it were his own book. He said, with feeling, 'I don't have Old He's courage, I've been ineffective all my life. I've become China's Oblomov.[16] Perhaps it's because I've always slept peacefully. I'm cultivated but poor, and I've always had a job. It's always been like that. I think it's better to be poor, though I'm afraid of the taste of poverty.' I gave him a glass of wine and had a good laugh with him. When I'm happy, I want to enjoy myself with people.

But who would have thought it would come to this? A publishing house decides to publish a book and a university Party secretary manages to stop publication? Shouldn't we talk about legality? Shouldn't we discuss principles?

'We have to stop it. We have to do it to protect He Jingfu. He mustn't lose his head, he can't think that any sort of revisionist rubbish will pass these days.'

That was what Xi Liu said in the Party committee meeting. I don't really know all the ins and outs of it but I do know he started the whole thing, though the person who introduced the question at the meeting was You Ruoshui. Just as it was about to end, he said, 'Comrade Xi Liu; there's a problem I think the Party should investigate. It isn't necessary for all the departmental Party secretaries to participate but Comrade Sun Yue of the Literature Department ought to stay.'

Xi Liu immediately nodded in agreement without asking what it was about or whether it was necessary to bring it up at a Party meeting. It obviously wasn't the first time he'd discussed it.

Of course I stayed to discuss this 'matter' which I hadn't heard anything about. To begin with, You Ruoshui brought out a mass of notes and listed the revisionist points he'd discovered in *Marxism and Humanism*, one, two, three, four, five . . .

'The most important and most dangerously revisionist point of view is where he says that there is no contradiction between Marxism and humanism, that they are interlinked. This is an emasculation of the Marxist doctrine of class and class struggle,' he said.

He wouldn't elaborate on why He Jingfu said Marxism and humanism were interlinked or what he saw in humanism. But I knew. He Jingfu's humanism was the complete liberation of all mankind. It meant not just the liberation of people from class oppression, but their liberation from spiritual fetters, from superstition, from blindness, and he wanted them to rise above their animal nature. He opposed the idea of class struggle as an aim, he opposed the broadening of class struggle under socialism because it created splits and suffering amongst the people. He thought that there ought to be more democracy under socialism, more freedom and equality. He wanted everyone to feel not just physically but also spiritually human, to value their power and individuality. Wasn't this right?

But You Ruoshui saw it all as revisionism: 'It's very simple. We Marxists have all criticised these points of view. And not just during the Cultural Revolution, we've criticised them for years – at times when the Party line was correct.'

I don't know if logic is considered a science, but it's very simple: Good times – Cultural Revolution – now; all right – not all right – all right. Three simple stages. Hegel is alive and living in China!

When You Ruoshui spoke, his pale face became red and his bald head glistened. He looked fixedly at Xi Liu though Xi Liu never looked at him. Instead, he looked at everyone else in turn, and finally his eyes rested on me and stayed there for a long time.

When You Ruoshui had finished, he put all his papers in his pocket. Xi Liu tore his eyes away from me, looked round the room and said calmly: 'We didn't know that the book was going to appear. If Comrade You Ruoshui hadn't heard the news from the individuals concerned and set out to investigate the matter, it would have been published without our knowledge.'

What was You Ruoshui up to? I had my suspicions.

'Comrade Sun Yue; did the Literature Department know about this book?'

I replied immediately: 'I knew.'

'Why didn't you say anything?' Xi Liu asked.

'It's a matter for the publishing house to decide. We have no power to intervene. He Jingfu is free to publish,' I said.

Xi Liu's cheekbones became frighteningly prominent, and he turned to the others. 'Is that how it is? Let's discuss it. Is the policy of "let a hundred flowers bloom and a thousand schools of thought contend" intended to allow bourgeois freedom? Does the Party intend to lead or not?'

How clear the river is today! Clear, with no fish visible. There

are no fish in the water because fish like muddy water. And
people? Do people like muddy water? It's a clear pool, do we
have to throw stones, mud and grass in to make it murky?

The oldest member of the Party committee spoke first. His
hair was as white as flax. He had a good heart; his eyes were
truthful and candid. In those 'turbulent years', I'd protected him
and, like a daughter, poured out my troubles to him. He always
used to comfort me, 'You're still young, it'll get better.' I
respected him very much.

'According to precedent, when the publishing house is going
to put out a book, they should contact the relevant department
and that way we all know about it. Now things have got to this
stage, we ought to find an amicable settlement. The writer is a
young man; let's settle the matter by persuasion and education
and ask him to correct the manuscript before publication. I think
his opinions are mistaken, we've criticised them many times
before. In the rectification of 1942 . . .'

I knew he was going to talk about the 'origins and development
of the criticism of humanism and human nature' from the time of
Pan Gu, the creator of the universe and the three sage rulers and
the five emperors. In the Cultural Revolution, every time there
was a meeting to criticise him, he always talked about ancient
history: the rectification of 1942 and the struggles against people
long dead and forgotten. He would always look at the Red
Guards with his truthful, candid eyes and say, 'I've never been a
revisionist. I've learnt from the Party over a long period, from
the rectification of '42 . . .' The Guards called him a 'stinking
exemplar', cursed him, slandered and laughed at him; but he
never acknowledged that he'd ever been a revisionist. For that,
I admired him even more. Over the last couple of years, however,
I'd felt distant. Life moves on but he was the same as he'd been
ten years ago, decades ago, always sitting as he did in the meeting
today, like a statue, always saying the same thing. You can admire
him but you can't discuss real problems with him. 'Little Sun,
don't rock the boat, we mustn't let this state of confusion drag
on. We Party members must take care of it. In 1942 . . .' When
I heard him mention 1942, my heart sank and I would have liked
to kick him. But I didn't.

'Things are different now. We don't normally expect publishing houses to make political investigations into writers but in the case of this particular book, they ought to have been more careful.'

That was a member of the Party committee of the secretariat of the Philosophy Department, a professional like me. As far as I knew, he was fairly liberated in his ideas; but had he been frightened by this 'particular person' and this 'particular book'?

'What is He Jingfu's attitude like within the department? Can we hear some opinions?' a woman committee member asked.

I said, 'Very good,' but inside I was thinking: how should this particular book and this particular person be understood? How far can we exercise our power in this 'particular case'? Anyone could present a 'particular case', anyone could discover that there were grounds for interference. Nobody is perfect, no gold is pure gold. This 'particular case', that 'particular case' . . . it's so difficult to control.

Perhaps I ought to tell them something about He Jingfu? I was afraid of talking about him there, I couldn't even think of him calmly. He'd not been to see me since Zhao Zhenhuan's visit. If we bumped into each other, we nodded and said hello, not a word more. I was finding it hard to bear: the distance between us was growing. I spoke of him more and more to friends, especially to Li Yining, and she always said: 'I don't want to see you hurt again. He Jingfu can't bring you peace of mind. You shouldn't marry him.'

It was true, He Jingfu wouldn't bring me peace of mind, yet perhaps it was precisely that that I found attractive. I'd already let him battle alone in the wind and rain; if the same sort of storm broke over him again, could I leave him to struggle alone? Could I find peace of mind that way?

'I've heard some opinions on He Jingfu; may I speak?' It was Chen Yuli who was taking notes of the meeting. Xi Liu nodded and she began:

'Ever since He Jingfu's case was re-examined and he was allowed back, he's been very over-confident. He often tells the students about his experiences and makes himself into a sort of fairy tale hero, and this influences the young people around him. He's always saying, "The Party ought to summarise the lessons that have been learnt," and what he means by that is that he has always been right and the Party has made mistakes; that he's brighter than the Party yet the Party has treated him shabbily. His book is propaganda in praise of the individual, and that's the sort of thing he's preaching to the students – the wave of anarchy in the Literature Department has a lot to do with him. Not long ago, Comrade Xi Liu criticised the students for writing love poems on the blackboards and a group of them made fun of the whole thing; that's also got something to do with He Jingfu. There are still students who ridicule Comrade Xi Liu, they've said they want him to be advisor to a Buddhist Association . . .'

Who sniggered? Was it that old lady and the professor next to her? He was a member of the standing committee and a professor in the History Department. He was the only professor on the Party committee so we all simply called him 'Professor'. He had his pipe in his mouth and was saying something funny to the woman next to him at which they both smiled. Xi Liu's face went red. He rapped the table with his fountain pen and ordered Chen Yuli, 'Come to the point!'

Chen Yuli realised that she'd lost her thread and blushed. She pulled herself together and pitched her voice higher: 'In summary, He Jingfu has failed to show himself worthy of the love and concern of the Party; he's continued to slip further and further along the road he took in 1957. Heaven knows where he will end up unless we help him soon. As for his personal life, I'd rather not discuss that here.'

With those last words, she looked meaningfully at me. I felt hot all over and my face went red. They say that if you've done something you shouldn't, the midnight knock at the door comes as no surprise. I'm not like that, I can blush when I'm completely guiltless, my heart can pound. Sometimes on a bus when someone's lost their purse and they are going to stop the bus and search for it, I get terribly nervous and terrified that they'll suddenly find the purse on me. Is this a neurosis developed from the irrational procedures of 'class struggle'? It's even more likely to happen over emotional issues. As soon as He Jingfu's private life was mentioned, I felt as if someone had thrown a bucketful of dirty water over me, and I couldn't stop my blushes.

Oh, Chen Yuli can speak beautifully! She's given them a 'particular case' – He Jingfu. If I wasn't in the Literature Department, if I didn't know He Jingfu, her speech could easily have given me a bad impression of him. I realised that people discriminated against those who held different views and this was the method they used: in front of people who didn't know the person, they said bad things, they used rumour and slander when the person couldn't explain himself. But I understood He Jingfu and I loved him. With every movement of Chen Yuli's pretty mouth, another He Jingfu appeared before me, an admirable, dear and lovable vagrant, my best, closest and most estranged friend.

Jingfu, I can't sit silent and listen to other people defile you. I can't let these comrades who don't know you retain a false image. I mustn't fear an explosion of my own feelings, I mustn't be afraid. It seems as if I've been waiting for this opportunity to announce my love for you publicly. I must speak.

I stood up, but before I could open my mouth another committee member spoke abruptly: 'If that is true, then we can't let him publish his book!' Someone else said, with more enthusiasm, 'If I had the power, I'd put the rightist hat back on his head. I've still got my doubts about his rehabilitation.'

I sat down again, remembering that I was in a Party meeting. My position was Party Secretary of the Chinese Literature Department and the subject under discussion was the question of how to deal with a person who'd written a book, not my relationship with He Jingfu.

'We must make education our main method. The Party's policy towards those who make mistakes has always been "to learn from past errors and to cure the disease to save the patient". In the rectification of '42 . . .'

I was touched by the goodness of the white-haired old man, but he never got the point.

I hoped the professor would say something. He was an honest and humorous man, unexceptional-looking though his humour gave him a certain fascination. He didn't often talk in Party meetings, perhaps because he thought that as the only professor on the committee, it was better to appear modest. He had a relaxed way of smoking his pipe. His house was full of pipes.

During the Cultural Revolution they were all confiscated, but he'd found ways of using bits of cardboard and parts of mosquito coil boxes to make his own. They were beautifully done and worked perfectly, and he made quite a few for pipe-smoking friends. People used to laugh at him and say, 'If you ever lose your job, you can always sell your handicrafts!'

His lips finally left the pipe-stem and he coughed lightly to show that he wanted to speak. He smiled before beginning: 'I've got a very confused impression from listening to Comrade Chen Yuli. On the one hand there's this over-confident chap and on the other there's this person who is immensely popular with the students. Friends, it's not easy to become popular with students. Of course we could argue that he's played upon their childish innocence, but you try it! I've been teaching for years, I'm in direct contact with students and I know that they aren't easily taken advantage of. They've got brains. If they're willing to be close to someone and to admire him, that shows he's got something we haven't got. For this reason, I fear He Jingfu won't be easily stopped. And if he really is as Comrade Chen Yuli says he is, I'm afraid it's not just a question of publishing a book.'

'He's saying the Party is wrong!' someone said, very agitated.

The professor puffed at his pipe. 'Can anyone say the Party has never made a mistake?'

The professor's intervention displeased Xi Liu, though he didn't say anything. He just looked from face to face, obviously hoping that someone would contradict the professor, who nudged the woman next to him. She smiled and nodded. Another of the most senior members of the committee, she was fair, elegant and pretty, not at all like a woman of sixty. I'd heard that she'd been an outstanding student at Beijing Normal College but had been expelled as a troublemaker. Since joining the revolution, she'd always done Party work and was head of the Party Propaganda Department.

'I've been wondering about something: shouldn't the committee discuss its criteria for judging this issue? We've been talking for quite a while . . .'

Xi Liu interrupted: 'Why do you raise this point?'

'What's the point of discussing criteria? Isn't practice the sole criterion for judging the truth? I think you've got ulterior motives; the target of attack is perfectly clear.' That was the person who wanted to put the rightist hat back on He Jingfu's head.

'We don't have to direct spearheads at everything,' the professor answered, smiling. 'We've already used up all our iron making such spears.'

'Look, two comrades have just expressed very different opinions. That shows we have to discuss the problem,' said the head of the Propaganda Department. 'If the Party can't investigate and make a decision about such an important question, then I'll have to resign.'

'We'll discuss criteria later, let's first hear your opinion on the He Jingfu problem,' Xi Liu interrupted her.

'Fine! I think that practice shows our most serious task is to oppose feudal remnants. I approve of He Jingfu's views and I think it is illegal for the Party to interfere with the publication of his book. That's all.' She explained her view simply and clearly and then whispered something to the professor.

'Does anyone else have anything to say?' asked Xi Liu; from his expression it was obvious he wanted to end the discussion. Finally, his eyes sweeping over our faces, he said, 'If there's nothing new to add, then we must make a decision. Two comrades think the book should be published. Does anyone else?'

'I do. I don't know anything about it, but I think that as there's a Party committee at the publishing house, we should trust it. We should abide by organisational principles.' This was the head of the Organisation Department. Xi Liu looked through him.

There were still a few people who hadn't said anything. I glanced at them one by one, but I knew they wouldn't say anything. They never said anything. Their only value was in voting but that couldn't be overlooked. Xi Liu relied on it. At this moment, they were models of indifference. They were as placid as kindergarten children who have been led to the gate of the park to enjoy the sun. I looked at them beseechingly, hoping that they would express a sober and fair opinion. It didn't just concern a person and a book, it concerned the implementation of Party policy. But each one of them avoided my eyes and stayed silent. It made me feel cold: now that a shoot was emerging from the ground with two tender leaves sprouting from it, how could they remain so cool and dumb?

'No one else approves? Then . . .'

I didn't wait for Xi Liu to finish, but stood up suddenly. He stopped and looked at me with surprise. After a moment, he asked, 'What is your opinion?'

'I don't think we can treat a person or a book so carelessly. This is a Party meeting and we ought to implement the Party's policy.' I was very agitated and my voice was shaking.

'And what do you think we should do?' Xi Liu asked impatiently.

'I think that some of the opinions just expressed about He Jingfu and his book are wrong.'

I couldn't get my ideas in order, I simply said what came into my head and I talked for a long time. What did I really say? I can't remember now. I can usually recall every word of what I've said or what I've written in a letter, but not this time. I probably talked in detail about my understanding of He Jingfu. But did I make it sound right? Chen Yuli laughed up her sleeve. Some people have very odd feelings and ideas; they can tolerate hatred between people and think it's quite normal, but they can't abide that people should love each other. They think that's abnormal. They can accept illicit relations between men and women but they can't bear real love. Let her laugh! If I've managed to convey the truth then I shall have no regrets. I also spoke about agreeing with He Jingfu's views and, yes, I asked You Ruoshui if he could tell us what revisionism was. He shrugged his shoulders and said, smiling, 'I don't think the question is worth answering.' I asked Xi Liu what he meant by revisionism but he also refused to reply, his cheekbones sharp. I knew they couldn't. They can't explain clearly what Marxism-Leninism is so how can they know what revisionism is?

The professor and the woman comrade who was head of the Propaganda Department approved of my speech. The others didn't react. They all looked at Xi Liu, ready to be led by the rise and fall of his cheekbones, all waiting for his response. It was like kicking a ball into a pile of cotton wool. What was the point? I sat down.

Habit, habit. Is there anything stronger or more powerful than habit? All eyes look up. A person's worth, including the worth of a person's views, all depend upon his position. The words of a prominent man are precious, the words of an obscure man are valueless. It may not be proper, but it's a fact. And facts are more convincing than abstract truths. Yet if these things can't be changed, what can we hope for?

I didn't want to say any more, I just wanted the meeting to end quickly. But Chen Yuli wanted to play a more brilliant part.

'Comrade Sun Yue's speech really surprised me,' she said. 'People who don't know might think there was some personal grievance between me and He Jingfu and that that was why I didn't speak well of him. In fact, I've never disliked He Jingfu, never felt any hatred for him – though I would like to encourage Comrade Sun Yue not to let private feelings of love blind her!'

There was a twitter of muttered comments and everybody turned to me. Of course they all remembered my past relationship with He Jingfu and were very interested in knowing how we stood now, in order to understand the motive for my friendship. I was the focus of searchlights. At first, I was confused, upset and ashamed, because I did love He Jingfu and that feeling had influenced my attitude to him. But I recovered; I asked myself: 'Have you abandoned the Party's basic principles, or got confused about right and wrong, because of your love?' And I answered myself, 'No.'

I stood up and looked directly at Xi Liu. 'Excuse me, Comrade Xi Liu, is the Party committee preparing to discuss my private feelings?' I was quite calm. Xi Liu blushed, as he had blushed earlier. It was unlike him, and I didn't know if it was because he was angry with my attitude or ashamed of what Chen Yuli had said.

'Sit down, Little Sun!' The woman from the Propaganda Department leapt up from her seat. 'Comrade Xi Liu, I am absolutely opposed to the discussion of personal emotions in Party meetings! What right have we to interfere in people's private lives? We are quite capable of judging Comrade Sun Yue's speech on its own merits; what has it got to do with her private feelings?'

If I hadn't made a supreme effort, I'm sure I would have cried. Over the last years, because of the spread of 'class struggle' into every aspect of life, we had hardly had any private life left. To mention 'private emotions' immediately made people think of scandal. Every single person thought he had the right to interfere in other people's private lives, what else was organisation for? Listen:

'Sun Yue has the right to decide her own private affairs but it is not permissible to replace Party principles with emotions,' Xi Liu said.

Had I replaced Party principles with emotions? I wanted to join battle with Xi Liu, to face him and all the party members, to be a Party member myself; I didn't want to hide my opinions, nor did I want to hide my emotions. Some of these people had been my superiors in the past, some had been fellow-students. None of them really understood me and it seemed as if I didn't really understand them. Let them try.

'I'm quite willing to talk about my relationship with He Jingfu at a Party meeting,' I said. 'When he was a student, He Jingfu was in love with me and he still loves me. His love is real, pure, and I feel very fortunate because I also love him. But for all sorts of reasons, I can't marry him and that makes me very sad. Those are my feelings.'

Several people put their heads together. What were they saying? 'What are we discussing this for?' I heard one man ask.

'It's not me that wants to talk about it; Comrade Chen Yuli raised the matter,' I said to him. I knew that he didn't care, he'd said it without thinking. I looked at Xi Liu again: 'I did not protect He Jingfu because of my feelings for him, I was trying to carry out Party policy and the law of the country. Even if He Jingfu's ideas are all wrong, you can't stop him publishing, you can only try and determine what is right or wrong through discussion. And if his ideas are proved wrong, then I'm willing to stand with him and take responsibility. No matter how serious the error is.'

Chen Yuli was laughing up her sleeve again. She's jealous because she's never known that sort of love. What Xi Liu feels for her can't be called love. Sometimes I've felt sorry for her, yet she even uses her pitiable position to harm others. Does that bring her comfort and contentment? If the fox can't reach up to eat the grapes on the trellis, he says they're bitter. That's understandable. But to set fire to the entire trellis so that no one can eat the grapes is unforgivable. I'd like to tell the fox to stop behaving like that.

Finally, Xi Liu could remain patient no longer and he waved his hand to make me sit down. 'We are not going to discuss Sun Yue's personal problems here,' he said. 'I shall summarise. According to the discussion, the majority of comrades do not agree to the publication of He Jingfu's book. The minority will have to bow to the majority, though they may keep their own opinions. Please will Comrade You Ruoshui tell the publishing house of the Party's view. If they don't agree, then the responsibility is entirely theirs. As for He Jingfu, I agree with the opinion raised, that we should rely on education and persuasion. If he'll agree to withdraw the manuscript and make fundamental revisions, we'll be happy. Please will the Party Secretary of the Literature Department carry out detailed and thorough ideological work on him.'

Now I've got to go and do this detailed and thorough ideological work on him. Detailed and thorough!

'Oh, Little Sun! What are you doing here? Come in! Come in! We're just about to eat and there's plenty!'

Why do I have to bump into You Ruoshui? He's just appeared at his doorway. I really can't stand him.

'What a coincidence. You can come along and help me do deep and detailed ideological work on He Jingfu,' I said bitterly.

'I'm rather busy this evening,' he excused himself.

'Then will you give me your material so that I can explain your views to He Jingfu? I didn't take notes at the meeting.'

Again, he excused himself: 'Just give him the simple outline; do it from memory. He'll understand. We haven't really worked on the material, it isn't in a fit state to be shown to anyone.'

'You mean you discussed half-formed opinions at a Party meeting? The committee made its decision on the basis of your 'unworked-out' researches? I can't believe you think it isn't important to prepare carefully for a Party meeting?'

His white face went pink and he stroked his bald scalp nervously. Then he said, as if to a dear friend, 'Little Sun, I'll be honest. I didn't want to do it. I was just carrying out orders.'

'So Xi Liu told you to do it?'

'I wouldn't put it quite like that. I think that if you're a Party member, you have to do what your superiors tell you; don't you?'

His round greasy face disgusted me. I said 'Humph' in answer and walked on.

He grabbed my arm and said, 'Don't go! It's almost time to eat. Eat! Eat! Eat and then go!'

I fought free of his grasp and said coldly, 'It's not food I need now, I need to think. I've got to think what to say to He Jingfu.'

He stroked his scalp again, and spoke with apparent sincerity: 'Little Sun, you must persuade him to withdraw the manuscript. He can get it published sometime in the future, it won't be too late. The road a person has to travel is never smooth – all the great people in history have gone through nine disasters and eighteen difficulties. Setbacks have their good points, they're character-forming. That's why Mencius said, "Heaven bestows great responsibilities on ordinary people."'

'You haven't encountered many difficulties; does that mean you aren't a great person? I sincerely hope that you will encounter a few setbacks. It's a pity you've always trodden such a smooth path, you have nothing in front of you but obscurity!' I didn't care if I insulted him, I hoped I had.

'Oh, Little Sun, when did you become so fiery? Be careful, too much bile will ruin your digestion. Off you go, go home and eat!'

I stabbed him with a needle and no blood appeared. I sliced at him with a knife but couldn't cut his flesh. It's rare for someone to have 'cultivated himself' to this degree.

This man, this virtuous man, sees the chaos of the ten thousand things as one. Because of his very existence, the world is emerging from chaos. Nothing can harm him; he would not drown in a flood that reached the sky. When a drought melts stone and metal and scorches the hills, he doesn't feel warm.

I'd been fascinated by the lofty attainments of the 'virtuous man' when I read Zhuangzi's[17] chapter *Carefree Wandering*, but, however much I tried, I couldn't emulate him. Now, in You Ruoshui, I seemed to see the 'virtuous man's' main attribute:

cold-bloodedness. Yet even he was only half cold-blooded, why didn't he go to the 'land where nothing grows, to the wasteland' instead of running the Party office? And all this 'Eat! Eat!', this 'We've got some nice dishes'. Did he want something from me or didn't he?

I left him and ran to He Jingfu's. I still didn't know what I was going to say.

There was a patch of wasteland nearby: it used to be a smooth lawn, but now it was overgrown with weeds. They said that the gardeners weren't willing to work until their pay had been settled – a question of the 'relations of production'. Were there problems in the relations of production in the realm of thought? If they weren't sorted out, a smooth green lawn could become a tangle of weeds. Xi Liu had thrown me a rope. He wanted to tie He Jingfu up and I'd been sent to pull the rope tight.

I knocked twice at the door. He Jingfu stood in front of me. Xi Wang was there, too. They seemed very surprised at my arrival.

TWENTY-FOUR

HE JINGFU

The storm has come.
Though I'd expected it, it's worse than I'd feared.

Her sudden arrival took me by surprise. I hadn't invited her and she hadn't warned me.

She didn't look good. I asked her to sit on the chair in front of my desk and I sat on the bed, opposite Xi Wang. He sat on the other bed. He didn't seem to want to go, though he knew it was the first time she'd come to my room. Perhaps he wanted to talk to her about something, though he didn't seem to know what to say. She wasn't really at ease with students, though she was used to teachers and cadres.

I wished he'd go, though I was embarrassed by my feeling and I could feel my face reddening and my ears getting hot. Not wanting to betray my confusion, I tried to look nonchalant and made her some tea. I also tried to lighten the atmosphere by saying:

'I'm sorry, I'm negligent in greeting my esteemed guest, Departmental Party Secretary! May I beg to know why you have come?' Xi Wang turned his face away, smiling, and she blushed suddenly. I dropped my pretence and sat upright on the bed, waiting for her to speak.

She looked round the room but said nothing. Xi Wang got to his feet. I thought he was probably going to eat and said, 'You go on ahead to the canteen, I'll come in a minute.'

'No, I'll go in a while. I'm not hungry. There's something I'd like to discuss with Teacher Sun,' he said; he had only stood up in order to help himself to some tea. My ears got hotter and Sun Yue glanced at me. 'Teacher Sun, I've been wanting to ask you if you know about the matter of Teacher He?'

'What matter?' she asked, and looked at me again.

'Do you really not know? My father has been trying to get the university Party committee to ban publication of his book. He doesn't dare to do it himself, he can't do anything himself and he doesn't really want to ask other people to do it. He's become an obstacle in the way of ideological liberation, though he's still very pleased with himself. In his view it's probably clever to trip other people up.' The boy spoke so sharply about his own father. As he spoke, he turned to stare at Sun Yue as if he wanted to find out whether or not she did know.

She shivered but quickly stopped herself. Casually, she answered, 'Really? How did you hear about it?' From her expression, it was clear she was concealing something but I didn't want to challenge her, especially in front of Xi Wang. Could he tell? There was the trace of a mocking smile on his face. I looked at him nervously: I didn't want him to upset Sun Yue; but he avoided my eyes and drank great gulps of tea. When he put his cup down, the mocking smile had gone.

I relaxed and said to him, 'You've told Teacher Sun what you heard and I won't go through it again.'

He smiled and nodded and said, 'Teacher Sun, I found myself playing the KGB, I didn't mean to, but I saw a bit of what went on behind the scenes.' She looked startled. 'I rather regret it now. I shouldn't have rowed with them. Otherwise I'd have been able to find out more.'

I laughed. 'We don't need inside information. The editor told me that when Chen Yuli went to see them, she was already "acting for the university Party committee".' They're all right, Chen Yuli, Xi Liu and You Ruoshui, they just want to use the name of the organisation to arrive at their own ends. And this is "inside information"! But I didn't tell Xi Wang because he's so impetuous. Things that shouldn't be concealed get concealed because there are some people who insist on doing things though they don't want their actions to be publicly known. As soon as things "go behind the curtain", they lead to such a lot of trouble. We Chinese waste so much time in concealing things and prying.

'I'm not as naïve as you two. If people conceal things then there will be others who want to find out what's going on. If people who hide things don't show their hands, why should we behave like gentlemen?' Xi Wang said, getting excited.

'I don't like furtiveness. It's too like politics,' said Sun Yue. She too was a bit agitated.

'Who does like it? But it's not going to disappear just because you don't like it. Do you think you can teach someone like Chen Yuli to be open and above-board? She's a typical meddling woman. She's got no interest in life apart from stirring things up. It's a pity there are so many women like her around. I suppose it's because men like them.'

Sun Yue raised her eyebrows. 'What's it got to do with men and women? It's a question of right and wrong. Young people shouldn't talk like that.'

Xi Wang looked with interest at her. 'Teacher Sun, I didn't think you'd react so strongly. I know what you're thinking; you want to uphold the dignity of women. But how? As long as women like Chen Yuli exist, it's impossible.'

He was right. In our society, women are still treated as dolls and in some places it is still true that a woman without brains is considered virtuous and a man without virtue is considered intelligent. I suspect Sun Yue was thinking of that; that was why she didn't want other people to talk about it and why she was proud. Chen Yuli must know it too, but she's lost her self-respect and become a doll. She dresses up the position and wants to keep other people in the same bind. It's a well-known psychological problem.

I was watching Sun Yue, scrutinising her. It was the first time she'd come to my 'home'. I hadn't imagined her first visit like this: she should have been more like the Sun Yue of twenty years ago, standing naturally in front of me, bombarding me with questions. I'd imagined the doors of two souls opening and me walking forward . . . Yet today, I didn't know she was going to come and I didn't know why she had come.

'Teacher Sun,' Xi Wang said again. She turned to him. 'What do you think ought to be done about the book?'

'Everything must be decided according to Party policy,' Sun Yue replied cautiously. The tiniest loss of hope appeared on Xi Wang's face and he sighed, got up and swung by his arms on the mosquito net frame above the bed, as if he was doing exercises. I knew he did it when he wanted to calm himself.

Sun Yue seemed to realise that Xi Wang wasn't happy with her reply. She smiled lightly, and said gently: 'What do you think ought to be done?'

'You won't agree with me,' he sighed again, 'but I think that the matter ought to be discussed openly by all the teachers in the university. And there ought to be articles in the papers. We ought to attack the deathly, crushing atmosphere in this university. I don't mind arguing with teachers, I'd like to make my views known publicly. All he can do is stop my pocket money. I could always get a job.'

Sun Yue shook her head firmly and turned to me. I said to her, 'I don't agree with him. We've tried it thousands of times but this kind of wide-open discussion doesn't decide things, it just makes them more complicated. We ought to wait and see what the publishing house thinks. Do you think they'll stick to their principles?'

Xi Wang shook his head. 'I've been thinking more and more that students of the fifties and sixties were completely different from students of the seventies and eighties. Anyway, I don't want to force anybody. All I'll say is this: I approve of your fine sentiments but I don't think they're much use.'

'You think our generation is backward,' Sun Yue said, smiling, though she sounded hurt.

'No, that wasn't what I meant. If that's what you thought I meant, then please forgive me.' Xi Wang was still excited, his eyes shining. 'I feel that both your generation and mine have suffered and we're all thinking things out. Our ideology and feelings are the same as yours, it's just that we aren't as cautious and indecisive as you. China's problems are piling up, how long can we remain patient? When are you going to stop worrying about the past and help us do something?'

Sun Yue's eyes softened. She was very easily moved. She opened her mouth as if to say something but decided against it. I could see that she was controlling her feelings.

Xi Wang stood up and said nervously, 'Teacher Sun, Teacher He, I must go and eat. You stay and talk. I've been monopolising the conversation.'

Sun Yue stood up too and put her hand on his shoulder. 'I'm not cross. I'd love to talk more to both of you. You must come over, any time, Hanhan is always reminding me to ask you.'

Xi Wang relaxed and he winked mischievously at me: 'Teacher He, don't put it off too long! Do you want me to fetch you something to eat?' I shook my head and he left.

'What did he mean you shouldn't put off?' Sun Yue asked.

'Kids like him say the first thing that comes into their heads. Who knows what they mean?' I answered. In fact I knew exactly what he meant, but all I could do was wait.

'I really love young people like that. I've often thought we've got a lot in common; thoughts and expectations. When I look at them I can see my past and I can see my future. The only thing I can't see is my present state. I haven't got their firm confidence, but then they are a bit extreme, don't you think?' she asked.

'Yes. But if you compare them with some of the sluggish and numbed people we've got around us, their extreme views and enthusiasms are quite attractive,' I replied. What were we going to talk about? Had she come round to talk about this?

'Do you see a lot of the students?' she said. I nodded.

'I'd like to know them better but I'm scared to. I don't want to expose myself too much to them; I'm afraid I'd have a negative effect. It's not easy to be an exemplar.' A tear trickled down her cheek.

I sat facing her, wanting to wipe away the tear; to stop myself, I went to the window and looked out. Picking up what she'd said, I went on:

'It's a matter of one's consciousness. I'm still called a teacher but the role has no significance for me. In my years on the road, I got used to doing what other people told me to do. So there's no difference between "Teacher He" and "Old He" or 'Hey you" – it's just what people call me, nothing more. I'm used simply to

being a person and going along with other people and not adding
any other conditions to my being a person. If anyone else can
understand and trust me, I'll be his friend. I'm quite happy to
bare my soul in front of others – it's not very different from any
other soul. In those days, if anyone had expressed an interest in
my feelings, I'd have torn my chest open to show him my heart
and not minded if I'd bled to death . . .'

I didn't finish. Scenes of my life as a vagrant rose before my
eyes, one in particular . . .

'You've got no papers, you're a vagrant, so what's it got to do
with you? Clear off and don't come back here again or I'll have
you arrested!'

It was 1970 and I'd arrived at a town on the banks of the Huai
River where the local movement to send people to do manual
work in the countryside was in full swing. There were about five
thousand people to be sent away, out of a population of ten
thousand. The local Party secretary said it was to 'abolish the
differences between town and country'. It was like arriving in the
chaos of war, with people being forced to move, adults weeping,
children screaming. Their houses were pulled down behind them
to 'avoid trouble'. There was one family of six, the father ran a
small general store and the mother worked in a noodle factory.
They had four daughters, the eldest just ten years old. Every
day the work team called to try and force them to move, but they
begged to be allowed to stay because they didn't know how their
daughters would manage if they were sent away. The Party
secretary said he'd already shown extreme forbearance but now
he had to take 'revolutionary action'. I watched this 'revolutionary
action'.

A group of big men with shovels, axes and billhooks turned up
at the door. First, the man was dragged to one side. His wife
crouched, weeping and imploring at the feet of the Party secretary. Naturally, it was no use, they began to pull the house
down. Suddenly there was an animal howl and I saw a completely
naked woman climbing onto the roof. She was trying to shame
them into sparing the house.

The crowd began to laugh and she was pulled down. Another

group of men moved forward and in no time the house was a heap of broken bricks and tiles. In her shame and disappointment, the woman continued to howl. A few brave women encircled her and dressed her.

I stood to one side. I felt as if it was my own mother who had suffered this humiliation. I wanted to spit out my hate and fury but I had no rights, I had to remain silent.

I watched the fate of the family after they'd been sent to the countryside, thinking I might be able to give them some help. A few days later, the woman went mad. Whenever she saw anyone, she tried to tear her clothes off. When the family discovered her in the stream, she was already dead.

That night, I sat beside the stream she drowned in and shouted my feelings, my love for my country and my fears for it, into the empty dark. For that, I was chased away; nobody wanted my feelings.

'Old He!' said Sun Yue. I couldn't turn round, and just grunted.

'What are you thinking about?'

'I was thinking that it's always better to expose one's soul than to be lonely.'

'Jingfu!' When she called me by my name again, I had to turn round, and moved one step closer to her.

'When I think of you being a vagrant, my mind goes blank. I just can't imagine it. I can't imagine what would happen if I found myself in those circumstances . . .' She avoided my eyes.

'You'd be like me, you'd carry on. There's no special trick, you just keep living, keep looking for the truth, and you have to learn to accept everything. Including insults and injustices . . .' I didn't want to tell her about the incident I'd just remembered, she wouldn't be able to bear it.

'I've always felt sorry . . . I feel as if I caused all your suffering . . .' she said with her head down.

'Sun Yue!' I came one step nearer.

She raised her head and I saw her eyes. Those two eyes full of tears, just like the young girl in *Put down your whips*. Those eyes had made me forget myself on stage. Now, I felt exactly the same and all I could do was hold out my arms . . .

I saw her eyes, hesitant and hurt, much more difficult to bear than the blazing anger of years ago. I let my arms drop and shook them.

'Misfortune won't kill us, there must be happiness ahead. Sun Yue, we can't go on feeling hurt,' I said decisively, to comfort her and to chase away my own doubts.

'What kind of happiness? I can't see it,' she replied, half smiling.

'It's freedom, spiritual freedom. We aren't going to be misled again, or be blind or naïve or rash. Won't that be happiness? And we're thicker-skinned than we used to be.'

She laughed. 'Happiness is being thick-skinned?'

I laughed too. 'Absolutely! It's the essence of happiness. When someone's self-respect and character are under attack, a thick skin can protect them. Intellectuals are very thin-skinned so they are always losing their stuffing to protect their "face", though "face" is unimportant. Whenever there's oppression, especially during the upsets of the last ten years, almost all intellectuals have had to submit to serious scrutiny. One result has been that their skin has got thicker and they are less afraid of losing face. And it's also made them more determined to stick to the truth. You want to criticise me? Go ahead! Do you want to accuse me of something or not? You won't raise my salary? Fine! Delighted!'

She laughed loudly, like a young girl, and said, 'You're so stimulating! You can make me laugh and you can make my cry. You can turn the bitter into the sweet!'

I moved one step closer. I wanted to grasp her shoulders and say, 'Then let's stay together always!' but I was afraid of her hesitant, hurt eyes. So I stepped back three paces and resumed my former position, steadying myself. 'Sun Yue, why did you come here today? Is it about the publication of my book?'

She smoothed her hair, as if she too had retreated, and said calmly, 'How did you know?'

'We used to say in the village: there's a storm coming, I can hear the wind.'

'What wind?'

What wind? I didn't want to tell her. Even I could hear the rush of blood to the head.

'Let's not discuss the slanders,' I said.

'What slanders?' she pressed me.

Should I tell her? It was what she most feared. I've been amazed by the inventiveness of some people. They've invented all sorts of misdeeds for me, and found all sorts of ways of communicating them to the publishing house. Amongst my sins, the worst, the most provocative, was that of breaking up Sun Yue's family. And there were three major aspects to this wrongdoing: rivalry – fighting with Zhao Zhenhuan over his sweetheart; sowing discord – inciting the break-up between Sun Yue and Zhao Zhenhuan; exterminating the enemy – when Zhao Zhenhuan came all that way to see his daughter, I hid the child and sent Zhao Zhenhuan away. And Sun Yue was said to be fickle and inconstant as well as selfish.

'Tell me!' she insisted again, fiercely.

I decided not to. 'What's the point in listening to rumours? They are of no interest. Let's get back to the subject. Tell me, has the rain started?'

'Who knows whether it's raining or snowing? The Party committee asked me to tell you of its decision.' She was serious again. I quashed the feelings that were rising in me, and listened.

'The Party has investigated the opinions and ideas of the masses and considers that your book can't be published without considerable revision. The committee decided to communicate with the publishing house directly but wanted the Literature Department to discuss it with you, and hopes that you will see it as an expression of concern for you and that you will take the manuscript back.'

It was like listening to a recording. Clearly spoken, well-expressed and to the point. Only the emotions were missing. Was this what she'd learnt during her years as a cadre? Or was it an inherent talent? I didn't like it.

Impolitely, I asked, 'Is the announcement over?'

'Yes,' she said softly.

'Now I'd like to hear your own opinion.' I stressed 'your own' heavily.

'I support you, Jingfu, you must know that. What are you going to do now?' She was meek and didn't quarrel with my attitude, and I felt less fiery. 'I know you didn't write the book for yourself. This news must be awful for you. Tell me, treat me as a friend . . .'

She was like a mother comforting an upset child. The motherly and womanly warmth was hard to bear. What was it that was hard to bear? Not being able to get a book published is something that happens often, both in China and abroad. I'm not the first to meet with this sort of problem and I won't be the last, nor is my case the most tragic. But why hadn't they made a final and definite decision? If they'd made a clear decision against publication, it wouldn't have surprised me. It might have been unreasonable, but it wouldn't have been surprising, it happens all the time. From what I'd heard, I'd been preparing for a soaking. If one escapes death by the skin of one's teeth, should one still fear a rainstorm? Yet I found it difficult to accept, very difficult, because it was a university Party committee decision and, according to both Party regulations and the law, it shouldn't be allowed. I didn't want to see the Party organisation deal with things like this. They remove the democratic rights of a Party member and call it 'concern'! I wish they'd concern themselves with the honour and prestige of the Party and worry about the trust and expectations of the ordinary Party members. Why do they have to lie? Why do they have to deceive? And what about the reputation of the Party committee? We should be honest and open with each other. I don't mind if they beat me and curse me, that's far better than this insincere 'concern'.

'Are you crying?' She patted my shoulders. 'Come, you're a determined person, aren't you?'

I'm fairly determined. But if determined people cry, it's not easy to stop. A brave general wears thick chain mail to protect a fresh red beating heart. If that heart is wounded, it won't just ooze tears.

'What do you think you'll do?' she asked again.

'I won't ask for my manuscript back. Please tell the Party committee that I think the decision is wrong and I'm waiting to see what the publishing house says. If they don't dare publish the book because of this, then I'll make a complaint to the higher Party organisation,' I said. I'd thought it out earlier.

She sighed. 'I knew that's what you'd do. Did I make you uncomfortable with my bureaucratic airs? I did, didn't I?'

Why was she being so nice today? Her smiling face was so sweet and natural. It confused me, I couldn't work out what it signified.

'Has Zhao Zhenhuan written again?' I asked cautiously.

Her smile faded, and in a reserved and solemn voice, she said, 'He's written to Hanhan. Quite a few letters.'

'That's good. You must let Hanhan console him.'

I don't quite know what I meant by that. It made her face and voice become even more distant and closed. 'Yes, that's what I intend to do.' She stood up. 'It's late; I must be getting back. I'll tell the Party committee what you said. Please take care of yourself. Don't worry too much.'

I looked at my watch: it was only two in the afternoon. Neither of us had eaten yet. 'There's some bread here and bits and pieces. Will you stay and have lunch?'

'No,' she said, walking to the door. Just as she reached it, she turned: 'You could still get a hot meal at the restaurant opposite the main gate.' I nodded and said goodbye to her.

As I picked up my grain coupons, ready to go to the restaurant, it occurred to me that I should have invited her to come with me. But she'd already gone.

TWENTY-FIVE

YOU RUOSHUI

I've never been able to create ideas in my own head, so I've always been ready to change with the wind and turn on those I sided with before.

My reasons for opposing the publication of *Marxism and Humanism*:
1. It has a revisionist viewpoint.
2. There are certain problems about the author, He Jingfu.
After three hours of revision and correction and an ash tray brimming with cigarette stubs, all I had in front of me were those two lines.

I wasn't at all happy with the subject. Did I really oppose publication? It's fantastic. When I first heard about the book from Old Zhang in the publishing house, over a month ago, I was secretly very impressed. He said to me, 'I've thought a lot of these things, myself, but I didn't dare speak about them, much less write about them. But now I think that relations between people should be less paranoid. I've had enough of having to carry out class struggle from morning to night. For years, I was afraid to speak openly in front of my own wife for fear that she'd betray me. It's pathetic!'

'I think it's quite right to talk about humanism and humanitarianism,' I replied. 'In this persecution of people, we've sunk lower than animals. Ants, geese, bees, there are quite a few species

that really care for each other.' He wanted to make it one of the
major books of the year and I quite agreed.

Now I've got to write: 'I don't approve of publication.' Am I
the chief editor? Am I the head of the provincial Propaganda
Department? What power have I got? Yet they want me to
'oppose'.

I blame Old Zhang. I told him Xi Liu's feelings about He Jingfu
and gave him all the details of the Party committee discussion of
the subject, but he assumed an official air and said, 'Of course we
respect the opinion of your Party committee. But a matter like
this can't be settled by the two of us. Our Party committee has
looked at it too and they want your side to send us a written
summary comprising two sections, one on the writer and one on
the Party committee's opinion of this particular book.'

Today's bureaucrats are highly skilled; no matter what they do
they have to calculate just how much work and responsibility will
fall on their shoulders. If I were to change places with Old Zhang,
I expect I'd do the same.

When I got back from the publishers, I went straight to see Xi
Liu and tell him about it. I thought he might be quite pleased but
he said, 'The committee is in a real mess now. Over the last few
days, the professor, the head of the Propaganda Department, the
head of the organisation team and several others, even some of
the leading cadres in the departments, have come to see me to
oppose the decision. They say it's against Party policy and that
teachers and students are against it, too. It looks as if He Jingfu
has really been stirring things up and pressurising members of
the Party committee. And I hear that Sun Yue and my precious
son are both helping him. Sun Yue is heading further along the
wrong track.'

I thought of saying, 'Well, let's leave it then,' but he said, 'A
lot of people in the Party committee were really frightened by
the Cultural Revolution and they're terrified of the masses. I'm
not! Will there be a second Cultural Revolution? Let it come! By
the time it happens I may well have joined Marx anyway!'

What about me? I'm only fifty-five; will I have joined Marx in
heaven by then, too? 'Why don't we use your name?' I asked.

'It won't do. I can't intervene openly. I thought we'd use your name to prepare some material. We'll send a copy to the university Party committee, and to the publishing house and to the provincial propaganda chief. I can add my own opinion to the material for the university committee and can go and see the provincial propaganda chief myself for a talk. I imagine he must have an opinion on the current ideological line struggle.'

'I thought he was in hospital and wasn't really concerned with this . . .'

'You don't understand. He's gone into hospital as a sort of silent protest. He hasn't had anything to do with recent events. But we are old comrades-in-arms so I still know him well. I'm sure he keeps up.'

It was very clear that he wanted to use his 'connections' and the 'backdoor' method. I knew it was the most effective way, since the head of the Education Department was the immediate superior of the head of the publishing house, and though Old Zhang might not be afraid of the university Party committee, he was certainly afraid of the head of the Education Department. Everybody in publishing circles knew that Old Zhang and the head of the Education Department had tangled in previous political movements and that their relations were still difficult.

Did I want to get involved in this? 'I can't do it! Comrade Xi Liu, think again. I'm only the head of the Party committee office,' I said, trying to get out of it.

'That's a position of considerable importance!' Xi Liu smiled. 'And you're still young. There's a saying, "At fifty-five, the mountain tiger comes alive". You're in the prime of life. Now that they're stressing that the leaders ought to be younger, you've got great possibilities.'

He meant that he had it in his gift. I could understand that. I'm fifty-five but I joined the revolution forty years ago. When I was fifteen I joined the army and became a Party member and I was one of the youngest of the leading cadres in the north-east; but I was thrown out during the troubles there in the early fifties. It's been downhill all the way since then. How else would I find myself working under Xi Liu? I know what he's doing. He brought me to the university and he's used me ever since because I can do the things he doesn't want to do. I wouldn't dare overtake him so he's got me by the throat. Now he's making promises! Yet I don't feel that his position is totally secure. If the ideological movement for liberation continues to develop, he won't be able to hold on and his promises may not be worth much. Will he still be in a position of leadership? A promotion from Xi Liu looks only about thirty per cent guaranteed. Yet as long as he is in power, I have to serve him. Otherwise there isn't even a thirty per cent chance of promotion, I'll have to wear small shoes all my life.

The more I thought about it, the more disagreeable my situation seemed. 'You Ruoshui, don't worry. I'm here if there are any problems.' He encouraged me as I remained silent. That's what one's superiors always say, 'I'll take care of any problems.' But if any real problems arose, I'd get the blame. They either get out faster than you can or they turn on you and refuse to take responsibility. I cope with this sort of method by 'turning on those I sided with before'. If they want to get out, I'll stop them. If they turn on me, as long as they don't go too far, I don't mind. I learnt this when we were 'fighting selfishness and repudiating revisionism'; after a really bitter criticism session, I was commended by the workers' propaganda team of the university. Nevertheless, I'm still prepared to turn on previous associates if the need arises. How else can I protect myself?

'I'm not worried. When I've written it, I'll show it to you,' I answered cheerfully. I'll do it if it makes him feel better. But I keep notes on all the conversations I have with him, preparing to use them against him if necessary.

So I have to write my condemnation.

If it all goes wrong, will I be blamed? Will this material count against me? Xi Liu told you to write it? Then he must take the blame. But are the views expressed Xi Liu's? That's not so easy. That's why this will have to be very carefully polished.

I'll have to change the title. This one is too clearly slanted.

I threw it away and wrote: 'On He Jingfu and his book *Marxism and Humanism*'. That was much less emotional.

'My God! What are you doing? Haven't you done anything about lunch?' my wife said when she came back. She's always nagging, just because she's ten or more years younger than me, she never lets me forget it. She works in the university library and her work isn't very demanding, but she always insists that I get the meal at midday. Today I took no notice of her and went on writing.

'One: the book's revisionist standpoint.'

That won't do, it doesn't follow. In the title, He Jingfu's name comes first so I must discuss him first. I crossed it out and wrote: 'One: He Jingfu.'

What could I say about He Jingfu? I didn't know him before and all I know of him now is his name. Could I include what Chen Yuli said about him? I'd asked her to write it down but she wouldn't. Yet at every conceivable opportunity she talks about his failings and always brings in Sun Yue. I'm not at all clear as to whether He Jingfu has done her wrong or whether Sun Yue has done him wrong. Never mind her. I'll write, 'According to some'. They will ask, 'According to whom?' And I will reply, 'According to Chen Yuli.' I've got notes of what she said at the Party meeting. And I wasn't the only one to hear it.

'Did you hear me? Put the rice on! I haven't got time!' Then she stuck two fingers in my ears. She always does that, even if there are people around. If she's cross, she does it. If she isn't getting her own way, she does it. I can't stop her.

I smiled, and said, 'You see how busy I am. Can't you do it for once, just this once?'

She bent down to look at what I was writing and drove her fingers harder in. 'What are you writing? Who told you to write it? Aren't you afraid of criticism? I certainly am!'

'It's an assignment from the leadership; I've got to write it,' I replied calmly.

'Leadership? Which leadership? You ought to tell him to write it! If you came into the library and listened, you'd hear all the teachers and students in uproar. They're all defending He Jingfu. What's he ever done to you?'

'For heaven's sake! Don't you see? I'm doing it for work, there's nothing personal.'

She pursed her lips. 'Huh! Under the "Gang of Four" I was always warning you. You always said it was "for work" and what was the result? Didn't you go weeping and wailing to Xi Liu and say you'd done it all for personal glory? I give up! What's happened to your brains? Have you forgotten everything?'

My ears were stinging, and now my face was burning too. She was right. She'd had plenty of occasion to stick her fingers in my ears when the 'Gang of Four' were in power.

'If you want to write something, then why don't you write something on your children's behalf? You could satirise the bureaucracy that's stifling talent!'

I've got three children. The child she meant was from my first marriage. He's a worker. This year he wanted to take the exam to become a research student but the factory management wouldn't let him and said he couldn't leave the factory. Management like that ought to be taught a lesson. I've thought of lots of things I could write, criticising the 'needs of work'. I've even thought of a pseudonym because I wouldn't want to use my real name in case it affected him.

'I'll write it when I've finished this. You realise Xi Liu asked me to do this . . .'

She didn't wait for me to finish: 'Xi Liu! His ideas are ossified! His work-style is all wrong. If I had the power to recall him, I would! All he cares about is his official hat and he'll never give it up! Not even if he had to become a counter-revolutionary. What kind of policy is that?'

'All right, all right. Your ideology is liberated and your ideas are correct but you're not Party secretary and I can't take orders from you. Go and make lunch!' I wanted to get rid of her.

'If you're going to do things like that, don't think I'll make meals for you! Haven't you got any brains? Haven't you got any ideas of your own?'

Have I? I'm not sure. But this task isn't to do with ideas. It's bad enough not having any but wouldn't it be more painful if I did? He Jingfu has brains and where have they got him? The students and teachers are all on his side. So what? It's not a question of words but of power. If you've got power then you can be calm. If you haven't, all hell breaks loose. If they want to leap to his defence, then let them.

I paid no further attention to her but went on writing; she'd soon calm down. The title still wasn't right, why had I put He

Jingfu first? Wouldn't it be better to change it to 'Some opinions on *Marxism and Humanism*'? I tore it up and started again. 'An introduction to *Marxism and Humanism*'.

'Didn't you hear?' I hadn't realised that she was going to get still angrier. Why? Hear what? All I could do was put my pen down and look at her.

'Everyone says that you're brainless, that you've got no soul, that you've got no backbone! Look!'

She held out a piece of paper. A cartoon: it must have been drawn by a student. Students nowadays! The caption was 'How can he float?' [a joke about You Ruoshui's name which means 'like water'] and there was a picture of a headless man floating between rocks.

My face burnt, my eyes felt dry.

'I'm embarrassed to show it to you,' her voice was lower and rather unsteady.

I scribbled out the words I'd just written, crumpled the paper and threw it away.

Was I headless?

'Wash the rice!' I said to my wife. She smiled.

After the meal, I stretched out comfortably on the bed. Let Xi Liu write it himself! He couldn't harm me.

Could a person live without brains? The cartoon was quite clever. Then I remembered there was a joke in some book about a man whose head had been cut off. He didn't realise and got up from the execution ground and went through the city gate, on his way home. Halfway there, he began to feel hungry so he went to buy some cakes. They wouldn't sell them to him because they said, 'If you haven't got a head, how can you eat?' but he was determined to buy some. Finally the cake seller agreed. When he tried to put one in his mouth, he discovered it had gone. 'I've lost my mouth, though he said I'd lost my head. I don't care about my head but how can I manage without a mouth? If I've lost my mouth, I'll die!' Miserably, he felt his cut-off neck, lay down and died.

What does it mean? That a mouth is more important to some people than a brain? You can lose everything except your mouth. The student must have read the story before drawing his cartoon.

'I'm going to work. Don't write it behind my back!' Half-asleep, I heard my wife and mumbled; I was exhausted.

Xi Wang pushed the door open and came in. He walked straight over to my writing desk, saw that the papers on it were blank and started burrowing in the wastepaper basket.

'I knew you'd do something like this! You've got no Party spirit and you could do with a bit of human feeling! Teacher He is brilliant and though you don't need to encourage him, you don't have to destroy him. Why is it that you want to pour freezing water and a coating of icy mud on the heads of talented people?' He was reading what I'd written. I couldn't see his face, as his back was turned to me.

'Don't blame the innocent, Xi Wang! It was your father who made me do it, I don't like suppressing talent. Even my own son has suffered from that,' I argued.

'So you don't like the fact that your own son has been thwarted! You only ever think of yourself.'

'It's because of your father!'

'You and he both use each other!' he said, his voice sharper.

I got up from the bed; I wanted to throw him out. How dare a student come into my house and accuse me? Who cares if he's Xi Liu's son? His father doesn't care much for him.

As I got up, I heard him laugh out loud.

'What are you laughing at?'

'I don't believe it! You've got no head!' he answered, still laughing.

'Rubbish!' I shouted. My voice sounded odd. What was wrong with my throat? I rubbed it. It felt swollen. Was I getting cancer?

Xi Wang laughed again.

'Get out!' I pushed him.

'How did you manage to replace your head so quickly?' he asked, pointing at my head. I looked at his eyes, gleaming and full of laughter. I'd got a new head? I went to the mirror. No! Xi Liu's head was growing on my neck. The throat I'd just been feeling was his.

'I must write. You sit down,' I – Xi Liu said to him. He obeyed and sat down, looking at me.

I spread out the paper and began to write out the title again: 'My reasons for opposing the publication of *Marxism and Humanism*'. Why had I used that title again? There was nothing I could do, my hands wouldn't obey me.

'This won't do, You Ruoshui! He wanted the opinion of the university Party committee, not your own views.' Where was Old Zhang? Why was he suddenly talking to me? I turned round and bumped into a large nose. Old Zhang's head was growing on my right shoulder. His beard was bristly. My shoulders seemed to have grown, perhaps to support his head.

'The publishing house has no right to interfere in university matters. People do have the right to express their opinions to the Propaganda Department.'

That was the voice of the head of the Education Department. Where was he? I turned round to look and met a pair of icy cold spectacles on my left shoulder. His head was growing there.

'Beautiful! This is a real eyeball-to-eyeball encounter,' I heard Xi Wang say.

It was enough to make anyone despair. Why was he here when I didn't want anyone to see me? I would lose face. And my head? Where have you hidden it?

'Don't worry! Your head is locked away in my trunk!' Chen Yuli's head floated in front of me.

I was frightened and angry. 'Thank you! Please go! I'm busy, I've got a report to write.'

'I want to see what you've written. I'll advise you,' she smiled, and came weaving towards me.

'Do you want to grow on my shoulders too? Look, there's no room left,' I said to her. Before the sound of my voice had died, two hands clutched at my throat, hard. My neck was twisted forward, Chen Yuli's head floated upwards, her nose against the back of Xi Liu's head.

'Write!' Xi Liu insisted.

'Write!' Old Zhang insisted.

'Write!' the head of the Propaganda Department insisted.

'Write!' Chen Yuli insisted.

'All right, I will.' My hands wouldn't move and I called out, 'Let my hands go!'

'Are you dreaming, Mr You?' It was Xi Wang's voice again.

Why couldn't I see him? I struggled to open my eyes and there was Xi Wang standing in front of me. I was still lying on the bed. I'd been seeing ghosts. That hateful cartoon.

'Have you been here long?' I stood up quickly.

'A minute or two. When I came in I heard you shout, "Let my hands go!" What were you dreaming about?' he asked, smiling. He seemed to be summing me up, just as he had done in my dream. Had he only been there a minute? Had I dreamed all that in a minute? I must have started dreaming after he came in. I must have sensed his arrival when I was half-asleep, half-awake.

'Do sit down. My nerves are very bad, I've been dreaming a lot. I was dreaming about playing basketball with some students and just as I was about to throw the ball into the net, my hands were seized. A crazy dream!' As I told him this story, I went over to the desk, affecting unconcern. I looked at the wastepaper basket; all the crumpled sheets were still there, it didn't look as if anyone had touched them. I am seeing ghosts! Why should Xi Wang want to look at the contents of my wastepaper basket? On the other hand, why is he here?

'What can I do for you, Xi Wang?' I asked.

'Well, nothing in particular . . .'

'Have you been home to see your father?' I suspected this might have something to do with it.

'No,' he said, apparently truthfully. 'I wanted to talk to you.'

'Fine, what about?'

'About the publication of He Jingfu's book. What my father is doing, he can't do without you. I'd like to know what you think about it.'

I thought of the cartoon again. Had Xi Wang drawn it? I didn't know he could draw. But young people these days seem to be able to do anything. Whether he can draw or not, I wouldn't like to say whether or not he'd drawn the cartoon, the nasty little beast. Had he come to gather material for more cartoons? They make me nervous, these brats.

'What's my position in the Party? I'm in charge of the office. It's not up to me to make any decisions at all. I simply implement them.' I chose my words with care.

'It doesn't matter whether you make or implement decisions, what do you think about it?' He seemed like my boss.

'Me? Of course my ideology is not as liberated as yours. But I am against the suppression of talent. My own son is someone who has suffered that.' It was just like my dream. I'm really seeing ghosts!

'Let's look at it this way. Some people, when they are suffering themselves, get very agitated. They may cry out, they may run away. Yet it doesn't stop them doing the same to others.' Xi Wang also sounded exactly as he had done in my dream. I looked at him, startled. What was really going on today?

'You Ruoshui, I know there's no point in my talking to you. But I still wanted to. You really must watch things as they develop. The tides of science and democracy can't be held back. My father takes no notice, his thinking is completely ossified. I can't change him, nor can you, but we can be of some use in diminishing his influence. You're a close colleague, I'm his son, and his opponent; we can diminish his influence even if we start from opposite positions, it's quite possible.'

I'd often heard people say Xi Liu's son was a complex character, though I'd never spoken to him. Today, I could see they were right. He didn't act like a young person; more like an experienced politician. I had to be careful. I thought for a while.

'I don't know what you're getting at. Comrade Xi Liu is a little conservative in his thinking but his position is different from ours. He has to look at things very thoroughly, from all sides. We aren't in the same position, we don't have his power. Maybe he's a bit extreme but don't you think we ought to just warn him of the problems?'

He laughed. 'We don't have to agree on his worth. I'm sure you know it better than me. But your own position makes it difficult for you to judge reality. Let me put it quite straight: if you don't write that report for him, then his campaign to suppress He Jingfu will be a waste of time. He won't show his hand openly.'

It was a shock. How did he know about the report? Without thinking, I moved the wastepaper basket away from him and pushed it behind my chair. I didn't want him to see it.

'What report?' I pretended not to understand.

'You don't have to pretend with me, I know all about it,' he said, looking hard at me.

Had my wife said something? Could she have?

'Xi Wang, I really don't understand why, when you have such wonderful conditions for study and the opportunity to go and study abroad, you worry about things like this.' I changed the subject, seriously thinking I might straighten him out.

'There's only one aim in studying at the university or doing further study abroad and that's to transform China. Everything I do now is towards that aim. I'm not a utopian.'

I couldn't believe this was Xi Liu's son, it didn't seem possible.

'Will you think about what I've said?' he asked.

'Naturally, I think about everybody's opinions.'

His eyes flashed briefly over my face and he seemed to smile. 'I've disturbed you. I'm not necessarily right but I'd be grateful if you would think about it.' He spoke very politely, and stood up.

When I'd seen him off, I sat down weakly at my desk. Should I write or not? Why don't I have another think? I thought of my son. Why don't I write that essay first and complain about the injustice my son has suffered?

I picked up my pen and wrote out the title: 'A criticism of the needs of work'. Just as I was about to continue, I heard a woman's voice outside the door: 'You Ruoshui, Xi Liu asked me to come and see you!' It was Chen Yuli. I quickly tore up the sheet of paper and threw it into the wastepaper basket. Better to serve the interests of the Party secretary than worry about those who were interested in the Party secretary. What was the point in disagreeing with Xi Liu? Let the son fight his own battles with his father.

'Comrade Chen Yuli! Come in! Come in! I was just in the middle of writing . . .'

Chen Yuli's head appeared in front of me. At least it was growing on her own shoulders.

TWENTY-SIX

THE WRITER

Why does a simple matter get so complicated? The main reason is the human factor.

I always like seeing He Jingfu and Sun Yue. The publication of *Marxism and Humanism* has become quite a news item in the publishing house.

I'm a very uncomplicated character. For me, a book has a definable scholarly value, and a writer is a citizen with democratic rights. If a publishing house accepts a manuscript, surely that's the end of the matter. Not in this case. Halfway through the process, the university party Secretary opposes the publication of the book and the presses are halted. We're always criticising anarchy; I'm not quite sure what you'd call this. Policy is of no use, even the law is of no use against flagrant interference.

I'd had high hopes of the chief editor, Old Zhang. Colleagues had told me he was very much in favour of He Jingfu's book and unhappy about Xi Liu's interference. He wanted Xi Liu to produce some evidence so that he could argue about the legal aspects. But after the head of the Education Department supported Xi Lui and sent You Ruoshui's report over with a note – 'I want the publishing house to consider the circumstances of the book and its author. It is a very serious matter' – he ordered the presses to stop printing. Old Zhang said to friends privately, 'What do I

care about You Ruoshui's report? It's garbled and contradictory
and makes an unnecessary personal attack on He Jingfu. But I
can't ignore the head of the Education Department. He's got
complete power over me.'

Old Zhang is no fool; would he want to take responsibility
himself? No, he's kicked the ball upwards. He wrote to the head
of the Propaganda Department of the province, explaining the
situation and asking for instructions, and he requested that these
instructions be issued, not through the head of the Education
Department but directly from the Propaganda Department. On
the football field, the referee is signalling 'take a break'. The
problem is suspended.

It's broadened my view. If someone were to ask me how such
a simple problem had become so complicated, I'd reply that the
main reason was the human factor. First, there are people with
all sorts of different opinions who want to stir things up; to them
should be added people who are scared for all sorts of reasons,
plus one hard-headed obstinate man. That's how simple problems
get complicated.

When God made man, He showed considerable ingenuity. He
made a He Jingfu and then He made a Xi Liu, thereby promoting
mutual growth and restraint between the five elements[18]. Then
He needed a You Ruoshui, to complete Xi Liu; those two make
up a pair and even their names are linked in meaning [Liu means
'to flow'; Ruoshui means 'like water']. But that wasn't enough.
He added Old Zhang and the head of the Education Department,
enemies at upper and lower levels. Then He added Sun Yue to
give colour to the whole affair, to make it more attractive. If one
of them had been left out, the whole thing would have been
much simpler. But who would one have left out? They're all
essential.

Sun Yue is especially important. I've heard it said that she and
He Jingfu have grown much closer as a result of all this and that's
wonderful for He Jingfu. It really is a case of 'the sun rising in the
east, rain falling in the west, the road ahead is both dim and
bright'. It's a perfectly ordinary thing to happen but I'm very
happy for He Jingfu. I do hope that these two lovers will make a
pair.

There were quite a few people gathered in Sun Yue's room: Xu Hengzhong, He Jingfu and Li Yining. Hanhan was also home. I greeted them: 'What luck to find all of you here!'

Sun Yue smiled and said, 'It's better to arrive at the right time than to be early. Today Xu Hengzhong is celebrating the successful arrangement of a match. The matchmaker Li Yining is here. We've just had a celebratory meal together.'

This was another piece of news. I'd heard that Li Yining had found a wife for Xu Hengzhong, a rich woman, but I didn't think it would lead so quickly to marriage. I clasped my hands together and bowed to Xu Hengzhong: 'Congratulations! Are you planning a party? I'll help!'

Rather drunk, Xu Hengzhong returned my salutation. 'It doesn't look as if I'll be able to avoid it. I'm a pauper and I don't enjoy such things myself. But my fiancée's family don't see it like that so we'll obey the local customs! I can't remain aloof from worldly pursuits and not offer a few baked meats. So I've consented.' He couldn't conceal his satisfaction.

I can't say I was overjoyed by the news. I turned to He Jingfu and asked, 'Is there any sign of a solution to the publication problem?'

Xu Hengzhong seemed particularly over-excited today and interrupted: 'It's getting more and more complicated. Xi Liu's son Xi Wang wrote a report on the blackboard in the Literature Department today entitled, "Legal government is people's government – thoughts on our freedom to publish after the setbacks to He Jingfu's book". He didn't merely describe the affair in a very original way; he's criticised Xi Liu and the university Party committee, using names.'

'What's wrong with that? If we let people speak, perhaps Xi Liu will come to his senses!' I said.

'You're very simple-minded,' Xu Hengzhong shook his head at me. 'Won't Xi Liu just say that He Jingfu encouraged Xi Wang? He may well drag Sun Yue into it too and say that she's behind them . . .'

At that point, he stopped and looked at Sun Yue. She was blushing. She glanced at He Jingfu, and at me, and finally said, with her eyes down, 'I'm not afraid of being dragged in. I don't

want to be, and I shan't say anything. I just wish I had the strength
to be the backstage supporter of Old He, but I don't.'

'Don't talk like that, Sun Yue. I'm very worried about it,' He
Jingfu said, not looking at her.

What was going on? Why was he being so polite and reserved?
Had he been cowed by the rumours and slanders? The problem
must lie with Sun Yue. Women are full of pride, which I can
understand, but Old He is so much in need of loving support. I
encouraged them.

'Old He, Little Sun, it doesn't matter what people say, you can
stand firm. Xi Liu hasn't got to the point of ordering you not
to love each other. You've been through a battering, it's not
easy . . .'

He Jingfu stopped me with his hand. 'Old Chang, don't go on.
I'll always be Little Sun's friend and comrade.' Sun Yue seemed
not to have heard what we said.

Fine! Fine! You'll always be friends and comrades. I really can't
understand you. I look at Xu Hengzhong and see that people can
get married without affection, and you two who love each other
can't get married.

'All right; about the publishing business, what are you going to
do now?' I returned to the original topic without enthusiasm.

'That was what we were just talking about. What do you think
we should do?' He Jingfu seemed to be sorry for interrupting me
and spoke with especial warmth and friendliness.

'Go to the Commission for Inspecting Discipline!' I said.

'But there are people just like Xi Liu on the Commission,' Xu
Hengzhong said immediately, negatively.

'Then what do you think should be done? I can't believe there's
no way out. Things are much better than they used to be, don't
you agree?' I was rather concerned, so I turned the question back
to him.

I'd always admired Xu Hengzhong and been irritated by him. I
admired him because he could often analyse a problem more
thoroughly and carefully than others, in his elder-brotherly way. He
irritated me because he always saw the worst side and painted the
most dismal prospects. Nobody could deny that the worst side existed
but the problem was he could never see the way round it, he saw

people as powerless. How did he get like that? He's not been through half the problems He Jingfu and Sun Yue have faced.

'Of course it's not hopeless. I think Old He ought to go and talk to Xi Liu. He ought to explain that Xi Wang's report has got nothing to do with him and he also ought to get Xi Liu's opinion of his manuscript and show willingness to change it. That way, the situation can be improved. But I don't think he will.' Xu Hengzhong looked for my support, glancing at me as he spoke.

Before I could open my mouth, He Jingfu said, 'No. It's not a problem to be settled between individuals, it must be decided through organisational channels.'

'But if you were to use organisational channels now, you'd get nowhere. We're always hearing that the legal system has been strengthened, but in the university the law is what Xi Liu says. Why not compromise? Just get the book published and leave it at that. If you tell Xi Liu you're willing to revise it, even if you don't actually do so, he won't be able to do anything. Leave him a bit of face, let him retreat to his proper sphere of influence, and then what can he do to hinder you?' Xu Hengzhong argued.

'Do you think Xi Liu has done this just to punish He Jingfu?' I asked him.

'No, of course it's not as simple as that. The reasons for his attitude are varied. And each reason produces its own result. But if you can get rid of one of them, then the others may change, too,' Xu Hengzhong replied.

'But for me, the most important thing is to break the stranglehold of dogmatism, not to gain the approbation of Xi Liu. I've got nothing personal against Xi Liu. What he thinks is his own problem. I can't think of using personal feelings to heal the split between us,' He Jingfu said suddenly, refusing Xu Hengzhong's proposal.

I agreed with him but what was to be done? I couldn't think of anything. I turned to Sun Yue. 'Can't we get the problem discussed openly by the department and the Party committee?'

She sighed. 'We've all thought of that but Xi Liu isn't willing to allow open discussion. He says it's nothing to do with them. It's been discussed once and nothing definite came out of that. You Ruoshui has only reported his own feelings, he's got no power. As for stopping the presses, that's the publishing house's business, we've got no power to intervene. Perhaps there isn't enough paper, perhaps their plans have changed. The publishing house hasn't asked our opinion, so what can we do?'

'But it's quite clear that Xi Liu and the head of the Education Department have actually intervened!' I said.

'Have you any real evidence?' Xu Hengzhong asked. 'If you aren't careful they'll accuse you of making a false charge. If a nobody makes a charge against a somebody and it doesn't stick, it's a false charge. But there's never any likelihood of failure if a somebody wants to discipline a nobody. Nobodies are in a very low position and who cares if they never rise above it?'

I sighed heavily.

'It's terrifying. We can't use the normal channels, all we can do is plot some underhand scheme or try and use connections or the "back door",' Sun Yue said, angrily.

She was right. What could we do? For all sorts of reasons, the affair had begun to seem like a bowl of treacle that had got into the machinery, clogging the works and stopping the engine. I've often met similar cases in the cultural office.

For instance, there was a play they wanted to put on. They'd applied for permission but for ages and ages no one said yes or no. There might have been all sorts of reasons, but the fact was that one member of the leadership opposed it and he wasn't willing to say so in so many words. The actors didn't dare talk about it openly either.

Someone who had been unjustly persecuted wanted to get work. He went backwards and forwards but nobody wanted him. There could have been all sorts of reasons, or it could have been pure coincidence. But the fact was that one member of the leadership didn't like him and that was why nobody else was prepared to like him.

I often make up all sorts of 'coincidental reasons' to explain these things. The leadership send me to 'explain things clearly' though in fact they want the truth concealed.

Is this what they mean by 'internal injuries'? Nothing to be seen on the outside whilst the internal organisation is dying. If we don't rule by law, then how can we overcome these things?

But if we don't overcome these things, how can the rule of law really operate? Did the chicken lay the egg? Or did the egg produce the chicken? The chicken laid the egg and the egg produced the chicken. The origin can transform the product and the product can transform the origin. If you rule the product, you'll rule the origin. If you rule the origin, you'll rule the product. Neither should be emphasised at the expense of the other.

How can we get rid of this treacle if our hands are tied? I couldn't think of anything. I said to He Jingfu, 'What do you want to do? It looks as if all we *can* do is wait and see what the provincial Propaganda Bureau says.'

Sun Yue replied for him: 'We've decided to write a joint letter to the authorities. We won't just write about the book, but also about our ideas on the liberation of ideology and the question of cadres.'

'Don't go too far!' It was Li Yining, who hadn't said anything yet. 'You two shouldn't write a joint letter, there's already far too much gossip. Haven't you gone far enough by now?'

'Gossip! Let them talk! Sometimes I'd really like to shout at them, I . . .' She stopped, suddenly.

I saw her look at He Jingfu; he was frowning at her. They quickly turned their heads to the corner where Hanhan was silently doing her homework, and just at that moment, Hanhan lifted her eyes towards her mother. My heart beat faster; I felt that I had suddenly begun to understand. But before I could think it over, Li Yining spoke again: 'You must consider whether or not it's worth it. Why don't you just write about the question of publication? Why mention the rest? There are a thousand million people in China, you can't be the only ones who see problems, can you?'

'You can't say that. People have got to do something,' I said to Li Yining. I didn't know her well so I was polite.

But she answered rather shortly: 'If that's what you think, then you do it. I hadn't noticed you raising such acute social problems in your novel!'

I was surprised at her sharp tone. What she said was true, I hadn't written about such things though I thought about them all the time. Every day I wanted to write and every day there was a new plot. But I hesitated when I took up my pen. It wasn't fear, what should I fear? It was just that I wasn't accustomed to being the object of criticism. It was like someone who'd never acted before suddenly making up and getting on stage in front of the footlights. I knew it was a lack of courage of a sort. But you have to cultivate courage. And to cultivate it, you need courage. It was the chicken and egg question all over again. I'd passed the optimum age. The chicken was an old hen and couldn't lay any more eggs. The egg had been in the nest too long and wouldn't hatch. I didn't want to live my life like this but I didn't have much hope for the future. I did, however, support other people's creativity with all my strength, I wanted them to open up new horizons. People's achievements gave me real joy. Wouldn't that do? Must I become a martyr, too? I said to Li Yining, 'I have neither the talent nor the courage. But does that mean I can't support other people?'

Did she feel she'd gone a bit far? Her expression and tone softened: 'Your support may harm them. I know what goes on in China, it'll never be properly run. Our slave mentality, our laziness, are too deep, too strong. Most people think they can't do anything or they don't want to do anything. They just hope other people will do things whilst they stand aside, retaining the right to criticise. They often pin their hopes on honest officials. When honest officials are in power, they dare to stick their necks out. But if they meet corrupt officials, then all they do is retreat and accept it, and they may even help the villains. Sun Yue and He Jingfu have spent half their lives in misery, do they still have to plead for other people? They ought to be able to pass a few years in peace and quiet.'

'I absolutely agree with you. There's nothing to be gained by making this pointless sacrifice,' Xu Hengzhong said.

'Well, I don't agree!' Sun Yue said excitedly. She turned to Li Yining: 'Why do you want to see China and the people like that? I couldn't bear to. I know we face enormous difficulties but I still love my country and I'm full of hope for the future. But if you think there's no hope for the country and if you think one shouldn't try and improve things for the people and the country, what's the point in living?'

Xu Hengzhong smiled. 'Does there have to be a point to life? I'm sure that ninety-nine per cent of the people have no aim in life, or else they'd say that living itself was the point.'

Sun Yue got more excited, raising her eyebrows and glaring at him: 'That's just avoiding the issue. You mustn't ridicule the people and the country. And don't throw cold water on our idea. Leave us to sacrifice ourselves. I don't believe that any sacrifice is ever pointless!'

He Jingfu also seemed exhilarated. He'd been watching Sun Yue, and when he heard her words he went over to her, and then stepped back. Though she seemed not to have seen his movements, she got more upset and began to cry.

Tears were flowing down her face. He Jingfu tried to give her his teacup and she started to take it; then suddenly she pushed the cup away and picked up her own cup from the table.

He Jingfu's face went red, briefly, and he retreated again. Li Yining and I looked at each other. She'd obviously noticed, too, but we both pretended that nothing had happened. In fact I don't know what really happened.

Li Yining didn't argue with Sun Yue's heated outburst. She took Sun Yue's hands in hers and rubbed them gently, as if she, too, regretted what she'd just said.

Xu Hengzhong didn't laugh any more. He shook his head and sighed, turning to me. 'I know exactly what Little Sun is feeling. Who doesn't love his country? But these last few years, I've begun to see through it!'

'See through what?' He Jingfu pulled his stool closer to Xu Hengzhong.

'I've seen through everything,' Xu Hengzhong said quietly.

'That's not possible.' He Jingfu patted his hand, and said with a smile, 'Someone who's seen through everything couldn't pursue a fiancée so energetically, could he?'

Xu Hengzhong suddenly blushed and we all laughed. He Jingfu patted his hand again and told him not to take offence, and then said seriously, 'Old Xu, I think what you've seen is that the way ahead is not going to be easy for any of us and that we're all going to have to make sacrifices. You've been frightened by the sacrifices and the price we'll have to pay, haven't you?'

Xu Hengzhong shrugged, without agreeing or disagreeing.

'What about me? Do you think I'm afraid of the sacrifices, too?'
Li Yining asked.

He Jingfu laughed. 'Little Li, I'm not a doctor. The person who
knows Li Yining best is Li Yining.'

'My appallingly lazy nature has done me a lot of harm! Little
Sun, you may not like what I say but you probably don't realise
that I hate myself for it. I love my country, that's why I haven't
gone abroad like my ancestors. Even when times were hardest,
I never thought of escaping and leaving China. I was always
waiting for the day when I could express my gratitude to my
country but the long wait sapped my determination. I grew lazy,
content with what I had, fearful of difficulties. I also thought that
since the past and the present were different there might be
some hope, though I'd really lost my spirit. What's needed now
is enduring, unslackening painful work and struggle. For that, a
person has eternally to maintain his fighting spirit, his spirit of
confrontation and his ideals. I just haven't got any of them.
Sometimes I think to myself how wonderful it would be to get a
chance to sacrifice myself, to show my feelings for my country,
but when will I ever get that chance?

'Sometimes I think of trying to re-inspire myself. But I'm used
to my life now, with its slow, measured pace. My limbs are
weaker, my brain's emptier and I have to comfort myself with
the thought that there would be no point. Maybe China is badly
run but I wonder if I could do any better?'

Li Yining spoke very sincerely and Sun Yue cried even harder.
Even I thought, as the poet said, 'There is emptiness in my
heart'. 'Li Yining,' I said, 'from what you've just said, we're all
very much the same.'

He Jingfu broke in: 'We're of the same generation but there
are differences. Our experiences have created differences
between us, which is very natural. Isn't it natural to "seek
common ground whilst reserving differences"?'

Did He Jingfu want to resolve the argument? While he spoke,
we all looked at each other and smiled. He saw that Sun Yue was
still very upset and said gently, 'Little Sun!' She glanced quickly
at him and turned her face away to smile at us all.

The atmosphere relaxed.

'What a joke!' Hanhan said suddenly as she was doing her homework.

He Jingfu went over and picked up her exercise book. He shouted, 'She's a fraud! She's only answered two questions. She's been listening to us!' He told her to show the book to her mother.

Hanhan saw that Sun Yue was smiling, handed her the book, and said haughtily, 'What do you mean listening? You've been talking so loud I'm practically deaf. It's been pushing into my brain and forcing me to respond. It's a perfectly natural phenomenon.'

She spoke like an actress, which made us all laugh. He Jingfu poked her in the chest: 'All right, natural phenomenon, tell us what you were laughing at.'

Hanhan smiled deliberately at her mother, seemingly pleased and proud of the attention He Jingfu was giving her. She said, 'I think you intellectuals are crazy, really mad. Sometimes you're like children, fighting one minute, making up the next.'

'We're not at all like you kids,' I teased. 'Our jokes aren't just for fun, they're about the great questions of the future of the country!'

Hanhan responded immediately. 'You think we just muck around? Don't despise us. Our concerns are no less than yours. We'll be the students of the eighties and you are the generation of the fifties; there are thirty years between us. You don't understand us, you always treat us like babies.'

She was fascinating. She put on a serious air but her face was still a round babyish circle. It was like being faced by a doll. But we didn't laugh at her, we all showed our approval. Only Sun Yue pretended to be cross and said, 'See what I've brought up!'

Hanhan grimaced at He Jingfu and he smiled tenderly. 'That's enough argument. Do your homework.' Obediently, she turned away and paid no more attention to us.

'Have you written the letter?' I asked Sun Yue and He Jingfu, returning to the original subject again.

'We were just getting down to it when you all arrived. We got involved in the great celebration of Xu Hengzhong's news,' Sun Yue replied with a smile.

Xu Hengzhong seemed to object. 'It's clear there's no point in trying to advise you, you've made your own plans. You stay, I ought to be getting back.' He went to the door and turned back to say to me, 'We'll have the party in ten days. Please come. It would be nice if you could come early and help, otherwise there won't be anything to eat.'

He had his own plans, too. I nodded: 'Don't worry, I'll be the first to arrive. I wish you all the best.'

He shrugged and laughed. 'In today's society, love is still a rare thing. I'm a very ordinary person and I don't have very extravagant tastes. Nevertheless, this has all made my life happier.' With that, he left.

Sensitive insensitivity. Elegant vulgarity. The keen insight of the ignorant. Directionless retreat. Unlooked-for love. Happiness without love. Xu Hengzhong was like everybody else, full of contradictory unities. The greatest unifying factor was material benefit.

'Our generation of intellectuals has really turned out very different types,' I said with a sigh.

'Yet we all grew up at the same time. If a woman has nine children, all nine will be different. We all reflect our time; the good points and the bad, the past and the present,' He Jingfu responded.

'We used to talk about violence and division but recently I've actually been feeling them,' I added.

'I feel them, too. I didn't realise that the eternal clamour of the Cultural Revolution would get under people's skins. Now it's got into their souls,' Sun Yue said.

'It's more painful now,' said Li Yining.

'But without pain, there'd be no creation,' said He Jingfu.

'It's like my homework. When I can't do it, it's agony, but after thinking painfully I finally work it out and that makes me happy,' Hanhan interrupted.

He Jingfu pointed at her. 'Well said! You've hit the nail on the head. I think there's probably more hope for your generation than ours. You'll be a modernised generation and you can throw us in the dustbin.'

Hanhan looked at us seriously. 'It depends on your attitude. If you won't transform yourselves, I'm afraid you'll be eliminated!'

I said goodbye to them all happily. Li Yining and He Jingfu left with me. I asked He Jingfu, 'What's really going on between you and Sun Yue?' To my surprise he shook his head and said:

'We don't talk about things like that.'

Li Yining chimed in, 'You've probably heard some story or other, haven't you?'

Rather saddened, I said, 'You don't seem as bothered by it as I do. What are you going to do now?'

'As Lenin said, life often opens up new avenues,' He Jingfu replied.

True. Life often opens up new avenues. Why should I worry?

TWENTY-SEVEN

ZHAO ZHENHUAN

I've lost what I ought to lose and I've found what I ought to find.

Wang Panzi gently put a letter on my desk with an insinuating finger pointed at the name of the sender. He behaved as if he was handling a top-secret document and reminding me of security.

The envelope was printed with the name of the university, but even if the name hadn't been there I would have recognised the letter as coming from Sun Yue. Her writing is like her, beautiful and strong.

Wang Panzi walked away and began whispering with another colleague. Was he waiting for me to open the letter? Well, I wouldn't. He waited a while and then left, making a face at his colleague as he went. I knew the grimace well; it meant 'There's something going on'.

And there was. Yesterday, Feng Lanxiang asked me for a divorce on the grounds that Sun Yue and I had resumed marital relations, because when I went to Shanghai I'd stayed at her flat.

I offered no explanation and simply said: 'Yes, I'll divorce you but you must let me have Huanhuan.'

When she heard that she began to weep and shout and came to the newspaper office screaming, 'Why don't you come clean? You've worked this all out with Sun Yue! And you think I don't know! I tell you I know all about your nasty doings with her in Shanghai!'

What had I done? When I hadn't gone home, more than one friend had said to me, 'Go back home. Wang Panzi and Feng

Lanxiang used to be very close but there's no need to believe the rumours.' I thought about it. If they had really been intimate then it wouldn't be a rumour. Everyone at the office knew they'd had an affair but I thought I'd managed to bury that knowledge for my own peace of mind. If Wang Panzi hadn't got a wife and children in the countryside, Feng Lanxiang probably wouldn't have chosen me. What I couldn't understand was how that ugly and vulgar man had managed to interest her. Yet she'd always admired him.

I don't know whether they'd worked it all out together and whether sending me to Hangzhou was a trap, with the intention of creating a scandal. I hadn't asked Wang Panzi to approve or pay for my rail fare to Shanghai because I didn't want to misuse public funds on private business, but he had insisted: 'We're old pals, can't I help you out? How did it go? Did you meet any old friends in the university? Is Sun Yue well?'

I didn't reply, nor did I give him my train ticket. Nevertheless, word soon went round the newspaper office – 'Zhao Zhenhuan is going to remarry Sun Yue. When he agreed to go to Hangzhou on business, he really went to Shanghai to get reunited with Sun Yue.' 'Did you know, Zhao Zhenhuan is going to divorce Feng Lanxiang?' 'Zhao Zhenhuan keeps up with current trends when he's choosing wives!'

Lu Xun said that a person who has to defend himself against a false accusation is to be pitied. I didn't want to defend myself against the false accusation. But I had gained something from going to Shanghai; I'd realised what unhappiness I'd brought to Sun Yue and Hanhan, and I'd understood that I'd have to pay a huge price to redeem my soul. I didn't want anyone to comment on or judge what I'd done in Shanghai.

If she wants a divorce then let's divorce. I want no part in this drama. There was no way we could have put my 'three-point treaty' into practice. I couldn't bear my spiritual loneliness and she couldn't bear the desolation of our daily life. I did feel sorry for her, but I didn't and couldn't love her, nor did I have the power to make her faithful to me. But I thought she deserved better than Wang Panzi. She ought to look for someone better than him.

My hands were shaking a little. I didn't dare open the envelope. What news did the letter bring?

When I left Shanghai, I shook He Jingfu's hand hard and said to him again, 'I wish you all the best. Things will work out and when they do, write to me immediately. I want to be able to congratulate you both.' Perhaps that is the news the letter brings me. Is it, Sun Yue?

Why didn't Hanhan give me a hint? She's written several times but she's never mentioned He Jingfu and Sun Yue being together. In the first few letters she talked constantly of her mother and how her mother had suffered. In her last letters, she hasn't mentioned her mother. Was that a hint?

My hands began to shake more violently and I could feel my face getting sweaty. I didn't dare open the letter. The colleague at whom Wang Panzi had made the face came over and said with concern, 'Old Zhao, you don't look at all well, why don't you go and lie down? There's not much to do here.' I shook his hand gratefully and left the office.

I shut the door of the dormitory tightly, got myself a knife and slowly opened the envelope. Carefully I took out the letter, unfolded it and placed it in front of me.

'Daddy, I've always kept this old torn photo. Do you think it can be mended?'

Hanhan! Did you ask your mother the same question? Probably! But is there any other news in this letter?

I smiled slightly and felt a little happier.

'Zhenhuan, my old schoolmate –' It was an intimate yet unfamiliar form of address. What did it mean? I read on and through very fast. It was odd, perhaps I hadn't understood, but the letter didn't seem to contain any news. At least not what I'd hoped, what I'd feared.

I calmed myself, lay down on my bed and read the letter more carefully. Then I understood what Sun Yue had written.

Zhenhuan, my old schoolmate:

I should have written before, but because of the twists and turns in the publication of Jingfu's book I've been very worried. Jingfu is always criticising me for it.

You came to Shanghai looking for forgiveness and understanding and I disappointed you. I was very selfish. On that score, I'm not up to you and Jingfu.

Seeing you raked up a very important part of the past. I don't know how many times I've thought of it, pondered it; yet I couldn't seem to see anything except the terrible sadness and the pointless sacrifice. So I'd never thought I'd be able to forgive you. Even less did I think that I'd ever ask your forgiveness. I was completely submerged in my own resentment; I saw myself as the rejected wife, as an object of pity.

In fact what happened between us can't be explained by rejection and being rejected. And what remains is not simply one person's resentment.

First, I think that I, rather than you, have to take responsibility for our tragedy. Because when I agreed to marry you, all I felt for you was friendship and excitement, certainly not love. You never attracted me the way He Jingfu did, nor fired me with enthusiasm as he did. You made me feel comfortable and friendly. I knew that I wanted and ought to have married He Jingfu, but I married you. It was because I didn't want to be ungrateful and I didn't want to get a reputation for inconstancy. And after He Jingfu became a 'rightist', I didn't want to be politically tainted myself.

I remember you often said that our life before and after marriage was the same. In your heart I was still a friend and not a real wife, and at the time I said it was because we lived apart. Yet secretly I used to ask myself, 'What if we lived together? Would I become a real wife to him?' My response was doubt. I thought that I wouldn't be able to get used to it, or that it mightn't satisfy me.

Why did I never explain what didn't satisfy me? It was because living apart gave me the chance to substitute illusion for reality in order to make up for my emotional dissatisfaction. I used to write to you regularly. In my letters, I tried to conceal my feelings. You used to say that my letters were like literature, that they made you think of me not as a wife, but as an immortal. That was it, Zhenhuan! I made of myself, and of you, almost unconsciously, different people, in order to comfort myself. I lost myself in the world I created and didn't concern myself with your real and concrete needs. You were always trying to get me to come back down to the world of mortals, to be with you. But from my position in the clouds, I persuaded you to wait until the organisation department arranged it.

In practice, I was always a faithful wife. But in my mind, I was only faithful to myself. I think it must have been me that first sowed the seeds of separation; how can I blame you?

History has already turned the page. I've often wondered if we couldn't turn it back. Because we have Hanhan. But every time I think about it, I conclude that the past is already far behind us. It's not that you have another home, another child, but that you've become a separate person.

You may say that it's all because of Jingfu. True. I think that if I had married him, we wouldn't have had to accommodate to each other, we'd have been one. When I married you, both of us had to accommodate and make sacrifices. Of course love must mean sacrifice, but sacrifice needn't be the foundation for love. So I should have chosen Jingfu, not you.

But because of Hanhan, I've always tried to bury my love for him. She's very confused. She loves Jingfu but she can't bear the loss of her real father. Isn't it understandable? So I can't satisfy the child with a latecomer and I don't want to hurt her feelings again by marrying Jingfu. I'm sure he agrees, he's stopped asking . . .

Because of the publishing problems, I've seen a lot of him. I can't leave him to struggle alone.

I often look at Hanhan and worry; I hope that she'll forgive me. Yesterday she gave me a slip of paper which read, 'Ma, I want to talk to you about something I shouldn't really mention: I want you and Uncle He to be happy. You don't want me to give up all my feelings because of you and I don't want you to give things up because of me.' I gave the slip of paper to Jingfu.

Zhenhuan, about what's happening to you now, He Jingfu and I are very sympathetic and worried about you. I quite understand that you are suffering right now but Lenin said that life opens up its own new avenues. Now that you recognise the contradictions, you've got the possibility of resolving them. Jingfu and I both hope you will, very soon.

I've told Hanhan everything I know about our relationship. She was quite upset and said, 'You made the wrong choice at the start. But if you hadn't made that mistake, I wouldn't exist. I can't take responsibility for your mistake, at least.'

Half-jokingly, I replied, 'You must learn from me and make absolutely sure that you don't fall in love before you really know what life is about and before you know yourself. Friendship and attraction for the opposite sex give rise to feelings that are connected with love but aren't truly love. Love is when you really know someone's soul.' She nodded, seeming to understand about half of it. What will become of her? But being a father or mother, one has to do everything one can to lead and advise a child. We can't let children repeat our mistakes.

I feel really sorry about not letting you see Hanhan. You and Hanhan don't blame me, but I blame myself. I brought her up, but that was out of duty, not out of kindness. If it was kindness, I wouldn't expect sacrifices in return. Please forgive me. This winter, I'll send her to stay with you in the holidays, definitely.

Hanhan thinks of you a lot. Jingfu and I keep telling her to write to you again. She says she will, but it is to be an unusual letter, and will take a lot of thinking about: 'This letter will be like a full stop in Ma's, Daddy's and my lives. It's going to announce that the old pattern is finished and to announce a new beginning.' Don't be surprised; since she made friends with Jingfu and Xi Wang our Hanhan has become quite a philosopher. Soon you'll see her, your lovely elder daughter.

Jingfu asked me to send his best wishes. He'll write to you soon, too. Right now he's very busy trying to get the publication of his book sorted out. He's made some progress because the higher Party committee has sent someone to investigate and we're very pleased about that. He often says that in life, you can't avoid gain and loss. People love to succeed and hate to lose. But loss isn't necessarily bad. Sometimes you have to lose in order to gain. I very much agree with him. Of course it's not easy to avoid being proud of winning and miserable about losing. But we're determined not to let losses and gains stop us.

Zhenhuan, our former relationship is over. From now on, we are once again fellow-students and friends. That's what we always should have been. After a rather tortuous journey we now know ourselves and each other better and we've established the right sort of relationship. I think we ought to be congratulated, don't you?

You're very welcome to come over whenever you can. Best wishes to Lanxiang and Huanhuan,

Work well, stay happy!

Sun Yue.

A gold hairpin draws a silver river, separating the past and the present, separating her from me. A flock of magpies form a bridge over the silver river and written on the bridge are the words: Friendship may cross, love may not.

So that was the news her letter brought. Now I understand.

I can't work out whether I am happy or sad.

I pick up the precious photograph: Sun Yue and Hanhan looking fondly at me. Sun Yue says to me warmly, 'You've lost me forever.' Hanhan holds out her hands, 'Daddy, I'm yours forever!'

I see the dream I had long ago, following a girl through the waves, and at last I see it clearly. The girl was Hanhan, not Sun Yue. Sun Yue was never meant to belong to me.

I want to cry. I want to cry loudly, on my own.

Smiling as you say goodbye to the past; that can only happen on stage. I'm going to cry as I say goodbye to the past.

Cry, Zhao Zhenhuan! Cry for what you have lost. Cry Zhao Zhenhuan, cry for what you have gained. Cry! Cry! Cry out loud!

'Old Zhao, Old Zhao!'

Wang Panzi was outside the door. He couldn't leave me alone for a minute. I didn't want him to hear me cry or see my tears. Wiping my face, I gathered up the photo and the letter, straightened my hair in front of the mirror and opened the door.

'Are you lying here all alone? How pleasant!' He was the same as ever; whenever he saw me, he made insinuating remarks.

I freed myself from his arm and asked what he wanted. Immediately he assumed a secretive air: 'Well? Have you had good news?'

I laughed. 'Yes! I've lost what I was meant to lose and I've gained what I was meant to gain.'

'What does that signify? It sounds allegorical!' As he spoke, he scanned my face, trying to see what I meant.

'What's so hard to understand?' I asked, evenly. 'What do you want? Tell me or I'll throw you out.'

'Now, now, you're being very fierce!' he said, tittering again. 'It's nothing much. I've just received a note from the court about your divorce!' and he handed me the note.

'Thank you.'

'You must think about it carefully. You must think about it for Huanhuan's sake.'

He pretended to be so concerned. Despite the 'Do Not Spit' notice I could hardly restrain myself. I opened the door for him and said, 'Please leave. I want to write to Sun Yue.'

He left and I shut the door firmly.

Yes, I must reply to Sun Yue. I want to say to her and He Jingfu, 'Congratulations, my friends, my warmest congratulations!'

And I must write to Hanhan. I want to say to her, 'Hanhan, my dear daughter, I've found my soul again, in you!'

Tears roll down my cheeks. I won't bother to wipe them; why should I? I've lost what I was meant to lose and I've found what I was meant to find. Why shouldn't I cry? The past is finished and a new era has begun, can't I cry?

Tears fall on a sheet of writing paper. On that sheet I write, 'Sun Yue, my friend.'

ENDNOTES

1 (*p.50*). Deng Xiaoping (born 1904). A long-time party member and distinguished military commander during the War of Liberation, Deng was bitterly attacked in the Cultural Revolution. He was brought back into power in 1974, only to become the butt of the Campaign to criticise Deng (1975-6), a last fling of the Cultural Revolution. He was criticised as a 'capitalist' and his rather attractive pragmatism – 'It doesn't matter if the cat is black or white as long as it catches mice'; 'Sooner or later the barefoot doctors will have to start wearing shoes' – was ridiculed. Since the death of Mao in September 1976, he has been rehabilitated to become the most important man in China, associated with successful liberalising economic policies, directly opposed to the 'ultra-left' ideas of the late Maoist period.

2 (*p.50*). Su Qin (died BC 317). A thinker and writer who was at first very unsuccessful, to the point where his wife would not spin for him, his sister-in-law would not cook for him and his parents disowned him. When his ideas for federating some of the Warring States were successfully adopted, he was warmly welcomed by those who had previously scorned him.

3 (*p.66*). Lin Biao (1907-1971). Army leader associated with the ultra-left ideas of the Cultural Revolution; he compiled the Little Red Book of quotations from Mao for use in the army. Though he was pronounced Mao's successor in 1969, he died in a mysterious plane crash, presumably fleeing to the USSR after serious disagreements, possibly because he wanted the Cultural Revolution to continue and his own power (through the army) with it.

4 (*p.79*). The leading slogan in China after Mao's death (1976), referring to the modernisation of industry, agriculture, science and the army. Compared with pre-1976 slogans, it is remarkably non-political.

5 (*p.90*). An early classification of villains in post-Liberation China,

including landlords, capitalist-roaders, counter-revolutionaries etc. Intellectuals were added as an afterthought, hence the number 'nine', and became particularly 'stinking' during the Cultural Revolution.

6 (*p.113*). A folk dance from the Yan'an area which became popular with the Communists in Yan'an during the Anti-Japanese war. After 1949, it was popularised as part of the Yan'an culture.

7 (*p.114*). 1967, a critical stage in the Cultural Revolution in Shanghai, when supporters of the new radical Workers' Headquarters denounced the Municipal Committee and started a series of strikes and occupations during which radical groups came to power in the city.

8 (*p. 140*). Sandor Petöfi (1823-49) was a Hungarian poet and national- ist. His reputation in China has varied with successive political move- ments. Praised in the 1950s as a nationalist (albeit bourgeois) and as anti-Russian, he was despised during the Cultural Revolution for his non-revolutionary, bourgeois approach.

9 (*p.141*). Sun Zi, author of a classic of military history, *c.* 4th century BC.

10 (*p.163*). 'Wine-and-meat friends' means 'fair weather friends'.

11 (*p.164*). Jia Baoyu: a character in *The Dream of the Red Chamber*.

12 (*p.190*). 'Black Guard' means the opposite of 'Red Guard', and was the object of attack during the Cultural Revolution. Many teachers were criticised and assaulted by their 'Red Guard' pupils at the time.

13 (*p.194*). During the Cultural Revolution, peasants were expected to produce for political idealism, and not to work on private plots or even want to possess them. Unrealistic demands and 'norms' fixed for communal work led to growing hardship and dissatisfaction. The problem has now been recognised by the government, which has made the family the basic tax unit in the countryside, replacing the communal team. The new system seems to work far better.

14 (*p.205*). Metaphor for the reconciliation of husband and wife.

15 (*p.257*). The Buddhist paradise is the 'pure land' of Amitabha.

16   (*p.272*). The main character in the eponymous novel by the Russian, Goncharov, published in 1859. Oblomov found it hard to get out of bed, and became a symbol of likeable laziness.

17   (*p.284*). Zhuangzi: philosopher from 4th century BC, whose cryptic and paradoxical works form part of the early Taoist ideas.

18   (*p.312*). Traditionally, the Chinese believed that the essential harmony of nature could only be achieved through balancing opposites like male and female, dark and light. Thus there is 'balance' in these two evenly-matched, clashing characters.

Current and forthcoming titles from Sceptre

ANATOLY MARCHENKO

MY TESTIMONY

ELIZABETH LONGFORD

THE PEBBLED SHORE

LAWRENCE OLIVIER

ON ACTING

ALLAN MASSIE

AUGUSTUS

BERNARD LEVIN

HANNIBAL'S FOOTSTEPS

BOOKS OF DISTINCTION